Talon

TALON

ANTONY MELVILLE-ROSS

LUME BOOKS

LUME BOOKS

This edition published in 2021 by Lume Books
30 Great Guildford Street,
Borough, SE1 0HS

ISBN 978-1-83901-333-1

Typeset using Atomik ePublisher from Easypress Technologies

www.lumebooks.co.uk

For David and Mary with great affection

Chapter One

Born of a gale a thousand miles out in the Atlantic the rollers, with nothing
to impede their growth, had achieved a formidable maturity before they
reached the end of their journey. Some of the racing mountain ridges
converted their energy into thunder and towering pinnacles of spray against
the streaming rock of islands. Others out-flanked those outposts and moved
remorselessly on towards the mainland, making the submarine heave slowly
up and down like some enormous lethargic whale.

'You'd better break off the attack. In weather like this nobody would
think the less of you.'

The officer at the periscope glanced at the two men struggling to maintain
depth at the hydroplane controls, at the gauges in front of them showing
forty feet, then at the speaker. What he had said made sense because there
was some risk of capsizing if the submarine broke surface in its unstable
submerged condition, quite apart from the danger inherent in the proximity
of the British battle-squadron and its attendant destroyers, destroyers it
was difficult to see in the storm rack.

For a moment he was tempted, then answered, 'No, not yet. If I can
get just a little more visual data on their course and speed I can go deep
and attack by sonar.'

He pressed his forehead against the rubber shield above the binocular
eye-pieces, feeling the dampness of his own sweat there, but saw only the
shifting pattern formed by wintry sunlight on the underside of the latest
in the endless succession of big waves. Grimly he waited for it to pass,
then, suddenly, his vision was back in the world above the sea taking in

7

the towering bulk of the leading battleship, noting the positions of the five destroyers, their whereabouts revealed more by the fountains they threw upwards than by their physical configuration.

They were well clear of him, the destroyers, and still unaware of his presence. For that he was extremely thankful although not particularly surprised. It would, he believed, be difficult for their sonar operators to differentiate between the submarine and the western point of Soay Island to which he was keeping as close as he dared. He was right in his belief and there was no way in which he could have known of the existence of the sixth destroyer about to round the point of land from Soay Sound astern.

'Bearing is that. Range is that,' he said, waited while the man standing behind him read off the figures from the azimuth ring and the range indicator, then added, 'I am thirty degrees on her starboard bow. Target confirmed as a British battleship of the *Nelson*-class with a screen of five destroyers.'

His mouth twitched when someone replied, '*Jawohl, Herr Kapitan. Gott mit uns!*'

More grey-green water covering the periscope's upper lens obscuring his vision. He sighed softly, nervously, before saying, 'Better to place our trust in the *Fuhrer*.'

'*Jawohl, Herr Kapitan,*' the other repeated. '*Heil Hitler!*'

The voice of the sonar operator broke in sharply.

'Loud sonar transmissions dead astern, sir! In contact, sir!'

The officer swung the periscope quickly to face aft. At first he could see only a wall of water, then it subsided to reveal the rearing knife-edged bows of a destroyer, bows that dropped jarringly to send twin curtains of spray hurtling skywards. For a fraction of a second, between the two soaring curtains, an image resembling numerous hair-thin parallel black lines imprinted itself on the retina of his eyes, then it was gone. Realisation of what he had seen came to him almost before the next second had passed.

'The bastard's fired "Hedgehog" at us,' he said and added in a near-shout, 'Shut all water-tight doors! Shut main vents! Blow main ballast!'

Steel doors had been clipped tightly closed and high pressure air was roaring into the tanks, but the submarine had not begun to lift towards the surface when two of the widely spread pattern of mortar bombs hit her. Both struck above the engine room, the double detonation less than that of a single depth-charge, but more deadly because "Hedgehog" bombs exploded only on contact.

The submarine sank by the stern, the angle increasing as she slid downwards to crash onto the ocean floor two hundred and fifty feet below the surface. When the series of shuddering impacts had ceased, she lay still with a twenty degree list to starboard, a slight bow-down angle and nineteen dead men abaft the engine room bulkhead. From forward someone began screaming.

*

High above the angry sea the admiral stood staring down at the battleship's main armament of nine huge sixteen-inch guns in their three triple turrets, guns which earlier in the war had reduced *Bismarck*, the pride of the German navy, to a mass of torn and twisted steel. He was trembling slightly with rage and sadness, unconscious of the automatic flexing of his legs against the jerky movements of the deck beneath his feet, not seeing what his eyes were looking at. With almost clockwork regularity the massive bows of the flag-ship butted ponderously at the Atlantic rollers sending tons of white water swirling along the upper deck, but he didn't see that either.

A lieutenant approached him and said, 'Full "Subsmash" emergency procedure in operation, sir.'

'Thank you, Flags.'

The brief exchange brought his surroundings to life around him and he looked gloomily at the islands of Rhum and Canna to port and the mountains of Skye to starboard, grey, desolate, ghostly in the March storm. During the years between the wars he had frequently sailed a ketch along the west coast of Scotland, enjoying the matchless scenery, the courteous soft-spoken people, the magic place-names like Tobermory, Ardnamurchan, Kyle of Loch Alsh, Scalpay and Raasay. Now it was spoilt for him, the names inimical signs pointing the way towards needless tragedy.

'Sir?'

'What is it?'

9

'Any orders for *Dart*, sir?'

There were only three destroyers in the screen now that *Demon* and *Dagger* were racing north to locate the mass grave *Dart* had dug. For a few moments he watched their plunging progress, then turned to his flag-lieutenant.

'What orders would *you* give him, laddie?'

Puzzled, frowning slightly, the young officer watched him questioningly. He didn't speak.

'I mean, having given due consideration to his probably highly emotional state, would you order his immediate return to harbour, or instruct him to join the others in the search for the wreck?'

'Oh I see, sir. Personally, I'd keep him busy searching.'

'So would I, Flags,' the admiral said tiredly. 'Kindly see to it. There isn't much else we can do for a Royal Navy destroyer captain who has just sunk a British submarine.'

*

The twentieth man to die did it under the crushing weight of a torpedo which had torn itself loose from its securing bands when the submarine struck bottom. Despite the heavy dose of morphine injected into his broken body it seemed to take him a long time and when he had finished doing it the end to his screaming left a silence more tangible than the absence of sound. There was a waiting with expectation of nothing but the moment for them to follow him one by one to wherever he had gone, a mute collective sigh acknowledging the inevitable. The wounded ship, with all her machinery stilled, appeared already to be dead until the strained hull creaked alarmingly in sharp protest at the enormous pressure of the water surrounding it.

The sudden noise broke the spell which had held them and men glanced quickly at each other, then away again, the fear that the inevitable had leapt much closer clear on their faces, but steel and water had reached deadlock. Nothing happened.

'Cover him up and secure that torpedo where it is,' the first lieutenant said. 'There's no point in trying to move it, or him. We'd just be burning oxygen. Switch half of those lights off and no unnecessary moving around.'

He turned away then and made his way slowly aft along the canted deck, pausing at each mess to ask the people in it if they were all right, to tell them to save electricity and not to move about more than they had to. When he got to the control room he retched violently, but nothing came up.

'You okay, Number One?'

'Yes, sir. Sorry about that. Leading Seaman Glenn didn't look very nice. He's dead now.'

The captain nodded. 'I see. Now, this is the situation as far as we have been able to establish it. Engine and motor rooms flooded for certain. Possibly the after machinery space too, but the only proof we have of that is that we can't raise anyone there on the telephone. Both sonars are out of action. The keel set must have gone when we hit the bottom and the one on the after casing – well, that's where the "Hedgehog" bombs hit us.' He shrugged his shoulders before adding, 'But we're not quite deaf. There are two or three of them up there in contact with us. You can hear them if you listen carefully.'

As if as an aid to hearing he looked up towards the curve of the pressure hull covered by a maze of pipes and valves above his head. The first lieutenant and everybody else in the control room followed the direction of his gaze, then stood listening to the faint bat-squeak of the destroyers' transmissions probing down with electronic fingers, pin-pointing them. There was a link of sorts with the outside world, but it made nobody feel any better because in such weather conditions it would need a miracle to strengthen it enough to be of any use.

'Give me that wheel-spanner. We're not completely dumb either,' the captain said, took it in his right hand and began to strike the big brass wheel of one of the low-pressure air blowing valves rhythmically. After a minute he changed to Morse, a sharp tap for a dot, a heavier one for a dash. 'Forty-three alive,' he sent and kept on sending it.

*

The captain of *Dart* crouched in the corner of the destroyer's gyrating bridge watching the plunging shapes of *Demon* and *Dagger* to starboard. Like *Dart* they had only sufficient way on to keep their bows facing the rolling sea. He was soaking wet beneath his oil-skin and very cold, but scarcely aware of either condition. Physical sensations seemed to have ceased to affect him since he had definitely decided to commit suicide immediately on return to harbour. Behind him the sonar pinged monotonously.

'Stop transmitting and set passive sonar watch on the same bearing for three minutes,' he said, but the wind tore the words from his lips and hurled them away.

'I didn't hear that, sir.' The officer of the watch's voice close to his ear. He repeated the order, heard it repeated again and the amplified sound of the transmissions cease. *Dagger*, he saw, was shipping more green water than either *Demon* or *Dart*.

'Too bad.'

'What, sir?'

'Nothing.'

He continued to watch *Dagger*, marginally less sheltered by land from the storm, bury her bows deep then tear herself free of the clutching ocean only to fall again into its embrace. Listlessly he counted the seconds between each immersion, unconscious of the water pouring over him.

'Captain, sir?'

'Yes?'

'Sonar reports faint tapping sounds, probably from the submarine. They…'

He pushed the officer of the watch fiercely out of the way and leapt towards the sonar cabinet, but a jerking roll of the ship threw him against the compass binacle. The pain in his shoulder was savage but, because he was dead inside, made as little impression on him as the cold and the wet and a moment later he was standing over the sonar operator.

'What have you got, Simmonds?'

'A tapping noise, sir. Could be Morse. Very indistinct though.'

'Would it help if I stopped the engines? I could do that for a minute or two.'

The operator sat staring in front of him, his forehead creased in concentration. He didn't speak.

'I asked you…' the captain began, but stopped talking when the man shook his head emphatically, took off his earphones and said, 'No need, sir. It's Morse all right. I'm not very good at it. Could you get a telegraphist up here, or maybe read it yourself?'

The captain whirled and staggering slightly with the motion of the ship, ran to the Tannoy public address microphone. He spoke into it.

Seventy seconds later, 'Message reads "Forty-three alive", sir. They're tapping it out over and over,' the petty officer telegraphist told him, then looked quickly away at the sight of his captain's face crumpling. When he looked again the officer had gone.

'Signalman!'

'Sir?'

'Is the flag-ship still in lamp range?'

'Yes, sir. Just about, sir.'

'Right, make "Message received from submarine *Titan* states forty-three alive on board". Repeat that to *Demon* and *Dagger*. Guns, get me three hand-grenades quickly. Never mind about the watch. I'll take over. Hurry!'

He stood, waiting for the grenades, doing nothing about the tears on his cheeks, knowing that they would be unnoticeable amongst the flying droplets of spray constantly in the air. Whether he was crying with relief that forty-three men were still temporarily alive, or for an unknown number who, from the wording of the message, were obviously dead, or just for himself, he had no idea.

*

The three separate cracks of grenades exploding in water were puny, but the sound reached the ears of every man still alive aboard *Titan*.

'Good show, sir. They must have heard you,' the first lieutenant said.

'Yes, I think we can assume that they have, Number One,' the captain told him, putting the wheel-spanner down and went on, 'So I'll stop wasting air. All officers go and settle down in the wardroom, please. There's nothing more to be done here.'

He watched them troop forward, four of his own, six of the Commanding Officers' Qualifying Course followed by their instructor, Lieutenant Peter

Harding. The captain was more than a little awed by Harding, a mild-mannered man of twenty-five with seven very successful operational submarine patrols in command to his credit and an impressive show of decorations beneath the left shoulder of his jacket. A lot of tales had been told about Harding's activities in the Mediterranean the previous summer as captain of *Titan*'s sister ship *Trigger*, not the least of which concerned the single-handed destruction of a heavily escorted troop and arms convoy. The action had lasted for a day and a night and left a trail of burning and exploding ships in its wake with *Trigger* herself reduced to a near sinking condition by the end of it all.

The battle had not been unique, although certainly a classic of its kind, but what most surprised the captain of *Titan* was that it should have been Harding who had conducted it. With his mousey hair and a shy expression on an unremarkable face he simply did not look the part to have produced a piece of history known throughout the Submarine Service as "Harding's Convoy Action". As if that wasn't enough he had now been entrusted at a remarkably early age with the instruction of first lieutenants recommended for commands of their own.

But what for *Titan*'s captain converted surprised respect into awe was Harding's recent marriage to the very lovely daughter of the Marquis of Trent. People said that Lady Abigail Harding was the most beautiful woman in London and from the photographs he had seen of her in "The Tatler" he knew that for once people hadn't lied. He followed Harding towards the wardroom wondering how he had achieved that and, because he was both a romantic and a realist, thinking what a tragedy it was that the newly-weds would never see each other again.

*

In the Clyde a converted liner renamed *Phoenix* and fitted with winches for heavy rescue work raised her anchor and turned towards the Mull of Kintyre and the open sea beyond.

In Scapa Flow tugs towed two huge lighters carrying lifting equipment southwards then took refuge in the lee of the Island of Hoy when the storm raving through the Pentland Firth threatened to deprive them of their charges.

At the Admiralty in London one rear-admiral said to another, 'It was no fault of *Dart's*, Henry. She had been detached from the Fleet and the signal authorising *Titan* to carry out a practice attack on it wasn't copied to her. We'll talk about a court-martial when the enquiry has established where the fault does lie. As for Yardley, the poor devil simply carried out a split-second attack which unhappily succeeded on what he had every reason to believe was a U-boat.'

At Fort Blockhouse in Gosport, the traditional home of the Submarine Service, an officer at the wardroom bar asked a friend if he had heard the buzz that *Titan* had gone down in over two hundred feet of water and a lieutenant of the Royal Australian Navy's Volunteer Reserve wearing a greying beard moved closer to hear what they were saying to each other.

In *Titan's* wardroom a tall, dark-haired lieutenant named Gascoigne said, 'I'm very sorry, everybody. If I'd taken "Teacher's" advice and broken off the attack we wouldn't be in this trouble.'

'It was Rooke's fault for talking German,' someone replied and laughed nervously at his own joke.

'John.'

Gascoigne looked at Harding. 'Yes, sir?'

'I warned you about the effects of oxygen deprivation when you were my Number One in *Trigger*. It seems to be getting to you already. You aren't thinking properly.'

'I don't understand, sir.'

'If you *had* broken off the attack,' Harding told him, 'you would *not* have seen "Hedgehog" fired, you would *not* have ordered water-tight doors shut and we'd *all* be dead.' He paused before adding, 'Incidentally, you don't have to call me "sir" any longer. All six of you have qualified and you'll be given commands of your own as soon as they get us out of here.'

Aboard *Dart* Commander Yardley, the hours between him and the harbour where he had promised himself release stretching unendurably far ahead, retired to his cabin and shot the top of his head off with a Webley .45 revolver.

Chapter Two

The Royal Australian Navy Volunteer Reserve lieutenant with the greying beard stood just inside the street door of a block of flats called "Northways" near Swiss Cottage in London in which three floors housed the operational headquarters of the Submarine Service. A rather fat able seaman stood beside him. Both were listening to a man talking on the telephone.

'It's a Lieutenant Blakie and, er, a rating, sir. They say it's important that they see the Admiral, sir.'

'It's fuckin' essential,' Lieutenant Blakie said and scowled back when the man frowned at him.

'No, sir. I don't know what they want and, no, they haven't got an appointment to see anybody.' 'Yes, I quite understand, but they refuse to go away.' 'What, sir?' 'Oh, in that case perhaps you'd like to come and tell them yourself. They won't listen to me.'

The man dropped the telephone onto its rest and busied himself at ignoring the visitors until a lieutenant-commander arrived and asked sharply what the trouble was.

'Let's move inside away from this desk and I'll tell you, cobber,' Blakie said. The Australian accent was strong.

'Just state your business and address me as "sir" while you're doing it.'

'Right, *sir*! If you want it shouted around be it on your own head. There's a grey lady lyin' raped on the sea-bed you know where. That's our business, *sir*! We're divin' experts and we've built some equipment you've never even heard of which…'

16

'That's enough! You come with me and explain where you got this information. This rating stays here.'

The lieutenant-commander began to walk away, but stopped when Blakie said, 'This *ratin'* comes with me, all the way to the Admiral and, by Christ, you'd better get us there fast if you don't want a lot of dead men on your conscience.' The words had been quietly spoken and the other watched him thoughtfully, then nodded when the Australian added, 'C'mon, sir. Let's stop arsin' about. This is vital.'

Forty minutes and two officers of ascending seniority later, Blakie and the able seaman were shown into the office of Flag Officer Subarmines. Their service raincoats were off now and the admiral noted the emblem of a qualified diver on the rating's arm and the blue and white ribbon of the DSC on the officer's jacket.

'Are you the Blakie who sank a German troop-ship in Kristiansund harbour?'

'Yes, sir. In X-51, sir. Sank a mine-sweeper with the other charge too.'

'Ah. And if I remember rightly you were subsequently expelled from midget submarines. Why was that?'

'Got crocked once too often, sir.'

'Yes,' the admiral said. 'So you did. Do you still have a drinking problem?'

'None, sir. No problem at all. I think I must have been born to it. It comes natural to me.'

The four-stripe captain standing behind the admiral's chair flushed angrily, but the admiral merely turned his regard onto the rating.

'You. What's your name?'

'Prescott, sir.'

'You're a bit old to be only an able seaman, Prescott.'

'Oh, I made petty officer once, sir, and leading hand three times, but they keep busting me.'

'What for?'

'Getting pissed with Lieutenant Blakie, sir.'

'Bert's a natural too,' Blakie said helpfully and the admiral moved his eyes slowly back to him before saying, 'Even if you consider it proper to call ratings by their Christian names, Blakie, I'm at least glad that you do not permit them to call you by yours.'

'My oath, I couldn't allow that,' Blakie told him. 'It's Cyril. You wouldn't want to be called by a stupid name like that, would you?'

The captain moved uncomfortably and the admiral lowered his head, staring at the blotter on his desk, only his deep concern preventing his shoulders from shaking, until the Australian went on, 'Now we've got the introductions over do you think we could talk about *Titan*, sir?'

'Yes, Blakie, I think perhaps we could. Forgive me for presuming to establish what sort of people I'm talking to first.'

'No sweat, sir,' Blakie said. 'Now, this is the form.'

He opened his jacket, drew a long metal bolt from the waistband of his trousers and put it on the desk.

'Two of them, sir, blasted through the pressure hull. We've got a sort of gun for that. This flange here stops it goin' right through and seals the aperture, with an assist from the water pressure. When they're lodged in place Bert and me fix armoured hoses onto our ends and tap out a message to the boys inside to unscrew their ends. Like this.'

The admiral watched the lieutenant pick up the bolt and twist it until the front section came away to reveal a smallbore, thick-walled hollow tube.

'Then we pump air down one pipe, exhaust it through the other and Bob's your uncle, sir. They've got somethin' to breathe.'

'What,' the captain asked, 'happens if the tube is distorted during penetration and can't be unscrewed?'

Blakie looked at him. 'Well now, sir, if I wanted a breath of fresh air badly enough I reckon I'd saw the fucker in half.'

The captain flushed again and the admiral said, 'This is a very interesting concept, but I wonder how it works in practice. What tests have you carried out?'

'Eighty-one to date, sir. Mostly on merchantship wrecks in the Portsmouth and Harwich areas. Proper balls-up to begin with. First the gun wasn't powerful enough, then the bolts weren't strong enough, then the gun was too powerful and we either blew a bloody great hole in the hull or had bolts ricochetin' all over the shop, but we've more or less got it sorted now for thicker steel than those merchantmen had.'

'More or less?'

'Right. More or less. The firm of Blakie and Prescott doesn't offer guarantees. Not yet it doesn't. But I'll tell you this, sir. U 291 was rammed by a destroyer off the Wolf Rock. She's lyin' in a hundred and seventy feet of water and we put ten bolts into her. Eight of them worked fine.'

'And the other two?'

'Made big splits in the pressure hull, sir.'

'I see.'

The admiral stood up, walked to the window and stood, hands clasped behind him, staring out of it at nothing. He stayed like that until Blakie spoke again.

'I know what you're thinkin', sir, but you don't have a lot of choice really, do you? There's no chance of their even startin' to raise *Titan* until the weather moderates, so by the time they get her up, *if* they get her up, the crew'll be dead. I don't give 'em more than thirty-six hours as of now unless you let Bert and me take some air down to 'em. The worst that can happen is for us to kill 'em off a bit sooner and a lot quicker and I don't reckon they'd object to that too much. I've been through the slow suffocation routine myself once or twice and there's nothin' funny about it.'

Without turning round, 'Two hundred and fifty feet is very deep to work at, Blakie,' the admiral said. 'Somewhere around eight times atmospheric pressure I'd guess.'

'Too right, sir.'

'Have you two worked at that depth?'

'Christ, no. We only *look* stupid.'

'Well, that's the depth *Titan's* at.'

'Yes, sir. We know.'

The admiral turned away from the window, moved back to his desk and pressed a bell-push on it. He smiled faintly at the two men, then looked towards the door and said, 'Come in, Susan. Lieutenant Blakie here has some urgent requirements. I'd like you to jot them down and set the ball rolling as soon as he's finished.'

A blonde Wren Officer wearing a beautifully tailored uniform seated herself beside the desk, crossed her legs and opened a shorthand note-book. Blakie found himself being regarded by a pair of very calm grey eyes, eyes lazy with self-assurance. They disturbed him.

'I'm no fuckin' good at givin' dictation,' he said, bit his lip and added quickly, 'Oh Christ! I'm sorry, miss.'

The eyes crinkled at the corners. 'Just talk, Lieutenant Blakie. I'll censor it for you.'

'Good on yer,' he told her. 'First thing, I want four more of these made as spares. Here's the specification.'

He took a piece of paper from a pocket and pushed it and the bolt across the desk towards her. The captain picked up bolt and paper and left the room, walking fast.

'Next, complete plans of *Titan*. Not just any T-class sub. *Titan*. That's very important because they all vary slightly dependin' on the yard they were built in and we don't want to fry ourselves by shootin' bolts into the electrics, or place them somewhere where the crew can't reach 'em. All right?'

'Certainly,' she said.

'Right. Charts. No, never mind about charts. We can get 'em up there. Armoured hose, one-inch bore, two lengths of four hundred foot each. One end of each length to be fitted with a female adaptor to accept the end of that bolt the captain just took away. The other ends suitable for connection to an air pump, or compressor, or whatever they decide to use. That's not my job. Come to think of it we'd better have four lengths to be on the safe side, but the first two really quick. Got that?'

'Yes,' she said.

'Right. That hose, the compressor, an air pump each for Bert and me to be placed aboard an ocean-goin' tug, or some such, with a hell of a lot of cable for anchorin' itself, plus two winches for us, telephones and all the rest of the standard stuff for hard-hat divin'. Divin' with a helmet I mean. I'll want a recompression chamber on board too.'

'Skipper?'

Blakie glanced sideways at Prescott.

'Yes, Bert?'

'Two recompression chambers, skipper. The way I see it we never had to do a job as quick as this before. You and me can start by working together, but what with the depth and the weather and all, we may have to separate and work alternate like. If you're getting *de*compressed and I have to come

20

up a bit sharpish, you don't want to be *de*compressed all the way to let me in to be *re*compressed. If you see what I mean, that is.'

'Good thinkin', Bert.'

Blakie looked at the Wren officer. She was crossing her legs the other way. He thought they were very pretty legs.

'Two chambers please, miss. I don't know where you'll find 'em, but Bert's right. We want 'em.'

'Two chambers,' she said.

'Then we'll want a big ship, the bigger the better, stationed broadside on to seaward of us providin' a lee. She won't be able to hold the position long without driftin' down on us, but if she can be there whenever we're gettin' in and out of the water that'll help a lot.' Blakie scratched his beard, then went on, 'We'd better have a back-up team of the two best divers you can find in case we f… in case we muck it up. We'll teach them the drill with the gun before our first dive. Am I goin' too fast?'

Her dawdling pencil had already stopped. 'No,' she said and her eyes crinkled again.

'Right, all that leaves is constant weather reports, the best the "met" boys can produce, direct to me, a van to Waterloo Station to pick up the gear we left there and take us to whatever airfield you say, a plane to Scotland and another van at the other end. That's all.'

'Wouldn't it be wise to have a doctor with you, Lieutenant Blakie? One experienced in treating aeroembolism?'

He looked startled for a moment, then grinned. 'Oh, "the bends". Too right, miss. Bloody good idea. Thanks.'

The admiral spoke for only the second time since the Wren officer had come into the room.

'One more thing, m'dear. A signal from me to Commander-in-Chief Home Fleet and all interested authorities requesting utmost assistance be given to Lieutenant Blakie and/or Able Seaman Prescott. Word it yourself.'

'Yes, sir,' she said, stood up, looked at the Australian and added, 'I think you give very good dictation, Lieutenant Blakie.'

When the door closed, 'I like that sheila of yours, sir.'

'Her name's Su… Oh, of course, Blakie. An "Aussie" expression. Yes, she's very competent. Decorative too. Well, carry on. All the things you need will be there as soon as possible after you arrive.'

The admiral neither offered to shake hands, nor wished them luck, but when they reached the door he called, 'When this is over come back and see me, you two.'

On the way down the stairs twenty minutes later, 'I never sat down with an admiral before, skipper. Nice bloke.'

'Yeah,' Blakie agreed. 'Like you, he's not bad for a Pom. But I'd give a lot to...'

'To what, skipper?'

'Forget it.'

'Oh, I see,' Prescott said. 'Bit of all right, wasn't she?'

Chapter Three

The single bulb burning in the passageway outside *Titan's* small, crowded wardroom cast high-lights and shadows over the faces of some of the men seated round the table and made barely recognisable silhouettes of others. The effect was sepulchral, but there was just enough illumination for the players to see the Ludo board. Not all those present were officers. Dice clattered and came to rest against the little barrier of books placed to prevent them rolling off the canted surface. Leading Seaman Massey peered closely at them and smiled.

'I'm afraid that's your lot, sir.'

'Damn. So it is,' Gascoigne said. 'How much do I owe you now, Massey?'

'At double or quits that makes – er – a hundred and twenty-eight thousand quid, sir.'

'Right. I'm afraid I haven't got that much on me at the moment. Do you want to give me a chance to win some of it back?'

'Not bloody likely, sir. Anyway I'm scheduled to play the petty officers now. Should clean up in there too with any luck.'

Massey smiled again, excused himself and walked away, moving slowly to preserve what air there was as they had all been ordered to do.

Gascoigne got up himself and went to the nearly dark control room to talk to the men there and play whatever silly game they wanted. The captain had asked all officers to mix with the crew and to keep on mixing. And that was right, Gascoigne thought, despite or because of the fact that the crew seemed to have just as much to give the officers as the other way around. He stood for several minutes watching a group squatting on the deck between the periscopes. The Chief Engine Room Artificer was performing sleight-of-hand tricks.

'I bet you couldn't fool us with that one in decent light, Chief,' he said.

The man looked up. 'Not worth my while taking you up on that, sir. I hear you already owe Leading Seaman Massey sixty-four thousand pounds.'

'Wrong,' Gascoigne told him. 'We've just played double or quits and I lost again.'

'Well, there you are, sir. Now, why don't you sit down and watch closely.'

He did so, part of him intrigued, part concentrating on the sound of breathing from those near him. It wasn't laboured yet. Just a little shallow and rapid as it would have been after a long day's normal diving. What was much more noticeable was the temperature. It was rising rapidly and that was one of the main reasons for most of the lights being switched off.

Gascoigne frowned, then composed his features and gave his full attention to the coins vanishing mysteriously from the Chief ERA's hands.

*

Harding sat astride the fallen torpedo with his back to the covered body of Leading Seaman Glenn putting the final touches to the sketch of the fourteenth and last man in the torpedo stowage compartment. He enjoyed drawing and was very good at it, but fourteen portraits in two and a half hours with people peering over his shoulders as he worked had tired him.

'Move your head back, O'Donnell. Your face is in shadow again.'

'Sorry, sir.'

He didn't mind the tiredness. There was nothing else to do anyway and for portions of those two and a half hours he had provided the men and himself with something to think about other than the death closing in on them.

'There you are. That's you.'

'Cor! Thank you very much, sir. Wait 'til my old woman sees this!'

'Hope she likes it,' Harding said, got stiffly up from the torpedo and began to walk aft.

'Please, sir?'

24

'Yes?'

'You forgot to sign it, sir.'

'Oh, did I?' He scrawled his name in the bottom right hand corner, dated it and left them showing the drawings to each other.

A bunk was vacant in the ward room. He lay down on it and listened to the never-ceasing sound of the destroyer's sonar transmissions. Bat-squeaks he sometimes called them although he wasn't sure if he'd ever heard a bat squeaking. A feather-light wire brush caressing the hull? No, bat-squeaks would have to do if, he thought with sudden irritability, it mattered to any of them what they sounded like. For all the good they were doing the destroyers might as well go home and take their ghostly noises with them. Suddenly frightened at the idea that, useless or not, they might do exactly that, he closed his ears to the sounds and let his mind drift. It settled without any difficulty at all in its customary sanctuary.

Acting on the orders of his superiors who considered him a valuable commodity she had entrapped him, tormented him, seduced him and nursed him through and out of a case of combat fatigue which had threatened to deprive the Submarine Service of an experienced commander at a time when there were too few available. Amazingly, although he had been only one of many subjected to her spell, she had returned his love and, after a brief agonising separation, sought him out and offered herself as his wife.

The discovery that Gail Mainwaring had been a government-paid harlot and was a titled aristocrat in her own right had been comparatively minor ripples in the surge of emotions she engendered in him. It was hard to believe that feelings of such intensity would shortly fade into nothingness. Bleakly he wondered what she would do when he was dead, what she was undergoing now in the knowledge that he was dying slowly on the ocean floor, then, with a fierce effort of will, forced misery from him and summoned Lady Abigail Harding directly into his head.

He was drifting into sleep with her arms around his neck and her red hair, like the curtains of some tiny magic stage, falling about his face when the metallic tapping on the hull began.

Everyone in the wardroom was standing when Harding rolled out of the bunk and he stood with them listening to the click and scrape of some outside agency.

The captain said, 'In God's name what's…'

'*Keep quiet!*'

The words were spoken with sharp authority and all heads turned towards Gascoigne approaching from the direction of the control room.

'It's Morse,' Gascoigne said. 'Listen.'

Tap – scratch. Scratch – tap.

'That's AN. The water resistance is too great for him to make heavy and light taps. He's using that scraping sound to indicate a dash. There he goes again.'

Scratch. Tap tap. Scratch. Tap scratch. Scratch tap.

'*Titan*! Somebody grab something and bang out letter "R"!'

Somebody did and the diver, presumably with his helmet pressed to the hull, heard. A longer message vibrated through steel.

'Air repeat air… to you… by new method… in 24 hours… hold on… good luck'.

'Send "Wilco and thanks",' the captain said, shook his head disbelievingly and looked around at the others.

'I'm sorry I shouted at you, sir,' Gascoigne said.

'You did all right, John,' the captain told him, then added, 'I don't know what the blazes they think they're talking about, but we're going to play along for all we're worth.' He moved slowly towards the control room and a moment later the Tannoy crackled into life.

'This is the captain speaking. We have been contacted by a diver with the message that air will be supplied to us by some new method in twenty-four hours time. I don't know how this is possible, but you may rest assured that it is no cruel joke. They would never play that on us. From this moment on there will be no more games, no more talking and no movement whatsoever, except that the First Lieutenant will issue water to each group of you every six hours. If you *have* to go to the "heads", go on the deck. That is all and good luck to each one of you.'

The public address system clicked off.

*

'It'd be plain crazy to try landing in this. The wind's blowing right across that itsy-bitsy air-strip. Look at her drift.' The pilot had to shout to make himself heard above the engines' roar.

Blakie watched the little runway below them seemingly sliding away to starboard, watched too the wind-sock at its end pointing due south, rigid as a bar. The sight gave him sudden hope.

'Ah, c'mon,' he yelled back. 'I've always been told you Yank birdmen can fly a square brick shit-house through a typhoon.'

The American grinned briefly.

'You really want to try it?'

'Not much, but I don't have much choice either. You know the priority on this flight.'

'Okay. So tell your fat friend to strap himself in tight. Here we go.'

The DC3 banked steeply, circled, levelled again and edged crab-wise towards the air-strip. It bucked repeatedly like a frantic horse, then the ground was rushing up at them.

'Fuck this for a lark,' Blakie said, but the pilot was too busy to hear him.

The plane bounced viciously when it touched down, did it twice more with decreasing venom, ran off the end of the prepared surface and slewed dramatically to a halt at right-angles to it. The landing had been brilliant.

When the engine-noise died, 'You've been takin' lessons you have, cobber.'

'Nope. Book-learning. That was my first flight.'

'Thanks. Bert and me are grateful.'

'So you should be,' the American said. 'You're both still alive.'

*

'Name's Brown, Commander Brown,' the small man in the black bowler and long fawn raincoat said. 'You can call me Commander Brown or Fred, as you like, but I'll not be having any of this Mister Brown stuff just because I'm a civvie now. I came up hard way through ranks and I'm proud of it.' He glowered belligerently at Blakie.

'Right, Fred,' Blakie replied. 'They mostly call me Digger, and this is Bert.'

The scowl vanished from the small man's face to be replaced by a smile which creased it like a very old apple.

'Welcome, lads. We're right glad to see you. Can you really get air down to sub?'

'We're here to try, Fred. What's your job?'

'If you don't succeed I'll not have one. I'm salvage master, but if the boys die we'll leave 'em in peace down there. What with bombs and hitting bottom hard *Titan's* in a right old mess. Easier to build a new sub.'

His expression puzzled, 'How do you know what sort of state she's in?' Blakie asked.

The crumpled smile came again. 'Miracle I reckon. Wind shifted, didn't she. Veered right around to east of north. *Titan's* lying in the lee of Skye now. Still pretty rough, but nothing to what it were like before and we got a diver down to her.'

For a moment Blakie was back in the rearing, plunging cockpit of the DC3 looking down at the wind-sock pointing towards the south. The hope he had felt then had been justified.

'I noticed the wind change,' he said. 'What did the diver find?'

Brown took his bowler off, inspected the greasy hat-band with apparent approval and put it back on his head.

'One "Hedgehog" bomb hit casing above engine room. Blew a lot of it away and cracked pressure hull over eleven feet. Another hit pressure hull direct and punched hole in it a bit further aft. Rudder's gone, both shafts bent, after hydroplanes torn off too and starboard saddle tanks crushed. But diver reckons she's sound from engine room bulkhead for'ard. Got a message to them that they'd have air in twenty-four hours.' He glanced at his watch and added, 'Talking of which I'd better go and see if your gear's on board yet.'

When Brown had left the mess room of the big tug Blakie turned to Prescott.

'Talks funny doesn't he, Bert? Only said "the" about twice in all that.'

'Scouse or Geordie I reckon, skipper.'

'Eh?'

'Oh, sorry. Keep forgetting you're from down under. Scouse is Liverpool. Geordies come from over Newcastle way. Most northerners talk funny. Like you do.'

'You'll go too far one of these days, my lad,' Blakie said. 'Hand me those plans of *Titan* and we'll figure out where we're goin' to fire the bolts into her.'

*

The air in *Titan* had little left in it the lungs could usefully extract. It tasted acidly of fear-sweat, ammonia and human excrement. The only constant sound was of dragging breaths. The captain thought it strange that it was his tongue rather than his nose recording the all-pervading sourness, but was not sorry that his sense of smell had been impaired. A moment after completing the thought he could not remember what it had been and that worried him because it seemed to be getting more and more difficult to think consecutively, to recall what had gone before. The idea of using the escape apparatus came to him and he was not aware that it had done so several times before and been immediately rejected. He leaned closer to Harding.

'Peter.'

'Yes, Keith?'

'I don't like the way this is developing.'

'Who the hell does?' Harding asked.

'Oh, I know, but I'm beginning to wonder if we shouldn't risk an escape attempt while we still have the strength. Didn't you tell me that you had some talks with a boffin at Blockhouse recently on DSEA techniques?'

When Harding didn't reply immediately Keith Bryers frowned and said worriedly, 'You did, Peter. I'm sure it was you. What do you think our chances would be? Or was it someone else I was talking to?'

'It was me,' Harding told him and frowned in his turn. It was silly of Bryers to clutch at straws, to break his own rule about not talking when he must know that their chances of surviving at the pressure outside the ship were zero. Or was oxygen deficiency really taking hold at last, making them all progressively mindless? It looked like it with the ship's captain making ridiculous suggestions and not being sure to whom he had talked. That being so it was essential to put him straight before he started giving orders which would kill everybody aboard if the engine room bulkhead didn't

29

collapse first and do it for him. The internal bulkheads weren't designed to withstand as much pressure as the hull and if…

Suddenly aware that his own mind was wandering, Harding dragged it back to the issue he was being asked to discuss. It seemed to take an almost physical effort to do that and summon up for presentation the information he had been given.

'Forget it, Keith,' he said. 'If you flooded to equalise the pressure at this depth you would be opening a particularly lethal Pandora's box before we even got as far as opening the hatch for the first man to leave. This bloke I talked to admitted that a lot of what he said was theoretical, but he had had some pretty nasty things done to himself in a pressure chamber or something which bore the theory out.'

Harding sat, remembering the doctor who had allowed himself to be used as a guinea-pig, marvelling at the man's courage in inducing physical and chemical changes in himself so that others might benefit from the observed results. It was a form of bravery he found beyond praise and almost beyond belief.

'What did he say, Peter?'

'What? Oh yes, of course. Er, he said there's a chance of getting oxygen poisoning if that's all you're breathing, like from a DSEA set, anywhere below periscope depth, although it takes different people different ways and some can use it much deeper. He couldn't explain the variation, but this deep it would be almost certain suicide. Then – Oh Christ!'

'What's the matter?'

'Nothing's the matter. It's just so difficult to remember with this fog in my head. Where had I got to?'

'Oxygen poisoning,' Bryers said.

'Yes. Well, then there's carbon dioxide. Five per cent or so is okay at atmospheric pressure. We aren't a lot above that at the moment, but you open those valves and increase it to what's outside the hull, say eight atmospheres, ten atmospheres, I dunno, and you're talking about a partial carbon dioxide pressure of at least forty per cent and the old system just won't take that, not by a long chalk it won't.'

His fingers massaging his eyes and temples Harding went on, 'Then he mentioned the danger of something called nitrogen narcosis. At a depth like this we'd be so much under the influence that we probably couldn't be bothered to escape.'

'All right,' Bryers said. 'You've made your point.'

'No I haven't,' Harding told him. 'It's a sharper point than that. We haven't even got as far as starting the ascent yet. That's when we run into the "bends". Less than five minutes exposure down here will give you a "bend" when you get to the surface, and that includes the time taken to flood the compartment. How many of the chaps do you imagine are going to get out of one bloody escape hatch before that?'

Bryers didn't reply and Harding asked another question.

'And how many recompression chambers do you suppose they've got lined up for us up there? Sixty-odd? Because that's what we would need if the people who get "bends" were to live!'

He had been speaking with increasing anger, as though the whole thing was Bryers' fault, then he remembered those already dead and added more quietly, 'Sorry, Keith. Forty-odd I meant. But anyway, even if they've got chambers that hold more than one person, they'll only have a couple of them. They'll have needed those for the divers, but what's the use of that to the vast majority down here?'

'Okay,' Bryers said. 'Let's shut up now and go back to saying our prayers.' He sounded depressed, but no longer irresponsible.

Thirty-eight minutes later the first of Lieutenant Blakie's bolts slammed home into *Titan's* pressure hull.

*

Blakie lay in one of the chambers aboard the tug waiting for the pressure to take effect, fighting waves of nausea and dizziness, trying to ignore the pain in his joints and abdomen, feeling the numbness which could lead to paralysis in his feet.

The two deep dives had lasted too long and had been too close together. Those things he was perfectly well aware of, but there had been no time to waste and now the "bends" had got him. What had she called them?

Yeah, aeroembolism. That was it. Aeroembolism. Wouldn't matter really if he could stay where he was long enough for his system to reabsorb the nitrogen bubbles free in his body, blocking small veins and threatening to block arteries. Everything would be all right given time, but time he hadn't got. Bert would be returning to the surface before long and the work couldn't wait. One bolt was already successfully lodged in *Titan's* pressure hull, protruding through it into the radio room which was clearer than most places of pipes and other obstructions, but one was no use. You couldn't pump a sub up like a tyre, for God's sake! You had to have an exhaust point too before you could give them air. They'd have spread carbon dioxide-absorbing crystals about of course, but that did nothing to ease the lack of oxygen. They'd be very low on oxygen by now, he knew. Gasping like stranded fish probably.

Blakie retched dryly, then wiped moisture from his eyes. There was that bloody "met" report as well, the wind backing to the west again within forty-eight hours. So little time for *Phoenix* and the lighters to lift *Titan* and the lighters hadn't even arrived yet! Well, that wasn't his problem, but it seemed so pathetic to prolong life only to see it snatched away by a storm which would snap the air-lines like cotton thread. That would finish them. With two open apertures in the hull, too right it would!

He began to wonder how far Bert would have got assembling the gun at its second firing position outside the torpedo tube space for'ard, but shrugged angrily. Bert would tell him and he'd see for himself when he got down there. Symptoms easing at last. There was something he had intended to do while he was cooped up in this tank. Of course! Write a letter. He had asked for writing materials before they shut him in so that he could do that. For a little while he sat thinking, then took pen, paper and an envelope from his trouser pocket.

*

The twenty-first man to die was the Chief Engine Room Artificer. The first lieutenant, dragging a water container along the deck because he no longer had the strength to carry it, found him. He knew that the Chief ERA was dead because his mouth was open and the expression on his face was silly. The Chief ERA had never looked silly. In addition, he didn't have sweat running on his skin like everybody else.

'Tough tit,' the first lieutenant said. He thought that was rather funny and giggled. Nobody in the group paid any attention to him, or to the dead man, or to the water he had brought. That seemed reasonable enough and he nodded as though in agreement with their indifference, staying on all fours beside them, listening to the breath rasping in and out of their lungs clear above the roaring in his ears. For nearly a minute he knelt there wondering whether or not he should report the death to somebody, then forgot what it was he was trying to decide and lay down on the deck.

*

The guiding line Bert Prescott had positioned had parted and Blakie grounded near the submarine's stern which, he thought, was bloody annoying when it was the other end he wanted and the vast, looming shape seemed to stretch as far as a city block before losing itself in the darkness beyond the range of his lamp. Sighing impatiently he began to move slowly ahead, his huge boots sending up drifts of sand which hung in the water about him like smoke. It was easier when he reached the hull and could assist his progress by grasping the occasional hand-holds it offered, but it still took him a long time to reach the mid-ships section where the armoured hose curved down from the bolt fired into the radio room. He had to leave the hull there to cross the hose where it began to run along the ocean floor before slanting up towards the surface otherwise his own lines would have fouled it.

It was a pity, he admitted, that he had allowed the row with the surgeon-commander to develop. The man had only been trying to do what he could for his patient, but he seemed to have no sense of either proportion or priorities and his suggestion that the back-up team of divers could handle this final tricky phase had been fatuous. They had had nothing but the briefest run-down on the bolt-gun. They didn't *know* it the way he and Bert did. Still, that was no reason for telling a surgeon-commander to go

33

and do impossible things to himself. Blakie sighed again and moved on towards the bows, wishing he felt just a little less tired.

Bert Prescott had done a very good job on positioning the steel framework supporting the bolt-gun, but then Bert would, which was why he had just recommended him for reinstatement as petty officer. Blakie checked the alignment of the bolt. It was pointing almost exactly at the small X he had scratched on the hull during his previous dive. Each of the four wires securing the contraption to the hull against the recoil of the explosive charge had a bottle-screw at its nearest end. He tightened one fractionally, found the aim to be perfect and began to bang on the hull with a spanner.

There was no reply.

'Oh you bastards!' Blakie said. 'Oh you bloody Pommy bastards! Don't you dare give up on me now!'

For two minutes he hammered the hull, feeling the strength draining from him, then dropped the spanner.

'All right, you fuckers!' he shouted into his helmet. 'See if you can hear *this*!'

He took hold of the lanyard of the gun and jerked it.

*

The combined thudding shock of the discharge and of the bolt piercing an inch of heavy-duty steel roused the Torpedo Gunner's Mate. He thought that the noise had come from his kingdom, the tube space a few feet from where he was lying. That was something irregular and irregularities required investigation. He crawled forward to investigate it, then turned and crawled aft again all the way to the wardroom, worming his way over two prone figures in his path. They were the twenty-second and twenty-third dead men aboard, but he didn't know that.

The captain was sitting slumped forward across the table and the TGM grasped him by the thigh and shook it.

'Cap'n sir! Wake up!' The words came out in a gasping croak.

'Oh, hello, Jenner.'

'It's Mallows, sir. There's another… another of them bolts in… in my tube space and somebody's banging on the… hull again!'

'Thank you, Jenner.'

'Bloody hell! Wake up… will you?' Mallows said and shook the trouser leg he was holding as strongly as he could.

Suddenly Bryers sat upright and looked down at the chief petty officer.

'Mallows! Did you… did you say… Yes, by God, you did! Anyone else awake in here?'

'Mmm,' Gascoigne said, but didn't move.

'Then pull yourself to… together. The air's… here. Second… bolt.'

For a long moment Gascoigne's face remained blank, then a degree of intelligence returned to it like sunshine trying to penetrate the overcast.

'DSEA set,' he said. 'Permission to use a set, sir? Think better with… with oxygen.'

He saw Bryers nod, dragged himself off the cushioned locker he had been sitting on and bent to lift the lid. It seemed to take him a very long time to fumble it open, pull out a Davis escape set and turn a small wheel to puncture the seal of the oxygen bottle. Then the mouth-piece was between his teeth and he took two long breaths. Immediately his head began to spin at the impact of the oxygen his body had grown unaccustomed to, but before he could fall he snatched the tube from his mouth and thrust it at Bryers, gulping again himself at the submarine's foul air. But his strength had returned miraculously, his brain was clearing and it was easier to talk.

'Only a couple of breaths, sir, or you'll pass out.'

Bryers nodded for the second time, inhaled, dragged the set across the table towards him and passed the tube down to the chief petty officer lying near his feet.

'Only a little, Mallows. You heard what Lieutenant Gascoigne said. As soon as you feel dizzy breathe the ships air. Carbon dioxide is the antidote for oxygen poisoning.'

Gascoigne was already hammering on the hull with a wheel-spanner. At once the monotonous rhythmic rapping from outside changed to the tap and scrape of Morse. Tap tap scratch. Scratch tap. Tap tap tap…

'Unscrew – ends bolts – anticlockwise,' Gascoigne read aloud. 'If jammed – saw off – confirm.'

Tap bang tap – R – Gascoigne sent with his spanner.

More Morse from outside. 'When done send OK.'

He hammered the letter R again.

'Take another DSEA set and unscrew the one in the radio room, John,' the captain said. 'Mallows, come for'ard with me.'

In the control room Gascoigne switched on more lights, stepped over sprawled figures and took a monkey-wrench from a tool box. In the radio room he breathed briefly from an escape set and started work on the bolt. One minute later he staggered back into the control room, gasping and sweating. The end of the bolt hadn't moved at all and, he thought, any saws would be in the flooded engine room. Awful to fail now of all times.

One of the group on the deck was a big seaman with wide shoulders and heavy arms covered in tattoos. He knelt beside him and held the mouthpiece of the set close to his face.

With very little pause the man opened his eyes and said, 'What?'

'I haven't said anything yet,' Gascoigne told him, 'but you look like the ship's Tarzan. Come and unscrew something for me.'

The sailor groaned and lurched to his feet. 'Me Jane today more like, sir.'

'Well, never mind. You look a lot stronger than me.'

Standing in the doorway to the radio room Gascoigne watched the big muscles tighten and the point of the bolt turn. From behind him, 'Captain says to tell you the for'ard bolt's undone, sir.' Mallow's voice.

'Thank you,' he said, took the monkey-wrench from the tattooed sailor and rapped out OK with it.

Forty seconds later a jet of cold fresh air was drying the sweat on his face.

*

Flag Officer Submarines, his mind preoccupied amongst other things by *Titan*, crossed the ante-room towards his office without looking at the woman who was both his confidential secretary and his flag-lieutenant.

Automatically, "'Morning, Susan,' he said.

It was not until he reached his own door that it occurred to him that she hadn't acknowledged his greeting and he looked at her curiously. She was sitting, cheeks sucked in, eyebrows raised, the eyes themselves very wide, staring at her desk.

'Are you all right, Susan?'

'They've got air down to *Titan*, sir.' Still she didn't look at him.

'Have they indeed? Thank *God* for that! Tell me about it.'

Instead of doing so she picked up a signal form and thrust it in his direction, her arm at full stretch. Never had he known her do anything like that before and a puzzled frown replaced the pleasure on his face as he walked to her and took the paper from her.

"First stage Operation Reclaim successfully completed", he read, "but regret inform you Lt. C. J. Blakie, DSC, RANVR died in achieving this. Full report follows'.

'Oh, I'm so sorry. Are you . .? Were you . .?'

'Good Lord, no,' she said. 'Except as part of the operation I haven't given him a thought since he was here and I only met him that once.'

'Then what's the matter?'

Another thrusting movement of her arm and he found himself holding an envelope. It was inscribed "3rd Officer Susan Somebody, WRNS. Office of Flag Officer Submarines, "Northways", London. Private and Personal. By hand of Able Seaman Albert Prescott".

'Are you sure you want me to read this?'

She looked up at him then, shrugged and said, 'You might as well. In fact you'd better. There's a message in it for you.'

He held her eyes for a moment longer before taking the single sheet of paper from the envelope and unfolding it.

"Dear Sue,

I've got this gut-feeling which I've never had before that I'm not going to get away with this one and I'm feeling a bit crook too which is why I'm writing this letter. I haven't got a girl of my own in this country, so I've sort of co-opted you, if that's the right word, and I'm sitting here thinking about your legs and the way your eyes screwed up at the corners when you were laughing at me in the Admiral's office. You could have been a good Aussie with those crow's feet.

I don't really know what the hell I'm telling you this for except

it makes what's in my mind more real somehow and I'd like you to
know that I think you're an extremely smashing lady. Sorry I used
bad language when we met.

   With my love,
   Cy Blakie,
   Lieutenant, RANVR

PS. With luck you'll never read this but, if you do, please tell the
Admiral that Bert Prescott shouldn't be no able seaman and to have
him rated petty officer again. It was always my fault he got boozed."

When he refolded the letter she said rather tonelessly, 'Crook is Australian for unwell.'

'Yes.'

For countable seconds there was silence then, 'It's so endearingly, childishly disarming, sir. It makes me want to howl.'

'Yes,' the admiral said again, 'I can understand that, but before you deluge the office remember that you gave him some happy thoughts.'

A funeral cortege left Portsmouth Barracks two days later. The label on one of the wreaths read "For Cy, from his girl Sue".

Chapter Four

It would have been difficult for anyone to recognise the girl sitting bolt-upright in a chair in an attractive room of a house off Sloane Street in London as a beauty. She was wearing an unbecoming dressing-gown and felt slippers, both too large for her, her red hair was tangled and there were dark circles under her slanting green eyes, eyes a little blood-shot set in a drawn face. The dressing gown and slippers were her husband's and she had been wearing them sitting, as she now was, with only the shortest of breaks, for more than thirty hours. During all of that time she had been willing the telephone beside her to ring and now it *was* ringing she was afraid to answer it.

The bell tinkled remorselessly on and she drew the upper part of her body slowly away from it as though it were some poisonous reptile then, as if pitting her speed against a cobra's, reached out and snatched the instrument from its rest.

'Yiz?' she said. It was the best she could manage with her teeth buried in her lower lip.

'Lady Abigail Harding?' A woman's voice.

'Yiz,' she said again.

'This is the office of Flag Officer Submarines. There's encouraging news about your husband. He's still confined to bed, but is breathing easily. Do you understand?'

Gail released her lip, tasted blood, wiped the little wound with the side of her hand and sighed softly.

'Are you still there, Lady Abigail?'

'Yes,' she said. 'I'm still here and, yes, I understand. What's the prognosis?'

'The doctors are cautiously optimistic. If there are no further complications there should be a complete recovery. I can't say more on the phone, but I'll keep you fully informed.'

'I'd be more than just grateful if you would,' Gail told 3rd Officer Susan Wade.

The receiver rattled when she put it down and only then did she realise that her whole body was trembling. Whether it was doing so out of relief or in the knowledge that the waiting had to go on she was unsure, but at least he was alive at this minute so now was the time, she told herself, to bathe, change her clothes, eat something and generally stiffen her spine. She'd start as soon as the trembling eased.

Gradually it did so and she fell asleep in the chair.

*

Commander Brown was an anxious man and that made him angry because he didn't hold with anxiety. He believed in facts, plain north country common-sense and his slide-rule, but this day he didn't like what his slide-rule was telling him. Or his common-sense.

It had taken sixteen divers operating sometimes in pairs and sometimes in fours over two days to work the enormous slings under *Titan's* hull. Their job had been complicated by the presence of the air-hoses which they dared not so much as touch, but now the submarine was rising, inch by inch, towards the surface.

Brown propped himself more comfortably against *Phoenix's* list, all 21,000 tons of her tilted sideways by her share of *Titan's* weight. The two big lighters were taking the rest of it, both of them deep down by the bows where the lifting equipment was. His glance took in the vessels of the small Armada, the masts of the destroyers far to seaward protecting them from U-boat attack, the tankers laden with water ballast acting as storm barriers, the tugs, the collection of smaller service craft. Behind him somewhere he knew that there was an anti-aircraft cruiser, but he couldn't see her from where he stood. Nor could he see the Spitfires waiting on air-strips inland, but he was glad to know that they were there and that there was no need for him to watch the sky. Watching the sea was more than enough with the swell increasing almost imperceptibly, but increasing. He was sure of it.

'Hello, Fred.'

He turned towards the speaker, but didn't immediately recognise the tubby figure in the peaked uniform cap, then he smiled.

'Bert! *Petty Officer* Bert Prescott! It's good to see you, lad, and, my word, that was a fast bit of promotion.'

Prescott nodded. 'Admiral told Digger and me to go and see him when our job was done, so I went. He said we'd done well and that Digger had recommended me for reinstatement as PO, so he fixed it on the phone with the commanding officer of *Dolphin*. You know, the submarine base at Blockhouse.'

'Aye. I know, lad. Likely be a medal in it for you too.'

'Yes, so they tell me,' Prescott said. 'Digger and me both, but I'd rather have *him* back, the screwy Aussie bastard.'

Brown contented himself with a murmured "Aye" and Prescott went on, 'I see you're lifting. What's the situation now?'

'She's resting on sloping under-water ledge near enough hundred and ninety feet down,' Brown told him. 'We've been using tidal lift. Lucky the bottom shelves here. It's all winches can do to handle weight of wires, let alone sub, but every time tide lifts *Phoenix* and lighters, *Titan* comes up too and we shorten in wires before tide drops again. Slow, but it works.'

'No trouble, then.'

'Not 'til about an hour ago, Bert.'

'What happened an hour ago?'

Four of the twelve massive flexible steel-wire ropes stretching down to *Titan* passed over *Phoenix's* side quite close to where they were standing and Brown looked at them. Thick as they were, thicker than his arms, they were thrumming with strain. That was all right. Let them, he thought. They were designed to thrum. Then he began to think about the thousands of yards of chain cable lying on the ocean floor, stretching in several directions, anchoring *Phoenix* and the lighters in position. Would they hold if the swell rose another couple of feet, or drag and let *Titan* slip out of her

41

cradle back to the bottom? He'd been through it all before, but his feeling of urgency was stronger now and he took out his slide-rule, then put it away again because common-sense could tell him more.

'What happened an hour ago,' he said, 'was that I got to feeling there was change in weather coming. "Met" boys say no, the northerly will last another twenty-four hours, but they were wrong before when they said wind would back westerly last Tuesday. Thank God they were then, or we'd never have got as far as we have, but I'm afraid they're wrong again. Swell's coming up. I'm sure of it, and that's bad news that is.'

'Then what are you going to do, Fred?'

Commander Brown stood motionless for a long fifteen seconds, the skirts of his fawn raincoat flapping about his legs. He looked down at the sea and up at the sky which, moments before, he had been prepared to leave to the RAF and the anti-aircraft cruiser, then jammed his hat more firmly onto his head. The action made his ears stick out ridiculously, but somehow he didn't look ridiculous.

'I'm going to recommend to skipper of *Titan* that he gives crew order to bail out while they still can,' he said. 'That's what I'm going to do.'

He turned away abruptly and walked towards the ladder leading to *Phoenix's* bridge.

*

'Yes, that's all perfectly clear,' Bryers said. 'We'll start at once. See you up top.'

Communication with the world above him had been easy ever since a diver had connected a telephone line to the radio aerial and his leading telegraphist had wired a hand-set to the aerial's inboard end, but he wished that he had not had to listen to this last message, a message which had reduced the probability of rescue for all of them to the possibility of escape for a very few.

Absently he replaced the telephone and stood staring at the strange bolt which had unscrewed to become a tube protruding through the hull within three feet of him, feeling the jet of air coming from it fluttering his hair and pressing on his eye-lids. It was pleasant, that pressure, and he let his eyes close under its urging as though resting from all the other pressures on him.

42

The days had stretched his nerves even as they themselves had stretched to unbelievable lengths. Two of them with the air growing progressively more foul. Another two, after the bolts had given some of them their lives back on temporary lease, listening to the periodic scrape of the slings being worked into position by divers who could not stay for long at such a depth. And yet another two when long periods of silence alternated with the hours of creaking and rasping as metal inched across sand marking their agonisingly slow rise towards the surface. The infinitesimal flick of the pointers on the deep depth gauges around their dials had recorded that rise, but now the pointers were still and would either remain so or reverse their direction with dramatic suddenness.

That knowledge, which the telephone conversation had given him, had calmed Bryers as if, like over-extended elastic, his nervous system was no longer capable of reacting effectively to any additional tugs of fear. He opened his eyes and walked to the wardroom, whistling tonelessly through his teeth.

*

To Harding he said, 'This is the end of the bus route, Peter. We get out and walk now.'

Harding looked at him and then at the depth gauge.

'Weather?'

'Yes. We're to leave at once. You and your class will go first from the conning tower and gun tower. The rest of us will be using the torpedo stowage compartment. Let's get cracking.'

It would, Harding knew, take much less time to flood the two towers than the big torpedo stowage space and that meant exposure to pressure for a shorter period for him and the officers of the command qualification course. "Perishers" was the slang expression for those who attended that course. Its derivation was uncertain although it could have come from "periscope", but when the word entered his mind then, he pushed it out again because of its more obvious connotation. It had, he thought, no right to have come to him anyway because Bryers was offering them a better chance of survival than he would be giving his own people.

'No,' he said. 'We'll leave before your officers, if you insist, but not before your men. Send some of your people who have families up through the towers.'

Bryers smiled tiredly at him. 'Yes, you had to say that, didn't you Peter? Now you've got it off your chest let me remind you that while you are senior to me I'm the captain of this ship and you'll go when and how I say you'll go. You and your chaps are getting the choice spot because you are of greater potential value to the Submarine Service than anyone else here. Also you are guests on board. That's my decision.'

Harding opened his mouth to say something but, before he could speak, Bryers added, 'It is also the order of Flag Officer Submarines passed to me from the rescue ship just now.' He injected the last sentence with just enough pomposity to make the lie credible and, because he did not want to be thwarted in what he guessed would be his last contribution to the war effort, was thankful for Harding's shrug of resignation.

'Right, that's settled,' he said. 'Number One, I want everybody for'ard with their sets. The Cox'n can give us a final run through the drill. He did a stint in the practice escape tank at Blockhouse as an instructor, so he's worth listening to.'

The torpedo stowage compartment was crowded with men and so that he could be seen Bryers stood on the torpedo lashed in place over the covered body of Leading Seaman Glenn and, head bent, looked down at their pale, stubbled faces.

'We're abandoning ship before the storm that's coming sends us back to the bottom,' he told them, 'but before we start I want you all to listen carefully to the Cox'n. Your lives will depend on your carrying out the correct procedure, so pay attention.'

He had had further talks with Harding about the possibilities of escape by DSEA after the air supply had reached them and knew that even at the ship's reduced depth only a miracle could ensure their safety, but he kept that knowledge out of his face and voice when he said, 'Carry on, Cox'n.'

A stocky man replied, 'Aye aye, sir. I'll have that tall lieutenant from the command course, please. You, sir. They can all see what you're doing. You're lofty enough.'

Gascoigne edged his way towards him and stood watching while the coxswain unhitched a reinforced canvas tunnel secured to the deckhead like a concertina. Hanging down it reached to within three feet of the deck and the coxswain fastened it in place with the cords attached to it. When he turned back to Gascoigne and spoke, his voice had taken on the tone, half hectoring, half wheedling, of the instructor who has used the same words hundreds of times before.

'Now, sir, you'll be going out by the conning tower or gun tower, not up this trunk, but most of the routine is the same so, tell me, when the space begins to flood and the water is rising up your legs and body what happens to you, sir?'

'I get wet,' Gascoigne said.

'Very funny, sir. The correct answer is that you experience a rapidly increasing pressure on the ears which you will clear by swallowing or blowing with your mouth shut and your nostrils pinched. You will also experience a desire to panic which you will suppress. This will be particularly so when the water starts to cover your face. Now then, the set. You've already got it on your chest, so you're ready to go. On nose clip, on goggles, crack seal on oxygen bottle by turning this little valve wheel, insert mouth-piece and breathe normally. If breathing is not normal adjust the valve until it is. All right, sir?'

'Yes thank you, Cox'n.'

'Then do it, sir, so everyone can see.'

Gascoigne did it, suddenly feeling almost as nervous at being watched by the crew while he carried out actions which should have been second nature to him but were not, as he was of the frightening ordeal to come. He was still berating himself for not having taken the trouble that Harding had to familiarise himself with all aspects of the technique, wondering if some aversion connected with superstitious fear had prevented him from doing so, when he found himself breathing easily from the set.

'Right, sir. Turn off the oxygen and remove the mouthpiece. That wasn't so hard, was it now?'

'Simple, Cox'n,' Gascoigne said, pushed the goggles up onto his forehead and looked around at the mass of men. The coxswain was explaining that the bottom of the canvas trunk would be submerged when air and water pressure equalised following the flooding of the compartment, that the escapers would have to duck under to enter it. None of that concerned him because he would be escaping from the conning tower, not through the trunk, and he had a moment to observe the crew. Fear manifested itself in many ways, he knew, from palor, sweating, trembling, through giggling to bored indifference. The symptoms were all there. Even the coxswain's rather supercilious demeanour he recognised as a defence mechanism. Muscles straining in body and limbs betrayed his own condition.

'Now, when you're outside the ship,' the coxswain was saying, 'push off very gently, avoiding all the gubbins like lifting-wires, the jumping wire, air lines, the lot. If you hit them you'll likely do yourself a permanent injury. You'll see them all right in the lights the divers have rigged. Then you proceed upwards. You'll know which way is up by watching your air bubbles and…'

Titan trembled as though in response to some distant explosion, then swayed slightly. The movement was small, but enough to set the closely packed crowd of men swaying in unison.

'Better hurry it up, Cox'n' Bryers said.

'Aye aye, sir. Right everybody. This lieutenant understands. Anyone here who doesn't?'

'I'd like to ask a question.'

Gascoigne looked down at the speaker, a small sailor standing beside him.

'What is it, lad?' The coxswain's voice.

'These rolled up rubber apron things under the set. I was taught we had to unroll them and use them like an anti-parachute to stop ourselves going up too fast.'

'No!'

Heads turned in the direction from which the sharply spoken monosyllable had come.

'I'm sorry to interrupt,' Harding said, 'but if you'll allow me, Keith, I think everybody should get to the surface in the shortest possible time so that they are exposed to the shortest possible period of pressure. These are

Scottish waters, it's March outside after a long winter and there's no question at all of people dawdling up trying to decompress themselves by stages. The cold would get them.' He almost added, 'In fact I don't give anybody much more than five minutes to live in this sea temperature,' but bit down on the words and substituted, 'Go up fast, reduce the oxygen supply on the way, then cut it off completely and breathe out hard, otherwise the oxygen in the lungs will expand and burst them when the pressure outside has gone.'

Before Bryers could reply, somebody screamed, 'Oh, Jesus! Oh, blessed Jesus!' Then there was a brief scuffle, a thump and silence.

'Very well,' Bryers said. 'You all heard Lieutenant Harding. Peter, you and your chaps go and man the towers.'

Commander Brown's new westerly gale pushed another tentative finger towards *Phoenix* and the lighters, making them rise and dip slowly, tugging at their multiple moorings. A hundred and ninety feet below them sand rasped against steel as *Titan* moved restlessly in the cradle in which they held her.

*

Crouched at the top of the conning tower, his knees almost up to his chin and the top of Rooke's head pressing hard against his buttocks, Gascoigne released the two heavy clips of the upper hatch. From below the sound of the lower hatch thudding shut reached him. Then the water came. He had expected it to flood slowly in, filling the tower gradually from the bottom to near the top where the air it had compressed would halt its progress, but it wasn't like that.

As though furious at having been so long thwarted of victory the sea's advance guard arrived in the form of a freezing jet which seemed to flail about the tower, soaking him, confusing his senses, until all that he was certain about was the presence of agonising pain in his ears. Then the fury stopped almost as abruptly as it had started, his ear-drums popped and the pain faded from his memory. He was sitting in water now with his head and shoulders in a pocket of highly compressed ship's atmosphere. Beneath him Rooke's head nudged impatiently and he pushed at the upper hatch. At first it didn't move, but when he pressed harder it opened to the accompaniment of a disorientating flurry of incoming water and outgoing air.

It was only when his shoulder jarred against the metal spreaders between the two periscope standards that Gascoigne realised that he had floated clear of the submarine. The impact stopped his rise, pushing him sideways, and in the lights the divers had secured to the hull he saw first Rooke and then another figure float up past him. The second man's arms were trailing, doing nothing to replace the dislodged mouth-piece dangling from its strap below the chin. He lost sight of them then because the blow on his shoulder had set up a slow turning motion and forget them too, noticing that he was rising again, listening to the rasping sound recorded by his inner ear as he breathed from the rubberised third lung on his chest, seeing the vast, partially illuminated shape of *Titan* apparently revolving beneath him.

Cold. Bitterly, terrifyingly cold. Somebody had said something about that and about reducing the oxygen supply on the way up. Disobedient fingers reluctant to turn the little valve wheel. Try again. Done it. Noise. Not in his inner ear. Waterborne. A screeching roar. From the surface? Look up. Daylight certainly, but nothing else. Look down. A shape rearing towards him, huge, menacing, increasing in size as he watched. Paralysis of superstitious fear, memories, half-forgotten, of a fabulous sea-monster – the Kraken its name was, wasn't it? – filling his mind. Then reason reasserting itself. It was only *Titan* swinging about her mid-ship section, her bows rising as the flooded stern dropped. Only *Titan* pivoting at the edge of the shelf she had been lifted to. Only *Titan*, receding now, finally succumbing to her last enemy, the storm he had watched through the periscope aeons before. Not cold any more. Just very tired. Darkness coming.

*

The thick steel-wire ropes were still rigid, held under tension by their own weight, but they had stopped thrumming with strain and *Phoenix*, no longer listing, rose and fell staggeringly under the gale's onslaught. Close at hand the anti-aircraft cruiser continued its slow circling, to seaward the destroyers shipped green water over their plunging bows, far inland the Spitfires waited on their air-strips, guarding a corpse.

'Right bloody shame that,' Commander Brown said. He said it lightly, but his face was stricken. Petty Officer Prescott glanced at him and away again, not speaking.

'*Here they come*!' A wind-borne shout from *Phoenix's* bridge. Heads bobbing in the water near the ship's side. A loud-hailer blaring orders to the small service craft pitching near-by. Heaving-lines and life-belts dropping. Men clambering down a scrambling-net towards the survivors. One, disdaining it, diving into the sea.

'Seven, Fred. At least you got seven.'

Commander Brown, knuckles showing white on the ship's rail, his face creased again like a very old apple, but with tears running along the cracks now, shaking his head.

'Not me, Bert Prescott,' he said. 'Thee. Thee and Digger Blakie. You two got them, lad.'

Chapter Five

'Sit down,' Flag Officer Submarines said.

They sat, Lieutenants Rooke, Little, Gascoigne and Chase, the four who had once been six. Their instructor, Peter Harding, sat down with them.

He was sorry, the admiral told them, that Leigh and Brewster had not survived the ascent and they made murmuring noises in reply, Gascoigne remembering the figure with trailing arms and the gaping mouth from which no bubbles came. That had been Leigh because Brewster had died in a recompression chamber aboard *Phoenix*.

'Rotten thing to happen to you chaps on the last day of your course, or on any other day for that matter,' the admiral went on. There didn't seem to be anything to say in reply to that and they remained silent until he added, 'Still, you're more fortunate than the rest,' when they murmured again. That was the only reference made to the loss of *Titan's* entire crew.

When he next spoke it was with sudden briskness. 'Right. Now, I want to talk with each of you about the future. I expect you would rather do that separately.'

Lieutenant Chase replied first. 'I don't mind talking in front of the others, sir. I've had it. The sight of the inside of another submarine would drive me stark staring bonkers. I'm most awfully sorry, sir.' He had kept his voice low and even, but the effort of doing so and the admission itself had brought beads of sweat out on his forehead. The admiral noted the fact.

'My dear boy, don't you go around being sorry. Yours is a perfectly normal reaction. Thank you for not beating about the bush. Think about what you would like to do in the surface fleet and come and see me after your survivor's leave and I'll do my best to fix it for you. See Susan Wade, my flag-lieutenant, about an appointment. She's the blonde Wren officer outside. Gascoigne?'

'If it's all right with you, sir,' Gascoigne said, 'I'd like to go to Blockhouse at once, go to sea in any boat there doing a day's exercise dived and spend half an hour in the practice escape tank. I'll know after that.'

'Good. You talk to Susan Wade too. She'll send the necessary signal and see that you're issued with a rail warrant. Rooke?'

Gascoigne leant back in his chair feeling grateful to the admiral for not having talked about getting back on a horse immediately after falling off it, listening to Rooke saying, 'I'm all right, sir. Quite correctly I've never been credited with much imagination and I can't imagine that set of circumstances occurring again.'

'You, Little?'

'I'd like to go to Blockhouse with Gascoigne, sir.'

The four were dismissed after that, leaving Harding with the admiral.

'May I ask a question, sir?'

'Of course.'

'Did you order Bryers to give us the safer escape routes?'

'No,' the admiral said, 'but I gather from your question that he told you I did. Is that correct?'

'Yes, sir.'

'Well he did absolutely right and it can't have been easy for him. He'd have liked to have sent up the youngest, or married men, I expect.'

'Exactly, sir. I just thought you should know.'

'Thank you for telling me, Peter. Now, how about you? Are you prepared to go on teaching?'

He had been expecting the question, but Harding still took time to consider it before saying, 'I don't think I should, sir. I don't feel as positively as Chase. By that I mean I doubt if I'd be driven round the bend, but I'd be an inhibiting factor, an old woman breathing down their necks all the time, using the periscope too much myself in the closing stages of a practice attack. That sort of thing. That's no way to instil self-confidence in…' He stopped talking and shrugged.

'What a damned nuisance,' the admiral said. 'What a bloody damned nuisance! I was afraid that would be the case.'

Harding nodded. 'I know, sir, but I'll stay with the job until you can find somebody to replace me, if you want me to.'

The admiral looked slightly startled for a moment, then smiled before saying, 'I meant what a nuisance for you personally. You could have done without this after your bit of trouble in *Trigger*. Still, you have a great deal to be thankful for. Have you had time to think about what you might like to do?'

'Yes, sir. I'd like to transfer to the Fleet Air Arm as a pilot.'

'Hopeless, Peter. You're much too old.'

'At twenty-five, sir?'

''Fraid so,' the admiral said. 'They like to get their hands on them at eighteen. In fact I was once told by one of those Battle of Britain types that they would have taken them at sixteen if the government had let them. Very fast reflexes at that age and too young to have developed the sort of imagination that makes you think twice. "Look, Ma, no hands" stage really. You'd better go for something else.'

'I understand their point of view, sir, but I have one thing in my favour. I can fly already. That should count for something.'

'How on earth did you manage that? You've been at sea ever since you left school.'

'My father was a pilot, sir,' Harding told him. 'Before the war he owned an Avro Cadet three-seater biplane. He kept it just for fun and taught me to fly it. I've done thirty hours solo.'

'Well, well, well. Still, thirty hours isn't very much, is it?'

'They put pilots into the Battle of Britain with about ten hours on trainers and six or seven on Spitfires or Hurricanes, sir.'

'Hmm. Why didn't you go into the RAF or the Fleet Air Arm in the first place? Some people might say you failed in your duty there.'

Harding frowned. 'I hope you're not one of them, sir.'

Frowning in his turn the admiral said, 'Now none of that, young man. I'm well aware of your record and your decorations prove that it is good. I was simply making an observation. Answer my question, please.'

'Aye, aye, sir. Firstly, I always wanted to be a submariner. Secondly, I was a school-boy when my father let me go solo. I thought I could have got him into trouble if I'd revealed that.'

'And that doesn't apply now?'

'No, sir, it doesn't. My parents were killed in the Blitz. Not that it would really have mattered anyway. I know that now.'

'I see. Well, if you're sure you know what you're doing put your application for transfer in to me. I'll see that it's forwarded.' The admiral nodded dismissal then added, 'If you talk nicely to Susan Wade outside she'll probably find you a car to take you home.'

No matter how briefly Harding had been separated from his wife he always experienced the same shock of astonished pleasure at the sight of her. It came strongly when she opened the door of their home off Sloane Street to him, a surge of surprise and wonder that anyone like her existed outside the covers of a fashion magazine, double wonder that she had married him. There was no trace now of the bedraggled woman in dressing gown and felt slippers who had kept her vigil by the telephone for so long. He was looking at a svelte, long-legged girl with dark red hair and slanting eyes in a hauntingly lovely face. The eyes regarded him gravely, but the face held no other expression.

'Hello,' he said.

Her only reply was to reach out and trace the lines of strain on his forehead and around his mouth with the tip of a finger. Then she took hold of his wrist and led him towards the stairs.

Fifteen minutes later Gail Harding spoke for the first time.

'Better, darling?'

'Much, much better.' His voice a whisper.

'Good. When we heard you were safe Daddy sent round a bottle of champagne. Let's go and open it.'

Only the sound of soft, slow breathing came from Harding. She smiled at his sleeping face, settled down beside him and drew the covers over their bodies.

*

'Are you the two officers for *Dolphin*, sir?'

'That's right,' Gascoigne said and walked with Little down the steps at *Vernon*, the Navy's torpedo school, to the waiting boat. Its coxswain cast off at once and the boat swung in a half circle to cross Portsmouth harbour to Gosport on its far side. At the start of the short journey their view of Haslar Creek and Fort Blockhouse was obscured by the bulk of the old chain ferry clanking its slow way from shore to shore, then they passed astern of it and could see the oddly old-fashioned shapes of three H-class submarines lying alongside the wooden jetty which constituted the only floating part of His Majesty's Ship *Dolphin*.

'My God!' Little said. 'Just look at those piles of junk.'

'Careful,' Gascoigne told him. 'You may be speaking of the H-boat I love. Neither of us is going to get anything better as a first command. Anyway, show a little respect for age. They glued them together towards the end of the last war.'

'What are they propelled by? Elastic?'

'Certainly not. They fix a piece of camphor on the back end. Like the celluloid duck you had in your bath when you were a kid.'

'Amazing. What will they think of next?'

'I hear they're experimenting with squares of convas you hoist up a mast,' Gascoigne said. 'Its code name is "Project Wind-power" and it's "Top Secret".'

They kept up the unfunny childish banter until they stepped ashore because neither of them wanted to look at or talk about the T-class submarine moored beyond the twenty-five year-old veterans. With her long, powerful grey shape and blacktopped casing she was indistinguishable from *Titan* and *Titan*, although dead and buried forty-eight hours before, lived on in their minds.

Standing on the conning tower of his ship the captain of *Talon* watched through binoculars as the pair climbed the jetty steps. He was wishing that someone else had been given the job of taking these two passengers to sea. Minutes later he greeted them as they came aboard.

'Hello chaps, I'm Kennaway. Which of you is Little and which Gascoigne?'

They told him.

'Fine. Come to my cabin, will you?'

They followed him down the fore hatch, then walked aft through the ship, looking about them, trying not to do it fearfully. Gascoigne would have felt a great deal better had he known that he was paying his first visit to a ship he would eventually take to war against the Japanese. The door of the captain's cabin slid shut behind them.

'Hello, John. Hello, Malcolm.'

Malcolm Little smiled, nodded. Gascoigne said, 'Hello, sir.'

'You don't have to call me "sir" now. Didn't Peter Harding tell you that? You've both qualified as commanding officers you know.'

Gascoigne smiled as Little had done, wondering if Kennaway's christian name was really Ken as he had heard him called by his fellow captains in the Algiers flotilla the year before.

'All right,' Kennaway told them. 'Thanks for playing along. You don't know me and I don't know you. You're a couple of destroyer types who are thinking of transferring to submarines. If anybody recognises you say you're your brother or something. That way if you turn green when we dive that'll be par for the course for two new boys, you needn't be embarrassed and I'll surface at once.' He looked from one to the other before adding, 'A silly question or two wouldn't hurt. Is there a window you can watch the fish through? – that sort of nonsense. You know the daft things people ask.' He smiled faintly and left them.

Little sat on the bunk, Gascoigne in the only chair. Both listened to the familiar sounds of a submarine preparing to sail.

'I think that was very clever of him,' Gascoigne said. 'At least we don't have to be scared of looking afraid now. That's often the worst part.'

'I know,' Little agreed. 'He's made a thorough job of it too. There's a notice on the board outside telling the crew to help the two General Service officers with any questions they may have because we may be volunteering for submarines. One thing's bothering me though. I can't think of any silly questions.'

'Neither can I, but I can think of a pretty convincing silly trick.'

'What's that?'

Gascoigne told him, then told a knock on the door to come in.

'Captain's compliments, sirs,' the petty officer standing in the entrance said, 'and we're just about to leave harbour. He says you are to go on the bridge, or stay in here, or walk through the boat, or do anything you want, but not to touch any levers or valves, please, because that could be dangerous. Any questions you've got, just ask anybody.'

They thanked him, promised to touch nothing and made their way to the bridge, then stood out of everybody's way on the Oerlikon cannon platform at the back of it. The ferry had halted its interminable journey along its own shore to shore cable in obedience to the "submarine manoeuvring" flag flying from the staff at the harbour entrance and lay stopped near the Portsmouth side. *Talon* slipped her last wire and water boiled under her stern.

'Did you know,' Little asked, 'that the ferry doesn't have "full ahead" and "full astern" on its engine room telegraphs. It has "full a 'Portsmouth' and "full a 'Gosport'?'

'Really?' Gascoigne replied and pointed at an enormous sign on the harbour wall advertising Brickwoods Beer. 'Did *you* know that the easiest way to bring your ship alongside at *Dolphin* is to go hard a'port when the second "O" of Brickwoods is exactly on the starboard beam? They keep a day and night guard on it in case a German agent moves the letters and everybody runs aground.'

Their nerves were still very close to the surface.

Fort Blockhouse sliding by to the right, the city of Portsmouth to the left, *Talon* beginning to pitch and roll as she increased speed down the mine-free channel towards the open sea, the wind snatching at their clothing.

Gascoigne shivered, whether from cold or fear he was unsure, but decided not to analyse the sensation. For a little while he watched the vista of the Isle of Wight opening up to starboard, then looked at the squat bulk of the Nab Tower ahead, a stone structure built to repel the French during the Napoleonic wars and now a platform for anti-aircraft guns. Not much shipping to be seen. That all seemed to be gathered in the crowded harbour astern of them, assembling for the invasion of France so people were saying. He thought that any interest he might need to develop in the invasion of France could wait until the next day and shivered again.

'Chilly,' Little said.

'Yes, I'm going below. You coming?'

'Yes.'

The strong current of air sucked down the conning tower by the big diesel engines chilled him more and flattened his hair about his face. When he reached the control room he stepped away from the vertical brass ladder to make way for Little then stood, pushing the hair out of his eyes, trying to look intrigued by the all too familiar surroundings, averting his eyes instead from the identical spot where the chief engine room artificer had died, seeing again the sailor with the muscular tattooed arms.

'You look like the ship's Tarzan. Come and unscrew something for me.'

'Me Jane today more like, sir.'

Dead now, that sailor. All of them dead. Fishes nudging their bloated corpses.

'That's enough of that!' Gascoigne told himself and with an enormous effort of will turned to a petty officer and asked to have the diving panel explained to him. It was the longest twenty minutes of his life before the crew went to their diving stations and when the klaxon emitted its harsh double squawk he started violently.

Talon had been at periscope depth for less than thirty seconds when Gascoigne realised that he was going to be all right. The ship was fractionally bow-heavy. He could sense it, feel it with the soles of his feet, see it from the angle of the hydroplane indicators and when he found himself wondering how long it would take the first lieutenant to spot it himself and order ballast water pumped from forward to aft he knew that he had nothing more to fear. Professionalism and the instinct born of long experience had taken charge of him. He was back in his element.

Shortly after that he knew that there was nothing wrong with Little either.

'I can't see anything through this telescope except some grey stuff. Oh, sorry, I meant "periscope",' Little said.

'You're probably looking at the sky, sir,' a sub-lieutenant told him. 'Try twisting that handle. No, the other one. How's that?'

'I'm looking at water now.'

'Well, move it back a bit, sir, and…'

'Ah, I've got it. Good Lord! You can see people on shore!'

Gascoigne sighed softly, feeling as pleased at Little's tomfoolery as at his own absence of nerves then, deciding that it would be wise to continue with the charade and play his silly trick, took a cigarette from his pocket and lit it.

'Sir.' An urgent whisper.

He glanced down at the sonar operator beside him.

'Yes?'

'You can't do that, sir. 'Ere, give it to me quick before one of the officers sees you or you'll be in dead trouble. No smoking when we're dived, sir. It's a rule, sir.'

'Oh dear. I didn't know,' Gascoigne said and surrendered his cigarette.

Ten minutes later Kennaway took down the tannoy microphone.

'This is the Captain speaking. We're going to put the ship on the bottom. Pay no attention to the bump.' He hooked the microphone back in place, looked from Gascoigne to Little and went on, 'Okay, the bottom's where you had your bit of trouble. Which of you wants to put *Talon* down there first? It's about forty feet below the keel.'

Startled, they both stared at him, then around at the group of grinning faces.

''Ow about a smoke, sir? 'Ave one of mine.'

'Want me to explain the diving panel to you again, sir? You didn't look much like you understood it the first time.'

Then Kennaway's voice. 'Yes, they all know who you are. You're really quite famous. Now, who's first?'

Gascoigne took in a long, slow breath, smiling at Kennaway. 'Thanks, Ken. I'll take her down.' His gaze moved from man to man in the crowded control room then, 'You bunch of conniving bastards,' he said and laughed out loud.

At Fort Blockhouse that evening the session in the practice escape tank was a ten-minute immersion in warmed water. Nothing more.

*

Gascoigne spent the last day of his survivor's leave in London, excited because of the letter in his pocket, bored because his three weeks at his family home in Hampshire had been boring and London looked like being equally so. He could hardly wait for the next day. At noon he had gone to Hatchetts bar on Piccadilly where the management kept a book for submarine officers to write messages in. Sometimes there were telephone numbers where friends on leave could be contacted, but the most recent entry, an indecent piece of doggerel proclaiming that the officers of the S-class submarine *Slasher* had had an enjoyable evening, was three weeks old. He left and walked to Gieves, the naval tailors, to cash a cheque. Gieves were always good for a fiver and he had decided that, failing anything else, he might as well get a little drunk.

Gieves was as crowded as the street outside had been with the difference that all the uniforms inside were Navy. There were a lot of senior officers about and he was making slow, tactful progress around and between them towards the cash desk when Peter Harding said, 'Hello, John. How nice to see you.'

Turning, he stood smiling down at his ex-captain, boredom dropping from him.

'Nice to see you too, s… Peter. What a very pleasant…'

'Darling, here's John Gascoigne. At last you get to meet my right arm from the *Trigger* days.'

It was as though he had been struck. That Harding had married a beautiful girl with a title was common knowledge in the Submarine Service, but this, he thought, was ridiculous. He heard himself say, 'How do you do, Lady Abigail,' and the words seemed to echo in his head.

The vision's mouth twitched as though suppressing a smile before saying, 'All right, you've said it, but don't say it again. My name's Gail. Hello, John Gascoigne.'

No, they were not in any hurry. Yes, they would love it if he would buy them a drink. He supposed he really ought to take them across the road to the Ritz, but it was cheaper at Hatchetts. Nobody objected. Of course she didn't mind sitting at the bar she said. Who would, he asked himself, with legs like that?

When their drinks were in front of them Harding spoke first.

'I was glad to hear that your trip in *Talon* went off well.'

'Yes, a few shaky moments, but it turned out okay.'

'Any news about an appointment?'

'I thought you'd never ask,' Gascoigne said, took the letter from his pocket and put it on the bar between them.

Harding picked it up, glanced down the lines, gave a satisfied nod and handed it to his wife.

"From Admiral Submarines, Northways, London, NW3.

Date 3rd April 1944

To Lieutenant J. N. P. Gascoigne, DSC, RN.
    You have been appointed to H.M. Submarine H.58 in
command and should report to Captain (S/M) Fifth Submarine
Flotilla a.m. on the 16th April.
    A railway warrant and expense claim form are enclosed herewith."

Gascoigne watched her reading it, feeling a little silly now. It wasn't much of a letter. Why wave it about? Much better to have replied off-handedly, 'Yes, they've given me an H-boat. I'm joining tomorrow.' After all it *was* only an old H-boat.

'I think,' Gail said, 'it must be the most exciting thing in the world to get a letter like this giving you command of a warship for the first time.'

He could have died for her, rolled on his back and put his paws in the air, let her walk on him. His mother's voice came back to him. 'How nice, dear. Will they let you wear four stripes like old Captain Maynard?' No understanding of anything, and yet this girl…

'Have you got any plans for today?'

'No, I'm just stooging around, Peter. Filling in time until tomorrow.'

'Then come home and have some lunch with us.'

'Oh, thanks awfully, but I couldn't do that. Too keyed up about tomorrow. I'd be awfully bad company.' You didn't accept invitations to meals in private houses, not unless you took your ration book or some food with you. He hadn't got either.

'We'll eat here,' Gail said, 'see the new revue at the Palladium this afternoon and scratch around in the store cupboard for something for supper.

You can take the early train to Portsmouth in the morning. Please don't say no or I'll never hear the last of it from Peter.'

It wasn't difficult to capitulate to the slanting green eyes, but it was much harder, sitting next to her in the theatre, to concentrate on the show. By the time they reached the house off Sloane Street Gascoigne was in a state of bemused infatuation. The condition surprised him because his height and good looks had always drawn women to him without any particular effort on his part, but never before had he felt such a magnetic force controlling him. Then he watched her walking up the stairs ahead of him and the surprise evaporated. There was simply nothing, he decided, to be surprised about.

The Hardings, he found, lived on the top floor of the house, the three below it having been requisitioned by the Army for the use of the general commanding some military area or other and his staff. London and the south east he thought he had been told, but wasn't sure and didn't care. The resulting flat was pretty and made more so by the presence of its owner. Afterwards he never could remember what the scratching around in the store cupboard had produced for supper, but his recollection of the moments following the simple meal were vivid.

Harding had said to his wife, 'Do you remember when you told me outside Algiers that…'

Gascoigne never did hear what she had said outside Algiers. His mind jumped back over six months and a thousand miles to a submarine called *Trigger* and Harding, her captain, fighting a grim battle with both the enemy and his own quivering nerves. As second-in-command he had eventually gone to Harding to offer whatever solace he could to a man he liked and admired intensely and, as a result of their conversation, Harding had placed himself in the hands of the doctors when the ship reached Algiers from patrol. The patrol had been very successful, as had most of Harding's, but on that one *Trigger* had buried her own dead at sea and limped into harbour a floating wreck.

The severely wounded submarine had been towed to Gibraltar for repair and refitting with Gascoigne himself in charge, knowing only that his then unmarried and totally unattached commanding officer was under orders to rest. That he would ever return to active command after receiving such orders was highly improbable, but five weeks later a seemingly completely recovered Harding had flown to Gibraltar to resume command of his healed ship. Now Gascoigne knew without a shadow of doubt the nature of his ex-captain's cure.

His abstraction must have become apparent to them because they were both looking at him standing, as he was, with a half-dried plate in his hand.

'A penny for them.' The words had come from Harding and he glanced at him, then his gaze settled on Gail.

'Thank you for giving me my Skipper back. I've only just realised.'

She smiled the very smallest of smiles, reached up with a soapy hand, drew his head down and kissed him on the cheek.

'What a nice thing to say,' she said.

The soft brush of her lips stayed with Gascoigne throughout a long, near-sleepless night, a night filled with fantasies and half-waking dreams centred on the girl lying one room away from him. For those hours he allowed himself to pretend that Peter Harding didn't exist, but with the coming of day he trod firmly on his imagination and got out of bed, feeling sullied by the tracks his mind had followed. He was glad he had an early train to catch.

To just how great an extent the chance encounter of the day before was to affect his life Gascoigne did not know, although the signs were already there to be read. Sitting in the train, staring unseeingly at the grimy London suburbs sliding past the carriage windows, he experienced a surge of ambition of an intensity he had never before known. In the past it had been enough to serve under Harding, to contribute to and share in his remarkable successes, to have his work recognised with a decoration. It had been more than enough to survive the *Titan* disaster, to have passed his command course well and to have been appointed as captain of *H 58*. Now, for the first time, it occurred to him that he was his own man at last, or as much his own man as the structure of the Navy would permit him to be. That realisation brought both exhilaration and a sense of urgency, urgency born of the fact that there was so far to go to catch up with his ex-captain's achievements.

Why he had set his sights on that particular target he was unsure, nor was he clear in his mind whether his new-found aspiration was directed primarily towards war or such a woman as his hostess of the previous night. The fact that the war was there, while the woman was not, temporarily settled his priorities for him, but the train was still half an hour from Portsmouth when they became unsettled again. War, as he saw it, did not include running a training submarine and, abruptly, the thought of his first command lost its glamour. It was never to regain it and that fact started Gascoigne along a path of disaffection leading to a frustration which was to plague him until his chance came to practice competitiveness. Even then he was to believe himself thwarted.

Not for the first time, exposure to Gail Harding had induced change in the character of a man and in Gascoigne's case it was not for the better.

Chapter Six

'This – is – London.' The BBC announcer's words, carefully spaced for dramatic effect, reached him faintly through the thin partition and Gascoigne lifted his head from the pillow the better to hear what London had to say.

'At dawn this morning Allied forces landed in strength on the coast of France.' The voice calm, sonorous.

'Oh, damn it to hell!' Gascoigne said, rolled off his bunk and began to dress rapidly, too angry to listen to any more of what the radio in the next cubicle was saying. Too impatient also to bother with a shirt and tie he pulled on his uniform jacket, tied a white scarf round his neck, and left his cabin in the building known as the Submarine Sheds at Londonderry. On the jetty he stood looking at his command moored alongside.

'Bloody H-boat,' he muttered to himself.

''Morning, sir! Have you heard the news? The Invasion's started!'

He turned to see his first lieutenant grinning at him delightedly.

'Yes, I heard, and here are we clanking up and down the bloody River Foyle for month after month like a bloody clockwork mouse for convoy escorts to practice on. It makes me want to vomit!'

'It's pretty important work, sir.'

Gascoigne grunted and walked away, even angrier now because his second-in-command had been absolutely right. *H 58*'s impersonation of a U-boat was essential to the training of the destroyers, frigates and corvettes which guarded the Atlantic convoys. That was obvious to anybody, but the knowledge did nothing to lessen his seething frustration. What part, if any, submarines could play in the Invasion he had no idea, but for weeks past the feeling that the real war was passing him by had been growing until four days earlier it had reached its peak in a most ill-advised personal request to the commodore for a transfer to the surface fleet. He had been told curtly to stop wasting the commodore's time and to get on with the job he had been trained to do. All that request had achieved, he knew, was a question-mark if not a black one against his name.

Then there had been the incident with the aircraft carrier. *H 58* had crossed its bows at a range of a mile and a half. It had been perfectly safe to do so, but the carrier captain had been angry at this discourtesy by the much smaller ship with its far junior commander and had reported Gascoigne to his superiors. It hadn't mattered much to anyone but Gascoigne, but him it had infuriated because of its pettiness.

There was his marriage too. After only four weeks of that he regretted it. She was pretty enough, the WAAF radar operator he had married, but it had taken him less than half of those weeks to discover that she was also remarkably stupid. Definitely unfairly, certainly quite correctly, he blamed Gail Harding for driving him precipitately into an unsatisfactory formal liaison. Had he never met Harding's wife and experienced her frightening allure he would, he knew, never have grasped so unthinkingly at the first physically attractive woman to come his way. That that was hardly Gail Harding's fault he was not yet ready to admit and his mood was black as, later on D-Day, *H 58* made her slow way across Lough Foyle towards the open sea. Not even the seals he normally liked to watch, sunning themselves on the cross-girders of the pylons marking the deepwater channel, drew a second glance from him.

The first part of the day's diving passed off without incident and when Gascoigne ordered the ship brought to the surface at the end of it the leader of the group of escort ships which had been hunting him signalled "Thanks for excellent exercise."

A combination of currents and the evasive action Gascoigne had employed to shake off his pursuers had carried *H58* to the south and the signal from the leader of the next escort group was less friendly.

The leading signalman said, 'Sir, message reads "You have delayed my exercise unnecessarily by surfacing outside area. Proceed to centre of area at best speed and dive".'

Gascoigne nodded.

Three minutes later the frigate's lamp began flashing again.

'He wants to know what the delay is now, sir.'

'Make to him "The delay is a twenty-six year-old submarine which was never very fast in the first place. See relevant page *Janes Fighting Ships* for H-class".'

A moment later, 'He says "Don't be impertinent", sir.'

'Get stuffed!' Gascoigne said.

'You want me to send that, sir?'

'No.'

Eleven minutes after *H 58* had dived she entered a zone of fresh water pushed outwards by the River Foyle. It was much less dense than sea-water, much less able to support weight and the submarine dropped dramatically, the depth-gauge needles moving fast round the dials.

'Blow main ballast,' Gascoigne said.

The old ship was getting dangerously deep before the downward motion was halted and she began to rise. There was no stopping her then, nor did Gascoigne wish to stop her until her trim had been corrected, and she broke surface uncomfortably close to one of the frigates.

'Pump a couple of tons out of her, Number One,' Gascoigne told his first lieutenant and clambered up the conning tower ladder to the bridge with the signalman following him.

'Signal, sir. "Now what's the matter?"'

'Make "Ran into low density patch. Now lightening ship."'

The lamps spoke to each other again.

'From the frigate, sir, "Then get on with it. I'll allow you two minutes".'

The rage which had been simmering in Gascoigne boiled over and he brought the side of his fist down sharply on the ledge in front of him. The action hurt his hand and he stood, scowling at it, flexing his fingers, before saying, 'Make "You paddle your own canoe".'

There was no reply to the injunction, but when *H 58* finally surfaced at the end of the day's exercise her radio room intercepted an uncoded message from the leader of the escort group to the commodore. Gascoigne was shown it scribbled on a piece of signal paper. "From *Elk* to Commodore Londonderry. I consider the commanding officer of *H 58* to be thoroughly undisciplined. He made a nuisance of himself throughout the exercise today and deprived my group of valuable training time".

It had been Gascoigne's intention to spend the night with *H 58* secured to one of the buoys provided as submarine moorings near the mouth of the River Foyle because he had to be out in the exercise area in the Irish Sea early the next morning. *Elk's* signal changed all that and he followed the long channel across the lough all the way back to Londonderry hoping that the commodore, an ex-submariner, would understand. He found him, at eight in the evening, sitting in his office with his feet on his desk.

'When I heard you were coming up river I thought it would be me you were after, Gascoigne.'

'Yes, sir.'

'Well? Tell me about it.'

Gascoigne told him.

'And he really said "I'll allow you two minutes"?'

'I promise you, sir. My signalman will vouch for it.'

'All right, I'm not doubting your word. I just wanted to be sure that you had got it right. Sit down.'

Sitting uneasily on the edge of a chair Gascoigne watched the commodore stretch out a hand and pick up a telephone, heard him say, 'Give me Belfast,' then waited until the older man had been connected with the authority he wanted.

'Is *Elk* alongside yet?' 'Entering harbour now. I see.' 'No, I don't want him to call me. Just give Commander Whitney my compliments and tell him that, except as an operational necessity, I shall take it most kindly if he never comes to Londonderry again.'

The commodore replaced the hand-set slowly, his eyes on Gascoigne. A clock he hadn't noticed before filled Gascoigne's ears with its ticking and he found himself counting as though the thing was a bomb set to explode in one minute. He had reached twenty-three before the commodore spoke.

'I have done what I have done, Gascoigne, because of a piece of insufferable attempted interference in the running of your ship by someone neither entitled nor qualified to interfere. Only a submarine officer is competent to judge when his ship is in a fit condition to dive, isn't he?'

'Yes, sir.'

'Good, we are agreed. Now, it has taken a lot of time, a lot of money and a lot of trouble to bring you to the degree of competence which enables you to exercise the professional judgement required of a submarine commander, but you've reached it, haven't you?'

'I think so, sir.'

'So do I, at least from the technical point of view. I simply wonder by what method you have succeeded in resisting becoming imbued with the traditions of the Navy which infect the rest of us automatically. There's quite a bit more to commanding one of His Majesty's ships than technical excellence you know. Things like patience, tolerance and tact.'

'I know, sir.'

'You know, do you? But you still think it's clever to tell an officer two ranks your senior to paddle his own canoe.'

'No, sir. I think it was very stupid.'

Throughout the interview the commodore had neither raised his voice nor moved his position. Now he swung his feet to the floor, stood up and said sharply, 'Get out Gascoigne! I hope you're not going to behave like a cunt all your life! I shan't always be here to hold your hand!'

Gascoigne walked back to his ship in a haze of uncertainty. Never before had he received a reprimand of such a nature from a senior officer with its sudden switch from sarcasm to a savage obscenity. That he had been shielded from the immediate consequences of his own folly and that he had got less than he deserved was obvious to him. He was grateful for both those things, but deeply worried that another question-mark would find its way by some indirect route onto his record.

By the time *H 58* had slipped her moorings to return down river in readiness for the following days exercises he had convinced himself that his chance of receiving an operational command had receded almost to vanishing point and with it his hopes of emulating Peter Harding.

*

Gail finished reading Gascoigne's letter, handed it back across the hotel breakfast table to her husband and said, 'He *does* sound down in the mouth. Will that little spat really affect his future?'

'I don't think so,' Harding told her. 'It might well have done with anybody but Captain Ash. Beg his pardon, Commodore Ash I mean. He's always been famous for what John describes here as an anatomical rocket, but I'm pretty sure he wouldn't have delivered one if he'd intended to take official action. Still, I wish John would watch it. He used to be the soul of tact and this just isn't like him.'

'So I've always gathered from you. Do you have any idea what the trouble might be? That wife of his perhaps? She's so wrong for him.'

Harding shrugged and poured coffee for both of them. 'Might be, I suppose, but I'd guess that he's worked himself into a panic in case the war ends before he gets given an operational boat.' He grinned and added, 'Silly ass.'

'Didn't you feel the same way before you got an operational command, darling?'

'No,' Harding said. 'In those days it seemed as though the war would never end. There wasn't any hurry then and there isn't any hurry now. After Germany packs it in it'll take another two years at least to beat the Japs. John ought to know that.'

He sat for a few moments staring sightlessly at his coffee, remembering the orders which had released him from the command of an old L-class submarine running training classes out of Blyth, Northumberland, and sent him across the country to the big Vickers-Armstrongs yard at Barrow-in-Furness to take charge of something called J. 4219. Busy weeks had followed before a bottle had shattered against steel and a woman he didn't know, wearing a fur tippet and a little hat with a nose-veil, had said, 'I name this ship *Trigger*,' and followed the christening of J. 4219 with the customary blessing as the submarine began to slide towards the water. In no particular chronological order isolated memories from the seven war patrols which had followed came to him. Ships long dead died again in his mind, some violently in a sudden fury of sound and colour, others with tired resignation as the sea flooded in through the gaping holes his shells or torpedoes had torn in their sides.

His last patrol figured in his brief day-dream too. He had rescued a wounded American from German-occupied Italy, but his ignorance, like most of the rest of the world's, of the team of men working in the New Mexico desert which the American was to join made it impossible for him to know that his estimate of the duration of the Japanese war was wildly wrong.

'Yes,' Gail agreed, 'I'm afraid you're probably right and if you're also right about what's troubling him shouldn't you have a talk with him? You've taught him so much in the past, teach him to be patient now he's out on his own.'

Harding heard himself say that Gascoigne didn't need that sort of advice and grinned again, rather sheepishly, when she told him that he was contradicting himself.

'Yes I am, aren't I? I think it's just that I don't like the idea of interfering.' He thought then of the forcible intrusion she, as a total stranger, had been ordered by her superiors to make in his life when he needed help. It was little enough she was suggesting he did for his friend.

'Of course I'll talk to him,' he said, 'but the only time I've got free is the week-end after next between finishing off at the "Attack Teacher" here and starting flying training. I don't much want to spend that in Northern Ireland. If he can get away shall I invite him to Sloane Street?'

His wife shook her head. 'No, if he can arrange a short leave ask him down to Wiltshire. There's more room for you to talk in private there and Daddy will enjoy making man-to-man noises with someone new.'

Something in her voice made him look at her curiously for a moment before saying, 'That's rather elaborate, isn't it? I can say all there is to say to him in ten minutes or so.'

Without prevarication Gail said, 'It'll be easier for him if we water the company down a bit, Peter. John's a little in love with me. Are you cross?'

'Furious. Why isn't he head over heels like everyone else?'

She stood up, smiling, then stooped and kissed him. 'You go and teach your brood how to sink ships. I'll miss the train back to London if I don't hurry. Call you tonight.'

Harding went with her as far as the front door, then watched while she walked to her taxi. She didn't like protracted goodbyes, or having small things like an over-night bag carried for her. He was glad of that as it allowed him to admire the movement of her long legs, legs so excellent that not even flat-heeled uniform shoes detracted from their appearance. There was aesthetic as well as sexual pleasure for him in her beauty.

The bill paid, he left the Queen's Hotel, Southsea, to make his way to the submarine "Attack Teacher" at Gosport, feeling enormously content. Due, he supposed, to his own small flying experience and Flag Officer Submarines' efforts on his behalf, the Fleet Air Arm had accepted him as a trainee pilot. He was grateful to both parties to the arrangement and particularly to his admiral for keeping him in his present job, despite his own protestations of inadequacy, during the time it had taken the Fleet Air Arm to make up its mind.

But, above all, he was grateful to Gail for her unquestioning calm acceptance of his proposed new career, her understanding of his inability to sit out the rest of the war in some safe job on the grounds that he had already done enough. Of what that calm acceptance was costing her he had no idea at all and he was smiling at the recollection of the night they had just spent together as he strode towards the bus stop.

Gail Harding lay back in the corner of the taxi and felt the weight of sadness pressing on her eyelids. She let it close them, hoping that the action would not produce tears. They had never been far from her, the tears, since her husband had told her of his intention to transfer to flying duties. That had been weeks before and now she was exhausted from the prolonged necessity to demonstrate to him with conviction the lie that she did not mind.

She felt resentment towards him too for adding the bitterness of days numbered to the sweetness of the future she had imagined she had won for both of them, the certainty firm in her that his life which one element had failed to take would be claimed by another. To her mind it could hardly be otherwise because to attempt to fight in the air as well as on and under the sea during the same world conflict was to jeer in the faces of the gods and there could be only one forfeit for that. That his decision had been born of the long drawn out anguish of the *Titan* disaster she knew, but the knowledge brought her no comfort. It was surely better to stay with the familiar devil.

A flicker of amusement came to her with the realisation that she was experiencing pique amongst her other emotions, pique that she, with all her allure, was unable to combat the blandishments of war. Not that she had tried to do so, but that fact did nothing to lessen the hurtful discovery that she had a rival at least as glamorous as herself. Several times she had decided that her job as a woman was to use her wiles to prevent him getting killed as once she had done before their marriage, but on each occasion the decision foundered on the obvious fact that such a hand could not be played twice to an intelligent opponent. No, she would not try to challenge her rival again, but it was ironic that, of all the men her duty had required her to take to her bed, the one she had fallen in love with had had to be both the most malleable and possessed of a sense of duty strong enough to take him away from her.

'We're here, miss. Railway station, miss.'

'Oh! So we are. Thank you,' Gail said and handed money to the driver.

Master Sergeant Harvey Yates made his way slowly along the platform through the crowd of pushing, shouting British servicemen. There was no hurry. All the seats on the train would be taken already. Every damned train seemed to be full within seconds of its arrival. That was war-time England for you. He supposed he should be glad to be going home to the States, but doubted if he would ever be glad about anything again. Yates was fifty-four years old, very tired after three nights without sleep and completely broken-hearted.

Not knowing exactly how he had got there he found himself standing in a corridor of one of the carriages trying to find a secure footing amongst the mass of kit bags, sailors' hammocks and other men's feet, trying to at least to stand vertically, but it was difficult against the alternating pressures of shoulders to either side of him. When he had achieved a degree of stability he rested his forehead on the glass of the corridor window, staring at the posters on the grimy building opposite him. "Be like Dad – Keep Mum". "Walls have ears". "Careless talk costs lives".

It wouldn't, he thought, have been talk that had cost Teddy his life. Just one of those crazy raids. Teddy had been the smart one of the family and had made lieutenant in a Ranger battalion, so it hadn't surprised him

72

too much when he had been told by the Padre that his eldest son was dead. That had been five days ago. Thirty-six hours later Jack had gone down in the front turret of a burning B-17 over Essen. He had been the youngest. Yates hadn't blamed the Padre for chickening out when the middle one, Kirk, had bought his in Normandy the following day. The Colonel had come and told him about that, said how very sorry he was and given him orders to go home to Akron, Ohio, to look after the boys' mother for a while, there being nobody else left to her. The Army could be quite human at times.

A series of wolf whistles sounded from amongst the group of sailors immediately to his left as the train jerked into motion and without interest he shifted his gaze to the platform, but there didn't seem to be anybody there worth whistling at. Then the sliding door of the First Class compartment at his back moved.

'Instead of standing there whistling at me why don't you come in, sit down and behave yourselves. There's plenty of room.'

A girl's voice, gentle, speaking very educated British English.

He turned his head, but she was hidden by the door frame and all he could see was the sailors' faces red with embarrassment.

'Sorry, miss.' 'Thank you, miss.' 'Are you sure that would be all right, miss?'

'I don't see why not. The train doesn't stop anywhere between here and Waterloo Station, so nobody else can get in.'

Three British sailors and one in Dutch uniform filed in and Yates moved thankfully into the space they had left, stretching his spine.

'Won't you come in too, Master Sergeant? There's still a seat left and it's a long way to London.'

Beautiful. Very beautiful indeed, and an officer in whatever the Limeys called their equivalent of the Waves. Wrens, wasn't it?

'Why thank you, ma'am,' Yates said and settled down beside her.

Nobody spoke again until the sliding doors were opened.

'Tickets please. Hello! What are you lot doin' in here botherin' the officer? Don't worry, miss. I'll soon have *this* sorted out.'

Yates looked tiredly at the train conductor, wondering how he had managed to force his way along the crowded corridor.

'They're not bothering me in the least,' the girl replied. 'In fact I invited them in. There's no point in being crammed into the corridor like sardines when there are empty seats.'

'It's not allowed, miss. Officers and other ranks in the same compartment I mean.'

'Look,' the girl said, 'why don't you just run your railway and leave the Services' side to the people in them?'

'As you say, miss,' the conductor told her. 'And that being the case anyone in here without a First Class ticket gets out. Now, let's be seein' you.'

Even the Dutchman had caught the gist of the conversation and the men started to get to their feet.

'Wait.' All heads turned to the Wren officer. 'How much is the excess fare for five?'

When the conductor had done some arithmetic on his pad and told her, she took pen and cheque book from her bag and began to write.

'Sorry, miss. We don't accept cheques.'

She wrote on, waved the slip of paper in the air to dry the ink, then handed it with her identity card to the conductor.

'You do from me.'

Yates heard the authority behind the quietly spoken words, but did not know that he had just listened to the arrogance of generations of position and privilege. He couldn't imagine where it could have been, but he was almost certain that he had seen the girl before.

For long seconds the conductor hesitated as if seeking the will to continue the exchange, then said, 'Very well, Your Ladyship,' handed back the identity card and began laboriously to fill out five forms. While he was doing it Yates reached for his bill-fold, but changed his mind. Not that way.

The man left at last. One of the British naval ratings giggled and another asked, 'Are you really a…?'

'Shut up, sailor,' Yates said. He didn't expect to be disobeyed and was not. After that, he and the girl talked quietly.

'That was kind, ma'am.'

'No it wasn't. It was all too silly with a war on and everything. Are you going to London on leave?'

'No. They're shipping me back to the States.'

'Oh, how nice.'

He supposed he had frowned because he heard her say, 'Oh dear. I hope there's nothing wrong.'

For almost a minute he sat in silence, gazing at his hands resting on his knees, then in a barely audible voice he began to tell her. When he had finished she took his hand, holding it between both of hers on her lap, and stared through the window at the Hampshire countryside.

Suddenly, 'You snivelling little bitch!' A fierce whisper.

He heard, but didn't understand.

'How was that again, ma'am?'

'I was talking to myself,' she said.

Master Sergeant Yates slept all the way to London. Although he was asleep he was somehow aware that his hand was still held. A kiss on the cheek woke him when the train stopped and he stood, watching her walk away along the platform. She hadn't spoken again.

*

An enormous bouquet of flowers was standing outside the door of the flat in the house off Sloane Street when Gail Harding got home from her job that evening. The card read "With gratitude and respect from the Yank on the train". The size of the flower arrangement and the Moyses Stevens label on it told her that it had cost roughly three times the rail fare from Portsmouth to London.

He had, she supposed, seen her name when she had shown her identity card to the conductor, or recognised her from a photograph in the papers or the glossy magazines. Whatever the answer it had been nice of him to go to the trouble of looking up her address in the telephone book and sending her the flowers. They were too flamboyant for her taste, but she knew, as she carried them inside, that she would always be grateful to the American soldier for giving her back her sense of proportion.

*

Harding saw Gascoigne's tall figure moving towards him along the platform at Devizes station in Wiltshire. It vanished for a moment in a cloud of steam emitted by the locomotive, then reappeared again and he called, 'Over here, John!' Gascoigne waved an arm and changed direction slightly.

'Hello, Peter. You shouldn't have bothered to come and meet me. I could have got a taxi.'

'You'd have been lucky,' Harding said. 'But you needn't sound so pleased. You haven't seen the transport yet.'

Moments later Gascoigne was staring in fascination at the old Austin. He walked right round it before saying, 'I thought marquises rode around in Rolls-Royces.'

'Oh, his nibs has got two of those and a Daimler, but they're up on blocks for the duration. He wouldn't get half a mile in any of them on the petrol ration, but this isn't his, it's Gail's. His is much worse. Be careful with that door when you get in. It's only got one hinge.'

Smiling, Gascoigne manoeuvred himself into the ancient car and asked, 'Talking of his nibs, how do I address a marquis?'

'You call him "Sir", you ass. What do you think? He's the older generation and, anyway, that's all you call the King.'

Gascoigne grinned. 'What do you call him? The Marquis I mean, not the King. Daddy or something?'

'No, I don't call him Daddy or something,' Harding said. 'Now why don't you keep quiet until I've got this thing into gear? It's a very technical business.'

The family seat of the Marquis of Trent was enormous and it and its grounds reminded Gascoigne of photographs he had seen of Versailles. He had gathered from Harding that the owner lived in four rooms of it. The Lady Abigail had an additional room reserved for her, but shared her father's bathroom. The Army occupied the rest, as it did in the town house off Sloane Street, although their numbers had shrunk since the invasion of France.

'Do you,' his host asked, 'know Sir William Gascoigne, attorney to the Duke of Hereford?'

They were sitting in one corner of the gracious stone terrace which stretched the full length of the house's southern elevation drinking awful coffee after a worse lunch than Gascoigne would have been served aboard the depot ship. He didn't mind about the lunch because he knew that the Services, particularly the Submarine Service, ate much better than the civil population. It just seemed strange in such magnificent surroundings.

'No, sir,' Gascoigne said.

'Oh? Pity. How about the author, George Gascoigne? The chap who wrote the essay on prosody?'

'No, sir. Never heard of him. What's prosody?'

The marquis raised his eyebrows in astonishment, then shook his head and turned to Harding.

'Tell him, Peter.'

'I don't know, sir, unless it's an unnatural act.'

'No it's *not* an unnatural act, it's…'

'Stop it, Daddy,' Gail said, and to Gascoigne, 'Don't pay any attention to him, John. The first man he mentioned died in 1419, the second in 1577 and prosody is the science of versification. The Duke of Hereford he was talking about became King Henry IV.'

Gascoigne smiled back at the laughing green eyes, feeling again the stab of desire her regard always induced in him.

'And how, my old beetroot top,' her father asked, 'do you happen to know all that?'

'Because you left the encyclopedia lying open at "Gascoigne" and I read it too. That's how.'

'Bloody women,' the marquis said. 'Come on, John. I'll show you the grounds.'

Gascoigne fell in step beside the short, slightly-built man, glancing down at his sparse red hair, its colour a carroty version of his daughter's. It was difficult to think of him as a marquis and even more so as someone extremely senior in the Secret Service, which Harding had told him he was, but it was very easy to like him.

'Come here to be lectured by your ex-captain haven't you, young feller?'

'Something like that, sir. Peter told you, did he?'

'No, no. He wouldn't do that. Gail did. Anyway, I can probably save him the trouble. Your admiral's a friend of mine and I had a chat with him about you at the club.'

'Oh yes?' Gascoigne's tone was guarded.

'No need to worry,' the marquis told him. 'You're all right. Quite well thought of actually. Still, you'll have to be patient. Our submarine losses in the Far East have been tiny compared with those off Norway and in the Mediterranean. Thank God for that too, but it slows down advancement of course. New construction is coming along well, but there are several men ahead of you in the queue. Don't get upset if you aren't given an operational command before the beginning of next year.'

They had crossed a hundred yards of lawn and were approaching a gap in a tall clipped hedge. The marquis led the way through it.

'Halt! Where do you think you're going? This is a military establishment, cock!'

A very young soldier in very new battle-dress was pointing a rifle.

'Sorry, cock.' The marquis turned back through the gap and rejoined Gascoigne.

'Won't they really let you in there, sir?'

'Oh Lord, yes, but that kid doesn't know who I am and I'm not going to have him telephoning the duty officer just to get me permission to walk through my own orchard. Let's go this way. What do you know about the American Navy, John?'

'Not much, sir. Pretty casual lot I should imagine.'

The older man stopped and looked at him.

'Yes? Well, you couldn't be more wrong and that's really what I wanted to talk to you about because you're likely to be operating under their command. Their signal traffic is a little unconventional by our standards, but for the rest they're elitist, professional and very very formal. Their disciplinary code is fierce too. Where you'd stop a man's leave for a week they'd throw him into clink for a month for the same offence.'

Gascoigne looked and was astonished.

'Really, sir?'

'Really. You see, they've had to do it that way. Their Fleet was shattered at Pearl Harbour which meant them starting virtually from scratch. Now, in a remarkably short space of time, they've built themselves a Navy almost as big as ours. It may even be *as* big, or bigger. They're launching ships every day and they've had to find crews for those ships. Thousands and thousands of men, many from the mid-western states who'd never so much as seen the sea before. It's been a colossal achievement and they've had to be tough and strict to turn all those landsmen into sailors. That's the difference between the US Navy and their other Services.'

They had started walking again, Gascoigne very interested, thoughtful, saying nothing.

His host said, 'Command is an almost sacred thing to them too. Do you know what would happen if an American admiral visited your submarine?'

'No, sir.'

'*He* would salute *you*, you a lieutenant, and say, "Permission to come aboard, sir?" and when he left he'd salute again and ask permission to leave *your* ship. Makes you think, doesn't it?'

'Yes, it does.'

'Well, that's an example of their code of conduct and I advise you to remember it. Many people over here think they are a bunch of slap-happy extroverted amateurs, but that simply isn't true. They're dedicated and, as I said, professional.'

'You seem to know a great deal about them, sir.'

'No, not personally. Your admiral told me. He thought you might be interested.'

'Oh dear,' Gascoigne said. 'So he has heard about my – er – falls from grace.'

'Not officially, I understand,' the Marquis of Trent told him. 'I got the impression that he was rather amused, but felt that you would be well advised to raise your level of respect towards your seniors.' He smiled faintly before adding, 'Come on. Let's go back and prevent the love-birds doing whatever they might be thinking of doing. I haven't forgiven my daughter for unmasking me as a charlatan yet.'

Gascoigne enjoyed the short week-end but, when it was over, he was again thankful to escape from Gail Harding's disturbing presence.

Chapter Seven

With New York only hours ahead the feeling came to Harding that the great Cunard liner *Queen Mary* had scented home like a horse nearing its stable after a long day in the hunting field. It was imagination, he knew, but the bow wave seemed higher, the wake longer on the shifting green Atlantic, the vibration from the huge quadruple screws more intense. Under his feet the deck trembled and, under his hands, the wooden ship's-side rail, bearing the carved names and initials of the countless American servicemen the ship had carried in the opposite direction, quivered in sympathy with it.

There were Americans aboard now, but far less than there would have been had the course been easterly, and of those the majority were wounded. Other nationalities were travelling to the States too: a group of French civilians, quiet, unsmiling men who kept very much to themselves, boisterous Polish officers who talked to anyone and everyone in remarkably good English, a lone Russian who spoke to nobody, some Dutchmen who wanted to communicate with others but could not and, of course, the British. Somewhere aft, above the engine rooms, German prisoners of war were confined, a large number of them, all being transported to America to ease the pressure on the swollen prison camps of England. Harding had caught glimpses of them being exercised under guard on the aftermost deck. It was, he thought, a strange population for a floating city.

He glanced up at the three big funnels, the red and black Cunard colours hidden beneath their grey wartime livery, down at the long sweep of planking on which he was standing which once had held rows of affluent passengers in reclining chairs and now supported gun positions and another kind of traveller, around him at the empty sea and a sky inhabited only by ever-present gulls. Apart from the gulls they had been empty, the sea and the sky, almost all the way across the ocean. The giant Queens, *Mary* and *Elizabeth*, sailed fast and they sailed alone, relying on their speed, which in rough weather escort vessels could not match, to keep them safe from U-boat attack. Neither British nor American patrolling planes stayed near them for long for they would have acted only as a beacon on which hostile submarines could home. But what a prize, Harding thought, for a U-boat fortunate enough to find itself on the hurtling leviathan's mean line of advance and pictured himself back aboard *Trigger*, his last command, taking imaginary periscope observations, giving rapid manoeuvring orders, trying to anticipate where the next leg of the zig-zag would place his target. Then he grinned a little ruefully. That was all over and done with. His interest now was the war in the air. Turning away from the rail he made his way down to the small cabin he shared with two others, glad to find it deserted because he wanted to finish a letter to his wife.

Letter writing had been an irksome task to Harding until he and Gail had married. After that, at least when he wrote to her, it had become a pleasure and he wasn't surprised to find that he had covered nineteen pages during the five-day voyage. Nor, had it been pointed out to him, would he have been surprised that his writing was a reflection of herself, she who had drawn him with ferocious tenderness out of a maze of introverted self-doubt and off the shivering quicksands of combat fatigue on to a firm platform no less steady for the soaring happiness of which it was built. It was not pointed out to him and the lone fact remained submerged beneath the tide of love which was Gail, a tide which had borne him through even the prolonged agony of *Titan's* death with little more than superficial mental damage.

But one part of this letter remained to be written. It related to their last two days together and her behaviour had been so outrageous that, deeply conservative by nature, he was at a loss how to refer to it with the memory of those hours still bringing grins and blushes alternately to his face.

The first three days of the short leave he had been granted before leaving for the United States were spent with her in the house off Sloane Street, but they were hardly pleasant. London had come under bombardment by what were variously known as pilotless aircraft, flying bombs, doodle-bugs and, finally, the VI. They had watched several of the little planes with their stubby wings which had pierced the fighter and anti-aircraft defences speeding towards them, eerily indifferent to barrage balloons or anything else, listened to the increasing throb of the pulse jet which propelled them, learned that as long as the jet continued to throb they were safe, learned also that when it ceased to do so close to them there would, after an eternity of seconds, be a shattering explosion and the thunder of collapsing buildings.

It was an unnerving experience, worse almost than the Blitz because of the moronic robot-like performance of the devices and after too many had fallen too close, 'Bugger this!' Lady Abigail had said indecorously. 'We're supposed to be on leave. I'd like to spend it in a bed, not under one. Let's go to an hotel in the country and pretend we're not married. I've got some money.'

Harding who, deprived of his submarine and command pay, had very little agreed nevertheless and they travelled south to the small town of East Grinstead in Sussex where, at the picturesque Felbridge Hotel, he registered them as Lieutenant and Mrs Harding. He did so happily and in all inno-cence because Gail preferred to be free of her title at any location where it was not already known and because he had not taken all of her suggestion seriously if, indeed, it had all been recorded in his mind. But the simple act of signing signalled the opening bars of a calamitous operetta for him.

'Oh you fool, Peter! Not your own name! That's all the proof Moira needs!' Gail's urgent whisper carried clearly to his ears and, from the way the clerk's hand hesitated before removing the room key from its hook, Harding knew that it had carried to his too. Wondering dazedly, stupidly, if Moira whoever she might be was supposed to be his wife, he met the clerk's questioning gaze with a scowl, nodded in reply to his carefully spoken 'Room number seven, sir' and followed Gail to the stairs.

In their room, 'Tra-la and fiddle-di-dee,' she had replied to his mild remonstrance and, when he had finished changing from uniform into civilian clothes before her, had suggested that he wait for her in the bar.

Sitting, pen in hand, in his cabin aboard the *Queen Mary* he recalled for the thousandth time, her entry into that crowded bar. The too tight black satin dress, the fishnet stockings, the anklestrap shoes with four-inch heels, the red hair released from all fastenings floating about her face, the instant descent of silence on the room and the eyes following her progress across it. Such attention was an everyday occurrence for her which she had no need to achieve that way and he remembered thinking, 'Oh God! She's really laying it on!'

'If only Moira could see us now,' she had said into the deafening hush when she reached his side and half amused, half fearful, 'Do stop talking about Moira,' he had replied.

She had agreed emphatically and loudly that they should put Moira out of their minds and enjoy their two stolen nights together, a sentiment shared by the score of people present who, openly or covertly, watched the demolition and demoralisation of Harding by his wife until it was time to go into dinner.

It had taken him a little while to notice that her wedding and engagement rings were missing and that the one she constantly fingered had come from some curtain. That lack of observation was brought about, he supposed, through fear of being asked to leave the hotel and because she had taken to calling him George and, occasionally, Harry. He suffered it all in an agony of embarrassed delight and by breakfast the next morning joined her in the game by saying, 'Moira says it's bad for me,' when she asked him in a voice which embraced the whole dining-room if he took sugar in his coffee.

After that it was simply fun, fun not even spoiled when he paid the bill on the last morning and the manager had smiled and told him that it had been a pleasure having him and Lady Abigail in the hotel.

'You knew?' he had asked.

'Of course, sir,' the manager had said. 'We're not all that far out in the sticks here. You're both rather well known, you know. Anyway, we all enjoyed it very much.'

It was not until he was on the train for Liverpool that Harding realised that Gail's disturbing role of courtesan had been deliberately played to distract him, to deaden the pain of coming separation, the first long separation of their marriage. Because he didn't know her as well as he thought he did, because he knew nothing of an incident in another train involving

83

his wife and an American master sergeant named Harvey Yates, because it had never occurred to him that he could be utterly indispensable to so beautiful a woman, he remained unaware that she had been seeking distraction also for herself.

His letter lay before him, still unfinished, still with no reference to the supposedly adulterous week-end she had contrived. He shrugged, smiled, wrote "I adore you" on the last page and, with a flourish, added the name "George". The postscript, suggesting an extra-marital expedition to a place in Sussex he knew of, was signed "Harry". It was the best he could manage.

The towers of Manhattan were piercing the horizon beyond the *Queen Mary's* bows when the submarine was sighted. 'There is no need for alarm,' the public address system said. 'The submarine on the starboard bow is American.' Harding went on deck to look at it and found himself standing at the rail beside two US Navy officers. Both were holding binoculars to their eyes.

'Recognise it?'

'No. They mostly look the same, but this one is new. Probably straight out of the New London "Electric Boat" yard.'

'Yeah.'

'Hey! Isn't that Gene Haggerty on the bridge?'

'I guess it is, and that's Dwight Meynell in back of him.'

'So that's *Harpoon*.'

'Right.'

The names meant nothing to Harding and no prescience told him that they would come to mean a great deal to his friend John Gascoigne.

*

Harding duly experienced the shock felt by most first-time visitors to Manhattan. Photographs had not prepared him for the sensation of walking along the bottom of some deep canyon, its sides soaring edifices obscuring most of the sky, producing in him a sensation of claustrophobia his years of submarine service had failed to do. But, for all that, he was enormously impressed by some of the architecture.

The Empire State Building he thought a bore, a graceless, overgrown lump of masonry it seemed necessary to cross either the Hudson or East River to see at all, although he found the view from its top breathtaking.

Not much further up Fifth Avenue he stood for a long time looking at what, for him, was the most beautiful building in the world, a towering castle of enchantment leaping skywards in progressive steps of gleaming white a full seventy storeys above the street. The RCA Building a passer-by told him it was, the focal point of Rockefeller Center and part of the complex which housed the Radio City music hall and its famous team of precision dancers, the Rockettes. People watched him curiously while he stood on the sidewalk sketching the scene for Gail on the back of an envelope.

But it was the night scene which really amazed him. They were having a dim-out, or a brown-out, or something, to save electricity somebody said. To Harding due, he supposed, to the contrasting black sky directly above his head, the degree of illumination seemed more positive than day-light and he found it impossible to relate the brilliance to what he understood to be war. A picture of the bath-tubs at home with the blue line painted round the inside only inches from the bottom came to him. To preserve power nobody was supposed to fill the bath above that line and here the power was draining away through advertising signs in their thousands and windows numbered in millions. The memory of a harsh-voiced air raid warden shouting, 'Put out that bloody light!' when he had struck a match for Gail's cigarette in a blacked-out London street made him grin and wonder if the man would have suffered apoplexy if suddenly transported to this spot on Broadway. He turned and made his way slowly to the Barbizon Plaza Hotel on Lexington Avenue, where he had been allocated a bed, marvelling at the volume of civilian traffic. There appeared to be no rationing of petrol and from the meals he had eaten none of food either. It was all very strange after the extreme austerity he had grown accustomed to at home.

An envelope he was handed at the desk contained his onwards routing instructions and he read them, frowning slightly because he had been told that his training would take place at the Pensacola naval air station in Florida but, the letter said, there was no vacancy for him there for the foreseeable future. Instead he was to join an RAF class at No 4 British

Flying Training School, Falcon Field, at a place called Mesa in Arizona. A seat had been reserved for him on a plane leaving Newark, New Jersey, in five days time for…

A finger of superstitious fear touched him, then, growing bolder, prodded him into freezing, storm-tossed water with empty lungs and the taste of rubber in his mouth. A voice shouting, 'Easy! Take it easy! You're all right now, mate!' Arms around him, dragging him over the side of a boat. A sling around his chest, the same voice yelling, 'Hoist away!' and a swinging ascent up a vertical grey steel wall to a ship's deck. More arms grasping him, tearing the soaking clothes from his body. Consciousness slipping away.

'You okay, Lieutenant?'

Harding looked at the clerk who had given him the letter and the images left him.

'Oh yes, thanks. I have to go to Phoenix and that just happens to be the name of a ship that – well, you know how it is.'

It was hardly an adequate explanation for what he assumed to have been his sudden pallor, but the American nodded.

'I know how it is. Take it easy, you hear.'

'I'll do that,' Harding said and walked away, thinking how strange it was that the man should have used the same admonition as the member of *Phoenix's* crew who had lifted him from the sea over *Titan's* grave. The double coincidence of name and expression troubled him all the way to his room. There he shook his head irritably to clear it of nonsense and began to wonder how he would get on with his RAF classmates. Apart from an occasional flight as a passenger with RAF Transport Command he had had next to no contact with the breed. Eventually concluding that conjecture was as profitless an occupation as indulging in superstition he turned his thoughts to how, alone in the big city, he could occupy himself for the next five days.

He need not have worried about that. New York opened its arms to him, as it had done to so many thousands of British Servicemen, and when his plane lifted from the runway at Newark on the start of its journey south and west across the continent five days later he carried blurred memories of overwhelming kindness with him. Elegant town houses and imposing apartments with spectacular views had been his to come and go much as he pleased. Their, to him, elderly owners had welcomed him and his kind with charming courtesy, provided food and drink and ensured that there were pretty girls to talk to. Everything had been free and even when, in an attempt to return some of the hospitality he had received, he had taken his chosen companion for the evening to "The 21" or "The Stork Club" it had cost him little because his uniform guaranteed him sizeable discounts. A pleasant and touching interlude, he thought, and set to work with paper and pencil to tell Gail all about it while the plane crossed the Allegheny Mountains towards the vast flat expanse of the American mid-west.

*

'Well, you're an odd one,' the flight lieutenant in charge of Administration at Falcon Field said. 'Wrong Service, wrong age, wrong rank and covered in bloody medals. What are you trying to do? Win the war single-handed?'

Harding nodded, smiling, not speaking and the RAF officer went on, 'I don't know what we're going to do with you.'

'What you're going to do with me is re-teach me to fly,' Harding told him. 'That's what you're going to do.'

'Re-teach you?'

'Yes. I did a hundred hours on an Avro Cadet before the war. Thirty of them solo. That's the only reason the Fleet Air Arm accepted me for this training course. Then last month I did the usual twelve hours on Tiger Moths at home to see if I still had any aptitude for flying.'

'And had you?'

'Look, get off my back, will you?' Harding said. 'You know perfectly well I wouldn't be here if I hadn't. Now, why don't you tell me what the form is around here instead of making dubious noises?'

The other grinned suddenly and began to talk. 'Fair enough. Form coming up. We run four courses of fifty trainee pilots each here. They're staggered, the courses I mean, so one group is passing out, being given their wings and all that, with the other three at various stages coming up behind them. You'll be here for thirty weeks which will include two hundred hours flying, plus Link Trainer time. That's a sort of flight simulator in which you'll practice instrument flying and other odds and sods. Heard of it?'

'Of course.'

'Okay. Until you get on to night flying, which happens pretty early, you'll do most of your intrepid aviator impressions in the morning. Afternoons are for desk work, meteorology, navigation problems, armaments and that sort of thing. Gunnery and bombing theory too.'

'I see. Who are the flying instructors? Ex-operational RAF types?'

'No,' the flight lieutenant told him. 'It's been found that they seldom make good teachers. All the flying instructors here are American civilian pilots. They're employees of the Southwest Airways Company, so you won't get any Service bull out of them, but don't let that mislead you. If you step out of line they'll chop you down fast enough. Also it's entirely on their say-so whether you pass or fail and whether you get directed to fighters or bombers.' He looked at his watch before adding, 'It's getting late. The Old Man will be addressing your class in twenty minutes. When that's over you'll be issued with some typed gen about the course. You'd better read that tonight.'

Seven hours later Harding finished reading the file he had been given and put it on the table beside his bed in the home of a Mr and Mrs Levett. There had been no accommodation for him at the base or in the little town of Mesa, but not far away, on the outskirts of Phoenix, the Levetts had taken him in. He liked them, the middle-aged parents and their pretty, almost beautiful black-haired daughter called Tansy, although he hoped that Mrs Levett would soon stop asking him if everything was to his liking. Tansy, he gathered, had recently graduated from the University of Arizona in Tucson majoring in thermodynamics and, lying back on the bed with his hands behind his head, he wondered briefly what she had wanted to do a thing like that for. Then his thoughts drifted away to Falcon Field and the group called "Thunderbird" of which he was now officially a part.

His first reaction to his fellow class members had been that they were incredibly childish with their talk of "wizard prangs" and exhortations to each other to pull a finger out. It was only when he was told for the third time in an hour by yet another of them that somebody he didn't know was a natural recipient of "The Highly Derogatory Order of the Irremovable Digit" that he realised that they *were* children, none of them over nineteen and, for the first time in his almost twenty-six years Harding felt old.

They had started by calling him "sir" in voices of respectful awe, respect, he assumed, for his two gold stripes and awe for his decorations, but he had put a stop to that on the grounds that they were all pupils together and that he might be taking orders from any one of them during formation flying. His edict had been greeted with cries of 'Whacko!' and offers of beer. Harding switched the light off and fell asleep while he was trying to remember what, just before war broke out, it had been like to be nineteen.

*

It began badly.

Harding walked up to the lanky, prematurely grey man who had been pointed out to him lounging against the side of the hangar. He introduced himself and when the man neither moved nor spoke asked, 'Well, what do we do first?'

'I don't aim to do nothing until you're properly dressed,' the man told him.

Harding glanced down at his khaki shirt and slacks, then at the similarly attired American.

'I seem to be dressed the same as you,' he said.

'I don't aim to be no combat pilot neither,' the man replied. 'You draw a flying suit this morning?'

'Yes.'

'Then go put the darned thing on and don't tell me it's a hot day. I know it's a hot day, but it'll be deal hotter if some Nip sets your cockpit afire. You'll be glad enough of the protection then. I don't care if you're naked underneath as long as you're wearing your suit. Start the way you mean to go on.'

When Harding returned wearing a regulation coverall the man stared at him for a long moment without any particular expression on his face before saying, 'You're older,' as though that were a misdemeanour.

Still smarting from what he saw as a deserved rebuke over his dress, although few of the RAF cadets were wearing flying suits, the statement and the American's manner nettled Harding.

'Yes,' he said. 'I had to go away and change my clothes. That must have made me a good three minutes older. Time flies, doesn't it?'

He was answered with a yawn and the question, 'What's your background, Harding?'

'Submarines.'

'That all?'

'Cruisers before that.'

'Jesus! Great experience for an ageing would-be pilot.'

Harding opened his mouth to speak, but the irritation turning to anger inside him made him shut it again.

'Ah well,' the American said. 'We might as well get acquainted. I'm Harrison K. Harrison Junior. On duty you call me "Harrison". If we get around to having a beer together some day, you just relax and call me "Harrison". Okay?'

'Whatever you say, Harrison.'

Harding had spoken without smiling and the lanky man shrugged, levered himself away from the wall and walked into the hangar. Harding followed suspiciously, very much on his guard. It was to take him a little while to discover that he had been assigned to the best instructor at Falcon Field.

Harrison pointed a finger at a large biplane with a radial engine. 'That heavier than air machine is a Stearman PT 17. You'll be doing some eighty hours in it, starting this morning.'

It looked very big to Harding.

'It looks very big,' he said.

'Yeah? Well that don't make no difference. It has similar handling characteristics to the Tiger Moth you already flew back home.'

He pointed to another aircraft. 'That's a Vultee BT 4. You could be sitting in that for another forty hours, or maybe we'll go straight on to the Harvard AT 6. Depends how you go. Either way you'll be logging some two hundred hours all told before we let you loose on a Martlett or a Corsair.' The expressionless stare came again, then, 'Always assuming you can fly anything.'

'Quite so,' Harding said.

'Right. What do you hope to fly eventually?'

'Seafires. They're the naval version of the "Spit".'

'So they tell me. There's a place called Montrose in Scotland where they'll maybe teach you to handle those, but I guess we're jumping ahead a mite. Let's take a look at this Stearman.'

Harrison showed Harding every inch of it, outside and in, then made Harding show him. It was almost an hour later before he said, 'That'll do. Now ask some of the hired help picking their noses over there to push this thing outside.'

Pulse faster than normal, the plane juddering around him, Harding sat, going through his cockpit checks. Throttle – Mixture – Pitch – Fuel. Doing it again. Finding it difficult to memorise the relative position of the instruments. Airspeed indicator – Turn and bank indicator – Oil pressure gauge – Fuel gauge. Throttle – Mixture – Harrison's voice in his earphones.

'Tighten your straps.'

'I have tightened them.'

'Tighten them again so it hurts. They'll slacken off during flight. When you're dead I don't want you coming to me with some dumb excuse about your harness wasn't fixed right.'

Harding tightened the straps.

Harrison talking to the tower and the tower replying, 'Taxi to runway oh-four. Call when ready for take off.'

'Move it, Harding.'

'What do they mean "oh-four"? There's only one runway!'

'Oh Jesus. Look, the runway is angled two-two-five to oh-four-five degrees. They leave off the last figure because they don't have all day to talk to you in. Someone in that tower thinks maybe you might like to take off up wind, so they're suggesting the oh-four end.'

Engine note increasing, the Stearman bumping forward, slewing slightly from left to right and right to left. Steadying, running more smoothly, turning on to the runway. The tower saying, 'Clear for take off.'

Harrison's voice – 'I have a cliché for you, Harding, and you'd better believe it. There are old pilots and bold pilots, but there are no old bold pilots. Now get this thing off the ground and if you feel me over-riding the controls that's because I'm chicken.'

Engine raving, runway streaming past faster and faster, tail lifting. Hold her down, hold her down.

'You figuring to drive us into Phoenix, Harding?'

For no other reason than obstinacy Harding held the plane on the runway for seconds longer, then he eased the stick back and the ground dropped away.

'Get your wings level and watch your airspeed, Harding.'

The valley opening up before him, a vastness of cactus-speckled sand ringed with jagged peaks. Visibility extreme. Elation beginning to elbow his anger at the man behind him aside. Check instruments. All well. No! Oil pressure dropping! Throttle back! Airspeed falling off, the Stearman wallowing, close to stalling-point. Harrison over-riding the controls.

'What the hell are you trying to do, Harding?'

'The oil pressure dropped sharply. I had to throttle back. Seems to be all right again now.'

'Oh great. So you saved the engine and lost the plane. That's dandy.'

'Frightfully amusing,' Harding said and his ear-phones replied, 'Not from where I'm sitting it ain't, but you British always did have a warped sense of humor. Try to turn this thing to the right on to a reciprocal track without laughing your head off.'

Harding's resentment at the constant nagging sarcasm exploded into fury which transmitted itself to his hands and feet. The Stearman stood on its wing-tips in a screaming vertical turn to starboard, then flicked level again on a precisely opposite course. Trembling slightly, it took Harding a second to realise that Harrison had not attempted to over-ride the controls during the manoeuvre. The trembling eased.

'Very fancy,' his ear-phones told him. 'You must have pleased the hell out of yourself doing that. Now turn back to the left and stop playing at being the Red Baron.'

For an hour Harding flew, sometimes well, sometimes badly. The quiet derision in his ears remained constant and he lost his temper three more times, but he came to know the Stearman. He learned the country around Falcon Field too and could place himself in relation to Superstition Mountain, Four Peaks and the San Tan Range so that he trespassed neither on the air space allocated to Phoenix Airport nor the approaches to Williams Air Force Base. When he was told to land he did so with moderate proficiency, bouncing heavily once.

Standing beside the Stearman Harrison said, 'You have your brain in coarse pitch again, Harding. Try getting a little nearer to the ground next time. Levelling off a goddam half mile high is bad for the plane and my nerves. Same time tomorrow.' He turned and ambled away.

'Harrison!'

Harrison stopped, turned.

'Yeah?'

'I'm applying for another instructor. I'll never learn to fly if I have to listen to all the shit you hand out.'

The American walked slowly up to Harding and prodded him hard in the chest with a forefinger, forcing him to take a step backwards.

'Don't you talk to me about shit,' he said. 'You're so full of it your eye-balls have turned brown. The right place for you would be one of the military flying academies where they make you eat square.'

'Make you eat square what?'

'Square nothing. Just square. You sit rigid, stick your fork into the food, lift it vertically in front of your face, pause, then move it horizontally into your mouth and return your fork to the plate by the reverse route.'

'And why,' Harding asked in an icy voice, 'would that be the right place for me?'

'Because the people who make men do things like that are charlatans and you're one too.' The finger prodded again, but Harding stood his ground and Harrison went on, 'You listen to me, buddy. When I asked you for your background you omitted a whole heap of important facts about your past, including the very relevant one that you already had a hundred hours to your credit, thirty of them solo.'

'Oh, you knew, did you?'

'Don't act stupid, Harding. You can't seriously believe that I'd have let you throw that crate around the sky the way you've been doing this morning if

I hadn't known. What I want to know is why you didn't tell me and don't say because you thought that wingless wonder in Administration already had. Did you want me to think what a miraculous student you were?'

Shaking his head, 'No,' Harding said. 'I was angry with myself over the flying suit business.'

Harrison relaxed visibly. 'That's more like it. And mad at me too, for sure. Wouldn't be natural if you weren't. I always needle new pupils on the first day to see how they react. You can learn a lot about a guy that way.' He paused, pulled at an ear-lobe, then went on, 'Your reaction wasn't so good, but I guess I know why. You were a big hero while the kids here were still in school and you've grown unaccustomed to being kicked around. Now you'll have to forget the past and turn yourself into a pilot. Shouldn't be so hard for you. You're half the way there already.'

He turned to leave, then looked back.

'Feel like that beer I mentioned?'

Harding accepted the olive branch at once.

'Yes, provided I can call you "Harrison" while I'm drinking it.'

The instructor smiled for the first time. 'You have a deal,' he said.

That was the end of the bad time.

Chapter Eight

The Allied armies were surging towards Germany in a flood never to be more than momentarily halted when Gascoigne left *H 58* to take command of the improved U-class submarine which, because all the names starting with U had been used, was called *Voodoo*. She was sleek, superbly engineered, brand-new and useless.

'Probably the last of her class to be completed,' the flotilla captain said. 'Damn nice little boats, but far too short-ranged for the Pacific. We're handing her over to the Greeks. Sort of Anglo-Hellenic lease-lend. I want you to take her out to Piraeus, they fly back with the crew. You'll get your orders within the hour.'

Gascoigne telephone his wife to say that he would be abroad for a few days and sailed for the Clyde to join a Gibraltar-bound convoy.

The passage across the Bay of Biscay and down the coast of Spain was not something he recalled with any pleasure. The job he saw as a waste of time, although he had nothing better to do, because he could not imagine what the Greeks wanted a submarine for with the European war moving inexorably to its close. The weather was bad, the visibility worse and the seventeen merchantmen of four nationalities nervous with a submarine, virtually indistinguishable from a German U-boat, in their midst. He had done what he could to identify himself by sailing up and down the three columns of surface ships with a board hanging over the side of the conning tower bearing the painted message "Look at us carefully. We're British", but there were still incidents. A Norwegian freighter tried to ram him one dark rainy night and a jumpy British gunner shot at *Voodoo* on another. When

U-boats did attack it was a uniquely unpleasant experience for Gascoigne to be on the receiving end. No harm came to the convoy and one of the U-boats was sunk by the escorting destroyers, but the experience brought home to him forcibly the reason for the merchant sailors' edginess. It was a relief to part company with them at Gibraltar and proceed alone, diving by day, to Malta.

At Malta he was given an escort of an unarmed motor-yacht, the sole purpose of its presence being to protect him from the attentions of friendly aircraft. Together they crossed the Aegean Sea to the Greek mainland.

Voodoo docked at Piraeus at ten in the morning and Gascoigne went ashore to pay his respects to the captain of the dockyard. When he had done that he had himself driven to Athens to repeat the process with the admiral. Officially, peace had come to that part of Europe and such ceremony was required of him.

He was waiting in the flag-lieutenant's empty office when the admiral walked in.

'Who are you?'

'Gascoigne, sir. Captain of *Voodoo*.'

'What the devil are you doing here?'

Surprised, 'Paying a courtesy call on you, sir,' Gascoigne said.

'But dammit, you're supposed to be on your way to Australia.'

Gascoigne blinked and the admiral went on, 'Well, obviously you haven't had my signal. Where have you been for the last hour and a half?'

'Calling on the Captain of the Dockyard and then coming here to make my number with you, sir.'

'Ah, that explains it. The signal will be waiting for you aboard your ship. Come into my room and have a glass of sherry. It's nice to know that some of you young chaps haven't forgotten your manners, despite the war.'

The admiral poured sherry, then spoke into the telephone. Gascoigne sipped his drink, trying not to look excited, wondering what was happening. Within a minute the missing flag-lieutenant arrived and was despatched to find a copy of the signal. He returned immediately, handed it to the admiral who passed it to Gascoigne.

"I am requested by Flag Officer Submarines to instruct you to hand over command of *Voodoo* to your first lieutenant forthwith and to proceed immediately to Fremantle, Western Australia, for the purpose of assuming command of *Talon* vice Lt. K. F. Kennaway. Routeing instructions and travel documents will be delivered to you by messenger. Acknowledge".

'You look like the cat that swallowed the canary, Gascoigne.'

'Well, sir, it does beat the hell out of running a ferry service for the Greek Navy.'

'I bet it does,' the admiral said.

Four hours later Gascoigne was back in Malta. He left the DC3 which had taken him there and was led at once to another about to leave for Cairo. On both sides of the aircraft the inward-facing metal bench-seats were crowded with RAF personnel in transit to somewhere, but they made room for him and he sat, a lonely figure in his near-black uniform amongst the pale blue of the Air Force. The plane had been air-borne for about ten minutes when a squadron leader appeared from the direction of the flight deck and walked down the aisle towards Gascoigne.

'Hello. You're wearing the wrong suit, aren't you?'

'I think I must be,' Gascoigne said. 'I feel as though I'm sticking out like the original sore thumb.'

'Like to come up the front end where the workers live?'

'Love to.'

He followed the pilot forward and stood, transfixed by the brilliance of the day, the silvery sheen of the Mediterranean far below, the wide angle of vision. It was exhilarating after the cramped gloom of the passenger section.

'I have her,' the squadron leader said from the left-hand seat. 'Push off, Harry, and let the Navy sit down.'

The flight-sergeant grinned, got out of the other seat, said, 'Leave some for me,' and left the crew compartment. Gascoigne took his place.

'Fly this thing while I get out the fixings, will you?'

'What did you say?' The engine roar was loud and Gascoigne had to raise his voice above it.

'Look, put your feet there and there and grab hold here with your hands. Just keep her level. That's the Libyan coast down to your right. Follow it. I won't be a minute. Oh, and don't make any sudden movements. Nice and easy does it.'

97

'You're out of your mind,' Gascoigne said, but the pilot had already left his seat and was rummaging in a canvas satchel hanging on the crew compartment door. The plane seemed to wallow heavily.

'Ease the stick forward gently,' the squadron leader told him from somewhere behind his back. 'And I mean gently. You're trying to hold her in the air by brute force. She's strong enough to do it all by herself.'

Gascoigne was sweating by the time the man he was beginning to think of as a dangerous lunatic had resumed his seat and there was anger in his voice when he spoke.

'Stop messing about! You've got about forty passengers back there in case you've forgotten!'

He got a wink and a paper cup half full of whisky in reply.

'Try some of that. It's good for the nerves. I have control.'

'Good, but I wonder how long for. Do you usually drink when you're flying?'

'Practically all the time, old son. Well, perhaps that's not absolutely true, but I do like to impress the advantages of flying Transport Command on the other Services. Hospitality's good for business. Don't worry, Harry will land the plane if I drink more than this tot. Cheers. You're Gascoigne presumably.'

'Yes. What's your name?'

'Peterson. It seems you and I will be together for a bit. After we've dumped the shower in the back at Karachi I'm flying this kite down to Ceylon with some Far East mail and you.'

The news was received by Gascoigne without enthusiasm. He grunted and asked what the route was.

'Cairo, Baghdad, Bahrein, Karachi, Bombay, Bangalore, Cochin and Colombo.'

'And how long will that take?'

'Two or three days. Depends on how many side trips they dream up for us on the way.'

It took seven. Three of them Gascoigne spent under canvas at a transit camp outside Karachi, lying naked on a cot in the 105 degree temperature, seething with impatience while engineers worked on faults which had developed simultaneously in the landing gear and the port engine. He grew short-tempered and snapped at Peterson when drinks in the mess were suggested by him. Nor did his mood improve when an unscheduled night stop was made at Bombay to await the arrival of passengers from Calcutta. But it was at Cochin that he exploded with rage.

He and the other passengers walked together from the DC3 to the boundary of the RAF field to smoke while the plane was refuelled and stood in a circle outside the sergeants' mess lighting cigarettes.

One of them laughed and pointed at the sign hanging above the mess door. 'I like that. Ye Olde Coach Inn. Cochin. Get it?'

'Yes,' Gascoigne said. 'I get it,' and glanced impatiently at his watch, anxious to be gone with only the last three hundred miles to Colombo to cover.

A sergeant came out of the mess then, saw the group and shouted, 'Heard the news? The Germans have packed it in! It just came over the radio! They're calling this VE Day! Who wants a drink?'

Gascoigne drank a beer in the sergeants' mess, thanked his hosts and went back to the plane. It was deserted, the fuelling completed. Suspicion stirring in him he found his way to the officers' mess and walked in. Peterson, surrounded by a cheering group, was standing on a table, waving a glass and making an impassioned speech in bogus German. He was more than a little drunk. Fury shook Gascoigne, but he fought it down grimly because it was already too late to do anything. There would be no more flying for him that day.

His anger smouldered throughout a near-sleepless night fuelled by resentment at being held back from his new war by someone he considered an irresponsible fool and the embers burst into flame when at seven o'clock in the morning he found Peterson lying in a drunken stupor on the floor of one of the bedrooms in the transit building.

Ten minutes had passed when, almost as wet as his victim, Gascoigne dragged Peterson out of the tepid bath he had repeatedly immersed him in and said, 'Now get across to the mess and drink coffee until it comes out of your ears!'

Peterson retched, bringing up a mixture of vomit and the bath water he had swallowed. When he could speak, 'I'll have you for this, Gascoigne! By God, I'll have you for this! In case you've forgotten, I out-rank you!'

'You won't out-rank anybody when you've been court-martialled,' Gascoigne told him, 'and if we aren't air-borne by noon I shall make it my business to see that that's exactly what happens to you. Now move!'

His rage had run out of him and he felt only disgusted contempt when he turned away from the dripping figure. Despite Peter Harding's views, to him VE Day meant only that time was running out.

At five past twelve the DC3 lifted from the runway and turned south-east towards Colombo.

Two days later Gascoigne discovered that Perth, Western Australia, was eighteen hours and forty-six minutes by converted Liberator bomber from a long air-strip carved out of the jungle somewhere in Ceylon. He got out of the aircraft, stiff and tired, clutching a diploma proclaiming him to be a member of "The Longest Hop Society" and was grateful to somebody in the submarine depot ship at Fremantle for having sent a sailor in a jeep to meet him.

*

A bosun's pipe wailed in salute as Gascoigne crossed the narrow plank and stepped onto *Talon*'s casing. She looked much as he remembered her at Portsmouth except that she was painted pale green instead of grey now and a twin-Oerlikon had replaced the single cannon abaft the conning tower.

The dapper officer with a carefully groomed black beard said, 'Welcome aboard, sir. I'm Cavanagh. First Lieutenant.'

'Hello, Number One.'

'This is Greensmith, Sir. Engineer Officer.' A tall man, almost as tall as himself, with a cadaverous face.

'Hello, Chief.'

'Norcutt, sir. Navigating Officer.' Small, fair, diffident.

'Hello, Pilot.'

'Parrish, sir. Gunnery and Torpedo Officer, sir.' Burly, ruddy complex-ioned, the only one to smile.

'Hello, Guns.'

Gascoigne moved on.

'Ryland, by all that's wonderful!' he said. 'How are you?'

The chief petty officer grinned at him. 'Fine, sir. Good to see you again. We 'eard you was comin'.'

'Ryland was Cox'n with me in *Trigger*,' Gascoigne told Cavanagh.

'Yes, sir. I know, sir,' the first lieutenant said, then introduced the rest of the senior petty officers to the new captain.

After that Gascoigne asked for a boiler-suit and inspected his command. Starting right forward he examined the torpedo tube space very carefully, almost inch by inch, then did the same in the long torpedo stowage compartment next to it. He was less meticulous in the accommodation spaces, but only marginally so, and it was two hours before he reached the control room amidships. There he spent forty-five minutes looking at everything – the diving panel with its dials and columns of levers and valve-wheels, the hydroplane controls, steering wheel, periscopes, sonar, radar, torpedo data computer, gauges and more gauges, the organised chaos of pipes and electric cables overhead. His officers stood near him, ready to answer questions that rarely came.

The radio room claimed his attention for only a few moments and the galley received little more than a glance. Then he walked into the longest compartment in the ship housing the big diesel engines and the electric motors. The starboard engine was partly stripped down.

'What's the situation here, Chief?'

'Just routine maintenance, sir. We're only at forty-eight hours notice to sail so there's loads of time to do it.'

Gascoigne nodded and stepped carefully over the pieces of machinery lying on the steel deck. He was mildly interested in diesels, but engineer officers, although responsible for most of their ship's mechanical equipment, were often particularly possessive about the main engines. There was no point in his incurring resentment by poking about in a department he didn't fully understand. When he reached the motor room he was back in his own element and crawled about behind the switch-boards and over the engine and tail clutches, peering into every crevice he could reach. That done only the after accommodation and machinery spaces remained.

Those he examined too before coming to a halt almost a hundred yards of densely packed technology from where he had started.

'We'll break for lunch now,' he said. 'I'll check the permanent stores and confidential books this afternoon.'

Talon, he had seen for himself, was kept in excellent condition and did not differ from *Trigger* in any major aspect. Both points were gratifying. The latter because he had known *Trigger* better than anything in his short life and knew now that he had nothing to relearn. In addition, he had served notice on the ship's company that there was nowhere he wouldn't probe. At least, almost nowhere. Later he was to find that he had read his engineer officer's mind correctly and had no cause to regret leaving him alone to do his own job.

At nine that evening a weary Gascoigne reported to the flotilla captain that he was ready to take over command of *Talon*.

'Thank you, Gascoigne. You're looking a little threadbare. Anything the matter?'

'Lord no, sir. I'm just a bit tired. It was a long and rather frustrating air passage out here from Greece. Not much sleep.'

'Hmm. What have you got left to do?'

'Oh, a lot, sir. I'll need a day at sea locally. I want to talk to Kennaway to get the low-down on his crew – my crew I mean – and any quirks *Talon* may have. I'd like to talk to you and the Staff about the conditions in whatever part of the war zone you…'

'Yes, yes,' the flotilla captain broke in. 'All of that, and you must meet the Americans as well, but you won't be sailing until today week. That's definite. *Tiger-shark* has requested a five-day extension in the area you'll be patrolling and I don't want the two of you clashing. Push off on leave for three days. I'm not sending any of my captains to sea with bags under their eyes.'

More delays, Gascoigne thought, and frowned. His senior officer misread the expression.

'Don't worry. You're not being cast adrift in a foreign land. There are several families not far away who make our people extremely welcome on their sheep stations. Charming lot they are too and the country's beautiful.

You just ride or laze around. I'd be obliged, though, if you would eschew rock climbing. Kennaway's broken leg is enough for one flotilla. The Padre will tell you what's available.'

Gascoigne nodded and said, 'Aye aye, sir,' but he did both without enthusiasm, absently, his mind scanning the vast gap separating his achievements from those of Peter Harding, fretting at this further postponement of his dwindling chance of closing it.

'John.'

'Sir?'

'All I'm asking you to do is rest up and get acclimatised. You new boys are all the same, pawing the deck like bloody bulls. That's the wrong mental attitude to take to war with you in this trade. You know that perfectly well. Simmer down.'

'Yes of course, sir,' Gascoigne said and smiled. 'It's only that all I know about a horse is that the tiller's in the bows instead of the stern.'

'In that case forget about the Padre,' the flotilla captain told him, 'and find yourself a bit of fluff. There's plenty of it drifting around here. Just stay away from the port for three days and don't come back with even bigger bags under your eyes.'

Gascoigne left Fremantle the next morning in one of the cars set aside for the use of commanding officers and drove fast along the Stirling Highway towards Perth. So busy had he been the day before that he had spared hardly a glance for his surroundings, for the beautiful Swan River with the two big depot ships, British and American and their broods of submarines, secured to the jetty near its mouth. He shrugged. That would have to wait now. It was while he was wondering gloomily how to fill his three days that the motor-cycle appeared in his rear-view mirror. Moments later it passed him, siren wailing, and he drew into the side of the road in obedience to a pointing finger.

'Where do you think you are?' the policeman asked. 'Bloody Monte Carlo?'

'What?' Gascoigne said.

'Don't act dumb with me. There's a 30 mph limit on this road. You were doing over sixty.'

'I'm sorry. I didn't see any road sign.'

'Christ, that's all I need – a Pom! There is no sign. Everybody in Western Australia knows there's a thirty limit on the Stirling Highway. How long you bin here?'

'About thirty-six hours. This is my first time ashore since I came from the airport.'

'Ah, shit a brick. All right, cobber, drive on and try to remember *you* may be upside down but your speedo's the right way up.'

Gascoigne smiled. 'Thanks.'

'No sweat,' the policeman said and walked back to his machine.

More sedately Gascoigne continued on his way to the club he had been told about off the highway between Perth and Fremantle. There was no need for membership provided that you were Navy, British or Dutch. The Americans had one somewhere else.

It was a pleasant place with a bar, restaurant, tennis courts and a pool. With a drink in his hand he glanced around him at the people in the bar, a group of four sitting at a table and a lone girl, a very big girl, standing watching him from five yards away.

'Hi, I'm Stella Forbes,' she said. 'You're new.'

Legs astride, hands on hips, pelvis thrust forward, challenging. So be it.

'Hi, I'm John Gascoigne. You're gorgeous.'

She moved closer to him and he was amazed to find himself staring into eyes on a level with his own.

'Too right,' she answered, 'and every inch of it genuine.'

He looked at her up-swept hair, its top-knot of tumbling brown curls held in place by a black ribbon making her seem even taller than she was. He looked at the big eyes and mouth in the big face, at the broad shoulders and the breasts straining the material of her blouse, the narrow waist, wide hips and long tapering legs. A lot of woman, he thought. Not beautiful. Not even pretty. Handsome he supposed the word was. Handsome and compelling.

'You'll know me next time.'

Unabashed, 'Yes, I don't think I'd overlook you. You must be what they call a bonzer sheila.'

'Too right,' she said again. 'What are you going to do about it?'

'Buy you a drink for a start. What would you like?'

'A gallon of beer, but not in this place.'

'Why? What's the matter with it?'

'My date's due in ten minutes. We'd better make ourselves scarce.'

On the way out to the car, 'In case you're wondering, I'm not a tart.'

'Just an enthusiastic amateur?'

'Too right,' she said for the third time.

Despite the complete lack of physical resemblance, her height, shape and boldness made her almost as attractive to Gascoigne as was Gail Harding. There was a bonus, too, in that she inspired no fear in him as Gail did, but only the desire to hold and crush. Never having imagined meeting any woman his own size the effect on him of the well-proportioned Amazon named Stella Forbes was electrifying.

Throughout the day, lunching, driving, walking, dining, passing her target of a gallon of beer with ease, they scarcely touched, but that night at the house of the Australian girl's absent POW husband Gascoigne was comprehensively unfaithful to his wife over several hours. He fought and won each battle, inevitably lost the war, and fell asleep with Stella's chuckle blending with her heart-beat in his ears.

Before the three days were over, she had abandoned her tough talk and an undemanding fondness had grown between them. Driving back to his ship, keeping carefully inside the 30 mph limit, Gascoigne smiled at the memory of the flotilla captain's words. A bit of fluff did not seem to describe what he had found for himself.

There was a packet of letters from England awaiting his return, most of them from his wife. He groaned and put them in his pocket unopened, wishing she could find something better to do than write to him every day.

*

'Thanks. How much is that?'

'No charge, Lieutenant.'

Gascoigne looked at the glasses of beer in front of him, then at the white-coated American barman.

'No charge at all?'

'No, sir. We ask a nominal price for some drinks, but beer's for free.'
The man moved away.

Parrish said, 'I should have warned you, sir. I forgot you wouldn't know.'

'Oh, that's all right, Guns, but who does pay?'

'The US Navy I suppose. They built this place for their own use because
their ships are dry, as you know, and made us honorary members. That's
why it's called "The Allied Officers' Wine Mess".'

'Civil of them,' Gascoigne said and looked around him at the smartly
decorated bar and games-room of the prefabricated building.

'Bit of embarrassment as well I think, sir,' Greensmith told him.

'Why's that, Chief?'

'Well, sir, we ask a Yank aboard the depot ship for a couple of gins and
all he can offer us in return aboard his is Coca Cola.'

'Yes, I see. So bang goes my magnificent gesture of buying you all a
drink. Ah well, some other time.'

For half an hour they talked and drank beer, Gascoigne and Greensmith,
Parrish and Norcutt. Cavanagh had pleaded pressure of work and stayed
behind. When they stepped out onto the sun-lit jetty the strains of "Anchors
Aweigh" were coming from the American depot ship.

'What are they playing that for?' Gascoigne asked. 'Are they going somewhere?'

'One of their submarines leaving for patrol, sir,' Norcutt said.

Gascoigne stopped walking and looked at him. 'In broad daylight with
that bloody band playing?'

'Yes, sir. They always do.'

'Christ! Why don't they just send the Japs a postcard?' Gascoigne said.
'When we go I want a hundred miles of sea astern of us before anyone
notices that we've left.'

He walked on, glancing seaward, wondering if there was a Japanese
submarine covering the approaches to the Swan River. If there wasn't, he
thought, there certainly should be. Strange people US Navy officers, with
their formal courtesy and love of ceremony, ceremony like that band amongst
other things. It was difficult for him to believe that what he looked upon in
his own Navy as the most silent branch of the Silent Service could make so
much noise in another nation's. Well, Gail's father had tried to warn him,

but there was no doubt that, whatever their idiosyncrasies in harbour, the Americans were very effective in enemy waters.

That afternoon he was taken to meet them, a fatherly, white-haired four-stripe captain who called him "Son" and several three and two-and-a-half stripers who addressed him as "Commander" although he was only a lieutenant. Some of them were submarine captains and of these the youngest, he guessed, was six or seven years older than he. It felt strange with nobody of his own age and rank present and he had to remind himself that at the beginning of the war, five and a half years earlier, the British equivalents of these men would have been of similar seniority.

They were helpfully informative, answering his questions and showing him whatever he asked to see, but he came away without any particular feeling of brotherhood and thought he detected relief among them at his departure. His greatest surprise had been what he considered to be the luxurious accommodation aboard the American submarine they had shown him over. Somehow he felt that such comfort must have been achieved at the cost of mechanical efficiency and to a small degree he was right, but he felt a pang of envy nevertheless. The emotion was to grow in him.

*

'All set, John?'

Gascoigne, already in an old sea-going uniform because there wasn't much point in wearing anything else when leaving for patrol in the middle of the night, nodded at the flotilla captain.

'All set, sir.'

'Very well. Now I want you to be...' The older man stopped talking, smiled and went on, 'You know what I want you to be, so I'll stop making mother-hen noises. Just don't push your luck too far during your first patrol in command.'

'I won't, sir,' Gascoigne said.

They leant on the depot ship's rail, looking down at *Talon*'s long, narrow shape, at the men moving about on her casing stowing away wires and fenders inside it, at Cavanagh calling orders from the bridge. Gascoigne was

107

worried about his first lieutenant. Cavanagh, never particularly welcoming, now seemed completely withdrawn, speaking only when spoken to, or when his work required it of him.

As though reading his thoughts, 'Quite happy with your officers and men?' the flotilla captain asked.

'Perfectly, sir, but I think they wish I was Kennaway, which is natural enough,' Gascoigne said and heard his senior grunt sympathetically beside him.

In the glow of the groups of lights he could see the current of the Swan River forming a little bow wave around *Talon's* motionless stem. Four knots at least, he calculated. He would head up-river and turn there before making for the open sea.

'Sir?'

They both turned to the depot ship's officer of the watch.

'American officer coming along the jetty now, sir. I think it's Captain Haines.'

'Thank you,' the flotilla captain said and to Gascoigne, 'You'd better get aboard. Good luck.'

'Thank you, sir.' Gascoigne saluted, turned away and ran down the ladder to his own ship. Once there, he stood on the casing waiting for the representative of Commander Submarines Pacific. Two minutes later he was facing the white-haired captain he had already met.

'Permission to come aboard, sir?'

But for the difference in accent it could have been the Marquis of Trent's voice.

'You're very welcome to come aboard, sir.' Gascoigne didn't know if that was the correct reply, but it seemed to satisfy the American who stopped saluting and took the final step onto *Talon's* casing.

Holding himself rigidly to attention the US Navy captain said, 'As you probably know, Commander, it is the Admiral's custom to visit with the captain of every submarine proceeding on a war mission. Unfortunately he had to fly to Sydney yesterday and has instructed me to offer you his apologies and best wishes.'

Formally Gascoigne replied, 'I'm honoured by the Admiral's interest and your presence here, sir. Perhaps I might ask you to convey my respects to him on his return to Perth.'

The visitor relaxed. 'I'll do that and I'll also get the hell out of here so you can get on with it. God speed you, son.' He snapped to attention again. 'Permission to leave your ship, sir?'

When he had gone Gascoigne made his way to the bridge, feeling strangely touched by the little ceremony.

'All hands aboard. Ship ready for sea, sir,' Cavanagh reported.

'Thank you, Number One.'

Gascoigne looked at the remaining berthing wires, then upwards towards the depot ship's rail, but could see nobody because of the lights in his eyes.

'Let go. Half ahead together,' he said.

Water boiled under *Talon's* stern and she moved forward into the darkness.

Chapter Nine

'Do you need the car this afternoon, Dad?'

'No, hon. You take it. The keys are in my pants pocket. The blue ones on the bed. Where're you aiming to go?'

'Peter has never seen the desert at ground level so I thought I'd drive him north towards Prescott or someplace,' Tansy said.

'Fine, fine. How are things going with you two? I seem to have detected some eye-lash fluttering on your part.'

Levett's daughter smiled at him. 'I wish he was as observant as you, Dad.'

'Oh, like that, is it? Strange. He seems glad enough of your company. Have you fallen for him badly, Tansy?'

'Perhaps, but I don't think so really. Well, maybe.'

Levett looked at his wife. 'Any hope of your being able to interpret that for me?'

'It means "yes", dear,' Mrs Levett told him. 'Can't you understand plain English?'

'He's a nice boy,' Levett said.

*

The ground was hard-packed gravelly sand strewn with small fragments of rock. There were no trees, but cactus in many forms, some drab green, others a whitish yellow, marched into the distance so regularly disposed as to give the appearance of landscaping. It was hot and very quiet. If there were birds, they were silent.

'What are the funny big ones with arms like policemen stopping traffic called?' Harding asked.

'Sah-wah-ro, spelt S-A-G-U-A-R-O. Some of them are fifty feet tall and two hundred years old.'

'Really?'

'Yes, really!' Friendly exasperation in the voice. 'And that's an Ocotillo, and that's a Chaw-yuh, spelt C-H-O-L-L-A, and that's a Barrel Cactus you can get water out of if you're ever lost in the desert, and that's a – Oh Peter, you are funny.'

Harding eased his shoulders against the side of the white Packard, propped a nearly empty beer bottle against a wheel and glanced at his companion. He thought that she looked very attractive in her fawn moccasins and matching blouse and skirt. The blouse was unbuttoned, showing part of a white brassiere and the film of moisture on the skin of her chest. It *was* very hot.

'Why particularly?'

'You're always asking questions,' Tansy said, 'but you never tell us anything about yourself. Why's that?'

As if seeking an answer there, he turned his eyes skywards. The sun was behind the car, placing them in a small area of shade, but its rays, playing on ice particles in some high, tenuous drift of cloud picked out the colours of the spectrum over an abbreviated arc like a section cut from a rainbow. He had never seen that anywhere but Arizona.

'I suppose it's because I'm curious by nature, but not very interesting,' he told her. 'Also, I belong to the Silent Service.'

'Gracious! What's that? Are you a spy?'

Harding grinned. 'No, I'm not. It's what the Royal Navy likes to call itself. Or what the newspapers like to call it. I don't know which.'

'*I* think you're interesting,' Tansy said, straightened the rug they were sitting on and lay down on her back with her head resting on his thighs. The blouse fell away from her body.

Whatever excitement Harding felt was swamped by a wave of agonising embarrassment and he found himself nervously stroking her long black hair, wondering frantically what he should do, what he should say, then heard himself ask fatuously, 'What made you study thermodynamics?'

'Oh no you don't,' she told him. 'I'm interrogating you now. What did you do in the Navy before you came here?'

Grasping at the straw with relief he gave her a potted version of his career, the words tumbling out of him to form brief sentences which held little of interest. To his dismay he reached the end of his account in about ninety seconds and, his life summarily disposed of, there was only her hair to stroke. He wished that he hadn't started to do that, but couldn't very well stop then.

'Hmm. If that's all that happened, what are all those ribbons on your uniform coats for, Peter?'

'Long Service and Good Conduct,' he said. It was the stock reply to the question, but he could have bitten his tongue for using it in case she took the last two words as a sarcastic rebuff. If she had noticed them she gave no sign, only making the doubting "Hmm" sound again before asking him if he were married.

'Yes, I'm married, Tansy.'

The statement seemed to intrigue her. 'Are you really? Is she cute-looking?'

Harding looked down at the eager, pretty face staring up at him and with what he later realised to have been appalling obtuseness gave the honest reply that his wife was not cute-looking.

'Hah!' The sound had a triumphant note to it and, as though she had made sufficient progress for one day, Tansy sat abruptly upright and buttoned her blouse.

'Come on,' she said. 'Finish your beer and we'll walk a little. Keep to the tracks. There are snakes about.'

He followed her, trying to decide whether or not her last sentence contained a double meaning, keeping to the tracks anyway because he was decidedly frightened of rattlesnakes.

*

The Vought F4U-1D Corsair crunched down onto the runway with such force that it was still oscillating up and down when half its landing run across Falcon Field had been completed. Harding nodded as though satisfied about something, taxied to the parking area and switched off the big Pratt and Whitney Double Wasp engine just as Harrison's jeep drew alongside. He pushed the cockpit cover back and climbed from the plane.

'What happened, Peter?'

'Just trying something,' Harding said.

'Trying what, for the love of Mike? You fell out of the sky from about fifteen feet up like you did with the Stearman months ago when we first flew together.'

Harding got into the jeep. 'I was playing aircraft carriers. They signalled from the flight deck that the stern was dropping fast so, as I was committed, I cut the power back and dropped in in time for the hook to catch the arresting wire. Might have ended up in the drink otherwise. Just thinking ahead.'

'Listen,' Harrison said. 'You're not the greatest pilot I ever met, but you're a good one. If the Navy has to scrape you off the deck of some flat-top that's their problem. Just don't make me have to do it off this runway. Oh, Mary says she's expecting you for dinner. That okay by you?'

'It certainly is. Thank you very much.'

Harrison nodded. 'Fine. I'll drop you at the Levetts and pick you up again around six.'

When Harding let himself into the house, Mr Levett was standing in the middle of the living room with a drink in his hand and Mrs Levett's back was disappearing through the doorway to the kitchen.

'Hi, Peter. Drink?'

'Er – no thank you, sir.' He had never known Levett to drink in the middle of the afternoon, never known him to drink anything much at all except orange juice and iced tea.

'How'd the flying go today, Peter?'

Harding looked at him closely and saw concern written plainly on his face. 'Something's wrong, sir,' he said. 'Do you want to tell me what it is?'

'Yeah, I guess I do. It's Tansy.'

'What about Tansy? What's happened to her?' It came out in a series of barks as though he were questioning a naval defaulter and when Levett didn't immediately reply added, 'For God's sake, Mr Levett, has she hurt herself?'

'Not in the way you mean, son,' Levett told him. 'She's in her room

113

and would be grateful if you would go and talk with her. So would her Mom and I.'

Both worried and perplexed Harding nodded and walked quickly out. When he reached the girl's door he knocked on it and said, 'It's Peter.'

'Come in, Peter.'

That she had been crying was obvious, but she was composed enough now to smile diffidently at him and say, 'Thank you for coming, Peter,' in a soft voice. Her blue dress was shapeless, its cut too young for her, and her long black hair was gathered in a bun at the back of her head. She was wearing no make-up. To Harding she looked as though she were doing penance.

'Why on earth wouldn't I come?' he asked.

Tansy smiled again, nodding. 'I have to make you a very big apology,' she said.

'What on earth for?' He didn't even notice that he had said "on earth" twice in two sentences.

She took the cord of the window blind in her hands, coiled it round her fingers, then let it drop.

'Peter?'

'Go on, Tansy. What's troubling you?'

'A few days after you got here,' she said, 'I started giving you the eye. I don't think you noticed, but you seemed to like being with me, so that was all right. It was more than all right because I was happy and there was plenty of time.' Taking hold of the blind cord again she fiddled with it for a moment before going on, 'Then the time started to slip away. You got your "wings" and began your conversion to combat planes. Is that the right word?'

'Conversion? Yes.'

'Well you see, I thought I should step up the assault a bit as you would be leaving before long and going goodness knows where and I didn't want you to do that before I had you hog-tied. That was why I kind of threw myself at you in the desert last Sunday.' She grinned suddenly and added, 'That scared you, didn't it?' Without waiting for an answer she sobered and said, 'I'm very sorry.'

'But there's nothing to apologise for, Tansy! I'm not very good at that sort of thing, but that doesn't mean I wasn't flattered. Honoured.'

As though she had not heard what he had said, 'You were going to get the works tonight, the full treatment,' Tansy told him in a sombre voice. 'I was going to come to your room and spread you all over the wall paper.'

Harding blinked, started to say something, but she forestalled him.

'No homely wife was going to stand in my way. No sirree! It wasn't until I got a bit hysterical around lunch time that Dad explained to me about the pit-falls of Anglo-American English. When you told me she wasn't cute it didn't occur to me that she could be a goddam raving beauty!'

There was anger and accusation in her words now and Harding said uncomfortably, 'She *is* rather good-looking.'

'She is rather – Oh you *British*! What's that tiara for? Is she a princess or something?'

Harding blinked again. 'So you found the photographs.'

'Yes, I found the photographs. I was putting some clean shirts in your drawer and I saw them sticking out from under the lining paper and...'

Tansy bit her lip and shook her head before saying, 'That isn't true. All men have photographs of their wives around somewhere. Mostly they show them around too. You never did. You never told me anything. Not even much last Sunday. I never suspected that you could be married until then. Anyway, I wanted to see what the old hag looked like, so I searched your room. That's what I'm apologising for.'

'Well, don't,' Harding said. 'It isn't important.'

For the second time a statement of his was ignored. 'I feel such a darned fool,' Tansy told the blind cord and threw it away from her, making it rap against the glass of the window, then asked, 'Why don't you put them in frames and stand them up like everybody else?'

He knew precisely why he didn't put them in frames and stand them up like everybody else. It was because they excited that kind of attention which demanded explanation and that, like having to account for his medals, made him shy.

'I don't know,' he said, 'but I do know that I wouldn't have distressed you for anything.' Guilt had hold of him, for what reason he had no idea, and he added, 'I'll find somewhere else to stay.'

'It would be kind if you would,' the girl said.

Before he reached the door her voice calling his name stopped him and he turned.

'Yes, Tansy?'

A pause, then a whispered, 'Nothing.'

He went out.

In the jeep Harding asked, 'Could you and Mary possibly give me a bed for the night? I'll be looking for new lodgings tomorrow.'

'Glad to,' Harrison said. 'But there's no call for you to look for anyplace else. You can stay with us 'til you go home on Saturday.'

'*Saturday*? The course doesn't end for another three weeks.'

'Right, but for some reason which is lost on me your country needs you. I just got through telling the Old Man I didn't have anything more I could usefully teach you, so you've finished. Stay with us, huh?'

'Well, thank you very much.'

'Sure. What happened back there? You negative Tansy's virginity or somesuch?'

Harding smiled rather tiredly. 'Not exactly, but I made a pass at her and her father didn't like that from a Limey.' The falsehood did a little to assuage his still not understood feeling of guilt.

'In a pig's ear!' Harrison said and snorted in disbelief.

'You have a wonderful way with words, Harry,' Harding told him.

Chapter Ten

Broken water sparkling under a brilliant sun, an endless succession of miniature rainbows living briefly above *Talon's* bow wave and around her engine exhausts, the blue dome of the sky paling to white as it reached down to meet the hard line of the distant horizon. Only darkness had altered the scene for the five days and fifteen hundred miles since Fremantle had faded from sight astern, but now there was a faint pink smudge hanging seemingly unsupported above the sea far away to the north. It looked like a cloud.

'It looks like a cloud, sir,' the starboard lookout said.

Parrish grunted and spoke into the voice-pipe.

Almost immediately he heard the hissing sound behind him which betrayed the presence of an ascending body partially blocking the passage of air down the conning tower towards the hungry diesels, then the sound stopped as Gascoigne pulled himself clear of the upper hatch.

'Where is it, Guns?'

'Fine on the starboard bow, sir.'

His elbows resting on the front of the bridge Gascoigne stared through his binoculars for a long minute. It had taken him a fraction of that time to realize what he was looking at, but he was waiting for his racing pulse to slacken its pace before saying anything. When it had done so he too lowered his head and spoke into the voice-pipe.

'Captain here. Ask the First Lieutenant to speak to me, please.'

'First Lieutenant? Aye aye, sir,' sounded loud in his ear and, more faintly, 'Forrest, the Skipper wants the Jimmy. Find 'im quick.' He smiled and waited until Cavanagh's voice said, 'First Lieutenant speaking, sir.'

117

'We've sighted Mount Rinjani, Number One. Go to full war condition, send our four best lookouts up here and ask the Chief to give me the most revolutions he can without shaking us to bits. I'm staying on the surface as long as I dare and we'll try to make the passage through the Lombok Straight tonight. Oh, and tell the Pilot he's made a perfect land-fall.'

Gascoigne stayed on the bridge while the peak of the twelve thousand-foot mountain took on substance and the beautiful cone of the volcanic Mount Agung grew out of the sea to the west of it. These marked the islands of Lombok and Bali and were the pillars of the gateway through which he must pass. The name Bali evoked images of girls wearing nothing but grass skirts. He grinned in amusement at the incongruous thought and from sheer exhilaration at the sunlit day, the wind in his face, the fact that for the first time in more than five years of war he was taking his own ship into battle. The steady thumping of his heart was a pleasant accompaniment to his mood and it was with reluctance that he shook it off, forcing his mind into more sober channels. There were enemy aircraft to be watched for now, calculations of tide and distance to be made, a destroyer patrol known to be a permanency in the Strait he must evade.

No enemy aircraft appeared but, ninety minutes before sunset, he decided that there would soon be the risk of being sighted from the shore and, at his command, *Talon* slid beneath the surface.

As soon as he had shut the door of his cabin behind him Gascoigne experienced a vivid memory of the first occasion on which he had stood there. He supposed it was his keyed up state which brought that about. It had been Kennaway's cabin then and Little had been with him that day at Portsmouth, both of them wondering if they would ever again be able to face being under water. That worry, then so intense, seemed laughable now, but when his mind took a further step back to *Titan* his euphoria vanished completely.

Pulling down the lid which converted the wash-basin into a desk, he sat and began to write notes for his patrol report as he had seen Peter Harding do so often. There didn't seem to be much to say except that his ship was poised to penetrate the Lombok Strait into the Japanese-dominated Java Sea. When he had written words to that effect he climbed into his bunk.

He wasn't in the least tired, but lying down made it less likely that he would succumb to the temptation of returning unnecessarily to the control room. Harding had never interfered with anything a capable officer of the watch could do for himself and he was damned if he would either, but he would have liked something to do for the next hour and a quarter.

'It's beginning to get dark, sir.'

Strange. He must have dozed off after all. Well, that was satisfactory enough. Good for his image.

Turning his head towards the doorway he said, 'Thank you, Number One. Take the last possible visual fix, then go down to eighty feet. Call me twenty minutes after that.'

'Aye, aye, sir.'

Alone again Gascoigne wondered whether he was trying to impress himself or his crew with the casual attitude he was adopting. A bit of both he supposed and concluded that he really *was* rather a charlatan. The piece of self-knowledge didn't distress him. His officers and men had observed Kennaway's approach to action on many occasions and now they would be waiting to make comparisons. That was inevitable, but whatever traits they read into his character he could at least ensure that a tendency to show anxiety was not one of them. Anxiety was highly infectious and an epidemic of it could be fatal to all of them.

Cavanagh's voice calling out periscope bearings reached him through the closed door, then the order 'Eighty feet'. He watched the needle of the depth gauge at the foot of his bunk move slowly round the dial and steady at that depth, then closed his eyes and waited to be called, worrying vaguely about the currents he might expect to encounter that night. If he were forced to dive their effect on his passage through the Strait could be significant. After a while he stopped worrying because the unpredictability of the tidal action around the huge necklace of islands stretching above Australia's head from Sumatra to New Guinea made conjecture pointless. The current would be running north, south or not at all. Which of those he would know when he got there.

The door sliding open again and Cavanagh saying, 'We've been at eighty feet for twenty minutes, sir.'

'Thank you, Number One. Come up to sixty feet and stand by to surface.'

Gascoigne swung his feet to the deck, picked up his binoculars and followed the first lieutenant into the dimly red-lit control room.

'Let's have some more of these lights out,' he said.

It was very dark with only the area around the depth gauges and the helmsman's gyro repeater faintly illuminated. The men by the diving panel were hardly recognisable.

'Can you chaps see to blow main ballast?'

'More or less, sir.'

'Can you or can't you?'

'Yes, sir. We can.'

'Right.'

'Sixty feet, sir,' Cavanagh said, then asked, 'Carry on up to periscope depth?'

'No, we'll stay here for ten minutes for night vision. After that, if Taylor can't hear anything, we'll go straight up. We'll see nothing through the periscopes until moonrise.'

The soft murmur of the ventilation system, an occasional click from the gyro repeater when the helmsman strayed a degree off course, the sound of breathing. Seconds dragging. Much too much atmosphere for a simple surfacing procedure. All of them silent because they knew so little of him or his possible moods. I should say something, Gascoigne thought, but nothing that didn't seem contrived came into his head. He shrugged and waited.

It was a relief when the time came for him to turn to the sonar operator and ask, 'Anything, Taylor?'

'Nothing, sir. Quiet all round.'

'Surface,' Gascoigne said and began to climb the conning tower ladder, his ears filled with the roar of high pressure air driving the water from the main ballast tanks. The sound cut off abruptly and he was listening to Cavanagh's voice chanting the depths. 'Forty-five feet, forty, thirty-five, thirty feet…'

At twenty-five feet he released both clips on the heavy hatch above his head and pushed. The hatch swung up and away from him, lifted to a vertical position by its counter-balance weights, and he clambered out on to the bridge with water which had not yet drained from it swirling about his feet.

Gascoigne was glad that the time he had allowed to elapse while his eyes adjusted themselves to darkness enabled him to see so well. He was much less glad about what he saw. On either bow the towering black masses of Rinjani and Agung, not beautiful any longer in their looming immensity but inimical, and between them a greater blackness which was the Strait. A tentacle of fear reached out and touched him, but he shook it off and swept the horizon quickly with his binoculars. There was no other vessel in sight and he opened the voice-pipe cocks.

'Control room?'

'Control room, sir.'

'Officer of the watch and lookouts to the bridge. Bring the ship to full buoyancy. Stop starboard. In starboard engine clutch…' Men were taking their places beside and behind him before he had finished his stream of orders. *Talon* gathered speed towards the ebony curtain of night guarding the entrance to the Java Sea.

Because to the west of the channel the hundred-fathom line reached nearer to the land than it did to the east Gascoigne had chosen that side to make his passage. There was safety to be found in the deep water under the keel and some advantage to be gained from hugging the shore because enemy ships should then be encountered only to seaward of him, with less chance of their detecting *Talon's* presence by radar, sonar or sight against the background of the coast. There might be shore batteries of course but…

Very close on the port beam the small island of Nusar Besar bounced the rumble of the diesels back to his ears, seeming to magnify it. He glanced uneasily in that direction for a moment, then concentrated on the darkness ahead, thankful to be almost through the narrowest part of the channel without incident, concerned that it had taken so long to get that far. From the bearings he had taken he now knew that the current was running due south at five knots subtracting five nautical miles an hour from *Talon's* speed of advance, quite enough to frustrate the attempt to break into the Java Sea if he were forced to dive for any appreciable period. The prospect of being driven ignominiously back into the Indian Ocean was, he decided, too grim to contemplate and, not without effort, forced himself to stop contemplating it.

'Control room, ask the navigating officer how long to moonrise.'

'Yes, sir. He says nine minutes, sir.'

'Thank you.'

Nusar Besar falling away on the port quarter. *Talon* nosing across the mouth of Badung Strait towards Bali. Gascoigne silently damning the rising moon, not knowing that he would be blessing it before the night was over.

'Gun flashes bearing Red 160, sir!'

So there *was* a shore battery on Nusar Besar. No sound or sight of shells, but the dull booming of artillery clear across the water.

'Thank you, Keats. Did anyone see where the bricks landed?'

Nobody had and there were no more flashes. The Japs had left it too late, Gascoigne thought. Probably they had had to check by radio to ensure that it was not one of their own ships they were firing on and now he was out of range. That was fortunate, but the obvious fact that his presence was now known to the enemy was not.

Far above their heads moonlight beginning to paint the peaks of Rinjani and Agung with silver, making the blackness below blacker by contrast, seeming to constrict further the already narrow channel. For Gascoigne it was like sailing through a vast Gothic stage set.

'Darkened ship dead ahead, sir!' the port forward lookout called and Gascoigne knew why the shore battery had not fired again.

'Starboard thirty. Full ahead together,' he said.

Talon curving in a great arc, the vibration increasing as the speed built up, the hull juddering throughout its length from the thrust of the propellors.

'Steady on 160.'

'160. Aye aye, sir.'

'Can you still see it, Hargreaves?'

'No, sir. Out of my sector, sir.'

'I can,' Able Seaman Keats said. 'About Red 120, sir. Getting fainter, sir.'

'What's it look like, Keats?'

'Dunno, sir. Just a long smudge.'

'Well done, Keats. Stay on it.'

'Aye aye, sir.'

A long smudge. That indicated that the ship was broadside-on to them.

It would be bows-on in full pursuit had they been sighted. *Talon* ran just to the east of due south, losing some of the distance she had gained at every turn of her screws. The moonlight crept down the mountains like a slow-motion avalanche towards the black water.

'Can't see nothing no more, sir.'

The image which Gascoigne had held briefly in his own binoculars had gone too and he ordered a succession of course alterations to the east, north-east and, finally, north. After that he reduced speed and the vibration faded to normal.

'That was a good sighting of yours, Hargreaves,' he said.

'Eh? Oh, yessir. Thank you, sir.'

The brilliance of the moon racing across the sea now, reaching, engulfing them, speeding on. Bali and Nusar Besar in full moonlight, Lombok still in silhouette. 'This cuts both ways,' Gascoigne told himself, but the illusion that only his ship was spot-lit stayed with him. After the hours of darkness he felt nakedly exposed.

'Darkened ship bearing Green 90, sir. Coming towards, I think.'

Talon turned west and ran again, but the black shape, up moon from them and astern now, continued to grow in size.

'Clear the bridge,' Gascoigne said.

When the officer of the watch had scrambled into the conning tower after the lookouts he raised his binoculars and examined their pursuer carefully with them. Destroyer definitely and closing fast. He lowered himself through the hatch, heard the klaxon snarl twice in response to the pressure of his thumb on the button and closed the hatch after him.

While he was securing the clips in place he shouted down to the control room, 'Go straight to 120 feet, Number One, and shut off for depth-charging.'

'Aye aye, sir.'

There was a studied indifference about the acknowledgement which made him frown and he was making his way thoughtfully down the ladder when Cavanagh and his resentment were driven from his mind by two cracking explosions which echoed back from the rocky shore. Three more depth-charges followed and Gascoigne found himself standing at the bottom of the ladder staring aft in the direction in which he had last seen the destroyer.

When he realised that his mouth was foolishly open he snapped his teeth together and turned to the first lieutenant.

'I don't know what all that was about, Number One. He's almost two miles away.'

'Delighted to hear it, sir.'

There was that off-handed tone again and irritation spilled over into Gascoigne's voice.

'All right. Group down and slow ahead together. If he hasn't any better idea than that where we are there's no point in waving to him!'

Talon sank slowly, silently to the depth he had ordered and for twelve minutes there were no more explosions.

'What's he doing now, Taylor?'

The sonar operator said, 'Hydrophone effect bearing Red 135 and fading, sir. Seems to be moving off to the south.'

A sixth detonation, less loud than those which had preceded it, added weight to the statement and twenty minutes later as quietly as she had sunk *Talon* rose again to periscope depth. There was nothing to be seen of the destroyer through the periscope, nor was she visible on the glinting water when Gascoigne ordered his ship taken back to the surface. *Talon* resumed her northward progress and covered fifteen miles before she was forced to dive again.

The third warship had appeared suddenly, moving fast and directly towards them from the direction of Lombok when they were almost through the Straits. That *Talon* had been sighted and that any attempted surface evasion would prove useless was obvious and Gascoigne submerged at once, feeling frustration and not a little nervousness. He had a lot of patrols under Harding and others to his credit, but no previous experience of having to force an entry to a war zone because in the Mediterranean a submarine had been in one as soon as it left harbour. The present game of tag with the type of surface vessel it was second nature to him to avoid at most if not all times alarmed him.

'In contact, sir,' Taylor said. 'Bearing steady. Attacking I think sir.'

'What does it sound like, Taylor?'

'Fast turbine, sir.'

That almost certainly meant another destroyer, Gascoigne knew, but he did nothing for a full minute. The enemy had still been distant when he had dived.

'Any change?'

'No, sir. Constant bearing. Closing.'

As before, the first depth-charge exploded some considerable way off. It was noisy but harmless. The second was closer and the third near enough to set crockery clinking. Only then did Gascoigne take evasive action, increasing to full speed, making a radical course alteration. Eight more single charges were dropped, two of them at about the same distance as the third, the remainder progressively further away. *Talon* was moving slowly again.

'Passed astern of us, sir,' Taylor said.

Gascoigne nodded and glanced round the control room. With the night above brilliant with moonlight there was less need for dimness to protect his night vision and he had given permission for two red bulbs to be switched on. They bathed the innumerable metal fittings and the faces of the men with pink, producing a soft, almost fairy-tale atmosphere.

'No hydrophone effect, sir.'

'Any transmissions?'

'No, sir.'

So the destroyer was lying stopped, listening for them.

'Pass the word for absolute silence,' Gascoigne told the first lieutenant, saw him reach for the Tannoy microphone and added quickly, 'No, not with that thing. By word of mouth.'

It was nearly a quarter of an hour before sonar transmissions and the sound of turning propellors were heard again. The destroyer made contact almost at once and its resulting attack was identical in form to its first except that only seven charges were dropped. None of them had the slightest affect on the submarine, but that brought no comfort to Gascoigne. He was losing time and being deprived of the distance he had gained by the tide. Half an hour later and after the fourth ineffectual depth-charging he was an extremely worried man. Twist and turn as he would the enemy ship regained contact sooner or later with, it seemed, little idea of its quarry's range but an accurate bearing on it. That the immediate outcome was as

125

nothing compared to some savage assaults he had undergone at the hands of Germans and even Italians was irrelevant because keeping his ship submerged for long enough would achieve the same object as blowing it to bits.

The memory of a solitary shattering under-water bombardment when more than a score of depth-charges had exploded almost simultaneously around the submarine he was serving in came to him. Peter Harding had been in command then and, after that near-fatal blow, had gone very deep to hide beneath a temperature layer which deflected the enemy's sonar transmissions. But that had been in the almost tideless Mediterranean where such layers built up. The likelihood of one existing in a channel through which the Java Sea spewed into the Indian Ocean at five nautical miles an hour was remote and Gascoigne pushed the recollection aside.

The fifth attack followed the same pattern as the preceding four and the realization that such a pattern had formed alerted him to what he must do, if the visibility was still good enough to let him do it.

'What are the longest and shortest times they've stayed stopped and listening between attacks?' he asked.

'Fourteen minutes and eight minutes, sir.'

'Thank you. Which tubes have the fish with magnetic warheads in them, Guns?'

'Er – I'll find out, sir,' Parrish said.

Keeping anger out of his face Gascoigne waited until he was given the answer, then, 'Very well. Stand by 3, 4, 5 and 6 tubes. Bow-caps to remain shut. What's the bearing, Taylor?'

'Red 50, sir.'

'Come to port on to 280. Bring her up to sixty feet, Number One.'

Gascoigne stood, listening to his orders being repeated, watching the slow march of the illuminated figures on the tape of the gyro repeater in front of the helmsman, feeling the slight tilt of the deck beneath his feet as the ship began to rise.

'Hydrophone effect stopped on Red 35, sir. No transmissions.'

The same routine as before. Good.

'Thank you, Taylor. Go straight to periscope depth, Number One.'

The waiting seemed interminable, but he dared not increase speed for

126

fear of alerting the hunter. At forty feet he gestured for the forward periscope to be raised and stared into the binocular eye-pieces, seeing blackness turn to grey and the sudden burst of brightness as the upper lens broke the surface. A moment later he cursed softly to himself. The moon was over Bali now, throwing Mount Agung into silhouette and the destroyer was invisible against the back-drop of the island. *Talon* sank back to sixty feet in anticipation of the enemy's sixth run. It came after nine minutes.

Sixty feet was, Gascoigne knew, dangerously shallow, but he wanted to be in a position from which he could return quickly to periscope depth and, as far as he could tell, the charges had so far been set to detonate much deeper than where he now was. He hoped fervently that one would not explode directly beneath and blow them to the surface.

Taylor's chanted report of the destroyer's progress towards them might have been a recording of those that had gone before and Gascoigne found himself counting seconds down to the point where the first in the line of charges would be dropped. It came and passed and there was no depth-charge. He frowned and looked enquiringly at Taylor.

'In contact, sir. Bearing constant. Revolutions slowing.'

So that was it. The careful calculated approach, making certain of the range as well as the bearing, with a concentrated group, a pattern of depth-charges surrounding the submarine, at the end of it. Quite like old times and very frightening with him sitting like a bloody fool, Gascoigne thought, at only sixty feet. The hairs at the back of his neck prickled and he ran a hand over them to rid himself of the sensation. The action did nothing to halt the increasing tension he felt and the feather-light brush of sonar transmissions caressing the hull, audible now without Taylor's ear-phones, served only to heighten it, but he still waited for the last possible moment before ordering full speed.

The vibration and the hiss of water past *Talon's* hull built up rapidly, but the sound of the destroyer's passage directly overhead, like the flail of some giant threshing machine, drowned out everything else. Then the waiting began, the waiting for the steel canisters to sink to their pre-set depths before erupting into a rippling blast of thunder and monstrous shock-waves. Some of the men were staring at the curve of the pressure hull above their heads, others had their eyes tightly shut, all had grasped some handhold, their knuckles showing white. Gascoigne found himself gripping the periscope hoist-wire, unaware of having taken hold of it. The waiting continued while the noise of the propellors receded, faded into silence.

Nothing happened. Nothing happened at all and Gascoigne let his breath out slowly, hearing others around him do the same.

'Do you suppose they've run out of ash-cans, sir?'

'Shouldn't think so, Pilot. They probably reckon they can keep us down without wasting any more.' And they probably could do just that unless he did something about it Gascoigne thought before adding, 'Starboard 20. Group down. Slow ahead together. Come up to periscope depth.'

To the east of *Talon* now the destroyer lay motionless on the flat water, spot-lit by the moon. She appeared to be about a thousand yards away and almost broadside on.

'Open bow-caps. Steer 097,' Gascoigne said. He had spoken slowly, calmly, but his mind was racing. So many unknown quantities. What would be the relative effects of the tide on a vessel floating on the surface and torpedoes speeding under it? Unanswerable without much more knowledge than he had of local conditions, so ignore and assume them to be the same. How long would it take torpedoes travelling at 45 knots to cover half a mile? Stupid! Not an unknown quantity. Answer, allowing for acceleration build-up, just over forty-five seconds. What distance could a destroyer cover from a motionless condition in what was left of three-quarters of a minute after her sonar operator reported the scream of a 300hp engine driving the first torpedo to be fired towards him? No idea. Depended on people's reaction times and the ship's acceleration capability. Would the enemy commander move ahead or do something crafty like going full astern? Assume ahead because any ship gathered speed much faster that way.

'Bow caps open, sir.'

'Very well. What's our heading?'

'Coming onto 092, sir.'

'Okay. Keep five degrees of starboard wheel on. I shall be firing on the swing. Stand by.'

'Standing by, sir.'

The vertical hair-line on the lens was invisible at night but when where he thought it should be was a ship's length ahead of the target Gascoigne said, 'Fire 3,' and felt the slight jolt and the small pressure on the ear-drums which indicated that a torpedo had left its tube. Such was his concentration the fact that he had just fired his first shot in anger escaped him.

Half a ship's length. 'Fire 4.'

The destroyer's bows in the middle of the lens. 'Fire 5.'

The bridge. 'Fire 6.'

Temporary loss of weight forward while the sea flooded back into the tubes to fill the space previously occupied by the torpedoes. Forward hydro-plane indicators showing full dive to counteract the tendency of the bows to lift. Depth gauges reading 29 feet. He made jabbing motions with a forefinger towards the deck, then crouched until he was almost kneeling.

'Enough,' he said and the operator stopped the downward motion of the periscope.

'All torpedoes running, sir.'

'Thank you, Taylor. Can you hear the target?'

'No, sir. Too much noise from our fish.'

'Very well.'

It didn't matter. His eyes were showing him now what the sonar couldn't hear. The destroyer was under way, her silhouette foreshortening. A bead of sweat ran down the side of his nose and he tasted the saltiness of it when his tongue licked it from his upper lip. God! The waiting was intolerable! Had he been right about the effect of the tide? Had the enemy captain…? Stop it!

'How long since I fired the first fish?'

The distinctive sharp crack of an exploding torpedo warhead came to all of them before anyone could reply and water covered the periscope at the same moment with *Talon* beginning to regain her correct depth. Gascoigne swore savagely to himself, stood upright and gestured for the periscope to be raised higher. Nothing dramatic had happened, no flames, no exploding magazines and because the dark shape seemed to be taller than it had the fear gripped him that the torpedo had exploded prematurely and that the destroyer was rushing in to counter-attack. There had been no premature explosion and he watched, deeply thankful, as one end or the other of his adversary

129

rose high above the sea and hesitated for a moment before sliding rapidly from his sight. Which end it had been he couldn't tell and it didn't matter.

Elation flooding over him then. He had sunk his first ship! Not just any ship either, but a destroyer and he wanted to shout 'We got the bastard!' but did not. Enthusiasm in front of his distrusting, supercilious officers was something he was not yet prepared to display.

'Port 20. Steer north. Stand by to surface,' was all he said.

He was conscious of people's eyes on him while he turned the periscope slowly in a circle, examining the night horizon, listening to the orderly confusion of the surfacing preparations, then to Taylor saying, 'Breaking up noises on enemy's last bearing, sir. Sounds like her bulkheads giving way.'

'Yes. Thank you, Taylor. She's gone down.'

'Bloody good show, sir.' Cavanagh's voice. He ignored it, continuing his careful visual search.

'Can you hear anything, Taylor?'

'Only the breaking up noises, sir. Quiet all round apart from that.'

'Parrish.'

'Sir?'

'If you ever again demonstrate such appalling ignorance about the disposition of your torpedoes I'll have your reasons in writing from you and enter your name in the ship's log as an incompetent. Do you understand?'

'Yes, sir. I'm sorry, sir.'

'Surface,' Gascoigne said.

*

The moon was low in the west and the curtain of intense blackness still hung between Rinjani and Agung to the south, but *Talon* was on the right side of it now, moving slowly further into the broad expanse of the Java Sea. Gascoigne leant against the twin-Oerlikon cannon at the back of the bridge staring unseeingly at his ship's short wake, the most it could achieve with the power of the diesel engines mainly devoted to driving life back into the depleted battery cells. He was feeling tired but exhilarated, a little light-headed at the release from tension and the night's success

The last had produced an immediate and remarkable change in the atmosphere throughout the boat. The level of conversation had risen, laughter, a rarity during the passage from Fremantle, had become commonplace and the men greeted him cheerfully. Only his officers still maintained a degree of cautious reserve towards him, but even that had lessened. Parrish alone, shattered by the public rebuke he had received, looked miserable. He could stay shattered and miserable for a while, Gascoigne thought. It would do neither him nor the rest of the wardroom any harm to realise that he would not tolerate inefficiency in any form, that he was watching them just as they were watching him. An aching yawn made the muscles of his jaw crack and brought him back to the present.

Dawn was less than an hour off and before they dived for the day Gascoigne had to make up his mind on whether or not it was worth breaking radio silence to report his sinking of a Japanese warship. His personal inclination was against doing so. It was little enough after all and he didn't want to provide the enemy with a radio fix on his present position. On the other hand his action might result in the strengthening of the anti-submarine patrols in a channel used constantly by Allied submarines. It would be best to alert everybody.

'I'm going below, Number One. Call me for anything at all.'

'Aye aye, sir.'

In his cabin Gascoigne wrote "Scratch one tin-can…" looked at what he had written, grinned and tore the page from the pad. The admiral might be American but that was no reason slavishly to employ their terminology. He started again, remembering this time to begin with a nonsensical identification phrase which was supposed to confuse the enemy's cryptographers. "Page one of tales of *Talon* + Large Japanese destroyer torpedoed and sunk north Lombok Strait + Intensified counter-measures may result + Now approaching patrol area + *Talon* sends +"

He took the sheet of signal paper to the wardroom for ciphering by one of the officers, but none was awake. The engineer officer did most of the signal work because he had no bridge or periscope watch to stand and Gascoigne was about to pull the curtain screening his bunk aside when he changed his mind. Parrish could do it.

131

Softly so as not to rouse the others he said, 'Sorry to wake you, Guns, but I've got a message here for ciphering. Get it off to Commander Submarines Pacific as soon as you can.'

'Yes, sir. Right away, sir.' Parrish rolled out of his bunk and although he was still half asleep his face registered relief that he was to be trusted to do something. Gascoigne noted the expression and was glad.

The reaction to *Talon's* transmission came within minutes.

'To all submarines Java Sea area + *Talon* has scratched family-size tin-can north Lombok + Use utmost caution in passage of Strait + ComSubPac sends +"

Gascoigne was smiling over the wording, thankful that his decision to transmit had been the right one, when he was handed another decoded signal.

"For *Talon* + Orchids to you + Go rip 'em boy + Your photograph is on the piano + ComSubPac sends + "

He smiled again, pleased but vaguely embarrassed because all he would have got from a British admiral would have been the single word "Acknowledged" or, at most, a simple "Well done".

After a moment's hesitation he gave the two messages back to Parrish.

'Here,' he said. 'You'd better stick these on the noticeboard.'

Chapter Eleven

'My love! My love! My love!' Gail Harding said. 'Oh, it's so good to see you! Hold me tighter. Much tighter. That's better. Let me look at those "wings" on your sleeve. No don't let go of me. Show me later. You're so brown! But you're thinner. I can feel your ribs. Haven't you been eating properly? Oh darling, *do* say something. I want to hear if you've picked up an American accent.'

Harding kissed her, stopping the flow of words. The kiss lengthened, became exploratory, and they stood locked together, unaware of the smiles of the people passing them on the station platform, unaware of the people, unaware of the station.

At last, 'Howdy, podnuh!' Harding said.

'Podnuh? What's…? Oh yes, of course. I'm your partner, aren't I? C'mon, podnuh? We can't just stand here. I want to look at you. Say something else American. There's so much I want to hear! Are American women as sexy as me? Oh, do come on!'

She took him by the hand, almost dragging him towards the exit and Harding, engulfed by happiness which brought him close to tears, grabbed the suitcase he had let fall and went with her.

Holding hands again they sat on the window seat in their room in the little Montrose hotel watching the storm clouds rolling in from the North Sea towards the Scottish coast, seeing them reach it and pass inland turning the bright evening into instant twilight.

'I see what Harrison meant,' Harding said, 'when he told me that for eleven months of the year any dummy could fly a plane in Arizona. Almost his last words to me were "You'll have to start all over when you hit that crummy British weather. Flyers here don't know they're born yet".'

'And what were his *last* words?'

Harding laughed. 'Professional to the end. He reminded me never to try to climb through a warm front.'

'What happens if you try to climb through a warm front, whatever that is?'

'Oh, the plane ices up, the boost pressure drops and you never come out of the…'

It was as if by speaking of it he had introduced ice into the room. Gail shuddered and the tremor was transmitted from her hand to his.

'Well, you don't want to hear all that technical stuff,' he ended.

For a moment longer his wife watched the angry sky then, 'Let's get dressed now and go down for a drink before dinner,' she said.

*

Dawn was paling the same section of sky when Gail mumbled something into Harding's neck.

'What, darling?'

'You didn't answer my question.'

'What question?'

'Are American women as sexy as me? I asked you at the railway station.'

'Nowhere near!' Harding said.

'That's gratifying to hear, but I'm not sure I like the conviction with which you spoke. It implied wide-ranging experience. Who were they, you lecherous swine?'

Harding grinned. 'Their names are legion, but you know me and my memory.' A lock of her red hair had fallen across his mouth and he brushed it gently aside before adding, 'Actually, only one came near me.' He told her about Tansy Levett and by the time he had finished Gail was staring searchingly down at him, her elbows propped painfully on his chest.

'And that was *all*? You just walked away without as much as *kissing* her?'

'Yes, of course.'

'Oh, Peter. You rotten bastard.'

'Look,' he said, 'do you think you could support yourself some other way. Your elbows are hurting me.'

'Good! I hope they crack your ribs. Poor Tansy. She asked you at least to kiss her.'

'She did not. She just – Oh, I see what you mean.' He looked up for long seconds at the green eyes regarding him, but could detect no message in them and asked, 'Are you being serious?'

For a moment longer she held his gaze, then smiled and said, 'No. I don't want to lose my husband to a college kid or anybody else. It's simply that I always forget that you don't know that you're attractive. Odd that I shouldn't remember one of your most endearing traits. Go to sleep now, my darling. You've got a plane to fly in a few hours.'

With the sharpness of her elbows replaced by the soft pressure of her breasts Harding was sinking into unconsciousness when he heard her whisper, 'Tansy. A little yellow-flowered plant with bitter aromatic leaves. Don't let it make you any more bitter, child.'

That he would never fully understand his wife, or her mercurial changes of mood, Harding was quite certain and not in the least distressed by the knowledge. Her hair had fallen across his lips again. He let it lie there.

*

'I'm sorry that's all the time I can let you have on Seafires, Harding,' Commander Flying said. 'You know how I'm placed. Too many customers chasing too little equipment. Virtually every Seafire that can fly is earmarked for our carrier force off Japan. Well, you're joining it, aren't you?'

'Yes, sir. I've been appointed to *Intractable*.'

'When?'

'I'm leaving for Australia in five days, sir. I suppose I join her whenever I can, wherever she touches land next.'

'I imagine you do. Right, what shall we do with you for the rest of the week? Put it this way, what are you shortest of?'

'Air to air gunnery, sir,' Harding told him. 'I've done very little of that.'

'Okay, I'll borrow a "Spit" from the RAF so you can have a few runs at a drogue target. Oh by the way, a Wren on the Staff of Admiral Submarines telephoned a message through for you. What did I do with that piece of paper. Yes, here it is. A Lieutenant Gascoigne has been appointed in command of the submarine *Talon* based on Fremantle. She thought you would like to know. Make sense to you?'

'Yes, it does, sir,' Harding said. 'Gascoigne and I were together for a long time. Thank you for the message, and for the Spitfire too.'

He walked out, glad that John Gascoigne had got the operational command he had so desperately wanted at last, wondering what had happened to Ken Kennaway, hoping he hadn't cracked as he himself had because he doubted if they would find anyone quite like Gail to pull him through it.

*

It was the latest in the long line of Vickers Supermarine Spitfires, arguably the finest fighter ever built anywhere, and this the best of them, the Mk. XIV. With its Rolls-Royce Griffon engine providing over two thousand horse power to a five-bladed propeller it had a formidable rate of climb and a level flight capability of 450 mph at 26,000 feet. Harding had been cautioned against power-diving the plane. There was something called a sound barrier the new jets were experiencing trouble with and the Mk. XIV would strike it even in a shallow dive. Just what the barrier was he didn't know and had no intention of finding out. Enough to be scything down towards the little white drogue trailing far behind its towing aircraft, enough to feel the plane stagger slightly at the recoil of its 20 mm cannons, enough to soar up and away until he could see the coast of Scotland stretched out below him from the Firth of Forth in the south to beyond Aberdeen in the north. Harding felt god-like.

*

She turned the little hotel room into a pleasure palace and their last night together into a fantasy, a fantasy of drifting chiffon, swirling hair and gleaming skin. The sleepy man who started the long flight east the next day to join the British Pacific Fleet was once again too happily bemused to recognise that the intensity of her love-making had been a manifestation of her fear for him.

Chapter Twelve

Day showed Gascoigne a sea blue, flat, transparent, so transparent that *Talon's* bow and stern were clearly visible to him through the periscope, so flat that the image of his own ship was hardly distorted at all by the water between it and the periscope's upper lens. He didn't like that with aircraft constantly appearing from the direction of Surabaja to the west of him, knowing that he must be almost as visible to them dived as he would have been on the surface. The night before had given him his baptism of command decisions and now he had another to make. To cover the approaches to Surabaja or, more properly, its port Tanjungperak, for a day or two as he had intended, or to move westward along the north coast of Java to longitude 110 East which was the limit of his patrol area.

It irritated him that it took him almost a minute to reach the obvious conclusion that the air activity was a direct result of his own actions, that the planes were looking specifically for him and that if they made a sighting they would direct destroyers to the spot. There was no question that the best place for *Talon* to be was somewhere else until the swarm he had disturbed settled again.

'Go down to 120 feet, Pilot, and steer 345.'

'120 feet, course 345. Aye aye, sir.'

He continued watching for aircraft until the periscope dipped beneath the surface. Able Seaman Wycherley had replaced Taylor on sonar watch he saw.

'It's all yours, Wycherley. We'll be running deep today. Report the merest whisper of sound.'

'Aye aye, sir.'

Gascoigne slept until mid-afternoon, then asked for something to eat and, with his plate beside him, started to write up his notes on the events of the night before. Half an hour later he had almost finished, but put down his pencil at a diffident knock on the door of the cabin.

'Come in. Oh it's you, Guns.'

'Yes, sir. Can you spare a minute?'

'Of course.'

'It's about last night, sir. I…'

Parrish hesitated and Gascoigne held his gaze, not helping him.

'I don't know what came over me, sir. I did know that the fish with the magnetic heads were in 3, 4, 5 and 6 tubes, but when you suddenly asked me I… well, I got muddled and dried up. Please believe me when I say I'm most awfully sorry, sir.'

For long seconds Gascoigne continued to stare at his gunnery and torpedo officer until the other began to fidget nervously and, eventually, looked away. When Gascoigne spoke it was slowly.

'I don't seem able to recall the incident, Guns, but I'm sure that if I ever had occasion to ask you anything about your department in future you'll have all the necessary information at your finger-tips.'

Parrish blinked uncertainly, then smiled and said, 'I absolutely shall, sir.' He bobbed his head in some sort of salute and left.

Gascoigne returned to his writing, but abandoned it and sat back, thinking about his officers. Parrish wouldn't be a problem any longer, he thought. A bond forged by inefficiency had been created between them. Parrish's inefficiency in not being able to answer a simple question for which he had been forgiven. His own in having needed to ask it – he who was supposed to know everything about his own ship. Well, there had been nothing to gain from pointing that out to Parrish, and his officers were there to remind him of things when he had a lot to think about, or even when he had not. The Pilot seemed all right too. He was a good navigator and Gascoigne was beginning to believe that his reserve was natural to him and did not indicate a deliberate withholding of friendliness.

About the Chief he had no worries. Greensmith was that type of ship's engineer who showed little interest in secondary matters like command provided that the occupant of that office did whatever it was he was supposed to do and left the maintenance of machinery to those who understood it. To Gascoigne the only surprising thing about Greensmith was that he was not a Scot.

That left only the first lieutenant, the most important of his officers, and what to make of Michael Cavanagh he had no idea at all. Most of the usual manifestations of character had come his way but this, he thought, was his first encounter with outright cynicism. Even Cavanagh's words, 'Bloody good show, sir,' when the destroyer had sunk had managed to convey indifference and a trace of disdain. He was wondering what could cause such joylessness when the depth-charging started. No succession of single charges this, but a pattern of five or six, the first concentrated pattern he had heard since leaving the Mediterranean.

'I'm coming,' he told a rapping on the door and walked thoughtfully into the control room. A similar pattern exploded just after he reached it and he stood, frowning slightly, chewing his lower lip, then looked at the sonar operator.

'Did that hurt your ears, Taylor?'

'No, sir. Bloody miles away I reckon.'

'So do I,' Gascoigne said. 'Can you guess how far?'

Taylor shook his head. 'No. I heard them once in the Med from two hundred miles off. Leastways that's what the Skipper said when we got back to Malta and he'd talked to the captain of the boat which got the bollocking. The times checked exactly and so did the number of charges and we was two hundred miles apart.'

Twice Gascoigne had had a comparable experience and been amazed at the distance sound travelled under water. The distance Taylor had mentioned was no record and the sound might even have been audible without sonar as faint clicks.

'Yes, I know about that,' he said paused while a third pattern exploded and went on, 'but these are far closer.'

'Oh yes, sir. Maybe only ten miles. Maybe fifteen. I can't be sure. It depends you see, sir.'

Gascoigne did not ask what it depended on. Taylor had done the best

140

he could and no matter which of his two estimates was the better it was all very interesting because there was no Allied submarine within a hundred and fifty miles of *Talon*.

'Shall we go up and take a look, sir?'

He turned to the speaker. 'No, Number One. I think that's what they want us to do. We'll stay down here until it's time to surface for the night. There's to be absolute silence throughout the boat until then.'

Not stopping to explain himself Gascoigne went back to his cabin.

With, he supposed, an eye to economy whoever was engaged in blowing holes in the Java Sea had reduced his patterns to single charges. They continued to detonate at irregular intervals for a further nine minutes, no nearer, no further away, then silence returned.

It was just possible that what he had listened to had been an attack on a shoal of fish mistaken by some sonar operator for a submarine. Such an error was not uncommon, but was normally corrected fairly quickly and at least long before the wastage of ammunition on the scale he had witnessed could occur. He didn't think it had been fish. Nor was a false submarine echo off a wreck possible because the water in which *Talon* hung suspended was in the region of three thousand feet deep and no sonar could probe that far. The thought came to him of how dangerously shallow the sea would become when he attempted to patrol as he must along the north coast of Java, a hundred feet and less, but that was a problem for another day and he pushed it aside, refocussing his attention on the suspicion which had sprung from nowhere that a trap had been set for him.

Analysing instinct was difficult and he tried to apply logic to the process. He had made a mistake in delaying the decision to transmit a signal to ComSubPac for so long after penetrating the Lombok Strait. Although the enemy would be unable to make anything of the ciphered message, their direction finders might have told them that he had set course to the west and north, while had he sent it immediately after torpedoing the destroyer in the mouth of the Strait they would never have known which way he had subsequently turned. 'Stupid. Think faster in future,' he chided himself.

That blunder would have cut down their search area enormously so what, apart from sending up aircraft which had forced him far down in the translucent water, had they done? Positioned an arc of anti-submarine vessels across his assumed line of advance? Quite possible and the absence of propellor noise meant nothing because they could be lying up there motionless on the calm surface with their sonars passive, listening for him, just as the destroyer of the night before had done between attacks.

Assuming that they were there at all he imagined that they would have expected the submarine to have risen from time to time close to the surface to make a visual observation of its surroundings, giving them the chance to sight its periscope, hear the flooding and pumping which would have accompanied the manoeuvre, or identify its under-water shape from a patrolling plane. But all that day *Talon* had remained deep and silent, moving very slowly in response to the small thrust of a single idling screw.

Had the random depth-charging been a bluff, an attempt to break the stalemate? '*We are driving off an attack on an important target by another of your submarines. Come up and look.*' '*Shouldn't you check on the force we have deployed while there is still light to see by?*' Fanciful, Gascoigne supposed, but he was committed now. He stood up and returned to the control room. Norcutt was on watch.

'How long to sunset, Pilot?'

'About twenty minutes, sir.'

'When I want an approximation I'll let you know. How long to sunset?'

'Er – eighteen minutes and forty seconds, sir.'

'Thank you,' Gascoigne said, then stood, trying to visualize in reasonably precise terms the speed with which darkness flooded over the world at the setting of the sun some seven degrees south of the equator. It was very short, he knew, the period of transition from full day-light to blackness and he might be going to need every second of that time.

'Ask the First Lieutenant and the Gunnery Officer to speak to me, please.'

They came at once, Cavanagh and Parrish, and said, 'Sir?' almost in unison.

'I want to start us on the way up as soon as you're ready, Number One, and I want it done as quietly as possible. Orders by word of mouth. You, Guns, close your people up at gun action stations equally quietly. Handle the magazine cover yourself and don't clang about with the thing. Make ready some 4-inch H.E. and Oerlikon ammunition. All right?'

Both nodded their heads and Cavanagh asked what was going on.

'Nothing that I know of, Number One,' Gascoigne said. 'Taking precautions, that's all.'

At sixty feet, 'I'm afraid I'm going to have to flood, sir,' Cavanagh said.

The ship would be expanding as the pressure decreased, the expansion barely measurable but significant when taken over its entire surface. *Talon* would, therefore, be displacing a greater volume of water for the same weight which would make her more buoyant and, for the same reason, the buoyancy factor would again be increased when the periscope was extended outside the hull.

'Yes, of course,' Gascoigne replied and looked at his watch. It told him that the sun was within one diameter of the horizon. The hiss of air venting from an internal ballast tank as seawater flooded in sounded loud in the expectant silence.

At forty feet Gascoigne ordered the periscope raised and stood waiting for its top to break clear of the water.

'Hydrophone effect bearing Red 145, sir,' Taylor said.

'What's it sound like?'

'Something small, sir. Fast revving. Could be a light diesel.'

The periscope, already trained on the bearing Taylor had given, broke surface then and Gascoigne remained motionless for two seconds before turning it rapidly through a full circle. Those in the control room watching him, and most were, saw him hesitate momentarily on the starboard beam. When he had completed his sweep words flowed from him.

'No need for silence now. Target for the 4-inch gun is a two-masted schooner bearing Green 90 range roughly four thousand yards. Man the gun tower. Open fire when ready. Oerlikon crew, your target is a motor launch bearing Red 145. She's closer and coming towards us. Follow me up the conning tower. Group up. Full ahead together. Blow all main ballast, Number One. Gun action. Surface!'

Gascoigne clung to the vertical ladder just beneath the conning tower's upper hatch, looking down past the Oerlikon gunner and his two loaders towards the lighted control room below. One of the heavy clips on the hatch was already off, his hand gripped the other, ready to jerk it free when the first lieutenant blew his whistle, the only sound likely to reach him above the roar of high-pressure air expelling water from the tanks.

To him it seemed a long time, but it was seconds only before the thin squealing reached his ears. He jerked the second clip free, thrust the hatch open and hauled himself onto the bridge pushing hair out of his eyes, clearing them of salt water. The crew of the 4-inch gun would, he knew, be a lot wetter than he because their hatch was lower down and would have been deeper below the surface when it was opened. But wet or not it was obvious to him that Kennaway had trained them well. He heard Parrish say 'Shoot!' almost before he had opened the voice-pipe cocks and the immediate heavy slam of the big gun so close to him made him jump. It was a temptation to watch where the shot fell, but there was no time for that with only a nail-paring of sun showing above the western horizon and the motor launch approaching fast from the port quarter.

'Control room. Stop starboard. In starboard engine clutch. As soon as we're going ahead on the starboard engine repeat with the port engine and tell the Engineer Officer I want revs for full speed as soon as he can work up to them.'

Enough of what he had said had been repeated back to tell him that his orders were understood before the words coming from the voice-pipe were obliterated by the mind-shattering racket of Able Seaman Lowry's twin-Oerlikon cannon engaging the motor launch. It was half a mile away, a machine gun firing steadily from the roof of its bridge. Where the bullets were going Gascoigne had no idea, but frowned in quick concern when a puff of smoke near *Talon's* stern caught his eye. A hole in the pressure hull would be fatal to them all, but could a machine-gun bullet produce such a clear visual effect? No, of course it couldn't? The schooner, then, with a heavier gun? The smoke came again and he sighed softly. It was only the starboard engine starting up. Feeling simultaneously relieved and ridiculous he looked back at the motor launch just in time to see its bridge disintegrate under the impact of Lowry's 20 mm shells. Behind him the 4-inch kept up its regular slamming reports.

The sun had gone completely now, but the western horizon still stood out sharply and he clambered up the forward periscope standard to search

144

through his binoculars for further patrol vessels in that direction. There were none to be seen and he turned his attention to the schooner. The enemy ship was little more than a black smudge against the darkness to the east, visible mainly because of the gun flashes coming from her and a small fire burning somewhere on her deck, but *Talon*, he guessed, must be presenting a clear silhouette to the Japanese gunners. As if in confirmation a column of water rose out of the sea fifty yards from him. Gascoigne jumped down to the bridge deck, pushed the navigating officer away from the voice-pipe and ordered a course alteration to the west.

The Oerlikon fell silent and Lowry called out, 'Launch is sinking, sir! Permission to engage the other feller, sir?'

His ears ringing, Gascoigne said, 'What? Oh, well done. No, hold your fire. The range is too great. I think we'll…'

A rattling clang from the 4-inch gun-deck and a voice shouting 'Barton's hit!' made him swing round, the sentence unfinished.

Another voice answered, 'No I fuckin' ain't! I just tripped over these fuckin' shell-cases! The fuckin' deck's knee-deep in 'em!'

He peered over the front of the bridge at the dark huddle of men around the gun.

'Cease firing! Are you sure you're all right, Barton?'

'Yes, sir. Thank you, sir. Fuck it!' Barton said.

Gascoigne grinned and stared astern through his binoculars. No more gun flashes were coming from the schooner and the enemy seemed to have the fire well under control, but that didn't matter. He had broken through their defensive arc and that was all that counted.

Talon ran fast to the west across the calm night sea.

*

"The small action was over in less than four minutes" Gascoigne wrote in his patrol report notes. "Able Seaman Lowry is to be commended for his handling of the Oerlikon, as are Lieutenant Parrish and my gun-layer, Leading Seaman Wedgebury, for their work with the 4-inch. Although out of 22 rounds fired only three were definitely seen by them to hit the schooner it should be remembered that this was achieved at a range of over two miles on a nearly invisible target. I decided against staying on the scene to complete the destruction of this second anti-submarine vessel because of the risk of encountering others of greater fire-power, even destroyers, in the darkness. In fact I would have attempted to avoid the engagement altogether had not the motor launch heard us taking on ballast water as we approached the surface, but after that had happened it seemed futile to sit around and be depth-charged by an enemy we could out-gun".

He read his description of the day's events again, put the papers on his bunk and took a folder from a drawer. It contained a letter from his father, three from his mother and six from his wife, the last two of which he hadn't bothered to open. For a moment he thought of writing to his parents or reading his wife's latest complaints about rationing, but decided that either was too much effort and put the letters back where they had come from.

The only other item in the folder was a photograph from *The Tatler* of some months before. The caption read, "Four other guests at Wednesday's Charity Ball – Lieutenant Peter Harding, DSO, DSC, RN, Mrs Cotter, Major Ian Cotter, MC, and Lady Abigail Harding". Smiling at the picture Gascoigne thought that it really was rather bad luck for Mrs Cotter, whoever she might be, to be photographed in the company of Gail Harding. The major's wife was attractive, but the eyes settled automatically on the figure to the right of the group. Even in the dim red lighting of his cabin it stood out.

To Gascoigne the cutting was a double yard-stick. The image of his ex-captain and tutor reminded him of how situations could best be handled when faced with the enemy. That of Harding's wife provided him with visual gratification and a gauge against which he measured the desirability of other women. His own private scale indicated that a girl more than half as attractive as she was worth trying to get into bed. Stella Forbes came into that category, but his own wife did not. Nor did any other woman he knew. For a while he had imagined himself to be in love with Gail, but now accepted that that was not the case because he was unable to equate love with the considerable alarm her perfection inspired in him. He resented people who made him nervous, so was content to resent, admire and desire her

146

from a distance. Taken together the three emotions afforded him immense pleasure without the complication of involvement.

'Captain, sir?'

He turned the page face down and drew the curtain screening the already open cabin door aside.

'Yes, Elliott?'

'Grub's up, sir,' the seaman who acted as the officer's steward said.

'You're hopeless, Elliott. You'll never get a job as a butler after the war.'

The man grinned. 'Sorry, sir. Grub's *ready*. Will you have it here or in the wardroom?'

Gascoigne elected to go to the wardroom, made his way there and sat down at the head of the small table, glad to find that the first lieutenant had just gone on watch. Elliott put food in front of him and he began to eat, then asked, 'Is Barton OK?'

'Sprained his wrist when he fell, sir, or strained it. I'm never sure what the difference is,' Parrish said. 'Anyway, the Cox'n has strapped him up.'

'You'd better replace him as loader until he's better. Who have you got?'

'Me, sir.' Elliott was passing plates across the table to the engineer and navigating officers. 'I've practised. Make a nice change from dishing out stewed kangaroo or whatever this is.'

Gascoigne saw Parrish nod and said, 'Good, that's settled.'

He began to eat again, trying to think of some way of getting rid of the big brass shell-cases over the side more quickly as each was ejected from the gun when Parrish asked, 'How did you know that lot was up there waiting for us, sir?'

'I didn't, Guns. For heaven's sake, you know that. It seemed likely they'd have surface ships out looking for us as well as aircraft, but they could have been ten miles astern of us or ten miles further on. Coming up right under them was pure chance.'

Parrish giggled and said, 'Williamson doesn't think so, sir.'

'Who's Williamson? I don't know everybody yet.'

'Leading Telegraphist, sir. He's the ship's poet. Does little verses on everything and everybody. Now he's picked on you. Read it out, Neil.'

Norcutt looked embarrassed and made a show of searching his pockets before saying he hadn't got it.

147

'Yes you have,' Parrish told him. 'You stuffed it down between the cushions when the Captain came in. Here, give it to me.'

Reluctantly Norcutt did so and continued to look uneasy while Parrish angled the piece of paper towards the single red bulb and recited,

'When the spin of a coin
Sent us Skipper Gascoigne
The Japs gave up all hope
For he can find them without sonar or even periscope.
Then whether it's a destroyer or a motor boat
The answer's just the same – it's not allowed to float.
The buzz is he has a private line to
God or the Emperor Hirohito.'

The gunnery officer giggled again and Gascoigne smiled, feeling rather pleased by the silly rhyme, but his pleasure ebbed with the passing days, days spent lying in silent wait for an enemy who never came, nights during which *Talon* prowled the southern Java Sea with, it seemed, nothing more urgent to achieve than the recharging of her batteries before the next dawn drove her under.

Occasionally very small motorized schooners were sighted close inshore, but their lack of size and the shallowness of the water on which they sailed combined to convince Gascoigne that they were not worth the trouble and possible risk of attacking. He had no desire to be caught on the surface by aircraft without sufficient depth beneath his keel into which he could retreat. In addition, those vessels which passed near enough for close periscope observation appeared to have no Japanese aboard and he thought it no part of his duty to murder natives of Java.

What had happened was obvious to him, but the knowledge did little to lessen his growing frustration. First, his less than stealthy entry into his patrol area had resulted in the halting of coastal traffic of any size because the enemy would be reluctant to permit a ship of real value to sail with a hostile submarine known to be in the vicinity. That, he supposed, was a gain, but not a particularly encouraging one from a personal point of view. He wanted to sink ships, not immobilise them, but consoled himself with the thought that they could not remain in harbour indefinitely and that his own recent enforced passivity might persuade them to put to sea again.

But his second piece of knowledge was the more depressing. Just as the Mediterranean had been a preserve for British submarines, so had the Java and Flores Seas for the Americans. They, for the most part, had moved on, the havoc they had left behind invisible only because the evidence of it lay on the sea-bed. Now, with their faster, longer range submarines, they were operating far to the north gathering a rich harvest in the South China Sea and around the islands of Japan itself, while he was left to pick up whatever scraps they might have overlooked. For a man who had taken part in the destruction of Rommel's supply lines, a major contribution to the defeat of the Afrika Corps which had once been poised to take the Middle East oil-fields and even India, it was galling to find himself playing second fiddle to another Navy in another war.

With Britain only recently relieved of Atlantic and European commitments Gascoigne supposed it was inevitable that she should be cast for some time to come in the role of junior partner in the Far East, but his own personal relegation to what he was beginning to think of as a practise pitch angered him. Obscurely he blamed the Americans, forgetting entirely that had Kennaway not broken a leg he wouldn't have had a command at all.

At noon on the ninth blank day he was sitting in his cabin seething with barely suppressed rage and jealousy. The decoded signal lying on the desk in front of him was from a U.S. submarine eight hundred miles to the north. "Hot dog + scratch one flat-top" it read. So they'd sunk another Japanese aircraft carrier, a bloody great aircraft carrier, and that was only the latest of a dozen messages reporting the destruction of major enemy units, while he…

The occasional week-long periods of crushing boredom when nothing that floated had been sighted even in such an intensive theatre of war as the Mediterranean were temporarily erased from his memory. He imagined this to be his first term of inaction and was tired of staring through the periscope at volcanic mountains, at teak and palms and banyans, at brown-skinned people with whom he had no quarrel. He was tired, too, of the humidity, the brilliant days, the velvet nights and the empty, glassy sea. But most of all he was tired of his boisterous allies and the exultant way in which they

149

signalled their frequent and undoubted successes. Simple envy was making Gascoigne anti-American.

At five minutes past noon Cavanagh sighted the Japanese destroyer.

At twenty-three minutes past noon the Japanese destroyer had a firm sonar contact on *Talon*.

'Shut off for depth-charging,' Gascoigne said.

The ship juddering to the drive of the propellors as she raced away from the coast. No point in silent running with the enemy approaching fast and confidently on a steady bearing. No point at all. Every point in trying to reach deeper water before the attack came, water deep enough at least to set them the problem of at what depth to detonate their charges, to give them three dimensions to think about instead of virtually two with less than sixty feet between *Talon's* keel and the seabed.

He walked to the chart table, picked up dividers and made a measurement. Four minutes at full submerged speed on this course, he calculated, before the bottom began to shelve, but the destroyer would be over them long before that.

'Starboard 30, steer 090,' Gascoigne told the helmsman. For the time being he had forgotten all about the Americans and their sin of obliterating Japanese sea-power. The war he had searched for unsuccessfully was coming to him, riding a line of sonar pulses. It arrived with a prolonged thundering concussion which made him grab for support, rattled the teeth in his head and set up such a vibration that for a moment he thought he had double vision. It also blew the stern up several feet and that saved *Talon*, her thrusting screws forcing her downwards. Some lights broke.

'Port 30, steer 360,' Gascoigne said and heard the first lieutenant ordering all compartments to report damage. The hydroplanes brought the ship level again and she swung slowly towards the north and deeper water. He let her run on at full speed for sixty seconds, knowing that there was little chance of the destroyer hearing their hurried progress until the water disturbance caused by the depth-charges had subsided. At the end of that time speed was reduced to dead slow.

'No detectable damage of any consequence, sir,' the first lieutenant reported and surprised Gascoigne by adding, 'I think that last-minute

150

alteration of yours must have thrown him off. If those charges had been anywhere else but astern we'd have been blown to the surface.'

Gascoigne did not particularly appreciate being told the obvious, but as the remark was the closest Cavanagh had ever come to expressing approval of his actions he contented himself with saying, 'Yes. Did anybody count how many they dropped?'

Opinions in the control room varied between four and seven, but were unanimous in the belief that they had been very close.

'Hydrophone effect and sonar transmissions bearing Red 5. Sweeping, sir,' Taylor said.

So the destroyer had not regained contact, but was almost directly ahead and barring their path to deep water. Gascoigne nodded an acknowledgement, but gave no instructions. There was nothing to be gained by turning and presenting the whole length of the submarine as a sonar target. The waiting began.

'What's the bearing now, Taylor?'

'The same, sir. No change at all. Still sweeping.'

Nearly three minutes passed before Taylor spoke again.

'Speeding up, sir. Bearing Red 10. Red 15 now, sir. Going quite fast. Red 20. Red 25. Seems to be passing clear of us down the port side. Now bearing…'

Four separate crashing detonations making *Talon* quiver and Taylor snatch his ear-phones from his head, grimacing with pain at the amplified sound.

'Group up. Full ahead together,' Gascoigne said. The charges had been appreciably further away and he made his own contribution to the obvious by adding, 'They've lost us for the moment.' Deep water was almost within reach when he once more ordered silent running.

An hour later and with two hundred feet between them and the surface Gascoigne watched the people around him beginning to relax. There had been no more attacks and the sounds of the destroyer's transmissions and propellors were fading on the starboard beam.

'What I particularly object to,' Parrish announced, 'is being depth-charged when we haven't done anything to deserve it.'

'What I particularly object to is being depth-charged at all,' Norcutt replied.

'Quiet, you two,' Gascoigne said. 'Port 20, steer 180. Let's get back to the coast and see if we can't find out what all that was in aid of. Bring her up to periscope depth, Number One.'

Tenseness reasserted itself at his words and he wondered irritably what they all thought they were there for. If they were under the impression that it was to lie in comparative safety away from the inshore traffic lanes they...

'Do you suppose something might be coming, sir?' Cavanagh's words cut across his line of thought.

'I hope so, Number One. I don't think that destroyer just happened to be passing by. With luck they'll start shipping movements again if they think they've seen us off.'

'Wacko!' Parrish said and that and the growling murmur of the men in the control room told Gascoigne that their tenseness was born of expectancy, that not only he had been affected by the long days and nights of frustration. The realization both pleased and angered him, but the anger was with himself for his lack of imagination, for his self-centredness. He had, he concluded, a great deal to learn still about command.

An hour and a quarter later Norcutt called him to the control room.

'What is it, Pilot?'

'I don't know, sir. It looked huge a second ago, now it's smaller and above the horizon. Very strong mirage effect, sir. Could be anything.'

The navigating officer stepped back from the periscope and Gascoigne took his place, adjusting the binocular eye-pieces to the distance apart of his own eyes, staring at the distant shape, a shape which altered as he watched.

'Can you hear anything on this bearing, Taylor?'

'Not a sound, sir.'

The shape narrowed and rose until it looked like a factory chimney.

'Now it looks like a factory chimney,' Gascoigne said. 'All right. It's got to be a ship of some sort. There's no land in that direction. Let's go and find out what it is.'

Talon altered course towards the object and increased speed, but a full twenty minutes passed before the distortion caused by light refraction lessened sufficiently to reveal the image of a modern freighter and Gascoigne could give the order 'Start the attack.'

'Bearing is that and I'm ten degrees on her port bow.'

The man standing behind him read the bearing aloud from the azimuth ring on the deckhead where the periscope disappeared through the pressure hull and Gascoigne went on, 'The range – er – use a mast-head height of… Oh, bloody hell!'

'Transmogrified again, sir?'

'What, Guns? Oh. Yes, that's exactly what it's done. It's as though I was looking at three separate buildings hovering just above the surface.'

'I shouldn't worry, sir,' Cavanagh said. 'The patrol before last we saw the image of a ship upside down. It happens in this part of the world quite often in certain light conditions.'

Intrigued to find that his first lieutenant *was* capable of volunteering useful information and genuinely interested, Gascoigne asked, 'Did you really?'

'Honestly, sir. Kind of optical illusion. It sorts itself out when you get close enough.'

It sorted itself within the next minute and the attack was resumed, ranges, bearings and angles being passed to the navigating officer at the chart table and the gunnery officer at the torpedo data computer known familiarly as the "Fruit Machine".

'Plot suggests enemy course and speed 087 at 10 knots, sir.'

'Right, use those figures and give me a course for an 80 track.'

Talon sank deep, or as deep as the shallow sea would allow, and ran in fast for three minutes on the course Gascoigne had been given, then cruised back towards periscope depth.

From the sonar set Taylor said, 'I've got her at last, sir. Fast reciprocating engine bearing Green 40 and I think I can hear turbines on roughly the same bearing. Not sure though.'

Gascoigne signalled with his hand and stood watching the gleaming column of the periscope, thicker than a telegraph pole, rise out of its well with a subdued hydraulic hiss. When it was fully raised he jerked the folded handles into a horizontal position, then waited while *Talon* completed the last few feet of her rise. Light struck at his eyes as the upper lens broke surface and he swung quickly in a circle, searching the horizon, before steadying on Green 40.

He swore softly before saying, 'She's zigged away. Bearing is that. Range is that. I'm seventy degrees on her port bow. Give me a course for a 130 track. Down periscope.'

Increasing vibration and the surge of water past the hull sounding clear as the submarine turned on to her new course and hastened to close the range on the surface ship. Gascoigne looked at the first lieutenant.

'You'd better shut off for depth-charging again, Number One. Taylor was right about hearing turbines. There's a destroyer up there too. It must have been hidden behind the target before.'

Cavanagh said, 'Aye aye, sir,' and spoke into the Tannoy microphone.

A droplet of sweat detached itself from Gascoigne's hairline and ran down his forehead into the corner of his left eye. He wiped it away, the action bringing home to him how hot it had become. It wasn't surprising. The air had been warm and humid when they had dived at dawn and the heavy battery discharge involved in evading the first destroyer that afternoon and manoeuvring for attack now had raised the temperature by many degrees. The deck covering the three battery sections each containing one hundred and twelve large cells would be very warm to the touch, he knew, and that heat would be transferring itself to the air around them. Well, there was nothing he could do about that and it would get hotter still before the day was over. He glanced at his watch. Another eighty seconds to go to the next periscope observation.

'Taylor?'

'Yes, sir?'

'Haven't you heard any sonar transmissions?'

'I might have done, sir, just before you speeded up and went deep this last time, but I wasn't sure enough to report them. I think we've got strange listening conditions.'

Like the visual ones, Gascoigne thought.

'Yes,' he said. 'Periscope depth please, Number One.'

He moved his position then, to stand by the after periscope, the monocular one with the thinner top. With the sea like a glass floor he could no longer afford the luxury of the bigger binocular and its better field of view, its sky-searching capability, its choice of magnification. It was possible, even probable he knew, that the smaller periscope too would be sighted by the enemy anyway if he kept it up for more than a second or so. Then there was the problem of aircraft seeing *Talon's* shape through the water. There had been no planes in sight when last he looked, but that didn't mean they weren't there now. Finally, there were his torpedo tracks to worry about. They would be as visible as chalk lines drawn across slate in the flat calmness. Gascoigne gave a small, angry shake of the head. There was nothing he could do about them except hope that they would not be sighted until it was too late.

'Up periscope,' he said and immediately, 'Down periscope. Target is altering course to port. Destroyer astern of her. Up periscope… Down periscope.'

He glanced at the depth gauges. The ship was almost three feet too shallow he saw and crouched, squatting on his heels.

'Get her back to thirty-four feet, Number One! Up periscope.'

As soon as the eye-piece reached the level of his face he grabbed the handles, jerked them horizontal, then pushed them vertical again.

'Down periscope. Target still swinging.'

'I've got the sonar transmissions now, sir. Sweeping,' Taylor said.

'All right.'

Gascoigne stayed crouched close to the deck, sweat running down his bare back and chest. The depth gauges read thirty-two feet.

'Bloody well flood if you can't hold her, Number One. Up periscope.'

He had to rise to a half crouch that time before the upper lens was clear of the water. 'High enough,' he said, paused, then turned quickly through three hundred and sixty degrees searching for aircraft before adding, 'Range is that. Bearing is that. Down periscope. Group up. Full ahead together. Sixty feet. Enemy is pointing directly towards us. We'll run on on this course and fire a stern salvo if she doesn't zig again.'

'Any sign of the destroyer, sir?' Norcutt asked when the information and orders had been acknowledged.

'Yes. Still astern of the target, Pilot.'

And that was strange, Gascoigne thought. The stern position for an escorting warship *was* the best from which to launch a counter attack on a submarine, but it was *not* the best from which to protect the ship in one's charge. Could this, then, be a trap? Were the Japanese prepared to sacrifice the freighter in order to destroy the submarine? Hardly. The target was a

155

fine modern ship, too valuable to stake out as a sacrificial goat and the first destroyer trying to chase them away didn't fit the ambush theory either.

'Periscope depth. Stand by 9, 10 and 11 tubes,' he said.

At his next periscope observation Gascoigne whispered, 'Shit,' before saying in a taut voice, 'Stand by 1, 2 and 3 tubes. Secure 9, 10 and 11. Angle the fish 90 right – repeat 90 right. Open bow caps. Down periscope. Enemy has zigged back to starboard and I'm now seventy-five degrees on her port bow.' He talked on while Norcott worked feverishly on the chart and Parrish wound the handles of the "Fruit Machine".

A quarter of a minute later, 'This will be a firing observation,' Gascoigne said. 'What's the Director Angle?'

'Green 99, sir.'

'Up periscope. Put me on Green 99.'

The man standing behind him put his hands over Gascoigne's, moving the periscope, pushing gently with one hand, pulling with the other, until the vertical line etched up the brass column was exactly aligned with the correct bearing on the azimuth ring above his head.

'You're on Green 99, sir.'

'Thank you. Stand by. I'll aim the first fish visually. Numbers 2 and 3 to be fired at seven second intervals by stop-watch.'

The destroyer was out of his field of vision, but the bow of the freighter was moving into its right hand side towards the hair-line at the lens's centre.

'Fire 1. Down periscope.'

Talon went fast and deep as soon as Parrish, stop-watch in hand, had sent the third torpedo on its way. Gascoigne stood, picturing the long gleaming shapes leaping from their tubes, turning like sharks as their angled gyros forced the rudders over to send them streaking away at ninety degrees to the submarine's course. Then he began to worry again about the trail of bubbles they would leave in their wake.

'All torpedoes running, sir,' Taylor said.

'Thank you.'

He continued to stand where he was, waiting as the seconds dragged, the tension in him mounting. Eventually he *had* to ask.

'How many seconds estimated running time left, Guns?'

'Eight, sir. Five, four, three, two, one.'

Zero came and went. Nothing happened. No torpedo explosions, no increase in propellor revolutions by the surface ships, no sonar contact, until, four minutes after firing, the destroyer dropped a solitary depth-charge. It made everyone jump, but was far too distant to do anything else. Gascoigne guessed that somebody aboard the freighter had eventually seen the torpedo tracks, probably after they had passed, alerted the destroyer by lamp signal, hadn't been believed and that the single charge had been merely a gesture. It seemed a bit thin, even to himself, but he was unable to think of any other explanation for the destroyer not counter-attacking. He sighed softly and ordered a course alteration to the east, glad only that it wasn't very long until dark.

'How's the battery, Number One?'

'Getting pretty low, sir. I'll have some readings taken in a minute.'

'All right. I'm afraid I can only let you have a running charge on one engine to begin with when we surface.'

'Are you going after them, sir?'

'Of course not. I'm going to stand here and scratch my piles!' Gascoigne said and walked to his cabin. That to speak to his second-in-command in front of the control room crew in such a way was, he was well aware, quite wrong, but he was furious with himself for missing his first moving torpedo target and it *had* been a very stupid question.

*

It was not until the existence of a fault in the electro-acoustic transducer of his sonar set was reported to him that the destroyer commander conceded that the submarine attacked earlier in the day by his sister ship might have remained in the vicinity and that the mast-head lookout of the freighter *Tuka Maru* could have seen torpedo tracks as he had claimed to have done. The necessity to admit to a merchant seaman the existence of a defect in his equipment and of intransigence in himself infuriated him to such an extent that he wasted a further ten minutes in reviling his chief sonar operator for his failure to detect the trouble sooner. When he had finished doing that, he stood staring gloomily at the dim outline of the ship in his charge two hundred yards ahead of him.

She wasn't very large, the *Tuka Maru*, but her cargo was important. Steam condenser tubes for a light cruiser immobilised in Surabaya with her own tubes corroded by sea-water, a propellor for a big supply ship lying helpless in the same port to which she had limped after striking a reef, spare engines by the dozen for fighter and bomber planes as well as many other things essential for the conduct of the war against the round-eyed American pirates swarming into his country's Greater East Asia Co-Prosperity Sphere.

Commander Toichiro Sakaniahi sighed. A degree of loss of face would be involved for him but having escorted the *Tuka Maru* in safety all the way from Singapore he could not risk losing her close as she was to her destination and therefore he had no option but to call for reinforcements. Reluctantly he sent for his communications officer.

Forty miles away and twelve minutes later the captain of the first destroyer read Commander Sakaniahi's signal and reversed course to join the little convoy.

*

Gascoigne's eyes were fixed on the dark line of the night horizon, but he wasn't seeing it because the image he was trying to recreate in his mind was the day-light one of the freighter he had failed to sink. For a long time the picture refused to form at all, something that caused him no surprise. First the mirage effect had been so strong and then the flat calm had limited his periscope observations to seconds but, for all that, he knew that his brain had recorded something of importance. Ships marched across his memory in endless succession as if offering themselves for comparison, but with little idea of the configuration of the one he wanted to compare them with the parade didn't help him.

'Bridge? Permission to relieve lookouts, sir?'

He lowered his head to the voice-pipe. 'Yes, carry on.'

Three men climbed the conning tower ladder and stood silently, waiting for their night vision to come to them. There was a lengthy pause before the fourth arrived.

'Can't you be on time once in your fuckin' life?' Able Seaman Barton's angry whisper carrying to him.

'Life. Life-boats. That's it!' Gascoigne said.

'What, sir?'

He looked momentarily at Norcutt standing beside him, then back at the horizon.

'That ship we missed this afternoon, Pilot. The one we're chasing now. It's much smaller than I thought. Probably about fifteen hundred tons and I thought it was three or four thousand. We must have been a lot closer to it than I estimated when we fired, and our torpedoes will have passed ahead of the target. Too much aim-off.'

'Yes, I see that, sir,' Norcutt said, 'but where do life-boats come into it?'

'Relative size,' Gascoigne told him. 'They looked very big. The life-boats I mean, and there were only two of them. One on each side. A bigger ship would have had more and they would have looked smaller by comparison. It's only just occurred to me. Tell them to warm up the radar.'

*

The bulk of Madura Island guarding the approaches to Surabaya loomed blackly over *Talon* as she lay unmoving on water so still that the stars were reflected in it. One diesel, disconnected from its propellor, throbbed quietly, charging the batteries. The other waited in readiness to force the submarine into motion as soon as motion was required and radar had indicated that it would be required very soon.

For most of the night Gascoigne had hurried east, using the radar sparingly for fear of detection, but enough to show *Talon* overtaking the pair of ships, drawing ahead of them and, later, the pair being joined by a third. At no time was there a visual sighting in the darkness, but it wasn't difficult for him to guess that the newcomer was the destroyer which had attacked him in the early afternoon of the day before. The knowledge was both encouraging and worrying because although it indicated that the freighter was a vessel of some value it markedly reduced his chances of sinking it.

'Break the charge. In starboard tail-clutch,' Gascoigne said and the rumble of the diesel died, leaving only the gentle sound of water lapping against the ballast tanks. He stood for a moment listening to the near-silence, picturing the three enemy ships moving steadily in line ahead towards the channel leading to Surabaya's port of Tanjungperak, trying to estimate how close he could get to them without being sighted.

With the mass of the big island surrounding him on three sides he was as well placed as it was possible for him to be. Echoes from the land would confuse both the enemy's sonar and radar and it would be difficult for their lookouts to distinguish *Talon* against it. Suddenly it occurred to him that the situation was very similar to his practise attack on the Home Fleet battle-squadron off the Scottish island of Soay in *Titan* all that time ago. The weather had been appalling then and he had been submerged, not lying on the surface, but his tactics had been the same. A cold finger seemed to trace the outline of his spine at the memory of that day and the days that followed and he rolled his shoulders to dispel the sensation.

'Starboard tail-clutch in, sir.'

'Thank you.'

Eyes watering a little from staring so long at nothing through his binoculars. Should he ask for one more quick radar scan in case the picture imprinted on his mind had altered radically? No, better not risk it. They would be in visual range soon, or sonar would pick up the sound of their screws. He let the binoculars dangle from the strap around his neck. It was so quiet on the bridge that he could hear the soft slither of leather on metal behind him as the lookouts moved their feet and the voice of the coxswain, waiting at the steering wheel in the control room below for the ship to get under way, reached him clearly up the voice-pipe. Some anecdote about a patrol off Norway was being related and Gascoigne raised his binoculars again, smiling at the sentences peppered with the amiable obscenities sailors appeared to employ as a form of punctuation.

'Darkened ship bearing Green 25, sir!'

'Well done, Barton,' Gascoigne said, then to the voice-pipe, 'Control room, enemy in sight. Stand by to start the attack. Slow ahead port. Steer twenty-five degrees to starboard.'

The submarine came alive then and the slight vibration seemed to coincide with the accelerated beating of his heart. Her bow swung and steadied on the bearing of Able Seaman Barton's sighting, presenting her narrowest silhouette. Only then did Gascoigne see it too, the black smudge on the sea much closer than the horizon. Gradually the smudge separated to become two and the two became three. Destroyer – freighter – destroyer.

'Stand by all tubes, bow and stern. Half ahead together.'

The wind of movement ruffling his hair as *Talon* began to surge forward out of the bay in which she had been lying towards the Japanese ships crossing its mouth. Already they were more distinct, not that the range had shortened much yet, but because dawn was close, paling the sea ahead while leaving *Talon* still in the deep shadow of Madura Island. Gascoigne began calling out bearings, angles, estimated ranges, forcing himself to do it calmly despite the racing of his pulse, fighting down the temptation to loose his torpedoes before the optimum position had been reached. As the passing seconds accumulated to become minutes he began to sweat with anxiety and cramp stabbed at both his hands. He glanced at them in astonishment, muttered something to himself and released his fierce grip on the torpedo night-sight. For fifteen seconds more he crouched, massaging his palms, staring through the binoculars clipped to the sight, then at last it was time and, incredibly, the enemy moved on unnoticing.

The fourth torpedo leapt forward from its tube just as Norcutt said, 'The leading destroyer's opened fire, sir!'

No shells dropped near *Talon*, nor was there any sound of their passing but, for Gascoigne, things began to happen with confusing rapidity. The whooping of destroyer sirens and the rolling thunder of the salvo whose flashes Norcutt had seen reaching his ears simultaneously across the water. The configuration of the leading warship changing, foreshortening, as it altered course towards him. Searchlights blazing into life, probing the pre-dawn greyness with violet-blue fingers and, behind his back, the seemingly instant arrival of dawn itself.

'Star-shells, sir!' one of the after lookouts shouted. 'Five or six of 'em. Bearing from port quarter to starboard quarter!'

He turned his head quickly to stare at the string of brilliant light-sources in the sky drifting slowly down on their parachutes, illuminating land and sea, ripping away his frail cloak of invisibility as though it had never been. Now he knew where the destroyer's fire had been directed.

'Clear the bridge,' he said and into the voice-pipe, 'Dive! Dive! Dive!'

The double snarl of the klaxon sounded from below, followed by the first lieutenant's voice.

'Captain, sir?'

'What is it, Number One?'

'Sharp explosion. Sounded like a torpedo, sir.'

'Okay.'

Gascoigne slammed the voice-pipe cocks shut, then looked again towards the enemy ships. The second destroyer was heading towards him now, but the first had turned broadside on and the jagged steel protruding from what was left of her bows was plain to see in the light from the star-shells. So was the column of water that soared skyward from the freighter's stem. Gun flashes rippled again and this time he thought he heard the projectiles pass overhead, but was not sure.

Talon was tilting, beginning to slide under water and Gascoigne dropped hurriedly into the conning tower, pulling the heavy hatch shut after him, calling down to the control room.

'Eighty feet, Number One. I think there's enough depth for that. And shut off for depth-charging.'

When he reached the control room, 'Did you hear a second explosion?'

'Yes, sir. Eight seconds after the first.'

'Right. We hit one of the destroyers and the freighter. Both well forward. The other destroyer's coming after us now.'

The attack, when it came, was savage, smashing bulbs, some gauge glasses, a lot of crockery and fracturing the bolts holding the electric cooker in the galley in place. Later a hair-line fracture was found in the casing of the port main motor too, but it had no effect on its performance. Nobody was hurt, but everyone was frightened, including Gascoigne who knew better than most that to be caught in such shallow water was to invite depth-charging to destruction.

He looked at the oven, lying at an angle, blocking the passageway between the control and engine rooms, and said, 'So that's what they think of our cooking, is it?'

Nobody laughed, but the coxswain replied, 'I'll 'ave the cook up in front of you as a defaulter as soon as we go to patrol routine, sir.'

Gascoigne nodded, smiling. 'You do that, Cox'n.'

A little later he ordered slow, silent running and looked questioningly at the sonar operator.

'Milling about astern of us, sir. Not even transmitting. Er – Sir?'

'Yes, Taylor?'

A second pattern of charges exploded before Taylor could say what he wanted to, but it was distant.

'Is this the same bloke that dropped that single charge yesterday, sir?'

'It's likely. There was a destroyer astern of the target both times we've attacked. Could have been the same one. Are you going to suggest that their sonar's on the blink?'

'Looks like it, sir. The transmissions sounded strange yesterday and now there's none. Maybe that first lot he dropped just now was done visual, like he saw where we dived, sir.'

'Good for you, Taylor. What's going on up there now?'

'Hang on, sir,' Taylor said, adjusted his head-phones and sat for a few moments slowly rotating the knurled knob in front of him, his eyes slitted in concentration, then he added, 'Hydrophone effect fading on Red 145, sir.'

Gascoigne felt both relief at their escape and pleasure at a successful attack. The relief stayed with him for some time, but the pleasure lasted only until he regained periscope depth.

Daylight had brought aircraft to the scene, several aircraft, but no change in the glassy condition of the sea. *Talon* began to sink down again, heading west towards deeper water.

'What's the form up there, sir?' Parrish asked.

'Lousy, Guns. We didn't sink either of them. One destroyer is taking the other in tow and the freighter is lying stopped off the southern arm of that bay we were in. They'll tow *her* in next and there are so many planes around they're practically queuing up to make a run over the area. We don't have a hope of getting close.'

Somewhere above them two bombs exploded with sufficient force to make the pieces of glass on the deck leap an inch into the air.

'See what I mean?' Gascoigne said.

*

It should have been obvious to anybody that for a first patrol in command, a patrol conducted in an area the Americans had already swept through like a swarm of locusts, Gascoigne had done rather well. It was not obvious to Gascoigne. A destroyer sunk, something many of the most celebrated submarine commanders could lay no claim to. Another damaged and out of the war for many months. A freighter crippled and an anti-submarine motor vessel sent to the bottom by Able Seaman Lowry's cannon. It all seemed so petty compared with the achievements of Peter Harding and so many others in the Mediterranean, trivial in comparison to what the Americans were doing to the north of where he now was. He *had* to do better and do it quickly before his recall signal was received.

Gascoigne sat through lunch, eating automatically, taking no part in the conversation, not even hearing what was said. As soon as he had finished he got up and walked pensively into the control room. At the chart table he stopped and stood looking down at the black pirate flag, deep in his own thoughts.

'Sorry, sir. I'll move this out of the way,' Leading Signalman Kirkwood said.

'What? Oh, no that's okay, Kirkwood. I was just daydreaming. Carry on with what you're doing.'

'Right oh, sir.'

The grinning white skull at the flag's centre seemed to take on a life of its own as the signalman's stitching moved the material.

'Nice to see a bit of red going on here, sir.' Kirkwood snapped the cotton thread and patted the red horizontal strip he had sewn on to record the sinking of a warship by torpedo. The Lombok destroyer. Above it were five similar strips in white. Kennaway's merchant victims. On the other side of the skull a pair of crossed guns recalled *Talon's* first sinking by gun action and the stars surrounding it subsequent ones. It amounted to a reasonable score, but remembering the flag Harding had flown in the *Trigger* days this one looked naked to Gascoigne.

164

'Yes,' he said. 'I suppose it is.'

'Can't I stick on anything for the destroyer and the freighter we torpedoed this morning, sir?'

'No you can't, Kirkwood. We didn't sink them.'

Gascoigne stayed where he was for a moment longer, trying to remember who had started the custom of British submarines flying the "Jolly Roger" on entering harbour after a successful patrol. He thought it had been Admiral Sir Max Horton during the first world war but wasn't certain.

Madura Island was hazy with distance when he looked at it through the periscope and if the air-search was still in progress the planes were no longer visible, even at high magnification.

'Come round to 180,' he told the officer of the watch. 'We'll try the north coast of Java again.'

'Aye aye, sir,' Parrish said and to the helmsman, 'Port ten, steer 180.' Then he turned back to Gascoigne. 'Anything special in mind, sir?'

'Not really, Guns. They'll probably halt coastal traffic again for a bit until the dust we kicked up this morning settles, but our chances of picking off anything out here in the deep-field are pretty slim. I just want to go and look.'

Talon closed the shore, found nothing and retired to seaward for the night. An hour before dawn she returned to the coast and dived in shallow water. Thirty minutes later one of the small motorised sailing craft Gascoigne had ignored previously was seen approaching and he decided to examine it.

'Guns, get your boarding party assembled and issue them all with .45s. We'll search this one. If there are any Japs aboard take them prisoner. Don't hurt the natives unless they attack you, which I can't imagine them wanting to do.'

'Right, sir. Are we looking for anything special – apart from Japs I mean?'

'I don't actually know,' Gascoigne said. 'Up in the Celebes the Japs are using little chaps like this to carry nickel ore, but I don't know if there is any of that down here. Just find out what the form is.'

Parrish turned to go but Gascoigne stopped him.

'Guns.'

'Sir?'

'I'll put our bow alongside. You board from there so they won't be able to lob grenades down the conning tower hatch, or do anything else comic. If we sight aircraft I'll blow a whistle and you get your people back aboard here bloody quickly. Okay?'

'Okay, sir.'

'Right, off you go. Stand by to surface, Number One. I want four lookouts on the bridge with me and two machine-gunners.'

Talon reared to the surface within fifty feet of the small vessel, dwarfing it. The crew appeared to consist of seven brown-skinned men wearing loin-cloths. For a moment they stood, staring in amazement, then lowered the three sails and stopped the engine. Gascoigne manoeuvred the bow alongside and watched Parrish and his boarding party of four leap down onto the wooden deck. Three of the party stayed where they landed. Parrish and the fourth disappeared below.

'You speak English?' Gascoigne called.

The crew smiled at him shyly, but gave no sign of understanding.

'Where you from? Where you go?'

The crew shuffled their feet and continued to smile. Parrish's head reappeared through a hatch.

'Nobody else aboard, sir. The cargo's fish.'

'Yes, I thought it might be from the smell,' Gascoigne shouted back. 'Any papers?'

'No sir. Nothing.'

'All right. Try to find out if they've seen any Japanese. Make faces or something.'

Gascoigne saw Parrish stick his upper front teeth out over his lower lip, pull the corners of his eyes upwards, then point questioningly up and down the coast. It must have been the funniest joke of all time. The seven-man crew clutched each other and laughed with total abandon watched by an astonished Parrish. They kept on laughing and Gascoigne glanced anxiously around him, but there was nothing to be seen except Java and the brilliant day.

'Machine-gunners go below,' he said. 'It's not going to be that kind of party.'

The Javanese had quietened when he looked back at them and one was holding a hand up, fingers spread. When Parrish did the same the man nodded, pointed at his own ship, shook his head vigorously and stretched

166

his arms wide as though he were telling a fishing story. Parrish copied him. The man nodded again, held up one finger and said, 'Tack – tack – tack – tack – tack.' Then he waved an arm towards the coast to the west.

'Tack – tack – tack – tack – tack,' Parrish replied, then shouted, 'Can we have the chart, sir?'

Gascoigne lowered his head to the voice-pipe. 'Number One, send up the chart and three bottles of whisky as quickly as you can.'

Twenty seconds later Able Seaman Lowry loped along the casing, handed the chart down to the gunnery officer and returned for the whisky bottles. The chart meant nothing to them. They examined it curiously, spoke a few unintelligible words amongst themselves and handed it back, smiling politely.

The whisky they understood perfectly and when Parrish ordered his boarding party back aboard the submarine they were stopped by authorative hands until an old piece of netting had been found, filled with fish and presented to them.

As the ships separated, Gascoigne waved and the brown men waved back. One of them made a Japanese face and that started them laughing again. They were still doing it and a broken-necked whisky bottle was being passed from hand to hand after *Talon* had slid beneath the surface and Gascoigne looked at them through the periscope.

'What did you make of all that, Guns' he asked.

'Well, sir, I think he was trying to tell me that there are five ships somewhere along the coast to the west of here. That arm stretching probably meant that they are bigger than his own, but I'm only guessing, sir.'

'Guess on. You're making sense to me.'

'Well, when he held up one finger and made that sort of machine-gun noise I thought he was suggesting that we went along and shot them up, but now I think he was telling us that they've got a warship with them. If he'd meant us he'd have pointed at *Talon*, sir.'

Impressed, Gascoigne held Parrish's eyes for a moment before saying, 'I think that's very good, Guns. We'll have to get you interpreter's pay. What language do they speak in Java?'

Parrish grinned. 'Tack – tack, sir. I took it for my School Certificate.'

'All right,' Gascoigne said. 'Let's go and find your armada.'

Chapter Thirteen

The bare-foot girl swung along the dust road winding down the side of the hill towards the little harbour laughing and waving to the men in the fields to either side.

'Hello, Ketut? You are well, Ketut?' they called, their hoes, rakes and work forgotten at the sight of her. She didn't reply, just laughed and waved, teeth flashing, dark almond-shaped eyes crinkling with happiness at their pleasure in looking at her beauty. Some of them she knew by name, some only by sight, but they were all her friends because all of her own people within fifty miles were her friends.

'When you are married, Ketut, bring your husband back from Bali so we may congratulate him,' one of them shouted and she nodded smiling agreement, pleased that she was wearing her best red skirt slit at the sides from ankle to knee for them to admire, sorry only to be wearing its matching sleeveless cotton jacket. The jacket was open down the front for coolness, but it covered her nipples so that the short soldiers with yellow skins from somewhere called Japan a million miles to the north should not see them. It was a pity about the little coat which she never wore in her village, because some of the people calling to her lived there and would have loved to have seen her pretty breasts once again before she left for Bali aboard the schooner. As if to compensate them for this lack she turned her head from side to side making her black hair, gathered at the nape of her neck and hanging to her waist, swing like a pendulum. The men laughed happily and she walked on, basking in friendship.

Sad as she might be at leaving them all it was still a wonderful day. For even more than a whole year now she had waited for the soldiers to give her permission to return to Bali and marry the man she loved more than all the others, the man who would stop her being a virgin. A tiny frown touched her forehead as she thought how silly it was still to be a virgin when you were nearly seventeen, then it vanished. That very morning the headman had sent for her and said that the soldiers had agreed to let her go. He had given her a piece of paper with strange writing on it and told her to go to the harbour eight miles away and show it to the men from Japan. It was inside the cloth bundle containing her belongings now she knew, but she prodded the bundle with a finger until the paper crackled, to make absolutely sure. She began to skip down the track until she real- ised that that made her jacket fly away from her body and she slowed to a more sedate pace.

When she reached the final corner, the inlet opened up before her and she could see the scattering of buildings at its head and the five big two- masted schooners lying along the jetty. The ugly grey ship with the square ends which belonged to the yellow-skinned men was there too, riding at its anchor in the middle of the creek.

Ketut was half-way down the slope and within fifty yards of the nearest of the schooners when the miracle happened.

Near its mouth the calm water of the inlet suddenly boiled into white foam and out of the foam rose the biggest fish anyone could ever have imagined. Pale green it was, as long as her village street and its dorsal fin stood higher than her parent's house. For a moment she stood transfixed, then looked wildly around her trying to remember where the holy man lived, but could not and she broke into a run, not caring now about exposing herself to the soldiers from Japan.

'Look! Look!' she cried. 'Look at the giant fish! Somebody fetch the holy man! Fetch him quickly to witness the miracle!'

But then she saw the greater miracle. Men were riding on the dorsal fin and others moving in front of it. Ketut dropped to her knees in the dust. It was at that moment that the great sea beast roared, a sharp coughing bellow of rage which made the air tremble and its breath was so hot that smoke burst from the side of the ugly grey ship with the square ends. A noise she knew to be made by a machine-gun began to come from the ugly grey ship and that made the huge fish angry, the snarl which came from it, like nothing she had ever heard before, going on and on with, every few seconds, the awful bellow of rage on top of it.

Mesmerised, she was unconscious of the soldiers running towards her pulling something on wheels until one of them took her by her long hair and threw her off the road. They set up their gun a few paces away, but she was not aware of that either until it started its chattering song. She wiped dirt out of her eyes then and sat up in time to see the ugly grey ship roll over, showing its underside, but the great fish seemed to have lost interest in it, directing its fury now at the first of the schooners. A mast fell tiredly over, bright flames ran along its deck and up the second mast. Behind it a house shuddered and collapsed in on itself, dust and smoke rising to mark where it had stood.

'Not the schooners!' Ketut screamed. 'Don't be angry with the schooners, great fish! One must carry me to Bali!' but the great fish did not hear her and the second in line vanished before her very eyes in a star-burst of vivid colours, bright even in the sunshine. The shock-wave of the explosion reached her then, lifting her, throwing her against the wall of a house with a force that drove the breath from her body and she lay dragging air back into her lungs, only dimly aware of the soldiers struggling to their feet around her and putting their fallen gun back on its cradle.

Her pretty red skirt had gone, snatched away by the hot wind. That made her ashamed and she sat with her back to the wall of the house, legs drawn up, arms clasping her knees. Beside her the soldiers' gun started chattering again, but she hardly noticed it because of the roaring from the water and the sight of the third and fourth schooners blazing. Where the second had blown up there was a gap in the wooden jetty, a neat gap, as though the men who had built it before she was born had made it in two halves.

It was drifting smoke which brought tears to her eyes, crushing disappointment and bewilderment such as she had never before experienced which made them flow. She looked woefully around for her bundle with her belongings and the important piece of paper in it, but her tear-distorted vision showed her only multiple images of the fires eating the little hamlet.

170

'Oh, fish,' Ketut whispered. 'Oh, fish. Why did you have to spoil the lovely day?'

*

Above the raving of Able Seaman Lowry's twin-Oerlikon cannon Gascoigne heard again the snapping sound of Japanese explosive bullets. They had to be very close for him to do that in all this bedlam he knew and as if in confirmation the flat water beyond *Talon's* bow became stippled by hurtling fragments of metal. He frowned anxiously, searching the shoreline through his binoculars. Lowry had destroyed the machine-gun emplacement on the end of the jetty while the 4-inch had been dealing with the square-ended tank landing-craft, but there was another gun somewhere.

A hand gripping his shoulder and Norcutt shouting in his ear, 'Sir, there are gun flashes coming from a few yards up the slope beyond the fifth schooner!'

'Well done, Pilot! Tell Guns to get the 4-inch on to it!' His voice was hoarse from the yelling he had done to make his constant orders audible in the uproar and from the cordite smoke blanketing his ship. It would be impossible, he decided, to make Lowry understand what he wanted from where he was standing and he pushed his way past the aircraft lookouts by the periscope standards onto the Oerlikon platform at the back of the bridge. Even there, as the navigating officer had done to him, he had to grasp the gunner's shoulder to make him stop firing. Lowry jerked at the unexpected contact and turned an excited, wild-eyed face to his captain. Two seconds passed before the look of killing-madness left it and recognition took its place.

''Ello, sir!' Lowry's voice was a shout.

'Can you hear me, Lowry?'

The able seaman pushed his forefingers into his ears, twisted them back and forth, then removed them.

'Just about, sir! Bit noisy, this thing!' He was still shouting.

In a bellow Gascoigne told him what to do.

'Got yer, sir!'

171

Gascoigne arrived back at the front of the bridge again just as the crackle of explosive bullets sounded directly overhead. He flinched, his skin crawling in anticipation of the stab of flying splinters.

'Pilot! Plot the position the tank landing-craft sank in on the chart! I don't want to run into it on the way out!'

More bullets exploded in the air to starboard.

'Aye aye, sir!' Norcutt shouted, then sat sharply down on the deck before falling against Gascoigne's legs. The Oerlikons opened fire. Grabbing the two forward aircraft lookouts by their wrists Gascoigne pulled them towards him, pointing down at the navigating officer, then at the conning tower hatch. The two men nodded in unison and lifted Norcutt in their arms.

Parrish saying something from the 4-inch gun platform.

'What?'

'Jammed, sir! Extractor won't work! Overheated I think!'

'All right!' Gascoigne called back. 'Get your people down below and shut the gun tower hatch! We're nearly finished here!'

The ammunition drums of Able Seaman Lowry's Oerlikons were loaded in repeated sequences of high-explosive, tracer, solid and incendiary 20mm shells. He "hose-piped" the bars of light left by the tracers in the smoke across the water, across the beach and up the slope to where the captain had pointed out the flashes. A whole sequence and a half struck a girl called Ketut before the stream of shells swept on to obliterate a Japanese machine-gun crew, but Lowry knew nothing of any girl.

*

Talon was moving fast to seaward three miles from the coast before the plane was sighted.

'Clear the bridge. Dive! Dive! Dive!' Gascoigne said, then stood listening to the hurried scuffing of shoes behind him, the click of the main vents opening and the hiss of air escaping from the ballast tanks. The air lifted plumes of sea-water skyward with it and the spray from the plumes drifted down on him. It was an extraordinarily pleasant sensation after the heat of the sun and the battle. He looked once at the still distant aircraft, then back at the pall of smoke hanging stationary above the harbour he had destroyed.

Like Lowry he was not aware that he had removed from the world someone of rare innocence and exquisite beauty and so was content as he lowered himself into the conning tower, sorry only about Norcutt.

When he reached the control room, 'Go straight down to seventy feet, Number One,' he said. 'There's enough depth for that. Run the echo-sounder on the way down and go deeper if you can. Keep twenty feet under the keel. I'm going to talk to the Pilot.'

'Aye aye, sir. Shut off for depth-charging, sir?'

Gascoigne shrugged. 'I don't think it's worth it. The thing was miles away when we dived, so it won't be a very accurate attack and it'll only be bombs, not depth-charges. Just tell the crew there'll be some loud bangs in a minute.'

In the wardroom he found Norcutt propped on pillows, one side of his face and head heavily bandaged. The coxswain was with him. He took him by the wrist in encouragement then, embarrassed by the gesture, pretended to be timing his pulse.

'How's your patient, Cox'n?'

'Doin' nicely, sir. Apart from tellin' me to fuck off, which ain't no way for a young officer to address the coxswain, 'e's made less fuss than Barton with his strained wrist. 'E'll be leapin' about again before we get back to Fremantle, sir.'

The bombs came then but, as Gascoigne had predicted, they were a long way away.

'We'll have to call you "Nelson" now, Pilot,' he said. 'Neil Nelson Norcutt. It has a nice ring to it.'

Norcutt smiled sleepily. 'Yes, sir. You're only the ninth person to say that, sir.'

'Am I? Oh well. Are you in much pain?'

'None, sir. The Cox'n's seen to that. Just drowsy.'

'Good, then go to sleep.'

'Yes, sir. Sir?'

'What, Neil?'

'I'm not sure if I'll be able to take star sights with my left eye. I've never tried it.'

173

Gascoigne bit his lip, then said, 'You just take it easy. I'll handle the navigation.'

Norcutt smiled again and Gascoigne gestured with his head to the coxswain. Once in the cabin he slid the door shut and pointed to the only chair. The chief petty officer sat down and he propped himself against the wash-basin.

'What's the form, Cox'n?'

'The splinter chipped a bit of bone out of the corner of the eye-socket, sir, nicked the eye-ball out as neat as you please and lodged in the nose cartilage.'

'I see. What do you feel about complications? Shock, infection, that sort of thing?'

The coxswain shrugged and spread his hands. 'Can't rightly say, sir. I only done a first aid course and that didn't stretch far, but I don't think shock's a problem.'

'No? Why?'

'Well, sir, 'e was knocked cold which was a good thing and I 'ad 'im doped up a bit sharpish when 'e came round. 'E's goin' to be bloody pissed off when it sinks in what's 'appened, but that's not the same as shock. Make sense to you, sir?'

'Yes, it does. Excellent sense.'

The other nodded and went on, 'As to infection, I'll just 'ave to watch it, sir. Keep 'im disinfected and everythin' sterile. We've got some of this sulpha-whatsit too, sir. I'll read up on that.'

'Okay. Now, would you like him moved in here? I could sleep in the wardroom.'

For fifteen seconds the coxswain sat frowning to himself, then he shook his head.

'Thank you, sir, but I don't think so. 'Im and the Engineer Officer is chums and Mr Parrish is always pullin' 'is leg. I think 'e'll be better off with them than mopin' in 'ere not knowin' what's goin' on. I would anyway.'

'Right,' Gascoigne said. 'I'm much obliged to you for what you've done and the way you've thought this through. Let me see the notes on Sulphanilamide, will you?'

The fire to the south was still visible when *Talon* surfaced for the night, but it faded rapidly as she raced towards the central Java Sea, putting

174

distance between herself and the disturbance she had created. When it was no more than an ember on the dark horizon Gascoigne went below to his cabin to put his account of the gun action on paper. He worked for half an hour, then finished the report by writing, "The destruction of the third and fourth schooners was achieved by the explosion of the very considerable quantity of ammunition constituting the cargo of the second without much further assistance from us. About this time, although resistance from the shore had ceased, with Lieutenant Norcutt wounded and the 4-inch gun jammed through over-heating, I decided to break off the action. It was then that I witnessed the remarkable power of the twin-Oerlikon cannon.

"The weapon has its obvious drawbacks, such as the difficulty in keeping it supplied with ammunition up the conning tower and the fact that it requires two loaders instead of one, but as I was turning to seaward Able Seaman Lowry fired the remains of his last two magazines into the fifth schooner and blew most of its side out from deck to water-line leaving its cargo of closely-packed wooden crates exposed. That a not very prolonged burst of automatic fire can inflict such damage on a 200-ton vessel is something you may wish to draw to the attention of commanding officers who are still employing the single version of the gun".

Gascoigne was reading all that he had written, changing a word here and there, when he was brought the decoded signal recalling *Talon* from patrol.

'Show this to the Navigating Officer and ask him…' He stopped there, bit his lip again, then said. 'Okay. Leave it with me.'

The recall was for two days ahead and he sat for some minutes wondering how best he could use those days, wondering also if he should not request permission to return to Fremantle at once because of Norcutt's eye. In the end he decided to compromise by cruising eastward so that he would be in position to make an immediate passage through the Lombok Strait when the time came for him to leave his patrol area.

Without getting up from his seat Gascoigne slid the cabin door open and leaned out into the passageway. 'Ask the Officer of the Watch to alter course to 090,' he said. It was to prove an unfortunate order.

Almost an hour after the alteration a radioed enemy report was received from an American submarine returning from the South China Sea with all her torpedoes expended. At once *Talon* turned back to the north and increased to full speed.

For the first time in Gascoigne's experience there was wind in the Java Sea, wind that shattered the mirror surface of the water which had caused him so much trouble, wind that smeared the sky with thin cloud blocking out the stars. Spray drifting back from the thrusting bow, the scudding overcast and the juddering vibration of the hull gave an added sense of urgency to their progress, but almost from the outset Gascoigne knew that urgency was not going to help him because he was already too late. But he kept on, mentally urging *Talon's* thundering diesels to a peak of performance they had never been designed to reach, even after the bright "blip" on the radar screen had shown positively that his quarry would pass far ahead of him in the darkness, too far for his torpedoes to reach and too fast for any submarine to overtake.

Later, Gascoigne calculated that he had failed to intercept the big Japanese cruiser the Americans had sighted by the precise distance he would have covered to the north had he not been thinking about Norcutt's wound. To blame Norcutt, the United States Navy, or himself for his misfortune was manifestly absurd, so he did none of those things, but the incident rekindled his jealousy and that, too, was to prove unfortunate.

*

'The name on the stern is *Tuka Maru*,' Gascoigne said and revolved the periscope handle so that the lenses realigned themselves to low power. Immediately the wounded freighter seemed to leap away to its correct distance from him and the name was no longer legible.

'The last internal tube with a fish in it is number 6, isn't it?'

'Yes, sir.'

'Okay. Stand by Number 6. We'll see if we can give them one right up the kilt.'

It had been the intense air activity over Madura Island which had drawn him back to the vicinity of the bay from which he had first attacked the freighter and its escorts, that and the storm racketing across the Java Sea. The waves were short, steep and running fast, their crests dissolving into drifting spume. Given that and the water darkened by the low overcast, he saw the planes more as a fortunate pointer to something taking place below them than any threat to *Talon*, for the chances of their sighting an under-water shape were very small in such conditions. What surprised him was to find the ship he had imagined to have been towed into Tanjungperak two days before still there. Then he realised that she was aground, probably deliberately beached by her master to prevent her sinking after the torpedo had struck.

Lighters lay alongside, moving uneasily up and down, able to remain there only because the water was calmer so near to the shore. Whether they were there to take off her cargo or keep her afloat he didn't know. There was no destroyer present and for that he was thankful.

Talon glided in to within a thousand yards, a single torpedo went on its way and Gascoigne watched *TukaMaru* die, settling slowly until only the foremast and a few feet of torn bow remained above the surface.

'Kirkwood.'

'Yes, sir?'

'You can sew that other strip of cloth onto the "Jolly Roger" now,' Gascoigne said.

The return passage of the Lombok Strait provided no problems, a six-knot southerly current sweeping *Talon* at sixty feet beneath the surface through and out into the Indian Ocean. If there were patrols about, nobody saw or heard them.

Chapter Fourteen

The sight of the black flag with its emblems of death and destruction fluttering from the top of the raised after periscope of the British submarine brought cheers and whistles from some of the men working on the upper deck of the American depot ship. Three or four of them waved and Gascoigne waved diffidently back, thinking how little he had achieved, wondering if any of the four submarines lying alongside was the one which had sunk the Japanese aircraft carrier. Still, he thought, it was nice of them to be pleased to see the pirate flag. They didn't fly it themselves, preferring strings of miniature Japanese flags, one flag for each ship they had sunk, and some of the strings were very long indeed.

Talon moved on, breasting the water of the quickly flowing Swan River. As the angle opened Gascoigne realised with a start of anxiety that he didn't like what he was looking at. There were two T-class boats of his own flotilla lying out in the stream to give him the inside berth in the second bank of submarines at the depot ship's side, but to reach that berth he saw that he would have to approach obliquely across the bows of the three submarines still secured in the first bank. In a harbour there would have been no difficulty in the manoeuvre, but in the fast river current running, he thought, at about five knots, there was a serious risk of *Talon* being swept onto the razor bows of her three sisters. He would have to go in very fast and with precise judgement, under the eyes of those he could see waiting to welcome him back.

A memory came to him of an incident in the Firth of Clyde at home when a submarine had rammed her mother ship, the bow tearing through the steel side into a fuel-oil tank. 'What ho! A gusher!' the submarine's captain

178

had said with supreme absence of concern, but he had been a man with an outstanding record and nothing worse had happened than a polite request to him from the Admiralty to refrain from repeating the performance. Gascoigne gritted his teeth and bent to the voice-pipe.

'Cox'n?'

'Yes, sir?' Chief Petty Officer Ryland said.

'There'll be some rapid wheel orders coming up in a few minutes. Stand by for them and warn the motor room that I'll want immediate action on the telegraphs.'

'Aye aye, sir.'

The Americans astern now, his own berth almost on the port beam. Was he going past too far? No, remember that current. Wait for it. Wait for it. The berth nearly on his port quarter. Wait. Wait. Now!

'Port thirty. Full ahead together,' Gascoigne said.

Talon's bow starting to swing left, her speed increasing.

'Midships… Starboard ten… Steady as you go.'

Ryland's calm voice coming to him up the voice-pipe, acknowledging the orders. *Talon* racing in at forty-five degrees to the jetty, aimed to miss the depot ship by two hundred feet, but the current carrying her broadside towards it, the jetty seeming to slide to the right bringing the great bulk of the depot ship with it. Aim-off only a hundred feet now. Had he turned too soon? Should he come more to starboard? No, it looked about right. Or did it? Impression of speed increasing with the ships so close. Slow down? Again no because of the tide. Towering grey wall of the depot ship looming over him. No aim-off anymore. Collision course.

'Starboard thirty! Stop starboard! Half astern starboard!' Keep voice down. No need to shout, damn it. Bow swinging right. Glance over shoulder to see the stern skidding to the left, missing the stems of the three submarines behind him by five feet.

'Midships. Stop starboard. Slow ahead port. Port ten. Half ahead starboard.' Steel-wire ropes snaking, tautening. 'Stop starboard. Midships. Stop port.' The tiniest quiver as the ships touched sides.

'Take over please, Number One. I'm going up to report.'

'Aye aye, sir.'

Gascoigne clambered over the side of the conning tower and walked along the casing to the gangway, feeling the sweat driven from his body by the tensions of the past few minutes trickling down from his arm-pits, aware, too, that his pulse was racing. He breathed in and out slowly, preparing himself for the meeting ahead. Because there had been no time to look at anything but what he was doing, he didn't know that the meeting was to be with Commander Submarines Pacific himself.

'We thought you had decided to go on up river to Perth, Commander.'

An American admiral, hand extended. Gascoigne shook it.

'Well, sir. I had to…'

'Sure, sure, son. I was only kidding. I know what you had to do and that was one of the neatest bits of ship-handling I've seen in a coon's age. Maybe I should have you come over and give the other half of my little family some instruction in how to do it.'

Gascoigne grinned. 'I don't think that would be a very good idea somehow, sir.'

'You're darned right, son,' the admiral said. 'Most of them get a mite uppity if even Captain Haines tries to persuade them to do it different. But come on over anyway. Gene Haggerty got in an hour ahead of you with a nice fat Jap scalp on his belt. I'll hear what you both have to say. Have someone follow on with a copy of your patrol report.'

'Aye aye, sir. Er – sir?'

'Yeah?'

'I've got a wounded officer on board. May I have five minutes to see him settled in the sick-bay?'

'Wounded? Wounded how?'

'He lost an eye in a gun action, sir.'

'Then goddammit, Gascoigne, why didn't you say so?'

'I just did, sir.'

The admiral frowned. 'Don't you get smart with me, son. I meant why didn't you signal?'

'Because there was no point in breaking radio silence for a *fait accompli* which nobody could do anything about, sir. I was almost due to leave patrol anyway.'

'Okay. I'll talk with Haggerty first,' the admiral said. 'Come as soon as you have your boy settled in.'

Gascoigne, his flotilla captain and a staff officer walked into the operations room of the American depot ship seven minutes later. Several U.S. Navy officers were seated at a long table, the admiral at its head. He looked up and asked, 'Your boy okay, Gascoigne?'

'Yes, he's all right, thank you sir.'

'Fine, fine. Be seated, gentlemen. Now, let me see. Everybody knows everybody except Gascoigne, I guess. John Gascoigne meet Eugene Haggerty who got himself a fine Nip flattop a week or two back. The guy on his right is Dwight Meynell, his Exec. That's the same as a first lieutenant in your outfit. That'll do for now. You can meet the rest later.'

Gascoigne nodded at the two men and they nodded back at him. It had to be that damned aircraft carrier, he thought. The thing seemed fated to haunt him, pointing a finger at his own inadequacy.

'Let's hear it, Dwight,' the admiral said.

'Sure thing, Admiral,' the executive officer replied. 'Like I said, we're running in on the surface at flank-speed. I have the deck and the con because the Skipper is below at the radar. It's blacker than hell, but radar has the son of a bitch pinned down so tight the darkness don't matter one bit. There are four tin-cans screening, but they don't know they're born yet. We're past them already when I let the first salvo go. Then it's wham! wham! wham! wham! and is he in trouble! Oh boy! I can still hardly see him, but the Skipper yells up that I'm getting too darned close, so I turn away and let him have four more from the stern tubes. Hot shit, Admiral! He really goes up! It's like the Fourth of July out there!'

The voice went on and Gascoigne sat, looking at his hands resting on the table. Very quietly he said, 'There I was, upside down, in a cloud, zero showing on the altimeter and smoke coming in in spirals through the wind-screen.'

Beside him the flotilla captain asked, 'Did you say something, John?'

Gascoigne inclined his head sideways and whispered, 'I was just wondering if they always talk like the RAF, sir.'

He got no reply, but noticed that Meynell was staring at him with unblinking eyes in an expressionless face which still managed to convey hardness. So he'd been overheard. So what? It interested him more that their formality pattern had gone out of the window.

It was another quarter of an hour before the admiral spoke. 'Nice going, you boys. Now let's hear from the British. I know that Gascoigne torpedoed a tin-can. That makes for a good start.'

'Two,' the flotilla captain said. 'I've just leafed through his patrol report. He blew the bows off another near Tanjungperak and sank the *TukaMaru* as well.'

At first the statement was received without comment, but all eyes were on Gascoigne, then, 'Son?'

He turned to the admiral.

'Yes, sir?'

'You taken a vow of silence? Like a Trappist monk maybe?'

'I don't understand, sir.'

'Well, let me ask you if there are any other *faits accompli* you've decided to keep to yourself.'

Gascoigne shrugged. 'Just bits and pieces, sir. Nothing to make a song and dance about. The whole patrol was rather a flop actually.'

'Rather a flop *actually*,' one of the Americans repeated and chuckled.

'Shut up, Russell,' the admiral said and to Gascoigne, 'You listen to me, son. A torpedoed destroyer, whether you sank it or not, is a destroyer out of the war. That's something we like to know about and, for your information, the *Tuka Maru* is a ship we've been trying to get for months. She's carried a lot of valuable cargo between Singapore and Surabaya, but she holes up for the night so you can't get to her when you're surfaced and she keeps in shallow water by day. How did you get to her?'

'By going into shallow water, sir.'

The admiral appeared to be waiting for further amplification, but when none was forthcoming he said, 'Okay, I'll read about it in your report. Balducci, get a signal off to the boys in that area saying there's no point them poking around after the *Tuka*. She's scratched.' An officer left the table and he turned back to Gascoigne. 'Tell us next time, son. Irresponsible use of radio is one thing, but withholding useful information is another.'

'Aye aye, sir.'

'Okay. Now this destroyer you torpedoed in the Lombok Strait, the one you *did* get around to telling us about, what made you decide to take the risk of attacking?'

'It had me boxed in, sir,' Gascoigne said. 'The tide was strongly against me and if I hadn't done something I'd have been pushed back into the Indian Ocean which would have been rather *infra dig.*'

Shortly after that the meeting broke up and, back in his own depot ship, Gascoigne called Stella Forbes. There was no reply and, amused at himself for feeling so put out by that, he decided to go and see Kennaway in hospital. He found him, his leg at last released from traction, sitting in a wheelchair. Gascoigne described the patrol to him, saying something of his own feelings of frustration because there were so few he could openly express them to.

'I don't know what you're complaining about, old boy,' Kennaway told him. 'It sounds as though you've done better than me. They'll probably give you a bar to that "gong" of yours for those two destroyers. You know, you shouldn't expect to find too much when the Yanks have been through the place like the Ten Plagues of Egypt.'

'Yes,' Gascoigne said. 'I listened to one of the plagues this morning. "Hot shit, Admiral! It's like the Fourth of July out there!" It makes me want to throw up. How they can spend part of their time talking like that and the rest standing around saluting each other I'll never know.'

Kennaway shrugged but didn't speak and after a moment Gascoigne went on, 'Talking of people it's difficult to understand, can you tell me anything about Cavanagh? He's efficient enough, but socially I can't get a thing from him.'

For several seconds Kennaway sat staring vacantly at the floor, then he pulled at his chin before saying, 'Perhaps that's because you already did.'

'Did what?'

'Get something from him socially.'

'What are you talking about, Ken?'

'Something well over six foot and 39–25–37 at a guess, but I can't actually vouch for the statistics. Brown curly hair too in case you know several women that shape.'

Idiotically, 'Stella Forbes,' Gascoigne said and sat down heavily on the bed beside which Kennaway was sitting.

'Bloody quick of you, old boy.'

'Oh Christ.'

'Quite,' Kennaway agreed and Gascoigne scowled at him.

'Why the hell didn't you tell me before? Why didn't you tell me when I asked you for a run-down on the crew?'

'Because, old fruit, the news hadn't percolated through these sterile walls until after you had left for patrol, so stop glowering at me.'

'Sorry,' Gascoigne said. 'Were they serious?'

'Cavanagh was.'

'Hmm. Now what the devil do I do?'

'You'll have to get rid of him, won't you?'

'Surely that's bit drastic. *He* hasn't done anything wrong.'

Kennaway moved irritably in his wheelchair and said, 'Oh come on, John. We're talking about the efficient running of a war machine, the one you're responsible for no less. What else can you do? Get rid of yourself? I don't think our masters would approve of that.'

'I'll think about it.'

'Well, I wouldn't waste any time if I were you. When are you going back on patrol?'

'I don't know,' Gascoigne told him. 'There's some depth-charge damage to the casing of one of the main motors and they suspect that the shaft alignment may be out of true. That could mean a spell in dry-dock.'

'I still wouldn't waste any time,' Kennaway said.

Gascoigne drove thoughtfully away from the hospital, trying to persuade himself that it would be best to leave matters as they were, but knowing all the time that Kennaway had been right, that he should act at once. Back aboard the depot ship he sent for Cavanagh. Their exchange was brief.

'I find that I've done you dirt, Number One. I can only say that I didn't know and that I'm sorry.'

'Isn't it your wife you should be apologising to, sir?'

That destroyed the single small hope of an amicable settlement and infuriated Gascoigne. It was not so much the impertinent reference to his wife which made him angry as the fact that his apology had been brushed aside, an apology he had had no need to make because it had been Stella Forbes who had made the first advance.

'I see,' he said coldly. 'You object to my disloyalty to my wife, but see nothing wrong with your association with somebody else's.'

'Are you trying to tell me that Stella's married?' Cavanagh had gone very red.

'I'm not *trying* to tell you, I *am* telling you.'

Gascoigne watched the flush fade from his first lieutenant's face, leaving it a pasty white. It occurred to him that Cavanagh might be going to faint.

Quickly he said, 'Look, we both seem to have got ourselves in a bit of a tangle. Shall we just drop the whole thing there and act as though none of it ever happened?'

Cavanagh shook his head. 'I don't think I wish to discuss the matter further.' There was a significant pause before he added the word "sir".

'Then you leave me no choice. I must ask for a replacement for you.'

'You do that,' Cavanagh told him. 'I hope you'll be very happy together.'

Watching his retreating back Gascoigne wondered whether he had been referring to the replacement officer or Stella Forbes.

Within ten minutes he found himself apologising again.

'I'm extremely sorry about this, sir.'

The flotilla captain looked at him, then down at his desk.

'I ought to have that girl declared a prohibited area,' he said.

'You know her, sir?'

'Know her! Your chap Cavanagh must be out of his skull going broody over her. The whole flotilla knows her. Even "Lofty" Wainwright had a fling with her once.' Wainwright was the most celebrated submarine commander in the flotilla and five foot three inches tall.

Relaxing, Gascoigne said, 'I wonder how he managed.'

'So did everybody else, so I asked him. He told me that he hooked his toes over the tops of her stockings.' The flotilla captain smiled briefly before adding, 'Look, would you accept Rendle as your first lieutenant? He's very good, but Volunteer Reserve. Don't ask me why but Birch doesn't really trust the RNVR and I'm sure he would be delighted to have Cavanagh in exchange for Rendle.'

185

'How very fortunate, sir.'

'Fine, I'll arrange it. Now, do you want to keep Parrish as your gunnery and torpedo officer?'

'No, sir. I'd like to push him up into Norcutt's job and put a new boy in charge of armaments. That'll put Parrish in line for first lieutenant in due course.'

'Good man,' the flotilla captain told him. 'That's the way to do it.'

*

A ring had been erected on the jetty immediately between the two depot ships. Tiers of plank seating on scaffolding surrounded it. Every seat was taken and Gascoigne sat on the top tier jammed between Birch, with whom he was exchanging first lieutenants, and his own Able Seaman Lowry, waiting for the first fight to begin. There were to be four of them, light-weight, middle, light-heavy and heavy-weight, each over three rounds. He looked gloomily across at the eight contestants sitting in a roped-off section opposite him, feeling the onset of embarrassment at the shambles he could foresee and wishing fervently that he had stayed away.

The four Americans looked well built, fit and professional in their maroon boxers' shorts with white piping and the matching towelling robes thrown over their shoulders. The British just looked silly in white shorts drooping to their knees, singlets, tennis shoes and blue uniform raincoats which had seen better days.

Suddenly, 'Good God! That's Barton!' Gascoigne said. 'What's he doing there, Lowry?'

'Middle-weight, sir.'

'I don't mean that, I mean what does he think he's doing? He's in no condition to fight. He's been at sea without exercise for weeks and, anyway, he sprained his wrist during that gun action.'

'Oh, I think that's better, sir, but it don't make no odds. 'E only uses one arm.'

'One arm?'

'Yes, sir. It's 'is style like, sir.'

Gascoigne subsided, groaning inwardly, and watched the light-weights prancing energetically about. Occasionally there was a flurry of gloves, but neither seemed to make significant contact and at the end of the third monotonous round the fight was awarded to the British. Having detected no superiority on either side, Gascoigne concluded that the American referee had presented an advance consolation prize to a team which was certainly not going to win anything else.

Then Barton climbed into the ring and looked around him suspiciously as though wondering where he was, while in the American corner a lithely muscular man shadow-boxed quietly. The bell rang, the fighters touched gloves and the American hit Barton hard three times in the face before dancing out of range. Barton shambled after him, his lower lip split and blood running from his nose. For a moment he seemed to sag at the knees as the next barrage of blows struck him and then it was all over.

The public address system cleared its throat and announced, 'Able Seaman Barton of the British submarine *Talon* wins by a knock-out after nineteen seconds of the first round.'

'Like I told you, it's 'is style, sir,' Lowry said.

Bemused, Gascoigne nodded absently, watching a bloody and still suspicious Barton leave the ring, his opponent not yet back on his feet.

It was, Gascoigne supposed, Barton's one punch victory which injected such venom into the encounter between the light-heavy-weights. Both contestants were cut and bleeding freely by the end of the first round and he was glad when the referee stopped the fight in the middle of the second. It was the third British win and embarrassment returned to him, but from the opposite direction now. He hoped that the big American negro would make the result 3–1 in the final fight, but it was not to be, although he so nearly lasted the three rounds against a freckle-faced Scots physical training instructor.

The outcome of the whole competition, as conclusive as it was unexpected, seemed to leave the audience stunned and it was in near-silence that the white haired Captain Haines took up the microphone and said, 'Thank you, gentlemen. We'll come better prepared next time.' The silence persisted while the crowd dispersed to its respective depot ships. That no good had been done to Anglo-American relations in Western Australia was clear.

'Pity about that,' Gascoigne said to Birch. 'There could be trouble ashore now. The Yanks are going to be resentful and our lot will be nauseatingly cocky.'

He was to remember his words.

*

'No objection at all,' the surgeon-commander said. 'In fact it would be a very good thing to get him out and about as much as possible before he's flown home. The socket is healing nicely, but it'll be some time before he can gauge distances with one eye, so look after him. I don't want him ricocheting off walls.'

'Thank you very much, sir,' Gascoigne said and he, Greensmith and Parrish took Norcutt to Perth for a farewell party. They were all rather drunk by the time Dwight Meynell walked into the bar where they sat. So was Meynell. He stopped by their table and stood, staring down at the gauze pad covering what had once been Norcutt's right eye, swaying slightly.

'You been peeking through key-holes, kid?'

'That's right,' Norcutt said.

'A deplorable habit in one so young. Why don't you buy yourself a book on sex and…'

Greensmith came to the aid of his friend. 'And why don't you shut your face? He lost an eye in a gun action if you must know.'

'Is that so? Then why isn't he wearing a goddam Purple Heart or something?'

Pompously Gascoigne said, 'Because, unlike you, we don't consider getting yourself shot sufficiently meritorious to win a decoration. The object of the exercise is to stay unshot.'

Meynell noticed Gascoigne for the first time.

'Jesus! The smart-ass Limey with smoke coming through his wind-shield. You know something, buddy? I didn't like the way you talked then and I don't like the way you're talking now. Are you going to get up off that chair or do I knock you off it?'

All his barely restrained hostility to Americans burst through the fragile

188

barrier containing it and flooded Gascoigne's system with adrenalin. 'Hot shit, Admiral, it's like the Fourth of July out there!' he said and part of him registered the fact that there was absolute silence in the bar as he got to his feet, towering over the stocky U.S. Navy officer.

His head was ringing strangely when, a moment later, he began to get up for the second time and the floor seemed to be shifting under the palms of his hands, but he staggered upright. The third time he had only reached a kneeling position when Greensmith and Parrish took him by the arms and eased him back into his seat. Meynell nodded as though satisfied and walked away.

'Okay, you. Outside!'

Gascoigne squinted up at the three figures approaching the table. Their outlines were hazy, but his voice was sharp when he said, 'Greensmith! Parrish! Get Norcutt out of here!' He stood up again.

'Leave the guy alone. He's okay.'

There was authority in Meynell's words and the figures stopped their advance.

'How so, Dwight?'

'Because he keeps getting up. You sisters would still be lying there,' Meynell said. 'Go find yourselves a fight someplace else.'

Slowly the hum of conversation in the bar returned to normal and Gascoigne looked apologetically at Norcutt.

'Sorry, Pilot. Afraid I ruined your party.'

'You didn't start the trouble, sir, and you jolly nearly had him too!'

'I *what*? I didn't even see him hit me!' Gascoigne said. 'But God bless your old Nelsonian eye anyway.'

He began to laugh, but that hurt his jaw and he stopped doing it.

*

The wardroom bar steward put his hand over the telephone mouthpiece and called out, 'Is there a Lieutenant Gascoigne here, please?'

'Yes, what is it?'

'Quarter-deck, sir. American officer to see you, sir.'

'Very well. Tell them I'll be along,' Gascoigne said.

189

He took his cap from the rack, walked out into the sunshine and saw a darkly handsome U.S. Navy commander standing near the gangway. The face was familiar but he couldn't remember where he'd seen it before.

'Balducci,' the commander said. 'We met a couple of days back at that patrol discussion.'

'Yes, of course, sir.'

'I'm on the Staff of ComSubPac, Gascoigne, and the Admiral sent me to say that if you have no previous lunch engagement he would be glad if you would take it with him.'

Apprehension took hold of Gascoigne. Would an admiral interest himself in an incident in a bar between two officers? He might. No he wouldn't. He would leave at least the British side to the British. Then what?

He kept the sudden worry out of his face and his tone light when he said, 'I don't think you have previous engagements when the Admiral sends for you, sir. Of course, I'll be delighted to join him for lunch.'

'Great. I have an automobile right alongside. Let's go. The Admiral eats at quarter of one.'

The big limousine with its Navy insignia carried them swiftly to Perth and despite his trepidation Gascoigne found time to be amused that no police patrol interfered with its 70 mph progress. Neither he nor Balducci spoke much.

'Nice of you to drop by, son,' the admiral said, and into a telephone, 'I'll be in conference for a half hour. Don't disturb me unless you have to.'

At his host's invitation Gascoigne helped himself to open-faced bacon and tomato sandwiches, cole-slaw and coffee from a side table. There was iced tea too, but he had never tasted that and didn't like the look of it.

'Push some of that junk out of the way to make room for your plate.'

'Thank you, sir,' Gascoigne moved some files aside to clear a space for his lunch on the corner of the admiral's desk, then sat down and followed his superior's example by beginning to eat.

'You don't like us too well, do you son?'

He blinked rapidly several times, startled, not knowing how to reply to the unexpected statement.

'Wait. That was a fool question. Leaves you stuck with "yes, I do" or "no, I don't". Let me rephrase it. Why don't you like us? Americans I mean.'

If, Gascoigne thought, there was an American he did like it was this one. Not that he had known him long, but what he did know fitted with the high regard in which he was held by the British portion of the Pacific submarine fleet. But he could hardly tell him that. That being so what could he tell him? The notion that when dealing with such a man the truth would serve him best came after a prolonged pause. He glanced up from his plate, saw that the admiral was demolishing a sandwich without any sign of impatience, and allowed a few more seconds to pass while he made certain of his thinking.

Finally, 'In one word – resentment, sir,' he said, then added, 'And I don't believe I'm alone in feeling that.'

'Uh-huh.' A neutral sound, neither encouraging nor forbidding and Gascoigne went on, 'I've only met the American Services professionally twice, sir. Once at home in the UK and now out here. I've experienced the same reaction both times.'

'What happened at home?'

'Well sir, my first command was an old H-class boat dating from the end of the last war and I spent months stooging around playing clock-work mouse for the Atlantic convoy escorts to practise on. I used to get very irritated at the conferences after the exercises in which American ships had been involved. Their captains seemed to go out of their way to indicate that they were running the show in the Atlantic, but were kind enough to admit that our lot had been of some help. I didn't see that as a fair picture.'

'Interesting you mentioning that,' the admiral said, put his coffee cup down and began rummaging about on his desk. 'They sent me the latest head-count on U-boats destroyed just the other day. Ah, here it is. Yep, U.S. surface and air forces did quite a job. 132 U-boats killed. But I *suppose* it's reasonable to say that your people were of some help. Their score was 505.' He tossed the piece of paper aside unsmilingly and went on. 'Then without any help at all your subs sank just short of a million and a half tons of shipping in the Mediterranean alone. That's one hell of a lot of ships. On top of that your Navy gets a big bunch of orchids for – Son?'

'Sir?'

'The expression on your face gives me the impression that I'm boring you.'

Gascoigne shook his head vigorously. 'Certainly not, sir. It's just that I don't believe that I made my point clear. What I meant…'

'I know what you meant. It was perfectly clear from what you said. You feel resentful towards us, so I was indicating a little appreciation as an antidote and I was *not* being sarcastic. Nobody gets sarcastic about figures like those I've just quoted, but hear this, Gascoigne, and don't interrupt, because I'm going to paint a picture for you. After that I'm going to tell you something for the good of both our souls and I hope you'll be able to hoist it aboard without a lot of trouble. Okay?'

'Yes, sir.'

'Okay. As you suggested yourself you are not the only Britisher to feel resentment towards us Yanks. Not by some millions, I guess, but let's keep this local. One specific complaint I get from the British here is that American submarine radar is a lot better than yours. They find that just a little strange considering that you people invented the thing and wonder why the production lines are favoring us. The answer is that they're not. Your quota of advanced radar went to those surface warships in the Atlantic which ran up that score of 505 U-boat kills. That was your own chosen priority and the right one. Ours was Pacific Fleet submarines and that was the right one too. You were trying to keep an island afloat, we've been striking back at a maritime empire and both of us forged our tools accordingly.'

The admiral made bludgeoning motions in the air with a clenched fist as though demonstrating how tools were forged before saying, 'That affected the design of our respective submarine fleets too. Yours for a European war, ours for longer distances. Those designs have worked well for both of us and to our mutual advantage. Your Mediterranean campaign cost you forty-one subs lost, forty-one the U.S. didn't have to lose and it freed our Navy of responsibility for a whole theater of war, which meant we could hit the Japs harder. Okay, now you've joined us in doing that, but I'll bet that you go along with the second standard British gripe which is being assigned to unproductive patrol areas.'

'Yes and no, sir,' Gascoigne said. 'I accept that we have range limitations which means that we could only spend a day or two on station in the South

192

China Sea, but surely there would be more point to that than wasting time messing about off Java.'

From the nodding of the admiral's head Gascoigne thought for a moment that he was being agreed with, then heard him mutter, 'No understanding of what war is about,' before saying more loudly, 'For two reasons you British are smarter at submarine gun actions than we are. The first is that for months we tied our own hands by putting to sea with that big cumbersome 5-inch gun it takes forever to open fire with. We've changed the darned thing for more suitable weapons now, but it left its mark in that today our people are torpedo minded almost to the exclusion of anything else. The second reason is that torpedo supply shortages forced you folks to rely heavily on your more suitable 4-inch gun and you gained a lot of practise and experience that way. So what do I do?'

'Send us into areas where there isn't much to torpedo, sir.'

'Hmm. I wouldn't have put it that way around. I send you to places where there is plenty to gun.'

'Yes, sir, but is it worth it?'

'Getting close to questioning my competence, aren't you son?' the admiral asked, but the crinkling of his eyes removed any trace of rebuke from the words. 'I want you to get it into your head that we aren't engaged in some Anglo-American competition to do with who can claim the greatest tonnage sunk. We're engaged in a huge combined operation to make it impossible for the Japs to move anything by sea *anywhere* by any means, big ships or small. That way when the Army and Marines hit the beaches they're going to suffer less casualties. In addition, we're draining their resources by making them search for us *everywhere*. Apart from the shipping you sank on your mission do you have any notion what you cost them in putting planes in the air and sending anti-submarine vessels to sea to try to find you?'

'No, sir.'

'Nor do I, but it was many thousands in anybody's currency and the currency they burnt wasn't the kind you can print and, as long as we keep creating mayhem of whatever nature, they have to keep right on burning it. When it's gone they die of cold.'

The American officer reached for the coffee pot, then left it where it was. 'That's cold too. Have I made you feel any better about life?'

'Quite a bit, sir.'

'Good. Now, having straightened you out on strategy, let's get on with my reason for asking you to come here. It concerns communication, ordinary verbal communication between people who share the same language, and what a trap that can be.'

Gascoigne watched curiously as his supreme commander stood up and began to pace slowly up and down. He thought he knew what was coming next, but was surprised at the form it took.

'Son.'

'Sir?'

'Your opposite numbers in the U.S. Navy are naive, vulgar and boastful. Right?'

Something close to alarm took hold of Gascoigne, the alarm which comes from the accurate reading of personal thoughts by somebody else. Searching for words of denial left him confused at the moment of realisation that there was nothing for him to deny.

'Okay,' the admiral said. 'So you agree, but do you know what they think of you? And I mean both you in particular and British officers in general.'

'No, sir.'

'I can sum it up with the words condescending, sarcastic, supercilious and, because they don't understand you any better than you understand them, dishonest too. Does that surprise you?'

For almost a quarter of a minute Gascoigne thought about the words, then he replied, 'The dishonest bit does, sir. Whatever else we may be I don't believe we are that.'

'Nor do I, youngster, but then I know you people a great deal better than my boys do. The wiser ones amongst them recognise your famous understatement for the irritating affectation it is, but those who haven't cottoned on take it at its face value and when the facts disprove what you say that automatically makes you liars. At best you confuse everybody by talking, as you did, about bits and pieces which are nothing to make a song and dance about and describing the mission as a flop. As it was just about as successful as it could have been given the shortage of targets, you

194

are, by implication, belittling other people's efforts and they don't like that one bit. In addition, telling us that to have the tide push you back into the Indian Ocean would be *infra dig*, and making it sound like the kind of thing that happens to lesser mortals but not to the British, doesn't help too much. *Infra dig* for Pete's sake!'

Abruptly the admiral stopped his slow pacing, sat down at his desk and said, 'What I'm asking you to do, Gascoigne, won't be easy, but can be done. It's to set aside the generations of reserve bred into you and leave it there until we've got this war out of the way. Don't contribute to distrust and misunderstanding between us because that is what the Japs want, just as the Germans did before them. There's no law against enthusiasm you know, so next time you sink a destroyer tell us you blew a tin-can to hell and gone and sound pleased about it. We'll understand you then and be pleased right along with you.'

Gascoigne's head was nodding in agreement, but the other talked on. 'Every Service in our two countries has had it's hour of glory since this mess started. This hour looks like it belongs to the American submarines for the most part. Don't begrudge them it. They've got the ball and they're running with it fast. Run with them and in a few more weeks the enemy won't have a darned thing afloat capable of interfering with the invasion of Japan. What do you say?'

'That I'm feeling remarkably childish,' Gascoigne said. 'Also that I'm extremely sorry for having put you to all the trouble of explaining the obvious to me.'

'No trouble. I have the speech off by heart. All I have to do is update it from time to time and remember whether I'm delivering the British or American version. The score stands at 17–15 in your favor as of now. Okay. Tell my driver to take you to your ship.'

Gascoigne was at the door when he was called back.

'Yes, sir?'

'When will I be receiving a British complaint about the un-officer-like behavior of Lieutenant Dwight Meynell?'

'Lieutenant Dwight who, sir?'

'Good boy,' the admiral said.

Chapter Fifteen

Harding slammed the Seafire down on to *Intractable's* huge, pitching deck and felt the straps bite into his shoulders at the extreme deceleration when the hook below the fuselage caught the arrester wire. The heavy landing made him think of his experiment at Falcon Field in Arizona half a world away, but he didn't think about if for long because the deck crew were already manhandling the plane out of the way of the rest of his flight coming in behind him. He released his harness, pushed the canopy open and scrambled hurriedly out to watch Blue 2 and Blue 3 plummet down in succession like hawks stooping. Then all three planes were pushed on to the big lift and sank out of sight towards the hangar deck.

They had only been in action for five days, but already he was a flight leader because McAndrew had vanished in a fire-ball over Shikoku and Jennings had ditched in the sea with a perforated glycol tank twenty miles short of the carrier force. Neither had been a friend of his, he had known them for too short a time for that, but he was glad of the two and a half Japs he had officially to his credit. They evened the score. The first and second he was certain about. One had blown up so close in front of his guns that he had flown straight through the debris and the other had shed a wing and spun down like a sycamore seed after his second burst of cannon fire when the rest of the flight had been miles away. The "half" worried him a little as he was pretty sure that it had been McAndrew's kill. The "Zeke" had been lurching, losing height, with its tail section in shreds before he had gone in and finished it off, but his leader had insisted that they share it equally. That had been nice of McAndrew.

All three had been "Zekes", the Mitsubishi A6M Zero fighter, the Intelligence officer had told them when they had described their victims to him. Interesting that was, he had added, because excellent planes that they had been the enemy had been less and less keen to commit them to battle since the Americans had given them such a pasting at the Battle of Midway back in 1942. It followed that the Japs were short of fighter aircraft. 'And you can get stuffed too. They've got plenty of the bloody things around here,' McAndrew had said to the Intelligence officer, but had waited until he was out of earshot to do it because the Intelligence officer was a lieutenant-commander and only Harding and Jennings had heard him.

Harding gestured to his two wing-men to follow him and walked away to be debriefed on this latest mission providing high altitude cover for a group of B-29s from the Marianas or somewhere attacking the Japanese mainland. Nobody had interfered with the American bombers and there was nothing much to be debriefed about, but they had to go anyway. It occurred vaguely to Harding that possibly the Intelligence officer had been right, but he was too tired to carry the thought through.

For almost all of nearly six years of war Harding had been tired, but it didn't seem to matter so much now because his weariness was physical and he could support that much more readily than the nervous exhaustion which had plagued him when he had commanded the submarine *Trigger* in the Mediterranean two years earlier. Now his responsibility was to his two fellow-pilots, his plane and himself, not at all a crushing burden by his standards.

He had left the flight deck but hadn't reached the debriefing room when the alarm bells set up their insistent clangour, followed almost immediately by the multiple concussions of the anti-aircraft armament which made the great ship shudder and reverberate like a giant drum, drowning out the slamming of watertight doors and shouted orders alike. Harding stopped where he was. There was nothing he could do until his plane was refuelled and they wouldn't be flying off under air attack anyway. *Kamikazes* probably, he thought, remembering the attack of the day before and the memory made him smile.

It wasn't that he was any less afraid of the damned things and their suicide-pilots than anybody else, in fact he felt his muscles tighten involuntarily as *Intractable* heeled first to port and then to starboard as she made rapid evasive turns, but no thunderbolt fell.

One had fallen the day before all right, a heavy, thumping explosion which had rattled his teeth, when a Japanese pilot, his plane and its bomb load had blown themselves to fragments on the forward end of the flight deck. There had been nothing amusing about that but when a signal from the American admiral had stated that he was detailing two destroyers to escort the damaged carrier to New Zealand for repairs and *Intractable's* captain had replied "Unnecessary, thank you – I shall be flying off aircraft in twenty minutes", he had grinned with satisfaction. The British carriers in the force had armoured decks. The Americans had not. That was what he was smiling about now. Then recognising the silly chauvinistic pride for what it was he wiped the expression from his face.

After a moment the guns fell silent and Harding walked on, trailed by his two companions, feeling the tiredness pressing on his eye-lids.

*

General Kishichi Horikoshi was tired too. He was also bored, depressed and disgusted – bored by his seniority which kept him grounded – depressed by the now certain knowledge that the only option open to Japan was unconditional surrender – disgusted with his fellow countrymen. It had been growing in him for years, the disgust, as more and more incontrovertible proof reached him of his own peoples' mindless savagery, their total abandonment of the manners and mores of the form of civilisation they claimed to hold so dear. No longer having any particular desire to be associated with them in victory it followed that he had even less to be of their company in defeat and, being in his own eyes an eminently logical man, General Kishichi Horikoshi decided to kill himself.

The decision had nothing to do with his forefathers, or loss of face, or any other manifestation of what he deemed to be the hypocritical nonsense his race indulged in. He had been brought up in America and such humbug had never taken root in him. It stemmed purely from the rabid behaviour of his nation.

His mind made up the general called for *saki*, wrote a letter to his wife and left his office with the drink untouched. On the airfield he walked slowly around the perimeter looking at the fighter aircraft parked there. They were a motley assortment, a sure indication of the straits to which the Army had been reduced, and he moved dispiritedly on, then brightened when he came to a Nakajima Ki-84 *Hayate*. Now there was a plane! The fact that he had never flown the type did not worry him because he knew he could get it air-borne and he had no intention of landing it again.

Men came running at his shout and bowed to him. Indeed it was, they told him when he asked if the aircraft was armed and fuelled to capacity and, guessing what he was going to do, bowed again very low.

*

'The target's a Jap light cruiser,' the briefing officer said. 'An American recce plane sighted her seven minutes ago steering north-east about here.' He tapped the chart with a ruler. 'I'll give you the co-ordinates. They didn't identify the class, but she has a small escort of two or three fighters. *Incomparable* is putting torpedo bombers up now. Red Flight, you engage the escorting fighters. Blue Flight, cover the torpedo bombers. The Yanks will follow up with dive bombers if necessary.' He talked on for another half minute, then asked if there were any questions. The leader of Red Flight shook his head, Harding said, 'No, sir,' the briefing officer wished them good luck and the six pilots trotted away to man their planes.

Sitting in his cockpit Harding could see the distorted area of flight deck where the *Kamikaze* had struck which the shipwrights had not yet succeeded in flattening. It was well to the right of his take off path and presented no hazard. He could see the rest of the force too, *Incomparable* to port, the three big American carriers to starboard and the destroyer screen spread out ahead. All of them were steaming into the wind so that planes could be launched. The slower torpedo bombers had already gone. Now it was the turn of the fighters.

Engine raving, shaking the Seafire, he tensed himself, waiting for the thrust of the seat against his back when the catapult fired. It came, coinciding with the downward sweep of the launching officer's arm. The flight deck slid away from under him and he was dipping towards the sea beyond *Intractable's* bows, gaining flying speed, then climbing slowly, waiting for the other two to join him. When they had done so he turned to the west of south, flying faster now to overtake the torpedo bombers.

General Kishichi Horikoshi sighted Blue Flight almost directly below him as it emerged from a bank of cloud at 19,000 feet fifty miles to the east of Yaku Jima. As being the most important, he chose the leading plane as his target and attacked at once knowing, but not caring, that by doing so the two following fighters would destroy him in his turn.

Pieces of metal flying from his engine cowling were the first indication Harding had that there was a plane in the sky other than those of his own flight and the group of torpedo bombers far down near the surface of the sea, then flame blossomed, boiling over the canopy, engulfing it, seeking admittance, gaining it, biting at his side and neck and head. He didn't think about his wife. He was too busy beating at the flames, trying to release his harness and gulping back the screams his stomach was forcing into his throat.

After a moment he began screaming anyway.

Chapter Sixteen

Water everywhere. Water exploding under *Talon's* plunging bow and boiling along the casing to explode again against the platform of the 4-inch gun. Water streaming from Gascoigne's oilskin and trickling down inside it. Heaving waves stretching from horizon to horizon offering no respite from its soggy assault. He didn't mind. The water was quite warm and it was good to be at sea again after such a long period of frustration.

Not all of it had been frustrating of course and certainly not the nights. Those he had spent in Stella Forbes's arms practising what she described as variations on a theme, but the theme had been frequently recurrent and the variations so manifold that he was content to be away from them now. There had been amusing days too after he and Dwight Meynell had discovered a liking for each other and the American had tried unsuccessfully to teach him how to ride a horse, but those had ended when the U.S.S. *Harpoon* had left for patrol taking Meynell and his captain Gene Haggerty with her. It was then that he had begun to fret about the delays plaguing *Talon* and the knowledge that impatience would achieve nothing only heightened his vexation.

There had been more than two weeks to wait before a dry-dock had become available for the inspection of the suspected misalignment of a propellor shaft. The shaft had been found to be perfectly in order and the trouble traced to its tail clutch, a job which would not have required docking at all. Returning from the dock to the depot ship, *Talon's* port propellor had struck a submerged log, slightly damaging the edge of one of its blades. Damage of such a nature would have affected any other type of ship not at all, but to a submarine it was a disaster because the sounds the distorted blade would produce would be clearly audible to enemy sonar. A return to dry-dock was essential as there was not the slightest prospect of carrying out the necessary work with divers in the swiftly flowing river current, but by then *Talon* was at the end of the queue again.

With too little to do and far too much time to do it in many members of the crew had found trouble for themselves ashore, mostly American trouble from sailors still smarting from the defeat of their boxing team. Feeling badly about it because of his own short-lived fracas with Meynell, Gascoigne dealt harshly with the culprits. Many were deprived of pay and the sight of men from *Talon* running up and down the jetty with rifles held above their heads became commonplace but, as Gail Harding's father had predicted, his punishments never approached in severity those meted out by the Americans to their own defaulters.

Only once had he been lenient. Two virtually unrecognisable sailors had been revealed as Able Seamen Barton and Lowry when the blood was washed from their faces. ''Appens once every time in 'arbour, sir, regular as clockwork,' the coxswain had told him. 'They're friends, you see, sir, and they never fights nobody but each other.' Gascoigne had done no more than deprive them of shore leave until time made them presentable enough to appear in public again.

But all that was behind him now. *Talon* was going back to war with officers he liked, a crew that accepted and trusted him and, thanks entirely to a wise American admiral, him at peace with himself and his allies. He hadn't even felt displeasure at the double invasion of his privacy represented by the mysterious appearance of another of Leading Telegraphist Williamson's awful verses on his bunk, nor had he asked who had put it there. With a grin on his dripping face he recited it silently.

'We thought the Skipper was tall,
But he's not tall at all
When standing near his girl.
She must be six foot six
In her black lace knicks
And she's got him in a whirl.'

He turned his head to look at the first lieutenant balancing against the ship's movement at his side. Rendle's straight blond hair was so wet that it clung to his forehead and scalp like a bathing cap.

'I was thinking about Barton and Lowry and their periodic punch-ups,' he answered untruthfully. 'In the Cox'n's words "they're sufferin' the defects of a mutually aggressional love-'ate relationship".'

'I'll ponder that later. It sounds significant,' Rendle said, then added, 'He's a very good coxswain from what I've been able to see, sir.'

'He's first rate,' Gascoigne told him. 'I've known him a long time. We were last together in *Trigger* in the Med.'

'Oh, you were Harding's number one, were you? That must have been quite an experience.'

'Yes, we had our moments. He was first rate too.'

For half an hour they talked easily, constantly scanning the empty sea, then Gascoigne went below to his cabin, stripped and towelled himself dry. It made a world of difference he thought, to have a second-in-command he could relax with. The RNVR officer had an easy manner, interests beyond the Navy and a professional competence the equal of any regular career officer of his rank Gascoigne had ever met. He was as grateful for his arrival aboard as he was for Cavanagh's departure. There was further gratification to be found in the fact that Parrish had stepped into Norcutt's shoes as though he had been navigating all his life and that Sub-Lieutenant Peebles, straight from his training course, was taking his job so seriously.

At Fremantle Peebles had driven the crew of the 4-inch gun to distraction with his daily practice sessions and insistence that everyone should be able to carry out everyone else's task as well as his own. Gascoigne had been leaning on the depot ship rail when, below him, the crew had come bursting out of *Talon's* gun-tower hatch for the sixth time that morning to load and train the gun on some imaginary enemy and then been ordered below again.

'Look, sir,' the disgusted gun-layer had said, 'we've been in action with this gun more times than you've had hot dinners. We've sunk a lot of ships with it too. We don't need all these exercises.'

'Maybe you don't, Wedgebury,' Peebles had replied, 'but I do and we'll keep on until I'm as good at it as you are. Right, I'm dead. Barton, take over as gun-layer. Wedgebury, get back here and give the orders for engaging that man on a bicycle across the river. He's a torpedo boat!'

There had been no more complaints from the gun's crew.

It was all very satisfactory Gascoigne concluded. He lay down on his bunk and stared curiously at the hand-set which had been installed near it just before they had left Australia. It was part of a short range ship to ship radio-telephone system and he was wondering if the opportunity would arise for him to use it for communication with other members of a submarine wolf-pack, for that was its purpose.

Twenty-nine hours later *Talon*, for the second time under his command, began the northward penetration of the Lombok Strait. Enemy destroyers forced Gascoigne to dive twice, but they made no sonar contact and he was able to surface again and lose them in the darkness. Before dawn he was back in the Java Sea.

*

'This is getting to be like last patrol,' Gascoigne said. He was leaning forward, hands flat on the chart table, staring down at the chart on it. 'Five days and not a sausage. Got any ideas, Number One?'

Beside him Rendle shrugged. 'Not really, sir. There is the bridge near Rombang. We could shell that, or it might fall down if we torpedoed the central support.'

From the forward periscope Parrish said, 'I've got a better idea than that, sir. We could sink this thing coming round the point now.'

As Gascoigne jumped for the periscope Taylor looked up from the sonar set and reported strong hydrophone effect straight ahead, then added that it sounded like a diesel engine.

Gascoigne studied the target from a moment before asking, 'What do you think it is, Pilot? You've been up here more often than I have.'

'I've never seen one before, sir,' Parrish told him, 'but it might be what's called a "sea-truck". That's a wooden-hulled freighter the Japs have started turning out. They're very short of steel and these are quicker to build than…'

'I've heard of them,' Gascoigne broke in. 'Stand by gun action. Load with high explosive. Semi-armour piercing would probably go right through and out the other side.'

'Stand by gun action! Stand by gun action!' the metallic voice of the Tannoy repeated and throughout *Talon's* length books and magazines were dropped, games pushed aside, bunks and hammocks disgorged their human contents as men jostled each other on their way to their appointed stations. Sub-Lieutenant Peebles arrived in the control room rubbing sleep from his eyes.

Gascoigne stepped back from the periscope. 'Come and take a quick look, Guns. This one's for you to open your account with.'

'Thank you, sir,' Peebles said. 'Point of aim the waterline, sir?'

'That's right. Able Seaman Lowry?'

'Here, sir.'

'You take care of the upperworks with your Oerlikon.'

'Aye aye, sir.'

The day was clear and bright with a breeze strong enough to have built up small waves. Gascoigne was thankful for that because the surface disturbance was sufficient to break up *Talon's* submerged image, making it less likely that she would be sighted by aircraft. He watched for them carefully while the submarine turned a slow half-circle to parallel the course of the approaching ship. It looked surprisingly large to him but, with its wooden hull, he had no idea what its displacement might be. If there were guns on deck he couldn't see them although the enemy vessel passed within three hundred yards.

When it was ahead, 'Range will be about five hundred,' Gascoigne said. 'Open fire when ready. Gun action. Surface.'

Of those times at sea when Gascoigne felt himself to be not in control of events, one of the most unpleasant for him was the brief period between giving that order and his arrival on the bridge. Deprived of hearing by the roar of high-pressure air expelling ballast water, his sight limited to a view of the inside of the conning tower and the legs of the Oerlikon gunners preceding him up it, his imagination took charge and painted vivid pictures of dramatic changes in the situation as he had last viewed it through the periscope seconds earlier. In his mind the enemy had miraculously reversed course to ram him, or it was a Q-ship with screens dropping to reveal the muzzles of heavy artillery or, out of an empty blue sky, bombers materialised. So it was a relief to feel the concussion on his ear-drums of the first shell leaving the 4-inch gun just as he pulled himself clear of the upper conning tower hatch and a greater one to reach the front of the bridge to find that nothing had altered except for a subsiding column of water marking the spot where the projectile had fallen short of its target.

The second round did not miss and he saw splinters fly and timbers cart-wheel from the stern of the merchantman. The third produced a similar result while 20 mm shells from Lowry's cannon tore at the enemy's bridge and no bombers materialised out of an empty blue sky.

They came instead, fast and low across the water, out of the mottled green back-drop of Java, two of them, almost touching the tops of the little waves, flashes of gunfire rippling along the leading edges of their wings.

'Clear the gun! Clear the bridge! Dive! Dive! Dive!' Gascoigne's voice was pitched high, whether from fear or the necessity to make itself heard above the uproar around him he was never afterwards sure. Whatever the reason, he *was* heard, his guns fell silent and the men scrambled rapidly down through the hatches, all of them except Lowry, but he was not aware of that then.

Gascoigne looked fearfully towards the speeding planes, cringing a little at the sight of the water between him and them torn into spray by their guns, finding no consolation in the knowledge that they had opened fire too soon because they would be over him long before *Talon* was fully submerged and then the bombs would come.

'Oh Christ,' he said softly. 'I've really been caught napping this time.'

It was while he was lowering himself into the conning tower, his eyes still on the planes, that the Oerlikons burst into a ranting fury of sound. For three seconds the shock held him motionless and, mesmerised, he watched tracer lancing towards the fighter-bombers. For two of those seconds they held their course directly into the storm of shells, but in the third they broke away, left and right, passing ahead and astern of the rapidly submerging submarine.

Lowry was swinging his cannon to follow the receding planes when, with no memory of how he got there, Gascoigne struck him across the side of the head, unhooked the harness holding him in position, dragged him to the conning tower hatch and forced him down it. Then he followed himself and slammed the hatch shut with the sea flooding over the bridge deck.

'Welcome aboard, sir. I was just about to shut the lower hatch on you.'

Dripping wet, Gascoigne looked down at the water swirling about on the control room deck, then at Rendle.

'So I should bloody well hope, Number One,' he said. 'Go down to eighty feet, shut off for depth charging and have this mess mopped up.'

Talon was at a safe depth by the time the planes had turned and made their second run. The bombs, when they came, were an anti-climax.

To Gascoigne's surprise and Peebles' delight the "seatruck" was burning furiously when sighted through the periscope twenty minutes later, but there were several planes about and Gascoigne ordered his ship taken deep again and went to his cabin. For almost an hour he sat in it wondering how best he could question Lowry, then decided that it would be pointless to do so in the face of such strong evidence. A serious breach of naval discipline had been perpetrated by the man's disregard of orders which had been heard by everybody else, including those immediately beside him responsible for feeding his cannon with drums of ammunition. There could be no question of his having misunderstood.

Gascoigne began to write down his report of the short engagement. When he had finished he re-read the last lines.

"It is abundantly clear from the foregoing that Able Seaman Lowry, with time to reconsider it, made the deliberate decision to sacrifice his own life in what proved to be a successful attempt to save the lives of his shipmates. That he did not, in fact, lose his own life, either through fire from the enemy planes or drowning when the ship submerged beneath him, is irrelevant. I would, therefore, submit that very serious consideration should be given to the degree of recognition he is awarded for his act and add my own recommendation that it should be of the highest."

He put the papers into a drawer and locked it.

*

'What's an atomic device anyway, sir?'

'Search me, Pilot,' Gascoigne said. 'Where *is* Hiroshima?'

'I've just looked it up, sir. It's south-west Honshu. You know, the main Japanese island with Tokyo and Mount Fujiyama on it.'

'Hmm. Well, it seems they've made quite a mess of the place with whatever it is,' Gascoigne told him, pushed the sheet of signal paper across the ward-room table and added, 'Read that, then lay off a course for the area we sank that "sea-truck" in the other day. There's bugger-all happening around here.'

For three days *Talon*, both surfaced and submerged, searched the north coast of Java from Madura Island to the Sunda Strait and found nothing worth attacking. The sea was empty even of fishing craft.

'It feels weird to me, sir,' Rendle said. 'I did three patrols up here before I joined you and it was never this quiet. Do you get a sort of feeling of – well, waiting?'

Gascoigne grinned. 'Yes, I do, Number One. Waiting for worthwhile targets, and I'm getting a little pissed-off with it, but our last patrol and a lecture I got from the Admiral taught me about patience.'

'That wasn't exactly what I meant, sir.'

'I know it wasn't,' Gascoigne said, 'and I know exactly what you did mean. Have you been shown the latest news release?'

'No, I've been in my bunk.'

'They've done it again.'

'Done what again?'

'Covered a city in X-rays or whatever they do. Nagasaki this time.'

There was a long pause before Rendle asked, 'Do you think this is the end of the war, sir?'

Gascoigne shrugged, but didn't reply.

*

Chief Petty Officer Ryland tapped on the frame of the cabin door and said, 'May I 'ave a word, sir?'

'Of course,' Gascoigne replied. 'Come in and shut the door, Cox'n.'

'Thank you, sir. It's about Lowry.'

'What about him?'

"E's been a bit strange ever since we got pushed under by them Jap aircraft the other day, sir. Sort of nervous like. So this mornin' I tackles 'im about it. At first 'e won't tell me nothin', but finally I gets it out of 'im that when the two of you was on the bridge together after everybody else 'ad come down below you gave 'im one right across the ear-'ole. 'E reckons that for an officer to 'ave done that, particularly the Captain, 'e must be in the shit up to 'ere.'

'Oh. What did you tell him?'

'Just that if 'e was in trouble you'd 'ave 'ad 'im up in front of you as a defaulter days ago, sir. I couldn't tell 'im nothin' else because nobody knows what 'appened up there except you and 'im.'

'And what did he say to that?'

'Wouldn't wear it, sir. Reckons you're goin' to 'ave 'im court-martialled when we gets back to Fremantle.' The chief petty officer hesitated, then went on, 'I been a coxswain a long time now, sir, and I know when one of the men knows 'e's done somethin' bad. Lowry knows, sir.'

For several seconds Gascoigne sat staring moodily at the coxswain's feet, then turned sideways and unlocked a drawer. He took a sheaf of paper from it, selected three pages and held them out.

'It starts half-way down the top page,' he said.

Ryland read slowly, mouthing the words, saying "Bloody 'ell" audibly four times before he reached the end. When he had finished he looked at his captain.

'This means the big one, doesn't it, sir?'

'Above and beyond the call of duty, Cox'n. That's what it's for, and I'll be very angry if they don't give it to him. However, you are to tell nobody of this. Nobody at all. Would-be heroes can get in the way at unfortunate moments, so I can do without any emulation. Understood?'

'Understood, sir. Is there anything I *can* say to Lowry? To cheer 'im up like?'

'Tell him,' Gascoigne said slowly, 'that I'm sorry if I hurt his ear, but as he had done all that was necessary I was drawing his attention to the fact that the ship was almost completely under water, as perhaps he hadn't noticed with all the noise he was making.'

Ryland smiled, nodded, murmured 'Aye aye, sir,' and left the cabin.

Chapter Seventeen

When the young American colonel opened his eyes the first thing they recorded was three shafts of early morning sunlight slanting through the gaps in the curtains of the hotel bedroom. He lay still for a moment, not yet fully awake, groping for the end of a memory strand which would lead him back to himself. It evaded him until his regard followed the rays of light to their destination, then recollection was instantaneous and complete.

The girl, half illuminated, half in shadow, was sitting at the dressing table, drawing a stocking up her leg, clipping it to a suspender. Her hair was tousled and she wore no make-up and that, he thought, made her even more attractive than she had appeared to him when he had first seen her the evening before. More like a woman, less like some beautiful, enamelled machine.

The colonel put his hands behind his head, interlacing his fingers, and said, 'Hi. You're an early riser.'

She glanced at him before reaching for her second stocking. 'Yes. I'm sorry. I didn't mean to wake you, but I have to go now.'

'Don't.'

'I must.'

'Why?'

'Just because.'

She finished dressing, using quick, economical movements, combed her hair, then walked to the side of the bed and stood, looking down at him.

'Poor sweet,' she said. 'You must be wondering what hit you.'

'You can say that again. Won't you please at least let me know who you are?'

'That's something I'm trying to find out,' Gail Harding told him, touched him lightly on the tip of the nose with a forefinger and left the room, walking quickly.

'Whoever he was,' the American said to the closed door, 'he sure was a lucky guy.'

It was on that day, the sixth since the news had reached her, that Gail resolved to try to pull herself together. Her dearest wish was to be allowed to cry, something she had been prone to do during her life from sadness, fury or happiness, but now at a time when she desperately wanted the release of doing so it was denied her. She decided to leave London for Wiltshire and face the inevitable commiserations there.

Seeing Jackman, invalided from the Army and wearing chauffeur's uniform now, waiting on the platform at Devizes station, cheered her, reminding her of his teasing encouragement when he had driven her back to school at the beginning of each term before the war. She had been very fond of him and was glad that it was him and not her father she would have to talk to first.

'Hello, Jackman. I'm so glad you're back with us. It's been a long time.'

'Six years, My Lady. You're looking very fine, if I may say so.'

'Thank you, Jackman. How's the leg?'

'Oh, it's all right, My Lady. It'll always be a bit shorter than the other, but I manage.'

Talking easily, like old friends, as they walked to the car, listening to him describe the gallant shambles that had been the Battle of Arnhem during the drive home. Not a word about Peter, thank God.

Gilchrist discharged from his job in an aircraft factory and looking every inch a butler again, hurrying down the broad steps towards the car.

'Welcome home, My Lady. I trust you had a good journey.'

'Splendid thank you, Gilchrist. Are you and Mrs Gilchrist keeping well?'

'Very well, and the better for seeing you, My Lady. Mrs Gilchrist was readying your room when we heard the car, but she'll be down directly.'

Standing in the great hall, Gilchrist taking her coat and telling her the plans for restoring the house following the Army's departure. Mrs Gilchrist damp-eyed but determinedly cheerful. Jackman waiting, a suit-case in either hand, a slight smile of respectful affection on his face. Not a word, not a single word about her husband. Her father strolling out of his study, hands deep in the pockets of an old tweed jacket.

'Hello, old fruit. I've just opened a bottle of rather nauseating sherry. If you'd care to…' Some nonsense about helping him finish it so Gilchrist could bring them something better.

Gail looked at them in turn, then, 'I love you. I love you all,' she said and burst into tears.

*

'Yes,' the Marquis of Trent said, 'I do think the Japs will surrender. No, you do *not* hope they'll hold out long enough for the Yanks to drop one on Tokyo.'

Gail sniffed. She had cried for nearly an hour in her room after the tears had first come and now she couldn't stop sniffing, but the frenzied madness she had been gripped by in London had left her.

'Sorry, Daddy. I've just finished saturating an old uniform coat of Peter's with salt sobs. That was vindictiveness talking. Not me.' She took the folded white handerkerchief he held out to her and blew her nose noisily before adding, 'I don't want anybody else killed anywhere at all. May I keep this?'

He looked at the handkerchief in her hand, as though surprised to see it there, nodded and said, 'The nights are the worst, aren't they?' It wasn't really a question.

She blew her nose again before saying, 'What do you mean?'

'Just making an observation. Have another martini.'

'Er – no thanks.'

Taking the glass from the coffee table beside her he refilled it and she accepted it without comment.

'Yes, Daddy. The nights are the worst. Have you been having me watched?'

'No, my old beetroot top. I have not been having you watched. Should I have done?'

'It wouldn't have been a very edifying experience for you if you had. I've

212

been behaving like a bitch on heat.' When he made no comment she went on, 'I always thought new widows went through a phase of vowing eternal chastity or thought about becoming nuns or something. Not me! I've been dragging strange men into bed and I'm not even ashamed of myself!' She sipped at her drink and the glass clattered when she set it down on the table.

'There's no need to sound so defiant about it,' he told her quietly. 'You've helped enough men through emotional plights of one sort or another. I don't find it exactly commendable, but it doesn't surprise me that you should seek to reverse the process when you're in one of your own. Anyway, the crisis is past or you wouldn't be down here.'

Gail sighed softly and said, 'I'm very fortunate to have such a wise and perceptive father. And if that sounds condescending it wasn't meant to. I've thought so ever since I was old enough to recognise things like that.'

The marquis shook his head. 'I can't accept your description. The word "perceptive" implies intuition which I don't possess to any marked degree. I just happen to have been in your shoes which enables me to know what you're going through. As to wisdom, age doesn't necessarily produce that, but it does provide one with a sense of perspective and those two facts together enable me to view what you say you have been doing with sympathy and understanding. You see, when that Messerachmitt shot up your mum's mobile canteen I was so lost that I spent six weeks making a fool of myself with Madeleine Pembury. That started almost straight after the funeral.'

'Oh, Daddy!'

'Ah. That shocks you, does it? We ancients should be immune from such feelings I suppose.'

'No, no, no! I meant "Oh, Daddy *darling*"! I was abroad when Mummy was killed and your letters were so calm and that made me go into my stiff upper lip routine and I never realised – Oh, Daddy!'

Gail flung out of her chair, pushed him back into his with her hands on his shoulders and kissed him fiercely on the forehead. After that she stood frowning down at him, wanting to comfort him, wanting to apologise for forcing him into the position of confessing his small weakness for her sake, but all that came out was, 'You'd better wipe that lipstick off. Dinner will be ready in a minute and Gilchrist might drop something if he sees you like that.'

He smiled up at her. 'Then perhaps, as you are in possession of my handkerchief, you would be good enough to remove the evidence yourself. Mrs Gilchrist can worry about it when she does the laundry.'

'Oh,' Gail said. 'Of course. I was forgetting. Here. Lick.'

When Gilchrist had announced dinner and withdrawn, the marquis stood up, his face grave again.

'As you are well aware, my dear, with your looks and rather extensive experience, men don't stand much of a chance with you. Please don't take advantage of that fact just to provide yourself with an emotional catharsis. You'll break other hearts than your own if you do. Wait until you find someone you at least like and who likes you. A lot can grow out of liking.'

'I'll wait,' Gail promised him, then gripped his arm tightly before adding, 'I lied to you a few moments ago. I am ashamed of myself. Very ashamed.'

'So I should hope,' he said cheerfully and led her into the dining room.

Chapter Eighteen

Dusk was close and *Talon*, doing little more than fill in time until her recall signal became effective, had almost completed a submerged reconnaissance of Bawean Island in the central Java Sea when Peebles made the sighting. Gascoigne burst from his cabin at the wailing of the alarm and the cry 'Cap'n to the control room!', thrusting sailors out of his way like a rugby three-quarter going for a touch-down. He brushed Peebles aside too and grasped the periscope handles.

It looked vast, a towering mass of unsymmetrically arranged steel plat-forms forming its bridge in the strange design favoured by Japanese naval architects. It also looked very formidable and so did its fleet of escorting vessels. How many there were of those he couldn't tell because they were still appearing round the point of land from behind which the squadron had come.

His voice taut, 'Give me the mast-head height of a *Kongo*-class battle-ship. Quickly now!'

Parrish told him, Peebles set the figure on the torpedo data computer and Gascoigne twisted the range dial until two images of the huge ship appeared in the periscope lens, one lifting above the other until its water-line rested precisely on the highest point of the one below it.

'Range is *that*! Bearing is *that*! I am 110 degrees on her port bow!'

The man behind Gascoigne called out numbers from the range indicator and the azimuth ring.

Peebles twisted handles on the "Fruit Machine" and said, 'Enemy course 280, range 11,000 yards, sir.'

Gascoigne was looking at a submariner's dream and a dream it would remain because the Japanese capital ship was near to extreme torpedo range and that range was increasing as he watched. If he fired immediately without even waiting to establish the enemy's speed, which would be a pretty pointless thing to do, his salvo would still fail to cover the necessary distance. He sighed softly, ordered the periscope lowered and stood staring at his watch. Two minutes later he took another range and bearing.

'The plot suggests enemy course 282, speed 14 knots, sir,' Parrish said from the chart table.

'Oh balls! Those bloody great things can do about thirty knots. They wouldn't be dawdling about like that.'

'It *isn't* balls, sir. If your ranges are right they're doing fourteen. It says so here and it's not a very difficult calculation.' Parrish sounded aggrieved.

'All right. Let's take another set of readings before the light goes,' Gascoigne said.

The results gave the same information.

'We could be ahead of them in an hour or so, sir.'

Gascoigne glanced at Rendle and nodded. 'We could indeed, Number One. Let's see if we can collect ourselves a battle-wagon. It's nearly dark now. Stand by to surface.'

*

The night was black, overcast, starless and that, Gascoigne thought, was a very definite plus. He would have the great bulk of his quarry in plain view long before it or its escorts sighted him. How soon his presence would be revealed to them by radar he was uncertain, but knew that American submarines had got surprisingly close to major Japanese targets without detection. His own radar, sparingly used, had confirmed the accuracy of his earlier periscope observations and that was another plus, but the number of "blips" on the screen representing escort vessels amounted to a minimum of twelve minuses. There might, he knew, be others on the far side of the battleship hidden from probing electronic fingers by its size. It didn't seem to matter very much with the odds against him already appallingly high.

Talon ran on fast to the west, parallel to the squadron, drawing ahead of it, her hull quivering to the thrust of her propellors. Her captain felt himself to be quivering too, but on a frequency of his own set up by the combined assault of excitement and apprehension on his nervous system. He breathed in and out slowly, deeply, in an attempt to rid himself of the sensation, but it had little effect. The self-evident hazards of the task he was about to undertake saw to that. Briefly he thought of the seventy men encased in the speeding steel tube beneath his feet, but that worry was too amorphous to grasp in its entirety and when his concern crystalised on the pity of Able Seaman Lowry never receiving his medal because nobody would ever know what he had done he muttered crossly to himself and pushed all of them out of his mind. It was their job to go where he led them.

'Good morning, sir.'

'Oh, hello, Number One.'

Rendle had replaced Parrish as officer of the watch, so it must be midnight.

'Nice night for it, sir.'

'Perfect.'

'The radio room tells me we haven't transmitted an enemy report yet, sir.'

'Look,' Gascoigne said, 'stop nagging me about it. There's one ciphered up and ready to go. We'll broadcast it in the final stages of the attack when it's too late for the Japs to react. They're bound to be keeping watch on our wave-length and we're close enough to blow their ear-drums in with our transmission. There's no point in letting them know we're practically sitting in their laps. Anyway, the nearest Allied submarine is north of Brunei, so there's loads of time.'

Out of the corner of his eye he saw the glint of Rendle's blond head nodding and asked, 'What's the state of the battery?'

'Over three-quarters charged, sir.'

'Good. We'll need all of that if the escorts force us to dive.'

'You're definitely in favour of a night surface attack, are you?'

'Yes,' Gascoigne told him. 'The escorts seem to be staying very close to the target according to radar, so I'm hoping to get off a full bow salvo of eight fish from outside the screen at, say, five thousand yards, then turn away and fire the three stern tubes.' He scratched at the stubble on his chin before adding, 'After that, we'll reload the six internal bow tubes and attack again if we haven't sunk it already.'

'You make it sound very simple, sir. Do you really see it working out that way?'

Gascoigne smiled in the darkness but, had it been visible, nobody would have detected humour in the expression. He was remembering the jealousy he had felt on his previous patrol at the size of the targets the Americans had been finding, telling himself too that having one of the biggest things afloat all to himself he was no longer in a position to complain on that score. For all that, there was more apprehension than excitement in him now for he could not bring himself to believe that any single submarine of any nation had ever encountered a lone man-of-war so heavily escorted. There were between twelve and fifteen anti-submarine vessels he estimated, ranging from small waspish chasers to large Fleet destroyers, at least five of the latter. His mind pictured the last minutes of his approach, the silhouettes of escorts shortening as they turned towards him, the brilliance of star-shells overhead, search-lights stabbing at his eyes, the rapid slamming of destroyers' guns, even the awful thunder of the battleship's broadside. *Talon*, her attack foiled, might submerge fast enough to survive all that, but then would come the depth-charging, and the depth-charging, and the depth-charging.

'No,' he said, 'I don't see it working out that way. We'll just get as close as we can as fast as we can and play it by ear. On the surface there will be the element of surprise and, I hope, resulting confusion in our favour. Dived we'd be faced with a much more slowly developing situation and with a dozen or so sonar sets pinging away the initiative would pass to them.'

Gascoigne heard Rendle say that it made sense to him, wished that he could agree or that he was somewhere else, because this looked very much like the final curtain for all of them aboard his ship and that seemed to be a terrible waste. His second-in-command's question of a few days before came back to him. 'Is this the end of the war, sir?' Although he had not committed himself he had believed at the time that it probably was after whatever the Americans had done to those two cities. Now, with the passing of the days, he was less sure but still thought it likely and wondered if the

218

Japanese squadron, hidden astern by the night, thought so too. Were they, perhaps, just trying to go home? They must, he knew, constitute the last concentration of enemy shipping in the Java Sea area and the slowness of their progress had interested him ever since Parrish had convinced him that their speed was only fourteen knots.

Three possible reasons for that had occurred to him. The first, that the smaller members of the screen could go no faster he had abandoned at once because had the squadron been operating as a task force the battleship and the destroyers would have gone ahead without them. The second and third, that the battleship was damaged or conserving a dwindling fuel supply were more likely, but now the fourth explanation took root in him. They wanted to go home and nothing else.

'And that,' he said to himself, 'is just too bloody bad. My orders are to stop you bastards going anywhere.' After that he spoke aloud. 'You'd better take charge down below, Number One, and send the crew to diving stations. I'll be starting the attack in about ten minutes.'

Despite the increased vibration with *Talon* moving at her greatest possible speed towards the enemy there was less sensation of movement. The alteration of course had brought the wind almost directly astern so that she seemed to be travelling through still air, air no longer able to dispel the stench of burnt diesel fuel expelled from her exhausts. The gas hung in a cloud about the six men on the bridge making them work saliva around inside their mouths and spit it out in an attempt to rid themselves of the sickeningly sweet taste.

Gascoigne coughed and bent to the voice-pipe.

'Bridge-Radar.'

'Radar—Bridge?'

'Another quick scan, please. Not more than fifteen seconds. Range and bearing of target and the two nearest escorts.'

'Aye aye, sir.'

Straightening, Gascoigne watched the whiteness of broken water curling away from *Talon's* stem and streaming over the ballast tanks to either side of the conning tower on which he stood. He didn't feel nervous any longer and he imagined that to be because he didn't feel anything very much except

219

vaguely sorry for his crew. It was, he concluded, as though he were already dead. Moments earlier he had seriously considered breaking off the attack and tracking the enemy squadron at long range so that others could do his job for him, but the voice of a BBC announcer had stopped that line of thought. His imagination replayed the announcement. "We interrupt this programme to bring you a news flash from the Java Sea. Lieutenant Gascoigne of the Royal Navy and the Emperor Hirohito of Japan have concluded a separate peace. We now return you to the Savoy Hotel in London and to the strains of…" Oh Jesus!

'Radar-Bridge.'

'Yes?'

'Target bearing Green 5, sir. Range 9.000 yards. Afraid that's all we got, sir. The set's playing up again. No definition on the smaller echoes.'

'Never mind. It's better than nothing. Cox'n, come fifteen degrees to port.'

'Fifteen degrees to port, sir. Aye aye, sir,' Ryland said.

Momentary loss of orientation because there is no clear horizon, no positive meeting point of sea and sky, only an occasional long wave-top pretending to be it. Diesels suddenly very loud. A trick of the wind, or his ears clearing belatedly after the air pressure change on surfacing? Engine note normal again. Just imagination. Where *is* the bloody horizon?

'I can see the battle-wagon, sir!' Peebles' voice sharp with excitement.

'How nice for you, Guns,' Gascoigne said tiredly. 'Now why don't you make a proper report so we can share the view with you?'

'Sorry, sir. Darkened ship bearing Green 20, sir.'

Gascoigne saw it too then and stared unblinkingly through his binoculars wondering if it *was* the battleship or a destroyer much closer to them. No, it was the target all right. There was no mistaking that towering superstructure.

'Can you see it, Barton?'

'Yes, sir,' the starboard forward look-out said.

'Very well. Ignore it. It's the escorts I want located now.'

'Aye aye, sir.'

Water churned to white scudding past, marking their passage. A touch of phosphorescence in it. Not much, but some. Would the escorts see it before he sighted their wakes? Probably. He was moving faster, causing more disturbance than they. Probably they already had seen it. Probably they had him pin-pointed by radar.

'Probably my arse.' A soft mutter.

'What did you say, sir?'

'Nothing, Guns. Mumbling to myself. Sign of old age.'

Courses converging, the great black shape growing and the cloying taste of diesel. Where the hell are the escorts?

'Two darkened ships bearing Green 70 and Green 90, sir.' An immediate answer to an unspoken question.

'Thank you, Barton.'

'Another one roughly in between them I think, sir.'

'Right.'

'Darkened ship dead ahead, sir. Crossing to port by the looks of it, sir.'

'Very well, Guns. Stand by all tubes,' Gascoigne said and cranked the torpedo night sight on to the director angle the "Fruit Machine" had indicated, giving the correct aim-off. More escorts sighted, reported, acknowledged. Difficult to keep track of them all, but only the one on the starboard beam really close. Destroyer by the look of it, but not pointing towards him. Not yet.

'All tubes standing by, sir. Bow caps open.'

'Thank you.'

The *Kongo*-class battleship looming hugely. Little or no chance of its avoiding his torpedoes now. Too close, too cumbersome, moving too slowly through the water for rapid evasive action. Only a few more seconds now before he sealed its death warrant and that of his crew. That he would be doing both he was virtually certain. Six out of eight of his bow salvo of torpedoes were fitted with magnetic warheads, warheads which would explode under the leviathan's keel where there was no heavy armour-plate. Then there was the stern salvo to follow if he was given time. As for his own ship, it was simply ridiculous to pretend that she could hope to survive the assault of so many anti-submarine vessels, an assault which would begin the moment they were aware of his presence.

Wondering with no great interest how fortune had contrived to keep him invisible to them so far, and what it was like to die in action, 'Fire one!' Gascoigne said.

'*Belay that order!*' A distant shout, but one that reached him clearly. Rendle's voice. Stupefied, he looked down at the voice-pipe as though it had taken on a life of its own.

'But the Captain, sir! 'E ordered…'

'Get your head out of the bloody way, Cox'n!'

The thing seemed to be arguing with itself, then Rendle's voice again, loud, clear, urgent. '*Don't fire, sir*! I repeat, *don't fire!* The war's *over!*'

For a long second Gascoigne thought about that before asking tonelessly, 'What are you talking about, Number One?'

'Signal from ComSubPac. Most immediate to all submarines at sea, sir. Cease hostilities against Japan!'

'Oh,' Gascoigne said. 'Really? Then hard a'port, Cox'n.'

''Ard a'port it is, sir,' Chief Petty Officer Ryland replied.

Talon swept in a half-circle, steadied on south-west and ran for her life. When it was definite that she was not pursued Gascoigne ordered her speed reduced. He was feeling strangely apathetic, taking pleasure only from the fact that with the wind in his face again he could no longer smell the diesel fumes.

Chapter Nineteen

Mount Agung to starboard. Mount Rinjani to port. Majestically friendly now, not forbidding sentinels. More the gent pillars of a triumphal arch spanning the Lombok Strait through which *Talon* sped towards the Indian Ocean with the fast southerly current helping her on her way. It seemed unbelievably strange to Gascoigne to be making the passage on the surface by day with a large White Ensign fluttering from the raised after periscope. He lowered his head to the voice-pipe.

'Who's on the wheel?'

'Barton, sir.'

'Barton, pass the word that there's a very dramatic view of Bali and Lombok from up here. If the crew wants to see it they can come on the bridge five at a time.'

'Aye aye, sir.'

They came and went in groups of five, some of the men entranced, some indifferent. Only three of the engine room staff bothered to make the climb up the conning tower ladder and one of those was the engineer officer himself.

'Troglodytes, your people,' Gascoigne said to him.

Greensmith smiled. 'It's always the same, sir. Submarines or surface ships. We "plumbers" have a healthy respect for the danger that lurks in fresh air.'

Ten minutes had gone by, Rendle was officer of the watch and Parrish had joined him and Gascoigne on the bridge when the airborne danger ceased to lurk. It revealed itself to eye and ear as a twin-engined bomber nearly in line with the sun, its nose pointing directly towards them. Its altitude was greater than that of the planes which had attacked *Talon* during the gun action with the "sea truck" off Java, but its intentions were so obviously the same that awareness of them overrode Gascoigne's shocked disbelief. He heard himself ordering the bridge to be cleared and the ship taken under water, then stood wondering stupidly what to do next, fear flooding through him at the realisation that there was nothing to do but wait. No Able Seaman Lowry manning the Oerlikons now. No chance of loading them in time from the ready-use lockers and firing them himself. No choice but to live through the next few seconds with the growing scream of the plane hammering at him, buffeting him, or was that sensation only his heart jerking frenziedly at the unexpectedness of it all? A moment of anger at himself for such pointless speculation, then the pressure-wave of the plane's passage on his eardrums and a gale of hot gases from exploding bombs turning the world about him in a sweeping circle.

Apart from a ringing inside his head he didn't seem to be hurt when he staggered to his feet, but *Talon*, half submerged and listing heavily to starboard, certainly was. The list increased as he watched and he grabbed at the side of the bridge for support. Forty degrees. Fifty.

'Oh God, she's going,' Gascoigne said, but there was nobody on the bridge to hear him and he was glad of that.

The angle not increasing any more, possibly lessening a little, but the sea closing over *Talon's* hull. He scrambled into the conning tower and closed the hatch after him. On his hurried way down the ladder he heard the words 'Shut off for depth-charging. Shut off for depth-charging. All compartments report damage. All compartments report damage.' It sounded like Peebles' voice.

In the control room the situation looked normal except that Rendle and Parrish were sitting on the deck and Peebles was in the first lieutenant's position, standing behind the hydroplane operators with the Tannoy microphone in his hand. The ship was level again, the depth gauges reading twenty-eight feet and sinking, but he could hear the sound of water jetting through the pressure hull somewhere. Or was that the singing in his ears? Not sure. Best to surface while it was still possible and try to fight the bomber off with gun-fire. Four heavy explosions in rapid succession. The plane's second run. Not close enough to matter.

'Compartments report no damage, sir,' Peebles said.

And that was difficult to believe, Gascoigne thought, but if that was what they said, that was the way it was, at least for the moment, but a flawed pressure hull could give at any time. The ability to think coming back to him, but his heart still hammering wildly. He took several silent deep breaths, trying to slacken its pace. Depth gauges reading thirty-five feet.

'Guns.'

'Yes, sir?'

'I want you to stand by to surface, then go very slowly down to fifty feet. If we start taking on any appreciable amount of water we'll blow main ballast.'

'Aye aye, sir.' Peebles raised the microphone to his mouth.

'No, wait! Get Lowry and his two Oerlikon loaders in here first, plus two machine gunners,' Gascoigne said and added to himself, 'Get your blasted priorities right, man!'

He looked down at Rendle then. 'What's up, Number One?'

'The bang caught the Pilot and me in the tower, sir, and the ship heeled over so quickly that he fell off the ladder and proceeded downwards at an acceleration of thirty-two feet per second per second. That's if I remember the laws of gravity correctly. Anyway, he thinks he's broken his ankle.'

'And you?'

'Hit my back on something, sir. I seem to be legless.'

'Legless?'

'I mean they don't seem to want to work, sir. My legs that is.'

Gascoigne knelt quickly beside him and pinched first one then the other of his calves hard.

'Did you feel that, Number One?'

'Yes, I did happen to notice it, sir. You seem to have rather strong fingers.'

'Thank God for that! You can't have broken your back in that case,' Gascoigne said and the other's deep sigh of relief explained the reason for his laboured levity.

'Depth fifty feet, sir. Ready to surface. Anti-aircraft guns' crews standing by. Compartments report no leaks, sir.'

Gascoigne turned back to Peebles. 'Do they? Then I think we'll stay

225

where we are. By the way, Guns, you handled all that very well. Very well indeed. Is anybody else hurt?'

The sub-lieutenant blushed, but replied only that there were no other casualties.

Sailors carried the two injured officers to the wardroom and made them comfortable there. Leading Telegraphist Williamson sat down and wrote another verse which ended with the statement, "There's simply nothing one can *say* for people who bomb after V-J *day*". Gascoigne and Greensmith walked through the ship, inspecting it for damage and talking to the crew.

Back in the control room, 'What do you think, Chief? Main ballast tanks?'

'Looks like it, sir,' Greensmith said. 'If she had just fallen into the hole the bombs blew in the water she'd have righted herself, but that didn't happen until we were nearly submerged and the port tanks were flooded. I think the starboard saddle-tanks are ruptured, sir. Some of them anyway.'

'Okay. We'll surface carefully after dark and see what the form is.'

'What do we do if all the starboard tanks have gone, sir?'

'Run her ashore on one of the islands and radio for help of course,' Gascoigne said. 'We wouldn't last long with her lying on her beam-ends.'

Not all the starboard ballast tanks had gone. Sixteen miles to the south of the Lombok Strait *Talon* surfaced sluggishly, moving slowly ahead through the darkness with a heavy list to starboard, her forward hydroplanes extended and at the full-rise position to provide a little more upward thrust in case the bow dipped under water.

Gascoigne leaned over the starboard side of the bridge shining an Aldis lamp like a small searchlight along the water-line. It told him nothing because the sea was lapping above where the tops of the ballast tanks began.

Over his shoulder to Greensmith he said, 'Tell them to blow main ballast for one second, Chief.'

At once a fury of enormous bubbles broke the surface immediately alongside and ahead of the conning tower, smaller ones abaft it. Then the disturbance ceased as suddenly as it had begun.

'Looks like numbers three and four, and possibly five, Chief.'

'That's what I thought, sir.'

'Thank heavens it's calm.'

'Yes indeed.'

Into the voice-pipe Gascoigne said, 'Open number four port main vent.'

He heard the vent click open and the whistle of expelled air as the sea rushed into the tank on the port side of the conning tower. Talon straightened a full five degrees, but settled lower in the water.

'Shut four port.' The whistling stopped and Gascoigne examined the water-line again with the Aldis lamp before ordering the vent opened and shut again. The list decreased to forty degrees, but still the starboard ballast tanks were not visible.

'That's the best I can do, Chief. We haven't much buoyancy left.'

'Okay, sir. I'll get cracking.'

Talon lay stopped on the gentle swell, men moving on the forward casing, working a heaving-line, weighted at its centre, from the bows aft under the keel towards No 3 external ballast tank. When it was in position Greensmith, clutching a waterproof flash-light and wearing only his underpants and a Davis escape set, lowered himself down it into the sea. When his head vanished from sight, only the movement of the heaving-line secured under his arms and the refracted glow of the torch betrayed his presence.

His head reappeared quickly and he removed his mouthpiece to shout, 'Tell the Captain there's a hole big enough to ride a bicycle through in number three! Can't fix it without docking, but the pressure hull seems okay! Just a bit scored, but not deeply! Move this bloody line aft to number four!'

Somebody called, 'Captain, sir?' and Gascoigne replied, 'It's all right. I heard.'

Greensmith, dripping, shivering, was back on the bridge fifteen minutes later.

'You got all that, did you sir?'

'Yes. Three and four are write-offs, but you can probably plug the splinter holes in five. Get a team on to that at once. I can't wait until daylight because that bomber could be back and if the weather breaks we'd be in dead trouble at this buoyancy.'

Gascoigne turned away without waiting for an acknowledgement and spoke into the voice-pipe. 'Tell the Torpedo Gunner's Mate I want to talk to him.'

A brief pause, then, 'Petty Officer Carrick speaking, sir.'

'Carrick, I want every torpedo on board out of the ship,' Gascoigne said. 'Fire the stern salvo first because the engine room staff will be working back there in a few minutes, then the bow salvo, reload and fire that lot too. When all the fish are gone, drain down the tubes and pump the water outboard. Got that?'

'Got it, sir. Nice expensive little operation.'

'I know. Can't be helped. I must lighten the ship. Don't wait for any more orders. Just get rid of the things and ask the Gunnery Officer to speak to me.'

'I'm here, sir.' Peebles' voice.

'Guns, have the magazine opened up and a safety-line rigged along the casing from the gun right for'ard. When that's done, open up the gun tower, send up enough men to form a chain and ditch every 4-inch shell we've got over the bows. The way we're listing warn them to watch their footing. Those things sometimes can explode if dropped. Leave the 20 mm and .303 ammunition. It doesn't weigh enough to matter and we may need anti-aircraft fire yet. Have you got that?'

'Yes, sir. Shall I start pumping out the internal ballast tanks too?'

'No,' Gascoigne said. 'That can wait until we're out of aircraft range. We may have to dive again which will involve taking on more internal ballast, not less, otherwise we'd never get under water after we've ditched all the ammunition.'

He sat down on the sharply tilted deck then, wrote out a signal describing where he was, what had happened and what he was doing about it, and sent it down to the wardroom for one of his injured officers to cipher.

Half an hour passed between the transmission of the signal and the receipt of the reply from Australia. Gascoigne spent it watching the water-filtered lights of the engineers moving eerily below the surface by No 5 external ballast tank, hearing the talk of the seamen handling the life-lines, watching the long shapes of 4-inch diameter shells and their brass propellant cases being passed from man to man in the crooks of their elbows, hearing the hundred-pound objects splashing monotonously into the sea near the bow, feeling more than hearing the repeated discharges as, one after another, his seventeen torpedoes were sent on their way to nowhere. That he was wasting many thousands of pounds sterling he knew, but did not care because he was gaining tons of reserve buoyancy and that might save his ship and, with it, the lives of his crew.

The strangeness of the scene was almost hypnotic. The motionless, listing submarine, lights flashing and glowing for the benefit of men who would never normally be where they were, made him think of smugglers of old, hastily repairing their damaged vessel and disposing of contraband before the arrival of an excise cutter. He was praying that nothing hostile *would* arrive out of the blackness beyond the flickering radiance of his men's lamps when he was handed the decoded message.

"For *Talon*", it read. "Help coming, son + U.S.S. *Harpoon* closing your position at flank speed on course 350 + Steer reciprocal if able + ETA approx noon today + Dwight Meynell says quote grab hold of the mane unquote + ComSubPac sends".

Gascoigne had been partly aware of the weight on his shoulders, but only realised the force of the pressure it had been exerting when it was so suddenly removed from him. He stretched luxuriously as though the weight had been a physical thing, grinning at Meynell's message, remembering the American's disgust at his total inability to stay on a horse and his final despairing advice. But this was one horse he didn't intend to fall off.

*

Eugene Haggerty said, 'What do you think we should do, Dwight?'

Meynell frowned thoughtfully before replying. 'Torpedo it maybe, Captain. It looks as though it's hurting, so that could be the kindest thing.'

Harpoon and *Talon* lay stopped within a few feet of each other, rising and falling slowly in time to the gentle swell, *Talon* leaning away from the American submarine, but only at an angle of twenty degrees now that the engineers had plugged the small holes in No 5 starboard main ballast tank. It wasn't completely air-tight, more like a tyre with a slow puncture, Gascoigne thought, but it would serve with plenty of air available to replace what was lost.

Haggerty looked across at Gascoigne. 'I hope you'll forgive my Exec, Commander. He's a country boy and thinks of everything in terms of horses.'

Gascoigne shook his head. 'I'm afraid I can't overlook his remarks and must insist that you assign him to other duties. Cleaning the "heads" would do as he spends his life ashore mucking out stables.'

'Either that or I could lend him to you,' Haggerty said. 'If you stay with "left" and "right" and don't go technical on him with words like "port" and "starboard" he'll get by.'

Despite the lightness of the exchange Gascoigne guessed that the offer was probably genuine.

'You're serious, aren't you Gene?'

'Sure. Now I have your Exec and Navigator aboard here you must be nearly fresh out of deck officers. I don't see you breaking any speed records with that damage, so you and whoever would be mighty tired by the time you made Australia.'

'Oh boy! This is like a dream,' Gascoigne said. 'All I have to do now is work out how the R.N. can court-martial a U.S. Navy officer. When I've done that I'll give him horseback riding!'

'No problem,' Haggerty told him. 'You're permitted to court-martial volunteers. Dwight just volunteered.'

Meynell came aboard *Talon* ten minutes later, swinging himself along a rope stretched between the two conning towers, and there was no levity in the formality with which he reported himself to Gascoigne. The voyage to Fremantle began at once.

*

Only the comforting presence of the U.S.S. *Harpoon* on a parallel course a mile away to starboard broke the monotony of the great expanse of ocean on which *Talon* rode. There had been no deterioration in the weather and Gascoigne was more than simply thankful for that. The streamlining of the starboard saddle tanks broken, the ship's forward motion was placing a strain on the now exposed flat bulkhead of No 5 such as it was never meant to withstand and rough seas could rapidly make that strain intolerable. If the bulkhead failed… Gascoigne shrugged. It had held for over a week and there was fast, efficient help within two thousand yards. He was more than simply thankful for that too.

There was virtually no lamp signalling between the two submarines. Two or three times a day Haggerty brought *Harpoon* close to *Talon* to talk about the situation. That morning Haggerty had said, 'Our resident medical genius tells me your boy Parrish can come up here and say hello tomorrow. There seems nothing wrong with his ankle. It was the metatarsus he broke. Rendle will take a little longer with his prolapsed disc, but he's coming along okay.' Gascoigne was unclear about the medical terms, but glad that his two officers were in the care of someone with more knowledge than he or Chief Petty Officer Ryland possessed.

'Permission for Lieutenant Meynell to come on the bridge, sir?' the voice-pipe asked.

'Yes,' Gascoigne said and glanced at his wrist. Five minutes early as usual. He had never known Meynell to be late in taking over what he called "the deck" or "the con", never "the watch".

It had taken the American less than twenty-four hours to win over the crew. Regarded with deep suspicion on his arrival, he had methodically worked his way from stem to stern asking technical questions of anybody and everybody. Such an approach, Gascoigne knew, was irresistible to British sailors who liked nothing better than to explain the intricacies of their part of ship to people less well informed than themselves or, for that matter, even to those with a superior understanding of it.

But there had been more to it than that. Meynell's attitude towards his temporary job had been highly professional. He could have been examining *Talon* with a view to establishing her readiness for combat under his command and Gascoigne found that quite remarkable in a man who had been a rancher with no interest in the sea less than four years earlier. Well known as their successes were to him it intrigued Gascoigne to be given evidence at first hand of the dedication of Americans as described to him by Gail Harding's father. Meynell's verdict on completing his inspection that *Talon* was a slow old scow, but that he would rather be depth-charged in her than in *Harpoon* was an indication of how much he had taken in and summed up neatly the necessity to compromise which had been the bane of naval architects for centuries.

'Hi, Captain.'

'Hello, Dwight.'

Despite being several years the older and the friendship which had grown out of early enmity, not once since he had been aboard *Talon* had Meynell addressed Gascoigne by his Christian name.

'No change?'

'No change, thank the Lord.'

'Amen to that. Why don't you go get some chow? I have the con.'

Gascoigne clambered down the steeply canted conning tower ladder content in the knowledge that Meynell would handle any emergency as ably as he could himself.

His faith never put to the test, Gascoigne manoeuvred his wounded ship without further emergencies into the Swan River nineteen days and eleven hours after the bombs had so nearly sent her to the bottom, astonished at a reception he knew he would not have received even if he *had* sunk the *Kongo*-class battleship. Flags fluttering, the sound of cheering and sirens almost drowning the strains of "A Life on the Ocean Wave" coming from the American depot ship, *Harpoon* close astern, following him like an anxious mother all the way to the dry-dock.

Standing at the dock's side, watching the water-level drop to reveal the gaping holes in *Talon's* saddle-tanks, 'Thanks for everything, Dwight.'

Meynell spoke formally to Gascoigne for the last time. 'My pleasure, Captain. If you and your officers feel the urge for a little drinking ashore tonight, it's on the United States Navy.'

'Go jump in the lake,' Gascoigne said. 'We're paying for this one.'

*

Gascoigne walked along the upper deck of the depot ship glancing self-consciously down at the two and a half gold stripes on the sleeves of the uniform a Perth tailor had delivered aboard. He was an acting lieutenant-commander now and that made him at least temporarily senior to Peter Harding. The fact embarrassed him, but the Admiralty had decreed that submarine captains should hold that rank to bring them more into line with their American counterparts. In his view the decision had been made just a little late. At the door of the captain's day cabin he knocked and went in.

'Hello, John,' the flotilla captain said. '*Talon* all right?'

'Yes, sir. I've just brought her alongside from the dock. It's a relief to have her floating upright again.'

'I bet it is. Pour yourself a drink and join us over here.'

'Thank you, sir.'

Glass in hand Gascoigne joined the group a moment later. Three depot ship officers and all the submarine captains were there.

'The subject is "Showing the Flag",' the flotilla captain told them, 'and the object is to show it, your boats and crews to as many people as possible. Consequently the flotilla will split up and you'll all go your separate ways to different centres of population along the south and east coast of Australia.' He drew a reverse L-shaped line with his forefinger on a map attached to the bulkhead as though there might be some amongst his audience uncertain about the location of the coast, then went on, 'Tasmania too.' Tasmania was stabbed by the same finger.

By far the smallest and easily the most heavily decorated man in the cabin said, 'Ten out of ten.'

The flotilla captain looked at him. 'What for?'

'Geography, sir. You're uncanny.'

'Any more of that-out of you, "Lofty" Wainwright, and I'll send you all the way round to Brisbane, which is here!' The finger stabbed the map again.

'Picture of undersized individual developing ghastly pallor,' Wainwright said. 'Please don't be unkind to a little old man, sir. I might manage to stagger as far as Adelaide, but I'd never make Melbourne let alone Brisbane. Why don't you send Gascoigne to Brisbane? He's younger than the rest of us.'

The flotilla captain smiled and looked at Gascoigne. 'Like to go to Brisbane, John?'

'Anywhere you say, sir,' Gascoigne said and by so doing altered the course of his life dramatically.

Chapter Twenty

Oh it's you, Jackman,' the Marquis of Trent had said. 'Come in and close the door.'

Jackman had done as he was told and been handed a slip of paper.

'That's a notification from the Great Western Railway about two packages awaiting collection at Devizes station. I suspect that they are Lieutenant Harding's personal effects. I want you to fetch them and bring them to me. On no account is Her Ladyship to see them, let alone have them. She had a letter from his commanding officer a couple of days ago and I don't want her distressed twice in one week.'

Fifty minutes later, 'Oh bloody hell,' the chauffeur said. He said it very quietly. The Lady Abigail had walked into the garage just as he took the suitcases from the car and that after Gilchrist had told him that she was out exercising her black mare "Liquorice Lass".

'Hello, Jackman. You're looking very furtive. What have you got there?'

'Good afternoon, My Lady. Some stuff Mrs Gilchrist's sister sent her. It came by rail.'

'I see,' Gail said, turned away, then back again. The suit-cases were covered in carefully stitched canvas with only their handles protruding not, she thought, the sort of packaging Mrs Gilchrist's sister could have contrived and wasn't that a Royal Navy stencil on the…

'Let me see those.'

'No, My Lady.'

'*What* did you say, Jackman?'

He met her astonished, imperious gaze levelly. 'Don't, Lady Abbie,' he said. 'Leave it. *Please*.'

Gail bit her lip, but that didn't prevent her chin trembling or the tears from coming. Jackman hadn't called her "Lady Abbie" since she had stopped wearing her hair in pigtails more than a decade before. After a moment he began to thump her on the shoulder as though she were a horse. He hadn't done that for more than a decade either. She gripped his wrist hard, said, '*Dear* Jackman,' then ran out of the garage.

In her room she stood, looking sharply around as if searching for something she needed quickly. There was nothing she needed quickly, nothing that the room held and, after a moment, her head stopped its bird-like movements.

'Idiot,' she whispered to herself, 'this really has to stop. It's over and there's no point in going on being emotional about it.'

She looked around the room again, slowly this time, as if expecting it to comment and her eyes came to rest on the uniform jacket lying on the bed, the same jacket she had first cried into, the one she held in her arms every night.

'This really has to stop,' she repeated, picked up the jacket, kissed it and put it on a coat-hanger. With the wardrobe door closed on it she waited to see if she felt any better, decided she did not, but knew that she did not want to look at any more of her husband's belongings. Not yet. Dear Jackman. Dear Daddy as well who, she guessed, had told him to keep the things away from her.

The strings controlling a puppet might have been cut from the way she flopped ungracefully into a chair and sprawled, head resting on its back, staring at the ceiling, feeling the crushing weight of her loneliness. During the twenty-six years of her life she had carried burdens in many forms, but never this one before. Her allure had seen to that, but it was useless to her now because of all the many men she knew, most of whom would have come running at her nod, none held sufficient attraction for her. Not after Peter. Darling, gentle Peter.

Well, perhaps there was one, she mused. John Gascoigne had endeared himself to her before ever they had met because of the support he had given her husband and Peter's high regard for him. Meeting him had done nothing to make her change her opinion. She had liked him and so had her father, something which counted heavily with her. But Gascoigne had gone and married that pretty Air Force girl with cotton wool in her skull. Silly man, she thought, and wondered both how they were getting on together and if she herself had been indirectly responsible for the marriage. That that was possible she knew well enough. John Gascoigne had been so transparently enraptured by her that his subsequent sudden wedding could easily have been an uncontrollable reflex.

For a few seconds Gail considered taking Gascoigne away from his wife when he returned to England, then put the thought from her. She had no moral scruples on the score but, also having no illusions about her desirability, thought it would not be fair. Unfairness she disliked intensely and as home-wrecking was unfairness that was that.

Getting slowly to her feet, 'Poor "Liquorice Lass",' she said to the unresponsive room. 'I mustn't keep her waiting any longer.'

Chapter Twenty-One

The day notification of the award of the Victoria Cross to Able Seaman Lowry was received aboard *Talon* began and ended badly for Gascoigne. A sea mist had kept him on the bridge most of the night while his ship nosed slowly through a heavy blanket of moisture which made the bow invisible from the bridge. Radar and the echo-sounder told him exactly where he was at any given moment, but the long hours were no less harrowing for that because the sea around him appeared to be full of ships which knew neither where they were nor what they were doing. Sirens boomed or wailed eerily, the direction from which the sounds came difficult to determine, and that set his nerves on edge until he had schooled himself to ignore them and rely exclusively on what Rendle, sitting by the radar set, told him. Once, he had dived when some large unseen vessel steering an erratic course had seemed intent on running him down and had stayed submerged until Taylor on sonar watch had said it was safe to surface again.

Visibility improved with the dawn but by then he was a long way behind schedule and reported the fact by radio so that his itinerary of public engagements could be revised. An amended programme reached him within two hours and with it the news of Lowry's decoration.

At 1050 that morning Gascoigne ordered the lower deck cleared and when as many of the crew as it would accommodate were jammed into the control room he read the citation, shook Lowry's hand and described to them all what had happened on that day in the Java Sea. Lowry endured the little ceremony in scarlet-faced silence, said 'Bugger my boots' in a wondering voice when it was over and allowed himself to be led away by his cheering shipmates. Forty-five minutes later he was deeply unconscious.

Before achieving that condition he had poured a bottle of ink over himself, urinated on the deck, ground Leading Telegraphist Williamson's glasses under his heel and struck Chief Petty Officer Ryland a glancing blow on the head with somebody else's shoe, all of it in the last minute of the half-hour since the daily issue of rum had been made. Then he had collapsed under the weight of three men and a great deal of alcohol.

As white with fury as earlier Lowry had been red with embarrassment Gascoigne summoned the first lieutenant and the coxswain to his cabin. The little space was very crowded with the three of them standing in it.

'Well?'

'Sorry about this, sir,' Rendle said. 'He must have had "sippers" from the tot of every man for'ard of the control room. It's all my fault. I should have foreseen this and...'

'It's too late to worry about whose bloody fault it is,' Gascoigne told them angrily. 'First of all, is he going to be all right?'

The coxswain nodded. 'Yes, sir. We forced water with mustard and salt in it down 'im and when that came up again a lot of rum come up with it. 'Is pulse is steady enough, sir.'

'Well, thank God for that, but what the blazes are we going to do now? This will ruin the whole "Showing the Flag" exercise! The ship was to have been the star turn, but now everybody will want to see Lowry, especially the press, and I'll have to tell them he's under arrest! What a flaming mess!'

'Can I make a suggestion, sir?'

'What is it, Cox'n?'

'Don't *put* 'im under arrest, sir.'

'But I've got to. He struck you. You know perfectly well that we can't have people going around striking chief petty officers!'

'Oh, I wouldn't say 'e done that, sir,' Ryland said. 'I 'appened to inadvertently strike that shoe 'e was 'oldin' with my ear. Clumsy I was.'

Gascoigne looked at him thoughtfully, then shook his head and was about to speak when the coxswain went on, 'Look, sir, I don't mind and the crew won't see it as laxness if you let's 'im off. 'Eaven's above, sir, 'e's a bloody 'ero to them and they knows it's their fault 'e's in this mess, or if they doesn't I'll bloody soon see that they does.'

It was long seconds before Gascoigne nodded and said, 'All right, Cox'n. In that case I'm very grateful to you for not pressing charges. We'll forget it. Send Able Seaman Barton to see me, please.'

The first lieutenant and the coxswain left and a minute later Barton appeared. 'You wanted me, sir?'

'Yes, Barton. We're trying to keep your pal Lowry out of the rattle.'

'Thought you might be, sir. The Cox'n's just started givin' them a right bollockin' for'ard for givin' him all that rum.'

'Good,' Gascoigne said. 'Now, listen to me. We'll be docking in a couple of hours and the press will be clamouring for Lowry. Obviously he's in no state to see them so I'll fob them off with some excuse or other and arrange a date for them with him tomorrow. Okay?'

'Yes, sir.'

'Right, that's point one. Point two is keeping him out of trouble for the rest of today. He may be in the same mood when he comes round as when he passed out and if he hits any more petty officers, or anybody else, he's had it.'

'Don't worry, sir. If he as much as blinks I'll flatten him.'

'I hoped you'd say that,' Gascoigne said, 'but are you sure you can? I mean if he gets awkward. You and he seem to come out about equal when you have your celebrated punch-ups.'

'Oh, that's only fun, sir. When it's serious like this I use my own system. Sort of secret weapon, sir.'

'I remember now,' Gascoigne told him. '"One Punch Barton". Well, don't hit him too hard.' 'That's quite a crowd, sir.'

'It certainly is, Number One,' Gascoigne agreed. 'How many would you say? Eight, ten thousand?'

'Something like that, sir.'

Both continued to look through binoculars at the mass of people waiting on the long stone jetty as *Talon* slid smoothly towards it, White Ensign and "Jolly Roger" fluttering. Already arms were waving and the sound of cheering reached them across the water. The cheering increased in intensity and volume as the distance shortened and when Gascoigne brought his ship alongside he had to shout his manoeuvring orders to make them audible above the din.

Standing on the casing near the wide gangway a crane had placed in position, listening to and hearing half of a speech of welcome from a man wearing a city suit and Homburg hat. Somebody from the Lord Mayor's office. Thank you very much I'll call on the Lord Mayor at his convenience. Please let me know when. To a senior police officer, yes open to the public as from noon tomorrow. Please arrange for a second gangway aft by the engine room hatch so that the people can come aboard here, walk through the ship, and leave from there. Right. One way traffic. There's not much room down below. To the press, sorry but it'll have to be tomorrow morning. I have official calls to make and Able Seaman Lowry is indisposed. Well, off the record I ordered him to "splice the main brace". That means a double tot of rum. Silly of me. He's very young. Too much excitement. Not used to drink. Fell asleep over lunch. Don't spoil his big moment by printing that. Yes you can have the run of the ship from 0900 to 1200. Yes Lowry and me too. Thanks for being patient.

Gascoigne went ashore after that, the police clearing a path through the crowd for him to a chauffeur-driven car placed at his disposal for the duration of the visit. He asked the driver to take him to the harbour master's office. That proved to have been a wise decision, his visit being as welcome as it was obviously unexpected.

'Just came to pay my respects and thank you for the use of your berthing facilities, Mr Strang.'

'Well, my oath, Commander! Nobody ever bothered to do that before! How about a beer?'

It was four o'clock in the afternoon, but Gascoigne said he'd love one.

'I'll have you connected to the shore telephone system before tonight,' Strang said. 'Meanwhile messages are being handled through this office.' He raised his voice and called, 'Anything for the sub, Flo?'

A smiling fat girl appeared in the doorway. 'Yes, Mr Strang. Message just came in. The Lord Mayor is free any time up to six if the captain calls to see him.'

'Thanks, love. Bring us some beer, will you?'

When Gascoigne was about to leave Strang asked, 'Mind signing a couple of autographs for my kids and maybe one for Flo too? She'll be too shy to ask.'

240

Gascoigne looked at him in astonishment. 'What on earth do they want them for? I'm not a film star.'

'No, you're better than that,' the harbour master told him. 'You're real and you'll find yourself signing quite a few before you leave this city.'

After Gascoigne had drunk a glass of sherry with the Lord Mayor it was time for him to attend his first scheduled function, cocktails and dinner as a guest of the Commodore and members of the Yacht Club. He was tired after a sleepless night and worrying day, but he found the occasion relaxing. It was good to be with people who knew about the sea and its hazards and the demands it could make, without having to have such things explained to them. To their pleasure and his own he stayed longer than he should have done and he was already late when he left for his next engagement. It didn't matter. His officers and men would be there.

'What's this Grand Ball thing in aid of?' he asked his driver.

'Well, you mostly, Skip. Sort of victory party built round your visit. I bet the organisers were sweating blood when that fog held you up last night. It's taken a lot of putting together. They've even got the finals of the "Miss Armed Forces" beauty contest going on. Well, that's over now, because we're running late, but the crumpet will still be there. Maybe you can cut yourself off a slice.'

'Maybe,' Gascoigne said and yawned shudderingly, wishing that he was in his bunk.

The ball-room was vast. Dozens of tables surrounded a large dance-floor with a band at each end. Many hundreds of people, scores of them dancing and, dotted amongst them, the uniforms of his crew.

'Ah, there you are, Commander. We'd begun to think you'd got lost.'

'I'm sorry. It was difficult getting away from the Yacht Club.'

He followed the official through the crowd, the noise, watching revolving lights cutting the smoky air with swathes of colour, wondering if his people were behaving themselves. Then Rendle was coming towards him.

'Hello, Number One. How's it all going?'

Rendle grinned. 'About what one might expect, sir. Five taken back aboard sloshed out of their minds and roughly the same number of "Probables", but there hasn't been any trouble. The Cox'n and his strong-arm squad have grabbed them as soon as they've got worse than just silly.'

'Good. What's the latest on Lowry?'

'Back in the land of the living,' Rendle said. 'Barton had to sit on his head when he first came round, but he's sober now and very, very sorry for himself. Ashamed too. Oh, by the way, talking of Lowry, there's a group of humorists who have come out in a positive rash of home-made medal ribbons. Not wanting to be outdone, I suppose. Anyway, I've let them keep them on for this party only and – Hey, Elliott! Come here and show the Captain your decorations.'

The sailor who acted as wardroom steward approached, grinning sheepishly. Oblongs of variously coloured material made up a row of improbable medal ribbons on his chest.

'Evening, sir.'

'Evening, Elliott. What are those things you've awarded yourself?'

'Well, sir, this one's the Bay of Fundy Fog Medal, sir. The next is the Under-water Meal Server's Star and this – I've forgotten, sir. No I haven't! It's the Cockroach Crusher's Cross! They don't come any higher than that, sir.'

Gascoigne smiled. 'All right, Elliott. Enjoy yourself, but I want to see your uniform back to normal tomorrow.'

'Of course, sir. Only a joke, sir.'

Elliott went away and Rendle said, 'Our table's this way.'

Not very tall. About up to his shoulder. Sun-tanned. Tawny hair half-concealing one side of her face. Tawny eyes. Fawn shoes and fawn jersey dress. Sleek. Svelte. Feline. Tawny. Something of Gail Harding. Almost.

'I don't think you've met Miss Fraser, sir.'

'Hello. I'm John Gascoigne.'

'Yes, I know.' Husky cat-purr, but without interest.

'So *you* won, did you?'

'So I won what?'

Puzzled, 'This "Miss Armed Forces" competition.'

'Oh God,' she said. 'All bosoms and waving hips. Is that how I look? Even if I had, what makes you think I'd come straight to *your* table?'

'Miss Fraser is in charge of government liaison and public relations for our visit, sir.' Rendle's voice. A little anxious.

The eyes watching him with nothing in them. Not even challenge.

'Well, good for her,' Gascoigne said coldly. 'Now, who wants a drink?'

He had to pose with the beauty queens while flash-bulbs popped and he danced with one of them. No, she hadn't won, but she had come third which wasn't bad for a girl from a place called Kingoonya she said and told him with her body that her bed was his. The arrival of Peebles, emboldened by alcohol to cut in on his captain, saved him the embarrassment of declining her unspoken offer and he made his way to one of the bars, still smarting at being put down so promptly, so emphatically by the girl called Fraser.

If it had ever happened to him before he couldn't remember when, and if it had happened it couldn't have mattered or he would have remembered. Now it mattered, although why that should be he was uncertain. There was Stella Forbes waiting for him back in Perth which should be enough for any man. That there was also a wife waiting for him back in England was something he considered less and less frequently these days and he considered it not at all now in his angry state.

'Drink, sir?'

He looked at the barman. 'Yes, please. Could I just have a beer if you've got one? I've already drunk my way through a dinner party.'

'No sweat, sir. That's the fuel this country runs on.'

She passed close to where he was standing, dancing with Parrish, animated, laughing, white teeth flashing in her tanned face. Why had she attacked him like that? Why had she attacked him at all? He hadn't done anything except make a mistaken assumption which was hardly an insult. Oh, forget her, he told himself, but found himself unable to do so. What had Parrish said her Christian name was? Oh yes, Candice. That had a pretty fatuous ring to it. Candice for Pete's sake! No good at all. Must do better than that. Too alarmingly attractive to be swept out of the mind by infantile ridicule. Awful mistake to have allowed that comparison with Gail Harding to enter his brain. That was the greatest danger signal. Not that she matched Gail of course. Nobody did that, but…

Gascoigne drank his beer and rejoined the group at the table, uneasy when she was at it too, uneasy when she was not. After half an hour of tension

243

which he knew he alone was experiencing, he went in search of his driver and had himself driven back to his ship. He hadn't spoken to her again.

*

His mood black after a broken night during which a girl with an arrogant face and disinterested gaze had intruded both on his waking and sleeping moments Gascoigne scowled at his reflection in his cabin's small mirror. That he was looking at an image of injured pride he was perfectly well aware, but that piece of self-knowledge only succeeded in making him crosser. Having his ego punctured by an attractive woman had been a unique and highly unpleasant experience for him. That he had been so carelessly brushed aside in front of his own officers made it worse. So absorbed was he in mentally replaying the brief exchange of the night before that he had finished shaving and put on his best uniform before he became aware of the almost total silence of his ship. The ventilation system hummed quietly at him, but there seemed to be no other sounds at all.

According to his watch it was five minutes past seven and *Talon* should have been long awake. Curious now he went to the wardroom. Empty. He turned back past his cabin to the control room. That was empty as well. Not until he had climbed almost to the top of the conning tower ladder did he hear any signs of life. Then he was on the bridge looking down at most of his crew standing to attention in three lines. Near them, in a group, stood Rendle, Parrish, Peebles and some petty officers, legs astride, hands clasped behind them, motionless. The only movement in the tableau was provided by Chief Petty Officer Ryland walking up and down in front of the triple rank of sailors.

'Not only you,' the coxswain was saying, 'does not want to march through the city, the Captain and other officers does not want to march through the city, I and other chief and petty officers does not want to march through the city.' He stopped then, both talking and walking, before shouting, 'But the city whose booze you 'ave already drunk most of wants you to march through it and that's what you are goin' to do!'

Intrigued, his depression momentarily forgotten, Gascoigne rested his elbows on the side of the bridge, watching and listening.

'So that you do not cause the city to fall about laughin'' the coxswain went on, 'you are goin' to march up and down this jetty firstly until you are all sober and secondly until you can do it almost as well as the Boy Scouts! Right? Right. Now then…'

Rendle had left the group on the jetty and returned aboard. He climbed the side of the conning tower, dropped to the bridge deck and saluted.

'Good morning, sir.'

'Good morning, Number One. Sensible idea of yours, this turn-out.'

'Well, most of them haven't marched anywhere in years. Same goes for rifle drill. I thought they'd better have a dummy run.'

'Rifle drill? We've only got half a dozen rifles.'

'I know, sir,' Rendle said. 'The local armoury is lending us the rest.'

'Oh, I see. Lucky you've got all this space to practise in. I was expecting the crowds back early.'

'That was the harbour master, sir. He's closed the whole jetty, except to the press, until we march off. I gather you made quite a hit by calling on him yesterday. He's being very helpful.'

'You *have* been busy, Number One.'

'Not me, sir. Candice has arranged everything.'

'Who?' Gascoigne asked. The word came out before he could stop it and immediately he felt petty.

'Miss Fraser, sir. She was down here by six and now she's with the police checking on traffic control for the march. Apparently she walked the route yesterday afternoon with a stop-watch to get the timing right at each intersection.'

'Little Miss Efficiency, eh?'

'She's efficient all right,' Rendle said. 'Arranged for the wreath for you to lay on the war memorial, several coach tours for the crew, a rugby match, theatres, entertainment in private homes, all sorts of things. I've got her list down below, sir. It covers your engagements too. I gather she'll be with you on those to make the introductions and so on.'

Gascoigne grunted, his eyes following the erratic progress of his crew along the quay, but not recording it, his feelings a mixture of resentment

245

at having matters which had never been in his hands taken out of them, and dismay at Rendle's final sentence. 'Ten days of that bloody woman!' he said, but this time he had the sense to say it to himself.

The press conference in the wardroom went off without trouble. Lowry was shy, almost monosyllabic, and Gascoigne told his story for him, trying to get across to his audience what it must have felt like to Lowry to be, as he had thought, the last man outside a sealed pressure-hull facing two fighter-bombers alone while his ship submerged under him, his only prospects death by bullets, bombs, drowning or all three. He felt that he had probably succeeded when the only woman journalist present said, 'Stone the bloody crows,' very softly and dabbed at her eyes with a handkerchief. Then it was time for the march through the city.

That went off without trouble too, he and about fifty of his officers and men, all that could be spared from duties aboard, striding in fair unison with the beat of a band of the Royal Australian Air Force which led them. The step got ragged at times because it was difficult to hear the music above the roars of the people lining the streets, but picked up again at Chief Petty Officer Ryland's bellowed 'Lep! Right! Lep!'

Gascoigne found it an emotional experience. The cheering which he felt to be over-reacting but heart-warming for all that, the flags of the League of Returned Servicemen which dipped in salute as the marchers passed them and the total silence of the crowd at the war memorial where he placed the wreath Miss Fraser had ordered. Sudden irritation at that thought quickly replaced by emotion again at the sight of the long double column of names carved in old stone headed 1914-1918 and the same on a board newly painted for the occasion bearing the legend 1939-1945. Singapore it read, North Africa, Italy, France, Germany. Even England. Who would they have been? Bomb victims? Fighter pilots screaming earthwards to dig their own graves in Kentish orchards or the Sussex Downs? Eyes misting a little at the thought of so many Australians dying so very far from home he stepped back and saluted. It was over and irritation returned to him at the sight of the two coaches provided by Miss Fraser waiting to carry the men back to their ship, or whatever else she had arranged for them. He hadn't had time to read her list of entertainments yet.

'Over here, Skip!' his driver called.

So she had even thought of sending the car to collect him at the end of the march.

'May we ride back with you, sir?'

'Yes, Number One, of course,' Gascoigne said. 'Pilot! Guns! This way. The car's over here.' Then to Rendle again, 'Where are the chaps going?'

'Checking their rifles in at the armoury first, sir. After that to a barbecue at a sheep station. Beer, bangers and hot and cold running blondes waiting for them. I'm very glad about it. The ship's going to be uninhabitable with all these thousands of people walking through it. Then there's this evening's cocktail party on board. We need all the space there is for that, so the crew have been given free cinema tickets. Somewhere for them to go until it's over.'

Gascoigne got into the car feeling thoughtful and the others followed him.

'You know, sir,' Rendle said, 'I hadn't really given all this much thought.'

'I hadn't given it any at all,' Gascoigne told him, 'but I suppose we can console ourselves that we didn't know what the form was until we got here. Have you got a copy of Miss Fraser's schedule with you?'

'Yes, sir.'

There were fifteen typed pages of it and Gascoigne was less than a third of the way through when the car came to a stop on the jetty. He was reluctantly deeply impressed by the wealth of detailed planning that had gone into the production of the document. Then the view out of the side window caught his attention.

Foot by slow foot *Talon* was swallowing a line of people which stretched the full length of the three hundred-yard jetty, drawing it in through the fore hatch and disgorging it again from the engine room access. When Gascoigne and his officers got out of the car those nearest to it broke away from the line and surrounded them, talking, laughing, many thrusting pieces of paper and pencils forward. Before he reached the safety of the wardroom by way of the conning tower hatch Gascoigne had signed his name twenty-nine times and been kissed by an assortment of women. The sight of Candice Fraser sitting in his chair checking a list of something or other with his engineer officer both startled and annoyed him, but he felt he should try to establish some degree of rapport.

'Good afternoon, Miss Fraser,' he said. 'I really must congratulate you on your meticulous arrangements and for giving so much thought to the social side. I could never have achieved what you have done.'

'It's hardly your field, Commander,' she told him, glanced up from her work and added, 'You'd better wash your face and change your collar. They're covered in lipstick.'

Confused, angry, he found himself in his cabin doing as he had been told like a small boy. He stayed there, listening to the chattering people moving endlessly past on the other side of his closed door, waiting for her to leave the ship.

At five o'clock precisely the last of the day's visitors left and an hour later the cocktail party guests began to arrive. Apart from the Lord Mayor and the harbour master Gascoigne had never seen any of them before and for twenty minutes he stood by the gangway saluting and shaking hands. When there seemed to be no more hands to shake he went below to join the noisily animated throng. The entire ship from the torpedo stowage compartment forward to the water-tight door leading to the engine room aft was crowded and he talked to group after group counting, for something to do, the number of times he said 'No, we don't get claustrophobia, but then the ship isn't usually as full as this.'

By eight most of them had left and he was hungry, anxious to go ashore to a restaurant for dinner, knowing that he had to leave at half past nine for some hotel two hours away by road, close to whatever it was he had to do the next day. He took the schedule from his pocket. Yes that was it. Some mining development he had to show himself at, tours of some factories and… The pages went back inside his jacket.

'Number One.'

'Sir?'

'Have you seen Miss Fraser recently? She and I have to leave at 2130.'

'Yes, sir. She went aft about ten minutes ago. I'll fetch her.'

'No, don't bother,' Gascoigne said. 'I'll find her myself.'

Gascoigne walked out of the control room, past the galley and radio room to the engine room and saw her standing at the far end of the long space by the main motor switch-boards, head bent in concentration, listening to one of his crew.

'Miss Fraser.'

Without looking in his direction, 'Don't interrupt,' she said. 'Petty Officer Finchley is explaining to me about rheostats.'

He turned furiously away, but stopped at the sound of her voice saying, 'And don't forget that the car leaves here at half past nine.'

He turned slowly back at that and said, 'Miss Fraser, the car leaves from wherever I say, whenever I say. The driver will tell you where and when that is.'

Dinner was spoilt for him and the two-hour drive with her in the back of the big limousine a lifetime he tried to live through by feigning sleep. Not once did they speak to each other, not even when they checked in at the pleasant U-shaped single-storey hotel, parting without a glance when they were led to their respective rooms.

Very tired now after the night at sea in the fog and the next which had brought him little rest, Gascoigne tossed and turned in his bed growing more and more wakeful until he abandoned hope of sleep, switched on his light and tried to read a book. When his telephone buzzed at a quarter past four his first thought was that something was wrong aboard *Talon*. He dropped the book onto the blanket and reached quickly for the receiver.

'Yes?'

'I can't either,' the ear-piece told him and his heart immediately began to thump heavily at the sound of the husky Australian voice.

'What can't you either, Miss Fraser?'

'Get to sleep. Would you like to go for a walk?'

'With you?'

'Well, I wasn't suggesting that you went by yourself. Of course with me.' There was laughter in the words and that was very nice because it made her human.

'Yes, I would. Give me a few minutes to get ready.'

'I'll meet you in the reception area at half past,' she said.

Looking across the dark garden of the hotel he saw a lighted window in the opposite wing as, presumably, she had seen his. He shaved and dressed quickly.

Except for an elderly man in hotel uniform reading a newspaper by the telephone switch-board the foyer was deserted when he reached it. Then he saw her walking towards him, the dimmed night bulbs glinting dully on her hair and painting high-lights which rippled on the black oil-skin of her coat as she moved. Gascoigne sighed softly, excitement growing in him.

'You talked one of my crew into giving you that coat. It's Navy issue.'

'Yes, I thought it would look better on me,' she said and smiled almost shyly before adding, 'You won't punish anybody, will you?'

'I won't punish anybody.'

A brief spatter of warm rain met them as they went out through the glass revolving door and a hundred yards from it the darkness had enfolded them so completely that they had to pause, waiting for their eyes to adjust. He took her arm then, the action as shy as her smile had been, and they walked on down the path leading to where she said the river was, talking quietly, telling each other the wrong reasons for their inability to sleep.

There was no lessening in the thumping of Gascoigne's heart. Her inexplicable presence beside him in the dark, secret world of the night, her hip brushing against his, saw to that. Silent now they reached the river and stood watching the faint sheen of it before beginning to walk along its bank. He wondered what he was going to do, wondered as well, in view of her earlier treatment of him, if he had the courage to do anything, fully aware of the wrongness of repeating what had happened in Perth. Sliding his hand down her sleeve and interlacing his fingers with hers was the feeblest of compromises.

'Not the heaviest pass I've ever had made at me, but it'll do,' she said and turned easily to twine her arms round his neck. It began to rain again, then stopped, but they stood unnoticing holding each other, mouths exploring. When she unbuttoned her oil-skin and lay down on the river bank her body stood out whitely against the dark material.

She cried out once, said 'Oh Pommy darling,' twice, then they lay still, Gascoigne drained of the tensions which had been increasing their grip on him by the hour and filled with wonder at an experience which had been like the first time ever.

'That's tidied up two things,' she told him.

'Which two things?'

'You'll have to stop calling me "Miss Fraser" now, and we'll be able to help each other properly over these frightful public engagements.'

The day had come close enough to show him that her eyes were smiling up at him, a gentle smile which was to affect him more and more deeply over the coming days. Wondering what had happened to the hard-bitch image she had projected, not yet ready to ask, he nodded his head and smiled back at her.

'You'll get cold lying there stark naked, Candy.'

'*Not* stark naked! I've still got my arms in the sleeves,' she said indignantly and drew him down onto her with them. When the next shower came she rolled on top of him, protecting him from it with the coat like the wings of a giant bat.

It was day when they got back to the hotel. They lay on her bed, both fighting off sleep suddenly so welcoming now that there was no longer any time for it, he with his face resting against the curve of her breast, she stroking his damp hair.

'Candy.'

'Yes, Pommy darling?'

Ready to ask now, 'Why did you think it necessary to soften me up like that?'

He felt her stiffen and slowly relax again, heard her say, with a trace of her old hardness, 'I was *not* softening you up. I'm not that sort of person.'

'Then I don't really understand.'

She took his head in her hands and said, 'How could you understand? I can't imagine anything much more confusing than having to contend with an insolent bitch who suddenly decides to throw herself at you, but I can tell you what happened now. I was waiting at the quayside to report to you after you had been officially welcomed, but you went off to pay your courtesy calls, so I couldn't. Well, you didn't see me amongst all those people, but I had a good long look at you and I thought that's for me, that's the one I want.'

For a moment she was silent, then began talking again. 'Before we met at that dance thing, I was given some potted biographies sent on from Perth. Yours and your senior people and Able Seaman Lowry. Yours said you were married. Hard luck, Candice. Hands off. He's not for you. That was a fair cow and the only thing I could do was put the shutters up right away because, being pretty conceited, I thought you might get smitten by me.'

Turning onto her side and holding his head close to her she went on, 'So I attacked you from the outset to put you right off me which didn't work in the way I meant it to, and then I had to watch you getting more and more perplexed and miserable because you didn't know why I couldn't even be civil. That was a fair cow too because my intention wasn't to be hurtful, it was to not cause a muddle and – Oh dear, I've lost the place. What was I talking about?'

'About not causing a muddle,' Gascoigne said in a muffled voice.

'What? Oh yes, of course. And then last night your light went on after you'd gone to bed and stayed on for simply hours and hours and I knew you were distressed – and – and I thought perhaps it would be better if we had each other while we can, so I've made a muddle after all. End of speech. Do you understand more now?'

He prised her fingers away from the back of his head and nodded. 'Yes, and I'm very grateful, to put it mildly. I didn't know how I was going to get through the coming days with you around.'

In a suddenly brisk voice she said, 'All right. Now suppose you get out of my bed. You were forceful enough to chop me down over the car yesterday, but not enough to drag me out to dinner and I, for one, want some breakfast.'

The day passed for Gascoigne in a haze of happy tiredness. At the mining development he gave his address from a flag-draped platform specially constructed to accommodate the senior management and the visitors. He was surprised at the intense interest shown by part of the large work-force in submarine warfare and answered their questions for more than half an hour. Throughout that time he was conscious of the almost tangible waves of sexuality being projected by the other and larger part towards Candice Fraser sitting decoratively at the opposite end of the platform. Being unable to blame them he didn't resent it.

Afterwards, 'I think you were up-staged, Commander,' the managing director told him. 'But never mind. They all liked that bit of yours about Australia being fastest on the draw in defence of the Old Country when war broke out.'

Another drive, a factory tour, another speech, then the same thing again.

The directors of wherever it was gave them lunch then and two more visits followed during the afternoon before they were free to return to the hotel and an early supper.

They ate a little, went to his room by unspoken mutual consent, undressed and were asleep within seconds of getting into bed, nestled together as closely as two spoons. Neither had moved when their morning call woke them at seven. Such total relaxation, such undemanding intimacy, was something Gascoigne had never experienced with his wife, Stella Forbes, or anybody else, and his slide into love with Candice Fraser gathered momentum.

*

Lieutenant Rendle was feeling angry with everybody in general, but mostly with himself for the naivety of his surprise at the frailty of human nature. He should, he knew, have anticipated pilfering even if, with such limited space to lock things away in, there was nothing much he could have done about it.

'Bloody fool!' he said.

'I'm very sorry, sir.'

He looked at Able Seaman Elliott. 'Not you, Elliott. *Me.*'

'Oh, I see, sir.'

Rendle picked up Elliott's empty scabbard, then tossed it irritably back on to the wardroom table. A bayonet was, he supposed, rather an attractive prize for a souvenir hunter.

'Have you any idea when it was pinched?' he asked, then added quickly, 'No, don't bother to answer that. It was a silly question. You'd have reported it immediately if you had and there's nothing we can do now anyway. Collect the sentries' bayonets, stow them away and tell the Cox'n they're not to be worn in future.'

When Elliott had gone he looked at the list of items taken by the sight-seers. That someone out of the nearly nine thousand people who had passed through the ship since the visit had begun had been able to steal a sentry's bayonet didn't surprise him particularly. In the press of people pushing and shoving around him the man would never have noticed the weapon being drawn carefully from its scabbard near his left hip. What did surprise and anger him was that the local citizens should want and, unobserved, be able to snip buttons, medal ribbons, even gold braid from uniforms not then being worn by their owners. That was mean because the uniforms were personal property and the men had to make good the deficiencies at their own expense, or suffer the consequences of being improperly dressed. Even things like soap and razor blades had vanished from the wash-basins.

Mean and petty too, Rendle thought. Who really needed a piece of grubby soap as a memento of a submarine's visit? Much less petty had been the theft of twenty-one pounds from the pocket of a pair of trousers Leading Seaman Wedgebury had left lying in his mess. The knowledge that Wedgebury needed his arse kicking for leaving the money there did nothing to dispel the nasty taste left by the fact of the criminal action and the possibility that one of the crew was responsible only added to it. To make it all worse the press had somehow got hold of the story and started a collection on Wedgebury's behalf. That, by implication, pointed an accusing finger at the public and cast the Navy in the role of a teller of tales. Rendle didn't like it and knew that his captain would be furious when he heard about it on his return. How much simpler and more pleasant it would have been to have kept the whole thing private and reimbursed Wedgebury for his loss out of mess funds. He sighed, put the list away and settled down to read a book.

'Two defaulters for you, sir.' The coxswain peering at him through a gap in the wardroom curtains.

'Who are they, Cox'n?'

'Lowry and Barton, sir. Another of their fights.'

Rendle sighed again, followed the coxswain to the control room and stood looking thoughtfully at the results of the latest Barton-Lowry encounter. Lowry had a swollen lower lip and a lump on his forehead which was little enough by their standards. Barton was slightly more badly marked and his uniform torn, but it seemed not to have been one of their epic clashes.

'Is there a police charge connected with this, Cox'n?'

'No, sir,' Chief Petty Officer Ryland said.

'Any other form of official complaint?'

'No, sir.'

'Then what happened?'

'They just come back aboard like that, sir. Like they often does. So I put them in your report, sir.'

'Were they drunk?'

'Not particularly, sir. Leastways, I'm not chargin' them with that. Just disorderly conduct in a public place.' The coxswain paused before saying for the second time, 'Like they often does.'

'Very well,' the first lieutenant said. 'I'll hear the two cases together.'

He listened, straight-faced, to the tortured phraseology which Ryland considered appropriate to the gravity of a charge which ended with the words, 'Which occurrence occurred on the aforesaid date when the ship was on a mission of good-will for the purpose of showin' the Flag to the Dominion of Australia thereby creatin' a breach of the peace to the detriment of good order and naval discipline, sir!'

'Has either of you anything to say for himself?' Rendle asked.

Lowry and Barton looked at each other, then back at him. Neither spoke.

'I asked you a question,' Rendle said.

'Well, sir, we were in this bar…'

'Go on, Barton.'

'It's a bit embarrassin', sir.'

'Then embarrass me, Barton.'

'She took her knickers off, sir. Sort of shimmied them down her legs and give them to Bert here as a keepsake. I mean Lowry, sir. Brown they were, with white lace. That was after she'd kissed him.'

'I couldn't have that, sir,' Lowry broke in. 'She wouldn't have liked it.'

'Then why did she give them to you, Lowry?'

'Not *her*, sir. Mabel I mean. That's Mabel Carter. We've just got engaged to be married, sir.'

'But you can't go getting engaged abroad without the Captain's permission, Lowry,' Rendle said.

'She's not abroad, sir. She's in Fulham. We got engaged by post. But that was before she heard about it.'

Rendle breathed in slowly, carefully, before saying, 'Well, if you don't tell Miss Carter, I won't either. I expect it was just a friendly gesture from this other girl. Just a keepsake as Barton says.'

255

'No, not the *knickers*, sir, my "*gong*"! Mabel hadn't heard about my V.C. when we got engaged. Nor had I. That's what caused all the trouble!' There was agitation growing in Lowry's voice.

A hand to his head Rendle asked, 'Do you think we could get back to this bar you were in? I'm not entirely sure what it is we're talking about. Perhaps you would be good enough to clarify the situation, Barton.'

'Yes, sir. There were these four girls...' Barton must have heard his tremulous "Oh God", Rendle supposed, because there was a pause before he repeated firmly 'There were these four girls,' then went on, 'They wanted Lowry's autograph you see, on account of his picture bein' in all the papers, so he's signed three and they're pattin' and strokin' him when the gingery one gives him...'

'No, it was the taller of the two blondes, Fred.'

Barton appeared to consider this, then nodded. 'Lowry's right, sir. It was the taller blonde. She gives him a lipstick, pulls the neck of her blouse down and asks him to sign his name on – well, on one of those, sir. So he does and she kisses him like I was sayin' and takes her knickers off and starts to shove them down the front of Lowry's jumper and he's grinnin' and lookin' a bit daft, sir, so I says knock it off Bert, Mabel wouldn't like it and this blonde says to me Mabel isn't gettin' it, I am, and you keep out of this anyway and that's when I snatched the knickers, sir.'

'Barton's right, sir,' Lowry said. 'Mabel wouldn't have liked it.'

It was nearly too much for Rendle. Nails of one hand digging into the palm of the other behind his back, biting the inside of his cheek, he fought to control himself. Barton and Lowry shifted their feet uneasily at the resultant ferocity of his expression. When he could trust himself to speak, 'What happened then?'

'Well, I only done it to return them to her, sir,' Barton told him, 'so that Lowry wouldn't have them, but she says you give those back you bastard and catches me across this eye with her handbag. Then the other three decides to have a go and I'm getting duffed up somethin' rotten until Lowry yanks a couple off me and we run for it. Very embarrassin' it was, sir, like I told you.'

'Have you...' Rendle hesitated, swallowed, then spoke steadily. 'Have you any proof of this story?'

'Yes, sir,' Barton said and, like a conjurer, produced a small garment from somewhere about his person. It was made of chocolate-brown satin with white lace edging.

A faint neighing sound escaped from Rendle's nose. He turned away, walked quickly to the wardroom, sat down and rested his forehead on the table. His shoulders were shaking. 'Mabel isn't gettin' it. I am,' he whispered to himself and that made the shaking worse.

A minute later, 'Thought I might find you 'ere, sir. What do you want me to do with them?'

He looked up at the coxswain's grinning face. 'Tell them to go away and not to come near me for at least a year, Cox'n.'

'Aye aye, sir,' Ryland said. 'And there was me thinkin' I'd heard it all before.'

His sense of the absurd still tugging at his facial muscles Rendle returned to his book in a happier frame of mind.

*

Gascoigne returned briefly but regularly to *Talon*, listened to the duty officers' reports, dealt with defaulters, listened also to requests, granting or denying them as necessary, signed whatever needed to be signed and departed again. On one of those occasions he was shown a cheque for the sum of three hundred and eighty-six pounds, the proceeds of the newspaper appeal on behalf of Leading Seaman Wedgebury. He sent it back at once with a covering note asking that the money be donated to the League of Returned Servicemen. On another day he found a letter from the flotilla captain at Fremantle awaiting him. It informed him of and congratulated him on the award of a bar to his Distinguished Service Cross.

The honour made Gascoigne frown because he could not believe that he had done enough to deserve it. As though such a reaction had been anticipated the next paragraph of the letter explained that his second destroyer had been found to have sunk before reaching harbour and that his attack on the *Kongo*-class battleship, thwarted by the cessation of hostilities, had been highly regarded.

The last paragraph told him that Peter Harding was dead.

So visibly shocked was he that Rendle gestured to the other officers to leave the wardroom, followed them and stood outside to fend off callers. It was the sound of his quiet voice turning somebody away that brought Gascoigne back to himself.

'Is that you out there, Number One?'

'Yes, sir.'

'Kind of you, but do come in. Did I go all pale and wan like a Victorian heroine?'

'White as a sheet, sir. Bad news?'

'Yes. Peter Harding, my captain in *Trigger*.'

'Bought it, sir?'

'Yes. He transferred to the Fleet Air Arm some time ago and it says here he was shot down south of Kyushu just before the end of the war. I was rather fond of him. Or, to put it another way, if you believe in best friends that's what he was.'

Rendle nodded but didn't say anything and after a pause Gascoigne went on, 'A quiet, shy, unassuming chap who pulled off a whole string of successes and always looked embarrassed about them. I came to believe that he was indestructible. Silly. Still I wish he could have lasted just those few more…' The sentence trailed into silence.

'Yes,' Rendle said.

Gascoigne nodded in his turn, went to his cabin and wrote to Gail Harding. He did it three times, destroying each effort before abandoning the task and leaving the ship. Working his way patiently from autograph to autograph through the ever-present crowd on the jetty which seemed never to get any smaller provided the distraction he needed to recover his equilibrium. Why he had lost it was a question he flinched away from because he knew that the answer did not lie entirely in sorrow. Later he wondered if he would have spoken of Gail to Candice Fraser that night had he not received the news of Harding's death.

They were in his room at another country hotel, she seated at the dressing table, wearing nothing but his pyjama trousers with the legs rolled up, brushing her hair, he lying on the bed, watching her reflection in the looking-glass.

'John.'

Except in front of others she had never called him by his name, but he was not surprised at her use of it now. She had been moodily unresponsive to his talk during the drive and it had taken no insight on his part to realise that something was amiss between them. For the past forty-eight hours he had nurtured his own worry born of her apparent indifference to the march of days towards the one on which *Talon* had to begin the voyage back to Fremantle. Such lack of concern fitted ill with her open pleasure at his company both in bed and out and with overweening disregard for his own proclivities he had begun to suspect her of being in the habit of taking temporary bed-mates. Justified or not, the suspicion gnawed at him.

Levelly, 'Yes, Candy?'

'You really must stop gazing into my eyes everywhere we go in public. It makes me extremely uncomfortable.'

'You're very difficult not to look at.'

'Then for God's sake look at my breasts or my legs like everybody else! Eyes are private!'

The cynicism of the words and the reflection of her angry gaze locked on his in the mirror shook him much more sharply than his own unvoiced fears had done and it was seconds before he could reply, 'I'd begun to hope that your eyes weren't private to me.'

She turned then to look directly at him, the hair-brush forgotten in her hand.

'Had you?' she asked. 'Why?'

'Because,' he said, 'although I wanted you from the first moment I saw you it took me longer to know what else had happened to me. I've only ever been in love once before and that was at long range. It took me a little while to recognise the condition for what it is.'

There was no more anger in her eyes and her voice was a ludicrous caricature of an Australian accent when she replied, 'Holy cow! Just when did you see the light, cobber?'

'Some days ago.'

'Well thanks for telling a girl! I'd come close to giving you the old heave-ho by tonight!'

'Sorry, Candy darling. It seemed trite to say "I love you" when I so obviously did. People are always saying it whether it's true or not, but I do love you and I want to ask you if you'll...'

259

Her voice was her own again when she stopped him by saying, 'Down, boy, down. Let's take things one step at a time.'

It was almost an hour later when she whispered something he didn't hear. 'What?' he asked.

'Who was your long-range lover and how long-range was she?'

'My – Oh, I see. Not all *that* long-range. She actually kissed me on the cheek once.'

'Sex-crazed bitch,' Candice said. 'Tell me about her.'

Gascoigne laughed softly and talked for a little about Gail Harding, then fell silent when the slow breathing of the girl at his side told him she was asleep.

*

Only one visit did Gascoigne make without her and that was to an experimental artillery range to which she was not permitted access. It was nearly two hundred miles away and when less than half the return journey had been completed the car broke down. He and the driver covered twenty miles on foot before they came to a house and it was half past four in the morning when he let himself into his hotel room. Candice frowned up at him from the bed.

'Okay, own up. Who is she?'

'I telephoned...'

Physical tiredness and the long period of fretting at the wasted hours away from her blocked further speech and did things to his face which brought her to her feet in one sinuous movement. Then they were kneeling on the floor with his head on her shoulder. How they got there he didn't know.

'Don't. Ah, don't,' she said. 'It's all right, Pommy darling. It's all right. I'm here and we've got the whole day free.'

He raised his head and looked at her questioningly, saw her nod and listened to her saying. 'It's true. There's measles at the two schools you were to visit and they've sent the kids home, so I'm going to take you on a mystery tour. Would you like that?'

'I'd like anything you suggest as soon as I've had a bit of sleep. It's been nearly twenty-four hours.'

'You can do that in the car. It's a long tour.'

They drank coffee from a thermos and ate fruit she had provided before she went to her own room to dress. Gascoigne bathed, shaved, left a message for their driver at the desk and walked out of the hotel.

The illuminated sign above the entrance and the first light of early morning had combined to bathe Candice Fraser in soft radiance. She was dressed in a white coat and skirt, a brown shirt and shoes to match it, leaning back against the door of the car in the attitude of unconscious arrogance which accompanied her unguarded moments. He had never seen her looking so breathtakingly lovely.

The overworked description did not so much spring to his mind as force itself physically on him when his breathing became shallow and speeded its tempo. That and fatigue produced a sensation of dizziness and he paused, watching tawny hair sway to the urging of the breeze. A lock disengaged itself, falling across her face, and the flick of her head which tossed it aside brought him within her field of vision. She smiled and he resumed his interrupted progress towards her.

*

'Wake up, Commander Gascoigne.'

That the car had stopped was his first awareness, but he was uncertain about what car and where he was. Then he opened his eyes and the world flooded in on him. She was half turned, laughing at him over the back of the driver's seat, the sunlight making a burnished bronze helmet of her hair.

'Hello,' he said.

'Hello to you.'

'What time is it?' He was too filled with languor to look at his watch.

'About twenty past ten.'

'Good God!' As quickly as his cramped limbs would allow he levered himself upright on the back seat of the Packard. 'You've been driving for five hours. I'm awfully sorry.'

'Don't be. We're used to it in this country. It's big,' she said, rummaged in her handbag and handed him a comb. 'You'd better tidy up. We're nearly there.'

He combed his hair, climbed stiffly from the back of the car and joined her in the front. It was a mystery tour she had said so he didn't ask where "there" was.

For a mile they drove through undulating grazing country before branching on to a narrow country lane and dipping down into a wooded valley. Gascoigne thought the trees were probably eucalyptus, but didn't know for certain and as he was too content to be curious he didn't ask about that either. Water exploded briefly as they crossed a tiny unbridged stream, then they turned left to follow a tarmac drive and climbed twisting up through the wood.

At the crest they broke into sunlight again and the rolling countryside spread out below marched away into the distance towards a range of blue hills on the horizon. There seemed to be sheep everywhere.

Directly ahead and slightly below eye-level a rambling two-storey house lay in a sprawl of out-buildings. The car rolled into a deserted yard beside it, but before it had stopped the yard was full of dogs. They milled around, barking, yelping, whimpering and scrabbling at the paintwork. Gascoigne guessed that there were thirty of them, but was later told there were only sixteen.

'Stay where you are,' Candice said.

'Or get torn limb from limb?'

She shook her head. 'Or drown in lick.'

From behind them a man shouted, 'Stow it, you stupid mutts and siddown!' The Australian accent was very strong, the voice commanding, and dogs sat, wriggling their rumps in frustration.

Candice got out of the car and said, 'Hello, Daddy darling.'

The dogs inched forward on their bottoms, tongues lolling, staring at her, then towards the male voice and quickly back to her again. Gascoigne sat motionless, waiting for the scarlet to drain from his face.

'I should have guessed. I bloody well should have guessed,' he whispered to himself. He heard the man say, 'Christ, you look sexy, Candy girl!' and her reply, 'I know, Daddy. Isn't it awful.' Then he opened the door and got out.

Fraser was a big man. Nearly as tall as Gascoigne and thicker through the chest. He was grey-headed, brick complexioned and the massive forearms which held Candice in a bear hug sprouted red hairs angrily. She disengaged herself, looked over her shoulder and said, 'This is Lieutenant-Commander John Gascoigne, Daddy.'

Fraser's gaze, when he turned it on Gascoigne, was almost theatrically expressionless and level and continued to be so for several seconds. After that he seemed to make up his mind about something and stretched out a hand.

'Commander Gascoigne. Nice to have you aboard.'

'It's nice to be aboard, sir.'

'Is it?' Fraser asked, turned to his daughter and said, 'Candy girl, you're a little bitch.' There was affection in the words, but a trace of anger too.

She pouted at him. 'Yes, Daddy. But why now particularly?'

'You never told him you were bringing him here.'

For the first time since he had known her Gascoigne heard a defensive tone in Candice's voice when she said, 'That's perfectly true. How did you know?'

'Jesus, girl, I'm not stupid. When a bloke says it's nice to be here with a look on his face like he's prepared to fight me to the death at the drop of a koala bear I'm inclined to suspect that something's wrong.'

'John.' Husky voice small, amber eyes huge, staring into his.

'Yes, Candy?'

'I'm desperately sorry. I...' She hesitated, breathed in slowly and went on, 'It was wicked of me. I was afraid, if I told you, that you wouldn't come and – and the two people here are the only ones in the whole world I can – Oh God.'

Fraser said, 'I think she's trying to say "show you off to".'

'Share you with,' Candice corrected him and Fraser nodded in acceptance.

Gascoigne looked from daughter to father, down at the dogs, then back at Fraser. When he spoke it was slowly, spacing his words.

'Sir, I thought Candy had done me every possible honour, but she did me another when she brought me here.'

'Stilted,' Fraser said. 'Bloody stilted. Takes a Pom to say things like that. Never mind, I like it. The name's Duncan Fraser. Forget the "sir". Come and meet the missus. She's hiding round the back somewhere.'

He turned away and strode towards the corner of the house, a snap of his fingers galvanising the dogs into action. Some tumbled and leapt around

263

him, some around Candice. One or two sniffed at Gascoigne's trouser legs before bounding off to join the others. Her face solemn, Candice walked to Gascoigne, rested her forehead on his chest for a moment then, hand in hand, they followed her father.

Mrs Fraser was about fifty and very lovely to look at. Her being so caused Gascoigne no surprise, but being confronted by an older version of Candice served only to heighten a shyness which, until this day, he could not recall being possessed of. Her smile, gentler, wiser than her daughter's, he found particularly disquieting. It offered an understanding he didn't want, or wasn't ready for, because it spoke of things he had thought to be known only to him. As he was introduced to her he found to his dismay that he was blushing again for the second time in five minutes, blushing for only the second time in his life.

'It was good of you to spare the time from your busy schedule to come and see us, Commander,' she said.

Wanting neither to take refuge behind a false shield, nor himself betray a secret, Gascoigne floundered.

'Actually, it was Candy who…' He stopped there, trying to think his way around a direct lie.

'Kidnapped you,' Mrs Fraser finished for him. 'Like mother, like daughter. I carried Duncan home in my teeth all unsuspecting too. Come and help me with the coffee, Candice.'

Gascoigne's cheeks were still burning as he watched the two women walk together towards the house and listened to Fraser saying, 'Pay no attention to either of those two beauts. If you do you're done for.'

'I'm already done for,' Gascoigne said.

'Yeah, I know.'

'Then you must be psychic.' Gascoigne heard the irritation in his own voice regretted it, but let the statement stand, his gaze fixed on the ground in front of him.

'Psychic? Too right, cobber. The power has always worked strongly in us Celts, although I'd better admit that Candy talking to us on the phone every day since you met and the expression on your mug when you look at her helped a little. Then don't forget I've known her all her life and that

I'm married to her mother.' Fraser pulled absently at the ear of one of the dogs before adding, 'So, before you start in on the *mea culpa* chorus my crystal ball tells me is coming up next, I'll make you free of my opinion that no mortal man stands a chance if one of them two puts the sign on him.'

Irritation had turned to strain and Fraser heard it when Gascoigne said, 'I might be able to handle these unusual and unexpected circumstances a little better if you'd stop being so damned nice. Somewhere during the past week I lost my identity. No, not somewhere. I know exactly where and I ought to be shot for it.' He jerked his face towards Fraser. 'It can happen, you know. Losing your identity I mean.'

'Of course it can bloody happen,' the older man told him. 'It's part of falling in love. You lose part of you and gain a lot more. Christ! I thought you Poms were educated, but you don't even know that. You don't even seem to know that *mea culpa* is Latin for an admission of guilt. Culpability, if you like. I tried to steer you round that one, but there you go heading straight for the sheep-dip.'

Gascoigne didn't speak and Fraser went on, 'Listen, John. I don't give a fart about guilt, but I'd be very concerned for Candy if I thought you were experiencing regret.'

'Regret?' Gascoigne said in a wondering voice. 'Regret? How can you regret the most incredibly wonderful thing that ever happened to you? It's been… It's been ridiculous. Absurd. Things just don't… but they did. I mean… so corny… string of clichés come true. She's so very… so very everything. I…'

He was aware of Fraser raising a hand then and realised later that it had been a signal because the women came out of the house. It was their similarity, he told himself, that made it necessary for him to blink rapidly before he could distinguish which of them it was carrying the tray.

'Coffee or beer, Commander?'

'Coffee please, Mrs Fraser.' It was some obscure point of pride. He wanted something stronger than coffee.

'Ah, give him a beer, love,' Fraser said. 'He's been in shock since I explained why the Poms will never beat us at cricket.'

*

The horses made soft equine noises just audible from the copse where they were tethered above the ten-foot rock face. A wood fire crackled lethargically, adding its heat to the spring sunshine to make a summer day. The remains of lunch lay on the grass and in the distance sheep were scattered like so much windblown paper.

'What was all that nonsense about wanting a three-legged horse?'

'I thought a missing leg might slow it down a bit.'

'But you don't ride badly at all.'

'You tell that to an American friend of mine called Dwight Meynell. He tried to teach me, but said I was so godawful that if I *had* to get on a horse the safest thing I could do was cheat and hold on to its mane. That's what I did today. He also stipulated a maximum speed of 3 mph, but my beast was under some compulsion to keep up with yours and its got defective brakes.'

Her smile no more than an indication that she had heard his words Candice gathered fragments of food and wrapping paper into a cardboard box and put it on the fire.

'You've made quite a hit with my parents. They like you.'

'I like them. Who wouldn't?'

'Make love to me, Pommy darling.'

*

Gascoigne went to call the ship to satisfy himself that all was well, found the telephone at the end of the hall where Fraser had said it was, then remembered that the number was on a card in a pocket of his uniform, not in the riding clothes he had been lent. Turning, he walked back along the hallway towards the staircase and Fraser's dressing room where he had changed. His feet made no sound on the carpeted floor and the drawing-room door was ajar.

'He's knocked for six, Candy.'

'Yes, I know he is.'

'You too, girl?'

'Oh heavens yes, Daddy. Right over the pavilion.'

'Well, what happens now? Has he asked you to marry him?'

'He started to the night before last. I stopped him.'

'Why, Candy girl? Because he's married?'

'No. I'd rationalised his wife out of existence before I allowed the affair to start, but I didn't want him proposing on a wave of emotion. He never has loved her and that helps me, although I would have fought her for him anyway, but a bit later I discovered that there is someone he does love, or is infatuated with. I'm not sure which.'

'And you're not prepared to fight her? That doesn't sound like you, Candy.'

A pause, then, 'I've never been a good loser, Daddy, but I may pluck up the courage to have a go. There's still a little time yet for me to decide in. She's every man's dream to look at, recently widowed, and has one of those top titles she carries with her regardless of whom she marries.'

'And he told you all this?' Incredulity in Fraser's voice.

'Good Lord no, Daddy. He just mentioned being rather taken with a girl called Gail Harding. I'm not surprised. Take a look in almost any one of those glossy magazines Mummy has sent out from England and you'll see what I'm up against. I've known of her for ages.'

As Gascoigne began to tiptoe up the stairs Candice's voice followed him. 'Yesterday the local papers carried an announcement of her husband's death. He was quite famous in the Mediterranean war. When John hears about that…'

He found the card with the telephone number on it and went back to the hall. Everything was in order aboard *Talon*.

*

'John, would you mind climbing back into that uniform of yours? The station hands are coming in in half an hour to carry out their monthly wrecking operation on my beer stocks. Like to have you all prettied up for them as it may be their only chance of seeing a real live submarine captain.' Then as though Gascoigne might object, Fraser went on, 'You'll have to have a shower anyway. You're exuding a strange mixed aroma of Candice's perfume and horse sweat.'

Candice looked demure and Mrs Fraser said, 'Don't be coarse, Duncan.'

Gascoigne was beyond blushing now. He smiled, nodded and walked towards the door.

267

Mrs Fraser called after him, 'John, I've moved your things into your room. Left at the top of the stairs, second door on the right.'

It was a big airy room with two long windows looking out across unbroken country. His uniform, brushed and pressed, hung over the back of a chair, his shoes, newly polished, stood beside it. The covers of the large bed had been neatly turned down. A pair of pyjamas lay on one pillow, a wisp of pale blue nightdress on the other. Gascoigne lowered himself slowly on to a window seat and put his head between his hands.

The day, the place, had become a love trap with each of his three jailers conspiring in their different ways to make escape harder for him. He didn't want to escape and was only too frightened that he would be ejected from the trap by the youngest warder because he did not know how to allay fears she had expressed in a conversation he was not supposed to have heard.

*

Dinner by candle light. Mrs Fraser at one end of the table, quiet and a little withdrawn, hiding her anxiety, gently charming. Colonel Fraser at the other, talking about cricket and the sheep station. Candice opposite Gascoigne, not looking at him much, but resting a leg against his. He felt as though he had known them all for years.

'Let's have some port. Haven't had any for months.'

'Not now, Duncan dear. Let them go. They have to leave at four in the morning.'

Candice sitting for almost half a minute staring at her fruit plate, saying nothing as though she had not heard her mother's words, or had lost interest in her surroundings. Only Gascoigne not aware that she was trying not to cry. Candice standing and, one after the other, holding her parent's heads against her, then stretching out a hand towards him.

Gascoigne, watching her undress, wondering how she could possibly have read so much into the little he had said about Gail Harding, trying to remember what he *had* said. Wondering too what he could do about it and thinking how strange women were, then forgetting about it all in her arms.

Chapter Twenty-Two

'Let go both springs,' Gascoigne said and heard the clatter and scrape as the two steel-wire ropes dropped from the jetty to the ballast tanks and were drawn aboard.

There were a few familiar faces in the crowd now. Mr Strang, the harbour master, and his secretary Flo. The senior policeman who had come onto the casing when they had first arrived and other police who had controlled the crowds for more than a week. The man in the Homburg hat from the Lord Mayor's office was there too and so were the people from the newspapers and the driver who had called him "Skip". But there were no Frasers, no Candice. Gascoigne didn't mind. She had promised to be in Perth not later than four days after *Talon* reached Fremantle.

'Let go aft. Slow ahead port. Half astern starboard. Starboard twenty. Let go for'ard.'

Water boiling under the stern as it swung away from the quay, the Air Force band which had led them through the city playing "Waltzing Matilda" now. The crowd beginning to wave, to cheer. 'Thank you for my lovely time, Pommy darling,' she had said and he had wanted to cry, nearly had cried. *Her* lovely time? He would never forget Australia or Australians and they were welcome to win at cricket.

'Midships. Stop port. Half astern port. Port twenty.'

'Twenty degrees of port wheel on, sir.' Ryland's voice from down below. *Talon* gathering speed astern, curving in a great arc to point her bow seawards.

'Stop starboard. In starboard engine clutch. Stop port. In port engine clutch. Half ahead together.'

The rumble of the diesels blending with the roar of the crowd, the crowd-noise beginning to fade with distance.

'Good-bye, you lot, and thank you,' Gascoigne said, but he said it very quietly, addressing not only the Frasers, but a lot of people and, amongst them, a dead lieutenant called Blakie to whom he owed his life.

*

Talon rising and falling monotonously over long pewter-coloured swells like the armoured cuirasses of giants breathing in their sleep. No sign at all of the vast continent to the north, no sign of anything much except heaving water, gulls and his own ship ploughing steadily west across the Great Australian Bight.

'What's the name of that three thousand foot peak in the Stirling Range near Albany, Pilot?'

'Something Bluff, sir. Um, no. Here it is. Bluff Knoll, sir.'

'All right. Have them warm up the radar and see if they can pick it out.'

Strange to be able to use radar without first calculating the odds, not having to worry about detection. Strange to have only two look-outs on the bridge. Strange to have no war to fight. There had been war for all of Gascoigne's adult life. It had been over for some weeks, the war, but he hadn't had much time to think about it. Now he had time and found his thoughts were filled with uncertainty. He only knew war. Peace was an unknown quantity and he didn't like unknown quantities. An era had ended.

*

The quay at Fremantle looking strangely deserted with no American depot ship there, no American submarines. Gascoigne pictured them arrowing back across the Pacific like hornets toward their nest, their terrible vengeance for Pearl Harbour exacted in such fullness that Japan had ceased to exist as a maritime power before ever those weird bombs had gone off over Hiroshima and Nagasaki. Where had Dwight Meynell said they had come from? San Diego, was it? He hoped he would see Meynell again some day.

The berthing operation quite simple, despite the fast-flowing Swan River. Just a matter of securing alongside another submarine, not having to cut across the bows of a whole bank of them as had happened before.

'Take over please, Number One. I'm going inboard to report to Captain Submarines.'

Aye aye, sir.'

*

Holding a glass of gin and water in the flotilla captain's big day-cabin.

'Yes, pretty successful, sir. I think we made quite a good impression and about twenty-four thousand people walked through the boat. Had a few bits and pieces stolen by souvenir hunters, but nothing of any consequence.'

'What sort of things?' the flotilla captain asked.

'A couple of wheel-spanners, a bayonet and a blanket, would you believe? Whoever took it must have wrapped it round himself under a coat. Some joker tried to nick the sights off the 4-inch gun, but he was nabbed before he could get them unscrewed.'

'You didn't press any charges, I hope.'

'Oh Lord no, sir. It *was* a good-will visit.'

'You were luckier than *Tiger-shark*. She had her steering-wheel pinched. Heaven knows how that was managed. Still, never mind about that now. How soon can you be ready for sea?'

Cold fingers clutching at the wall of Gascoigne's stomach, kneading it. Oh, Candy! Not for at least five days, please God!

Very calmly, 'As soon as we've fuelled and provisioned, sir,' he said.

'Ah. So *Talon* has no major defects. That's excellent. The whole flotilla is moving up to Hong Kong. The Japs smashed everything there before they left, so you chaps will be pumping amps into the dockyard's electrical system until the mess is sorted out. You are floating power-houses after all and there's no other type of vessel as well equipped for the job.'

'Quite, sir. When do we sail?'

'A week from today,' the flotilla captain told him.

The coldness receding from his stomach, but sweat pouring down from his

271

arm-pits as though relief had opened two tiny taps. Seven days and she was arriving in four. That should be enough time to get everything settled with her.

It was to be more than enough.

*

On the night of her arrival Gascoigne took Candice to dinner in a small, little-frequented restaurant in Perth. They had finished eating and were getting ready to leave when Stella Forbes said, 'So that's why you never came back to my bed, lover. Can't say that I blame you. Still, any time you get tired of her, give us a ring.'

Very tall, hips thrust forward challengingly, just as he had first seen her. She grinned and stalked away towards another table, towing a naval officer he didn't know in her wake.

'Well, that does rather simplify things,' Candice said, eyes downcast, smiling faintly.

'What do you mean, Candy?' He had a terrible feeling that he knew exactly what she meant.

Tawny eyes raising slowly to meet his.

'I was prepared to fight your wife for you, John. I had even nerved myself to do battle with the lovely Lady Abigail, but not every girl in every port. Not girls like that.' Voice familiarly husky, but toneless now. A sideways jerk of her head in the direction of the adjacent table.

Urgently, 'I don't understand! There's nothing between Gail and me!'

The ghost of a smile still about her mouth Candice said, 'You may really believe that here, at this moment, but there was a fascinated awe in your voice when you spoke of her. Not a very good omen for me, particularly now her husband's dead. Then, as I remember, you did crumble awfully easily when I made my play for you.'

The appalling injustice of her final sentence seemed to deprive Gascoigne of air. It was a moment before he could speak and when he did so it was through clenched teeth.

'Would you have thought more highly of me if I had thrown you into that river?'

'I'm sorry,' she told him. 'That last bit was silly and cruel, but had a certain logic. Think about it.'

She stood up, gathering her coat and handbag with a controlled sweep of one hand as though she had practised her exit, then stooped and kissed him on the forehead before adding, 'On the other hand, don't think about it. Be happy, Pommy darling.'

The pain was to come quickly enough but, as though anaesthetised by shock, his consciousness registered only the fading warmth of her lips above his left eyebrow and the sight of her walking out of the restaurant.

*

Gascoigne stood in his cabin, reading the last letter he would receive until the flotilla reached Hong Kong. Messrs Mather, Bletchley & Crouch – Solicitors – informed him that on the instructions of their client they were instituting divorce proceedings against him on the grounds of his adultery with a Mrs Stella Forbes of Perth, Western Australia. It took them a page and a half of close type to say as much and to assure him that they were in possession of attested evidence of his prolonged association with the co-respondent.

Bitterness so strong that he could taste it flooded through him. The bitterness was neither against his wife, nor against Cavanagh who, he knew, had laid the information against him, for the former's action suited him very well and he was not interested in his ex-first lieutenant's spiteful revenge. It was against a fate which had put a vital card into his hand when the game was already over. If only he could have told Candice that his wife was…

'Captain, sir?'

'Come in, Number One.'

'*Tiger-shark*'s under way, sir, and *Tornado* is just about to leave. Our turn next, sir.'

'Thank you,' Gascoigne said. 'I'll come up at once.'

*

The tall, ungraceful grey bulk of the depot ship moving endlessly to the west of north across the Indian Ocean, the pale green shark-shapes of eight submarines trailing her in arrowhead formation. Ahead Java and memories he welcomed. A thousand miles astern, Perth and an anguish which distance had done nothing to lessen.

Both by day and night Gascoigne spent long hours on the bridge, often sending the officer of the watch below because he wanted something to do and didn't want to be talked to while he was doing it. More and more he found that he didn't want to be talked to at all. Only one subject could have provided him with temporary relief and that subject could never be broached. He took to eating most of his meals in his cabin.

From Europe the news was not good. The Russians were becoming increasingly intractable, even belligerent in their attitude towards their war-time allies and he found gloomy satisfaction in the thought that he might soon be fighting them. It would, he knew, take all the might of the Anglo-American armies to drive the Russians back where they belonged, but total victory at sea would be a foregone conclusion, with no American help necessary. A few units of the Home Fleet alone could smash a Navy which had been ineffectual to a degree throughout the war and little more than a token force since the Japanese Admiral Togo had destroyed its predecessor at the battle of Tsushima in 1905. Gascoigne badly wanted *Talon* to be one of those units.

Once, before the Java Sea was reached, he was given the chance to demonstrate his readiness for such a combat. Each night, on orders from the flotilla captain, submarines were detached from the formation to carry out practice attacks on the depot ship. Most were content with a fast surface approach under cover of darkness firing a flare to indicate the launching of torpedoes, the whole exercise over in thirty minutes. As the most junior commander Gascoigne was given his opportunity last and he made a meal of it.

All that night *Talon* ran parallel to the group, tracking it, plotting its course and speed by radar, evading imaginary destroyers and other non-existent escorts, then forging ahead to dive close to its projected track at dawn. It was good to grip the periscope handles again, to provide the information and give the orders which would theoretically send six torpedoes lancing towards their target, to play the deadly game he had been trained for and played well, the only game he thoroughly understood. Gascoigne was almost happy during those hours and would have been more so had the situation been real. But when he ordered *Talon* brought to the surface and sent his estimate of the depot ship's course and speed by lamp signal, the reply "Very good attack – five hits" gave him no satisfaction. The endless black tunnel of reality had already replaced the solace of make-believe.

In the Sunda Strait he looked without interest at the low-lying shape of the island of Krakatoa. Once it had been a mountain until, some sixty years before, a gigantic volcanic explosion had blown it to pieces, altered the configuration of the whole Strait and, so somebody said, the shock-wave had travelled twice round the globe. It could have split it in two for all Gascoigne cared and he wished that he was looking at the awesome beauty of Mount Agung and Mount Rinjani, standing guard over the Lombok Strait far to the east, at the start of a war patrol.

The wish stayed with him all across the South China Sea, an area he had never penetrated before and the battle-zone he had so envied the Americans, then was temporarily forgotten in the strangeness of Hong Kong.

Talon never did provide power to the badly damaged dockyard. Within hours of his arrival Gascoigne was sent for by the flotilla captain.

'You're a lucky chap, John. You've only been out East for half a dog-watch, but your crew has been abroad longer than any other, so you're off home. The signal arrived a few minutes ago.'

Gascoigne agreed that he was a lucky chap and set sail for England two days later. It was a better place to fight Russians from than Hong Kong.

Chapter Twenty-Three

The bout of trembling was the worst that Harding could ever remember, worse even than the spasms which had shaken him after he had destroyed the Sicily convoy. He decided that he had no choice but to hand over command of *Trigger* to Gascoigne. Thank God for Gascoigne who understood about his nerves and was so quietly efficient. It would have been intolerable to have had to surrender his authority to anyone else. 'Tell the First Lieutenant I want to see him at once,' he said to one of the men standing just outside the door of his cabin, but the bushes screening the mouth of the small cave neither answered him nor moved to do his bidding. 'You there!' he shouted. 'Didn't you hear what I said?' Again there was no reply and Harding was almost thankful for that because he couldn't recall what he *had* said, couldn't recall anything much at all with the sudden assault of biting cold making the shakes uncontrollable and sending his teeth into a frenzy of chattering.

Parachute, some part of his mind prodded. Wrap yourself in that. He groped for it until some other part of his mind reminded him that he had buried it, buried his flying coverall too, as soon as he had dragged himself out of the sea and across the little beach to the trees all those days ago. Or was it weeks now? It wasn't important, but it worried him that he had buried the coverall. Harrison K. Harrison Jr had told him that he should wear it, but he wasn't sure why, or who Harrison K. Harrison Jr was and, anyway, flying gear had no relevance at all to whatever it was that he had decided he must do about *Trigger*.

The cold slid away from him then, retreating before a tide of growing warmth. Darling, beautiful Gail. Warmth still increasing, becoming uncomfortable, unbearable. Not Gail and, Christ, the plane's bloody canopy was jammed! Flames enveloping it, penetrating. Harding screamed.

A hundred yards through the trees, 'What was that?' a Japanese soldier said. 'Sounded like cats mating,' another replied.

The first grunted and the group of men loped on their way. They had been gone for two and a half days when Harding regained consciousness.

The fever had left him terribly weak and with griping pains in his stomach, but his brain had cleared and the pulsing agony in the side of his head and neck had eased to a nagging ache with a sharp, stinging sensation when he touched the tender skin. It was the feel of skin that told him that the huge scabs had fallen from him. There was no sign of them near where he had been lying and he guessed that insects had broken them up and carried them away. That reminded him of the necessity to eat. First he drank from the muddy pool near the cave wondering without much interest if that would bring the fever back, then he began to hunt for grubs, pushing them into his mouth like a monkey eating its own fleas. Later in the day he killed a small snake with a rock and ate it raw, promising himself a rabbit or a cat when he was strong enough to snare one.

Harding wasn't particularly worried about his situation. The threats to his life from starvation, exhaustion, exposure, a recurrence of fever or a new infection of his burns were so manifest without even taking into account what the Japanese would do to him if he allowed himself to fall into their hands that he didn't know which to worry about first. That lack of knowledge and an ever increasing lassitude blunted the cutting edge of anxiety. For no very good reason he spent a lot of time trying to remember how he had got out of the burning Seafire, but without success. Finally, he assumed, and assumed correctly, that he had been blown clear when the plane exploded and that he had pulled the rip-cord of his parachute automatically. His second correct assumption was that his long immersion in sea-water had probably saved him from dying of blood-poisoning set up by his burns. Those points settled he went back to hunting for grubs.

The onset of autumn and the cooler weather it brought nudged him into more positive action. He had read something of the severity of Japanese winters and, although he didn't know if that applied to the whole country or only to the northern end, it was obvious that he would need clothes to supplement those he had stolen from the rock they had been spread out to dry on near some village when he had first come ashore at whatever this place was.

The expedition was both unsuccessful and very nearly fatal with armed Japanese, almost as ragged as he was, passing within five yards of the tall grasses in which he was lying at the village's edge. After that Harding restricted his movements to the immediate vicinity of his cave. Food was scarce there and death from malnutrition and exposure pressed ever closer to him.

Eventually the soldiers found him and he lurched staggeringly towards the arc of advancing rifles, dragging the branch of a tree, he meant to use as a club, but no longer had the strength to lift from the ground. When they took his stick away he cursed them savagely and flailed about him with the tears of impotence running down his cheeks. When one of them picked him up, cradling him in his arms, Harding was conscious only of astonishment at the man's gentleness.

Chapter Twenty-Four

The extent to which peace had broken out was brought home to Gascoigne when he walked out of a room in Chatham Barracks in England. The room had housed the officers of a Board of Inquiry and the Board had found him guilty of inadequate security precautions resulting in the loss of a bayonet, two wheel-spanners and a blanket from the ship under his command. He had been told by the senior officer of the Board that he would not be required to pay for the lost items but that a report of negligence would be entered in his record.

Gascoigne did not know whether to laugh or cry over the pathetic stratagems employed to give the impression of efficiency and industry when the Navy, far too large a Navy now, had no war to fight. During hostilities if you lost a ship they gave you another. In time of peace, he had now discovered, if you lost a spanner they gave you a Board of Inquiry so that the members of the Board had something to do.

He walked slowly out of the barracks towards the dockyard thinking about the long passage home when he had had so little to occupy him. During the long days which separated Colombo from Hong Kong, Port Said from Colombo and Gibraltar from Port Said he had achieved a deep tan. In a week of battling north through an Atlantic gale he had lost it again. Not a great achievement for so many thousands of miles covered, but then his crew was efficient and Parrish probably a better navigator than himself. Gascoigne had felt like a passenger.

At the edge of a drydock he stood looking down at the unrecognisable shape which was all that the yard's workmen had left of *Talon*, a gutted hulk of a ship reverberating, like the empty steel tube she was, to the incessant assault of pneumatic tools. Parts of the upperworks had gone and orange sparks cascaded where the blue-white oxy-acetylene burners cut into more of them. He stayed there for a long time watching what was going on, but without any particular interest, thinking that in her dilapidated state he and his command had much in common. When the cheap cynicism of the thought came home to him he snorted angrily and began to walk briskly up and down a twenty yard stretch between two cranes with his hands behind his back as though he were on a quarter-deck, trying to raise some enthusiasm for the new *Talon* which would be born from the shell of the old. The first-class radar he had always wanted and a *schnorkel*, the thing the Dutch had invented and the Germans had developed which would enable him to charge his batteries without surfacing. The Oerlikon would have to go to make way for the great steel breathing tube, of course, and that made him sad. They had served him well, Able Seaman Lowry VC and the twin-cannon he had handled so effectively. It didn't matter. Nothing mattered.

At five, when a whistle blew and the workmen left *Talon* in peace to go to their homes, he went aboard, stepping carefully over abandoned pressure hoses, electric leads and anonymous objects the purpose of which he had no idea, very much aware of the long drop on either side of him to the bottom of the dock. He went down the fore hatch ladder and made his way slowly aft, looking at the havoc revealed by the naked bulbs of the temporary lighting. The partitions between the living quarters had gone and with them the bunks and other furnishings. The deck was up in places, laying bare the gaping empti-ness of the battery tanks which had housed the 336 huge cells for so long. The control room was a barren waste, most of its maze of pipes, valves, leads, levers and dials spirited away. The periscopes and radar mast had vanished too.

He passed the radio room and galley, both innocent of any fittings and stopped at the water-tight bulkhead leading to the engine and motor rooms. The wreckers hadn't been at work in them yet and they looked much as they always had. Gascoigne tried to conjure up the roar of the big diesels, but they didn't respond. Instead, from the far end he seemed to hear a husky voice saying, 'Don't interrupt. Petty Officer Finchley is explaining to me about rheostats.'

Turning, he went quickly ashore, deeply depressed, glad only that the wardroom bar at the barracks would be open by the time he reached it, but before he got there a sudden impulse made him change direction towards the railway station.

Afterwards Gascoigne was never certain whether it was at that moment or later in the London train that he decided to call on Lady Abigail Harding. That he should have done so before he was well aware, but had continued to put it off for three reasons. The first two were his failure to write to her from Australia or anywhere else and the inevitable sadness of the meeting. The third, which he was forced to admit to himself, was that he was still frightened of his friend's beautiful widow, an emotion no other woman had ever induced in him. When he had pressed the bell button beside the door of the house off Sloane Street he did nothing for his courage by persuading himself that she was most unlikely to be at home, that he could leave a note saying that he had called, that he was so sorry.

'John! John Gascoigne! Oh, I'm so very glad to see you!'

Genuine pleasure in her voice. Nothing to fear in that, but the visual impact unnerving as ever, the star-burst of reawakened desire for the unobtainable doubly so. Black dress, black shoes, very sheer black stockings. Mourning, or a foil for her red hair? Rather festive, he thought, for mourning, the low neck-line, the delicate stockings and the shoes with their high heels.

His silence taken for embarrassment, 'Consider it said,' she told him. 'We both loved him in our different ways, Come in, my dear.'

Watching her begin to mix a drink, 'I was wondering if you'd have dinner with me, but it looks as if you're going somewhere,' he said. He had had no intention of asking her to dinner. The words just came out.

'Love to.' No hesitation, no arch consideration. 'Put whatever you like into these gins while I make a call.' The sound of dialling while he poured tonic into the glasses.

'Daddy, it's me. John Gascoigne has just walked in. He's been in the Far East. Can you get Maggy to do your hostessing for you tonight?' 'No, he would *not* like to come to dinner. He's been given another medal and wants to celebrate it with me.'

Dear God, did the girl ever miss anything? He'd only had the raincoat covering his uniform off for one minute, but she had noticed the silver rosette in the middle of the blue and white ribbon on his chest, a rosette which had not been there when last they'd met, and by noticing had completely switched the evening's point of emphasis, negating the reason for his visit.

'Daddy, you're a darling. 'Bye.'

'We'll go to the Savoy,' Gascoigne said.

'We'll do no such thing. Controlled prices or not you'd end up paying through the nose. We'll go to Soho.' She blinked and added, 'Oh dear, that was pretty bossy, wasn't it? Of course we'll go to the Savoy if you want to.'

They went to Soho, Gascoigne intensely uneasy.

When their food was in front of them, 'Tell Aunty,' she said.

He put his knife and fork down, 'Tell Aunty what?'

'Girl trouble, wife trouble, whatever it is.'

'Why should it be either of those things? Or anything at all?'

'*I* don't know why, but I'll bet it's one or the other. Or both. You keep shying away from me as though I were a faulty fuse which probably means you aren't too keen on women at the moment. Then there's your turning up out of the blue this evening when you've been back in England for weeks.'

'How do you know that?' he asked.

'There was a picture in the papers of *Talon* arriving at Chatham with you standing on the bridge.'

'I'm sorry, Gail. I should have come to see you before. About Peter I mean.'

'Yes, you should, shouldn't you? But I can guess why you didn't, so you're forgiven. Now tell me all about it.'

Neither sure that he wanted to be forgiven nor on what grounds his behaviour was being excused Gascoigne frowned and dropped his gaze to his plate, trying to gather together the thoughts the regard of her slanting green eyes had scattered. They had never failed to do that on the few occasions he had met her, something which created both excitement and resentment in him. So did the rest of her. She was too perfect and the new lines traced on her face by recent sorrow served only to make her more so.

'All right, John. I'll stop being inquisitive. What shall we talk about?'

Gascoigne looked up at her then, to find her watching him, elbows

282

propped on the table, chin resting on the backs of interlaced fingers. Still not realising that that was what he had come for in the first place he knew suddenly that he wanted to tell her, that for some reason it was important to tell her.

'Forgive me,' he said. 'It would be a relief to talk to you.'

For twenty minutes, while their food grew cold, he described what had happened in Australia, leaving out only the references to her, neither underlining nor attempting to disguise his emotions. For that reason he told his story well, ending it without embroidery with the words 'That's all.'

'Good for Candy,' Gail said and moved for the first time since the recital had started, sitting back in her chair, letting her hands drop to her lap.

Whatever Gascoigne had expected to hear it had not been that, not just that, and in a strained voice he asked, 'Is that all you've got to say?'

'What more do you want me to say, John? Do you really need telling what a bastard you've been? Do you need reminding that you had a wife? For goodness sake, I've heard all about *your* feelings, but have you given any thought to hers?'

Without waiting for a reply to any of her questions Gail went on, 'You should never have married her of course, but that's no sort of excuse. Why did you marry her? Was it because of me?'

Gascoigne didn't answer, but she nodded as though he had before saying, 'As for Candy, can't you imagine how soiled she felt, how completely shattered at such an ending to her lovely time?'

He knew that the blood had drained from his face because he had felt it doing it, leaving the skin cold and clammy. The sensation brought home to him how much he had hoped for his companion's good opinion and that in turn produced bewilderment at how he could have allowed himself so stupidly to throw it away. What, he wondered, had he really been seeking from her? Sympathy? Comfort? Perhaps even compensation in kind for his loss? No, at least not the last. He hadn't the nerve for that.

'Oh God,' he said. There was a tremor in his voice and he flinched at the touch of her fingers on his wrist, then listened to her saying, 'Don't get in a panic. I haven't walked out on you yet, but don't blame Candy for doing so. Surely you must be able to understand why she did.'

After a moment of silence, 'Yes,' he told her. 'Now I can.'

'Good, then let's go home and I'll make a sandwich. This stuff has congealed and they aren't allowed to serve us any more, because of the rationing. You sea-going people have probably forgotten that.'

There was nowhere he wanted to go less than back to the house off Sloane Street, nobody he would rather have been away from than Gail Harding. He kept assuring himself of those two facts while he paid the bill for their uneaten food and sat well back in his own corner of the taxi, but he did nothing about it. Trying to engender disdain for her because of her suggestion that he might panic, and for the threat implicit in her saying that she hadn't walked out on him yet, didn't work either.

Making the sandwiches she had promised, heating soup, Gail let the silence between them drag on for several minutes before saying, 'I don't understand you, John.'

'Tell me if you ever do,' he replied. 'I'd like to be the second to know.'

At that, she put down the knife she was using, turned to him and placed her hands on his shoulders. 'Ah no, my dear,' she said. 'Don't make smart alec remarks. Not to me. You used to be such a gentle, considerate chap. I knew that from Peter and saw it for myself. What changed you? Was it me again?'

For the second time Gascoigne didn't answer and for the second time Gail nodded. 'I seem to have a lot to answer for, don't I?'

'No,' he told her. 'It wasn't like that.' But he said it uncertainly, a little defensively, aware that he was admitting to change in himself, knowing that he wasn't being entirely truthful, wishing that he had the courage to say "I love you".

Suddenly she grinned at him, a friendly urchin grin, and asked, 'Why don't you tell me to mind my own damned business?'

It was easier after that. At what point his confused resentment gave way to a comfortable companionship Gascoigne was unaware, knowing only that it had done so. For the first time in months his self-pity loosened its strangle-hold to be replaced by an objective awareness of others and his surroundings. He did experience envy when she spoke of Peter, but he was envious because she did it with such pride, not from physical jealousy. It would, he thought, be very nice to be talked about that way by a woman. Under the spell of her gently charming voice it was a short step from there to the realisation of how likeable his beautiful hostess was, how pleasant to be with, only a little frightening and that because she looked as she looked and was who she was. Even the previously devastating pangs of physical desire for her became, without lessening, supportable.

It was after midnight when, afraid of destroying a newly found intimacy by making a fool of himself, Gascoigne got to his feet.

'I must get back to Chatham.' He knew that the last train had gone.

'The last train's gone,' she said.

'I'll manage.'

Rising too, she stood rather primly before him, feet together, hands clasped loosely in front of her.

'I've given you the basic routine, John,' she told him. 'What else do I have to do? Dance on the table in my underwear? I will if you insist, but it would be a bit of a come-down. I'm supposed to be irresistible, even in an old sack.' She smiled, but the movement of the facial muscles expressed only a wry humour and a little sadness, not invitation.

Gascoigne's heart began thumping heavily, heavily enough, it seemed to him, to be shaking his body. It wasn't a pleasant sensation for him because he had always disliked external forces which could affect his involuntary muscles over-strongly. Incongruously his thoughts flicked for an instant to the Japanese bomber in the Lombok Strait. That incident had alarmed him badly by happening after the war had ended, when he had subconsciously lowered his defences to the extent that he had been caught mentally as well as physically unawares. Having been welcomed happily, scolded fiercely, soothed like a spanked child and offered her body, all in rapid succession by a woman he idolised, but dared touch only in his imagination, his defences were in disarray again.

'I won't pretend I don't understand what you are saying, Gail,' he told her, 'but I can't believe you're saying it.'

The small smile came again, still wry, still sad. 'Oh, I'm saying it all right. When I knew you were back in England I very nearly came to you and said it then, but I couldn't quite do it. Funny that. A brazen hussy like me developing scruples. Then you come here tonight and tell me that your wife is divorcing you and all the rest of it and I – Look, if we keep standing here like this I think I shall probably start to cry which would be very boring. I shall probably start to cry anyway, but you might as well sit down while I'm doing it.'

They sat down facing each other, ten feet apart.

'You're not in love with me, are you, Gail?' It was more statement than question.

'That's quite right,' she said. 'I'm not in love with you, but I like you and I find you sexually attractive. Does it shock you, my saying that?'

'No.'

She nodded, satisfied, then went on, 'In addition, I'm very lonely and sorry for myself, as you are, which is pretty feeble.' She frowned at him and added crossly, 'I *hate* feeble people, but as that's what we both are we could try propping each other up.'

'A girl like you lonely? With your looks?'

'Oh, they all come sniffing around. I thought you might like the job of keeping them away. I don't want any of them and if you think that's a compliment to you you must be right, mustn't you? Oh and I'm sorry for saying you acted like a bastard. You did, but not long ago I behaved much more badly, so who am I to talk?'

He shook his head vigorously in simultaneous rejection of her need to apologise and disavowal of her admission before saying, 'You're offering me the moon, Gail.'

She was out of her chair and standing over him, eyes blazingly green, red hair still swaying from the rapidity of her movement.

'You're very tall, Gascoigne!'

Startled by the use of his surname, the obvious statement and her equally obvious anger, 'Yes, I am rather.'

'Then reach up and lift me off this blasted pedestal you've parked me on! I am *not* a goddess! I'm just another girl, damn you! A girl you've wanted since the first moment you saw her!'

'Damn you too, Lady Abigail!'

He was standing in front of her with no recollection of getting to his

286

feet, hands gripping her upper arms, shaking her back and forth. Her head rocked in time to the movements, but her eyes, smiling now, never left his.

'That's better,' she said. 'No, don't stop. Get it out of your system, there's a nice man.'

Chapter Twenty-Five

The medical team from the military hospital boarded the U.S. Navy transport minutes after its anchor splashed down into Tokyo Bay. They went below at once, moving with a purposefulness born of long practice, checking the particulars of each Japanese soldier against the lists they carried. When they had done that the prisoners who could walk were shepherded to the waiting boats by armed Marines and taken ashore. Stretcher cases followed them. A medical officer and a major of Marines stood near the gangway watching the transfer.

'Where did this lot come from, Major?' the doctor asked.

'Islands around Tanega-shima. A few from Tanega-shima itself.'

'Usual thing?'

'Yeah, just bunches of nuts who refuse to believe the war's over. Takes forever to get it into their heads that it is. You don't get many thanks for your trouble either. This trip a whole group of nine suicided with grenades as soon as we had them convinced. Crazy, huh?'

'Sure is. Okay, let's go to take a look at our boy. Hiding from the Nips, was he?'

'I guess so,' the major said. 'He tried to fight the guys who found him. Reckon he's a little mixed up. He's been under sedation and on intra-venous feed since we picked him up.'

They went into the ship's hospital, walked to the only cot still occupied and looked down at the emaciated man lying in it. A bandage covered his eyes, the left side of the neck carried the multi-coloured whorls and furrows of burnt tissue and the left ear was missing altogether.

'Where are the ship's doctors, Major?'

'Went ashore with the stretcher cases. They'll be right back.'

'Uhuh. Do you know what's the matter with this man's eyes?'

'Not a lot, they tell me,' the major said. 'The first time I saw him he had a long beard and long hair, but you could see that the eyes were surrounded by pustules. Just some infection they're clearing up for him. He's suffering from malnutrition, exhaustion and exposure according to the doc. He's had fever too.'

'What type of fever?'

The Marine officer shrugged. 'How would I know? I only collect 'em. The medics do the nursing. But he's not about to infect anybody if that's what's worrying you.'

'No dog tag?'

'No dog tag. Peasant clothes. Stolen I imagine. No means of identification at all.'

Nodding, the medical officer sat down on the side of the bed, put his hand on the man's shoulder and shook it gently.

'Can you hear me, son?'

The bandaged head lifted an inch from the pillow and turned fractionally, as though listening.

'Son! Can you hear me?'

'Yes, I can hear you.' Speech slurred.

'Ah, that's great. Like to tell me where you're from?'

'No,' the man said. 'I wouldn't like to tell you where I'm from.'

'Why not? You're among friends. This is a U.S. Navy ship.'

'Then why is it crawling with Japs?'

'What makes you think it is?'

'I've heard them jabbering. Hundreds of them.'

'Oh, those were…'

The medical officer stopped talking when the man shouted, 'Harding! Lieutenant Peter Harding, Royal Navy! That's all I'm obliged to tell you under the Geneva Convention, if you've ever *heard* of the Geneva Convention!'

'Nice going, Lieutenant,' the major said. 'Now how about giving us your number? That's permitted under the Convention too.'

The man showed his teeth in a humourless grin before replying, 'That proves you're Japs all right. Royal Navy officers don't have numbers. Put *that* in your Intelligence file and stick it up your arse.'

The Medical officer looked up at the Marine. 'Sure sounds like a Limey.'

'He does at that,' the major said. 'I'll have him checked out with the British.'

*

Gail Harding lounged on the side of her bed, eyes unfocussed, listening to the faint hiss and clicking coming from the telephone receiver at her ear. She stayed like that for almost a minute before her eyes came alive and she sat upright.

'Hello. My name's Gail Harding, Miss Fraser.'

Long seconds passed while the ear-piece continued to make its own little secret sounds, then it said, 'Hello, Lady Abigail.'

She blinked rapidly several times before saying, 'You know about me?'

'Certainly. John carries quite a torch for you. I imagine that's who you're calling about. We don't have anything else in common.'

'*He* talked to *you* about *me?*'

'Yes.'

'The bloody, bloody fool!'

'Hardly the language I'd have expected from you, Lady Abigail.'

'Oh, do stop calling me "Lady Abigail",' Gail said. 'What an idiot that man is.'

'I've thought of other names for him,' the receiver told her.

'I expect you have. I called him a bastard after he'd told me what happened in Australia and I meant it.'

'So it's been "True Confessions Day", has it?'

'Not exactly. It all came out over a month ago, before we started living together.'

There was another pause before the husky voice spoke again. 'I'm glad he's achieved his dream. Now, do you mind coming to the bloody point? I'm sure you'll forgive that word from me as we Aussie sheilas don't have your advantages, and I'm not terribly interested in your sex life.'

'Very well,' Gail said. 'I'd like to tell you some points of fact if you're prepared to listen. If you're interested.'

'It's your phone bill and I'm sitting comfortably.'

It might be going to be all right Gail thought. What little she knew of Candice Fraser made her believe that she would not listen out of morbid curiosity, that she would have ended the conversation by now were she not interested. She breathed out slowly before saying, 'The first point is that my husband has been found alive and more or less well. He'll be coming home soon and as I love him very much I no longer constitute any threat to you. Actually I never would have been a threat if you two had stayed together.'

There was no reaction to her words from the other end and after a moment Gail went on, 'Point two is that John's wife has divorced him. The very tall girl who lives in Perth was named as co-respondent.' She paused for comment and when none came added, 'The third point is that at certain – at certain happy moments he calls me "Candy". He doesn't realise that he does that.'

The longest silence of all followed and, not surprised, Gail waited patiently, then, 'I'm happy for you about your husband,' the receiver told her.

'Thank you,' Gail said. 'I have no other facts for you, but I'll give you an opinion if you like.'

'What is it?'

'I think John's grown up now.'

'I see.'

No encouragement at all in any of the Australian girl's words, but across half the world Gail felt that she could detect the stirrings of life in what had been a dead voice. The next five words seemed to confirm the impression.

'Is he with you now?'

'Yes, he's downstairs working on some papers about *Talon*. Would you like to talk to him? He doesn't know anything of this conversation, or about my husband yet.'

A whisper which sounded like 'Oh Pommy darling' then, '*Talon*? I never expected to hear that name spoken again. Yes, I would like to talk to him, please. But first, even if you don't like being addressed as one, I think you must be rather a nice lady.'

'Don't go away,' Gail Harding said, put the receiver on the bed and walked towards the stairs.

Printed in the USA
CPSIA information can be obtained
at www.ICGtesting.com
LVHW041544160924
791204LV00005B/97